WINTER'S WRATH

BACKLASH

BIANCA SOMMERLAND

Also by Bianca Sommerland

Winter's Wrath Series
Backlash

The Dartmouth Cobras
Blind Pass
Game Misconduct
Defensive Zone
Breakaway
Offside
Delayed Penalty
Iron Cross
Goal Line
Line Brawl – Coming 2016

Also
Deadly Captive
Collateral Damage
The End – Coming 2016

Solid Education
Rosemary Entwined
Forbidden Steps
The Trip

Acknowledgements

When I started writing this book, I knew it was going to be different. I've said a few times that I haven't been this excited about a book since I stepped into the world of the Cobras. But with the excitement came a lot of fear, and I have so many I need to thank for helping me get past that, I'm not even sure where to begin.

Stacey, you're my rock and my voice of reason. If I thank you every time we speak, and in every book I ever write, it still won't be enough. Jennifer, you're an amazing friend, but you deserve a medal for putting up with all my crazy and managing to talk me down when I was ready to toss it all in the fire and go back to writing what was safe. Stella, your grit, your attitude, and your advice has me willing to take chances and knowing I'll survive in this industry.

To my crit partner, Cherise, thank you for always pushing me to reach a bit deeper. To Lisa, thank you for letting me pick your brain and for telling me all about the experiences you had with bands, not all that long ago. ;)

To Digital Tour Bus for sharing insights into the lives of all the bands I love. And Brian Stars, for showing the fun side of the musicians.

And as always, most importantly, to my daughters. As you're getting older, you've shown me, despite all the bumps in the road, you're both growing to be amazing young women. Our time together is so precious, and every time you laugh and smile, tell me about your day while snuggling, or dance and sing with me in the kitchen while we're acting nuts, I'm glad to know I've taught you the most important thing. Those moments are what holds us together and makes us strong enough to face anything.

Always.

Subsist

(Whispered) Red gifts, teeth, and candy. So many innocent lies. Let me believe. Let me always
believe.

(Growl)Crushed little bodies,
Caved to reality.
(Scream)Hold back until they stand,
Rise despite your bitter truths.

(Background Singer)Ordered perfection,
Ugly as sin.
Paint the world in dull hues.
Leave the monster under my bed.

Chorus-
Upon quivering wings.
Iced and shattered 'til they fall,
Again and again and again.

Smother the laughter.
Cut away the smiles.
Again and again and again.

(Growl) Forbidden High,
cut the strings.
(Scream) Drop down and get in line,
I will the price I pay.

(Background Singer) Take your honesty,
I've inked my reality,
On my flesh, in my skull,
Blood rain and Frost's games.

(War Cry)

Upon quivering wings.
Iced and shattered 'til they fall,
Again and again and again.

Smother the laughter.
Cut away the smiles.
Again and again and again.

(Solo)

I'll be good, I promise,
Don't tell me this anymore.
The demons are with me,
I love it when they smile.

Again and again and again. Again and again and again.

Dedication

For Dimebag, The Rev, and Lemmy.

Chapter One

Fucking Poe. *Again.* His brother was going to ruin the band before they ever got to headline a goddamn venue. Not that Edgar Allen's poetry wasn't great and all, but how much inspiration could the lead singer of a metalcore band get from the ratty old book he'd read a thousand times?

Back braced on the wall at the head of his top bunk on the tour bus, Alder Trousseau continued polishing the dark wood of his guitar, breathing in the rich aroma of maple and the sweet scent of carnauba wax. Holding his metal pick between his lips, he began humming the melody he'd been toying with for a few days now. Between practice and travel and appearances, he hadn't gotten a chance to pull out the sheet and jot down the notes. But as soon as they got back on the road, he was getting the guys together and writing this shit down. If it was still in his head after this long, it would stick with the fans.

Which covered the guitar, and the bass and the drums were easy enough to pull into a mind-blowing harmony, but without the lyrics, they had nothing. Braver "Brave" Trousseau, lead singer of Winter's Wrath and Alder's brother, was the lyrics guy. And he was a fucking god at whipping together terrifyingly beautiful phrases out of nowhere.

Only, considering how much time Brave had spent staring at that book during this tour, their next album was gonna be all 'Ravens' and 'Nevermore'.

"Stop staring at me, asshole." Brave pushed off the opposite bottom bunk and tossed the book at Alder's head. His long, wavy black hair covered half of his face as he glared at Alder. "You're not the only one working his ass off for this band."

Alder picked up the book, pitching it back to his brother. "Is this work?"

Rolling his broad, heavily tattooed shoulders, Brave nodded. "Yeah. Poe was a master at using words to freak people out."

Great. I was right. Alder sighed. "So we're singing about the birds?"

"That's Alfred Hitchcock, dumbass." Brave rested his forearms on the side of Alder's bunk, amusement slanting his lips. "We're singing about Santa Claus."

Shit. Alder scowled and dropped his gaze to his guitar. No use in asking Brave if he was joking. If he was, he'd make Alder feel stupid for believing him. If he wasn't...well, that was a scary thought.

Horror poetry and Old Saint Nick. Wouldn't Krampus make more sense?

Smacking the mattress, probably just to make Alder jump, Brave let out a gruff laugh. "Pussy. You just stay there, stroking your wood. I'm gonna go fuck your boyfriend."

Yeah, and I'm the asshole? Not even blinking, Alder waited until Brave was about halfway across the bus before he spoke. "Daphne Du Maurier wrote The Birds. Evan Hunter did the adaption for Hitchcock's film. Jesse isn't my boyfriend, but if you wanna get him fired from the crew, go for it."

"He's not getting fired for letting me fuck him."

"No, he'll get fired for not getting the van loaded. Damn it, Brave, go get a groupie to suck your dick. You're a real bitch when you haven't gotten laid in awhile." Alder had to fight to keep his hands from shaking as the rage he'd suppressed bubbled to the surface. They'd been on the road, on this fucking bus, for way too long. They were usually on their way home from a gig before he and Brave started on each other, but they'd had twice as many shows booked this time. Their manager was pushing them to another level, which made tolerating his dick of an older brother more than worth it.

Their hard work would pay off. If they didn't kill one another first.

Thing was, Brave would probably be easier to deal with after he fucked Jesse, but even though Jesse was one of their best roadies, their manager, Zach Cole, wouldn't hesitate to fire him for slacking off. No matter whose fault it was. A roadie like Jesse was a lot easier to replace than a vocalist.

Right, and wanting him around has nothing to do with the fact that you're in love with the man.

The narrowed eyed look Brave gave him meant one of two things. Either he was gonna have a cold comeback, or he'd figure out his comment about fucking Jesse had actually gotten to Alder. Either way, Brave was gearing up for a fight.

The front door of the bus slid open, cutting through the tension. Alder grinned when he saw the band's lanky young drummer, Tate Maddox, bounce onto the bus with his usual wild energy. The long part of his golden brown, semi-mohawk fell over the close shaved side of his head as he gave them a sideways look.

"Are you guys at each other again? Three more shows before we're in Vegas, baby! I'm putting all my savings on the tables. Need you guys to keep Cole off my ass so I can win enough money for us to make our first epic music video! No more cheesy lyric shit." Tate made devil horns with one hand and brought it to his lips to wiggle his tongue between his fingers. "I'll put on black lipstick or whatever he wants, but I need my pretty mug all over MTV!"

"MTV hardly ever shows music vids anymore, Tate. Not sure you were even born when they did." Brave rolled his eyes, sidling past the drummer to make his way off the bus.

Nice. Alder slid off the top bunk to sit on the one Tate had claimed beneath it. Of the five guys in the band, Tate was the only one who still had his head in the clouds after years of hard work and little reward. The band was doing well, taking where they'd started into consideration. They opened for huge names and none of the guys needed steady jobs to make a living. So what if they didn't have mansions and guitars that cost more than most cars? They were living the dream.

The dirty, endless days and sleepless nights dream.

Reality as a metalcore band wasn't what they'd all imagined as kids, but they had fans. People who bought their shirts and screamed their names. Who knew all the words to the songs on their debut album.

Granted, Winter's Wrath had a few chart toppers, but they'd only reached the top 10 on iTunes. Very few radio stations would play their music, because it was too intense. Brave had gotten an interview in the Metal Spade magazine, but nothing they'd done so far was very mainstream.

But they'd made enough money to upgrade from a makeshift sleeper van to a bus for the last two tours. They all had new guitars and Tate had the drum set he'd been drooling over for years. The poor kid had been using a second hand set he'd gotten in high school for the first three years the band was together. He kept it in the best shape he could, but in an interview for their debut album, a journalist had asked about it. Tate's face had gone red and he'd talked about his drum instructor, the man who'd given it to him. Said he wouldn't have gotten this far without him and having the kit on stage was like dragging a comfy blanket on tour.

He had one of those, too. Said blanket was draped over the small couch in the front lounge of the bus. A quilt his grandma made for him the first time he joined them on the road when he was just seventeen. The thing was fucking cool, with photos of all his favorite bands and their albums for the squares. Everything from Slayer to Motionless, surrounded with a drum pattern border.

Tate's grandma was one of the coolest ladies Alder had ever met. She'd had the whole band over for dinner the last time they were in Detroit and had taken four requests for quilts. They had her business cards on their merchandise table at every show and she had plenty of orders to keep her busy, but she'd insisted on doing blankets for the members first.

One of the *many* reasons Tate was a great addition to the band.

Resting his elbow on his knee, Alder grinned as Tate pulled a box of cookies from the side of his mattress. Cookies were Tate's go-to when he was having a good day. On bad days, he'd be chugging vodka or smoking some rank shit.

First tour, when Alder wasn't much older than Tate's twenty-one, he'd have been toking right along with him. After a couple years on the road, it was rare he even touched a beer outside of the after parties.

Crumbs sprinkled all over the bed as Tate yanked out the plastic cookie tray. The drummer groaned when he found only one inside. "Shit. Do you think I have time to run and grab a few boxes?"

Alder frowned. "Send one of the roadies."

"Why?" Tate looked over, then rolled his eyes. "We're in Ohio. Last night was a fluke. I'll be fine."

Maybe, but Alder wasn't willing to risk it. They'd opened for Horizon at a new venue whose owners had the ambition to pull off big shows, but didn't know the first thing about preparing for one. Metal and hard rock could mix quite well in most cases, and the majority of fans had seemed to enjoy themselves. But there wasn't enough security, and dozens of fans had crashed the stage. One nut had slammed into Brave and grinned in his face, wrapping one hand around Brave's neck as he'd whispered 'You'd be immortal if you died today.'

The cops had been called in, and after ejecting the crazies in the crowd, the show had been allowed to go on. But Brave had been shaken and Cole had told them all to stick close to the bus. Smart move.

Tate was the youngest member of the band. The restriction was gonna mess with him, but too bad. Either a roadie went for cookies, or Alder would go with him. Not getting cookies wasn't an option. During the band's first tour, Tate had been offered hard drugs by several fans and only intervention from Alder and the bass guitarist, Malakai Noble, had kept him from falling down that particular black hole. His sugar addiction had Alder wondering what exactly was in the joints Tate used to smoke, but since Jesse handled all the weed the band used now, he wasn't too worried. Jesse looked out for them better than any of the venue security they dealt with on the road.

Clearly, since no one would have gotten that close to Brave if Jesse had been backstage. Unfortunately, he'd been stuck in the roadies van when Cole found out he wasn't feeling well. Probably just bad takeout, but Cole was paranoid about any member of the band getting sick. Threats didn't really register with him, which was probably why he hadn't commented until the clip ended up on YouTube around midnight.

And even then, he'd just stood in front of them all, arms crossed, a sneer on his lips. "Let the media have their fun with this. We all know there are morons looking for their fifteen minutes of fame at every show. You good, Brave?"

Brave had nodded and let out a hoarse laugh. "Always."

There were bruises on Brave's neck today. Alder felt like an asshole for thinking shit about his brother reading Poe. Whatever, Brave would tell him to fuck off if he showed any sympathy.

Tate, however, wouldn't recover from this shit as quickly, and he'd be an easy target. He had his 'pretty mug' up on all the magazine covers the band hit. With their long hair covering their faces in most pictures, Alder and Brave might have a few seconds when a fan might not be sure if it was really them. With his golden brown hair shaved on the sides and a spiked semi-Mohawk on top, Tate was easily recognizable. Never mind those fucking eyes of his, which were such a pale blue-grey they didn't seem real.

Wrinkling his slightly crooked nose—the only thing on his face that wasn't model perfect—Tate waved his hand in front of Alder's face. "Dude, why you looking at me like that?"

Alder shrugged and stood. "Just thinking of you getting jumped on the way to the store. You're too cute for me to not give a fuck. Come on, we can ask Jesse to make a run. I need some shit anyway."

Tate licked his bottom lip, cocking his head slightly. "You think I'm cute?"

"Everyone thinks you're cute." Alder ruffled Tate's spiky hair to shift the mood before the kid got the wrong impression. "Kinda like having a puppy on the bus."

"Gee, thanks." Tate knocked his hand away and popped off the bunk. "I get it. Shit, I'm gonna have to pay to get a guy to fuck me, aren't I?"

Not this again. Alder sighed as he followed Tate out to the parking lot. Brave wasn't the only one suffering from blue balls. Malakai and Connor Phelan, their rhythm guitarist, had both hooked up with chicks at the after party last night. Bathroom stall and back alley quickies just weren't Alder's thing, so he'd checked out early, a little surprised when both Brave and Tate joined him on the bus.

Brave seemed to have gotten sick of being pawed by barely legal groupies, and he'd been pissed off about the crazy fucker at the show, but Tate usually had no trouble finding a nice, older woman to teach him a thing or two. He was going through a weird phase lately, hitting on guys and getting in trouble with Cole. Cole was pretty cool about most things. Yeah, he didn't want them getting plastered and acting like assholes in public, but when they slipped up, he usually just reminded them that they were supposed to be professionals. This wasn't the fucking 70s.

Their manager hadn't gotten with the times on the whole 'Love is love' thing though. Metal equaled *straight* to most fans and Cole wouldn't let any of them fuck up that image.

Which was kinda funny, considering not a single member of the band was completely straight. Cole'd had high hopes for Tate—the kid hadn't had much experience with either sex when he'd joined them.

He should have known we'd corrupt the boy. Alder caught up with Tate and put his arm over the drummer's shoulders. He wouldn't fuck Tate just to satisfy the kid's curiosity, but there were other ways he could help. "You'll get everything you want in Vegas, Tate. I promise."

"Yeah?" Tate grinned, brightening up instantly at just the mention of his favorite city. "Cole can't watch us all the time, right?"

"Fuck no. And we're there for a few days, so we can finally get a bit of a break." A *much* needed break. Maybe Alder would be less inclined to murder his brother once they got some time away from one another.

Rounding the corner of the trailer, where there was a frame tent set up, Alder stopped in his tracks, spotting Brave pressed close to a shirtless man against the side of another band's bus. Ripped jeans and wavy, dirty blond hair…*Jesse.*

Maybe fratricide wasn't such a bad idea after all.

"Shotgun? I don't want much."

At Brave's request, Jesse Vaughn almost choked on the smoke he'd inhaled and dropped his joint in the dirt. He'd gotten most of the equipment loaded in the trailer and was taking a quick break. Brave wasn't usually up this early—early being before noon. He still looked fucking good though. His long, black hair spilled wild down his back in soft waves, and the black liner he hadn't bothered to wash off last night was smudged, making his golden brown eyes even more brilliant. He didn't look tired though. More like a dirty, rugged angel that had just crawled out of the trenches. Hot and sweaty and ready for all kinds of trouble.

Trouble Jesse should avoid if he wanted to keep his job.

Crushing the joint under his boot, Jesse pulled out his cigarette pack to get some rolling paper. He had to roll a fresh joint now, so he'd keep it low on tobacco so it didn't fuck with Brave's voice.

"You sure this is a good idea?" Jesse couldn't remember the last time Brave had smoked anything.

"No." Brave let out a throaty laugh. "But we should do it anyway."

Yeah. Trouble.

But he *really* loved his job. Even though he hadn't been with the band the longest, Jesse pretty much ran the crew. Not the career path he'd originally planned on, he'd grown up with dreams of becoming a rock star. Or a professional wrestler. He'd gotten a wrestling scholarship for college, so his life had been set.

Until an assault charge against a rich kid and a year in jail royally fucked all his prospects. Jesse was lucky he had connections in the music world to fall back on. He'd worked as security at a venue in Detroit for a few years, where he'd met Brave and Alder at one of their first shows.

One of their roadies had fallen off the stage and broken his arm, so Jesse filled in. During the show he'd restrung Alder's guitar and tuned it for him when the man's stupid metal pick snapped a string. The band decided they needed him. And he'd been with them ever since.

Keeping his head low and doing his best not to piss off their manager, Cole. He didn't give them shit about using their position to get as much pussy as they could, but they weren't supposed to get too friendly with the band.

Fair enough, but Brave made it hard. Real fucking hard.

There'd been a time or two Jesse had come close to crossing the no-fucking-the-band line. With both brothers. What could he say, they were hot. Both tall, with black hair and similar features, but other than that, very different.

Brave was long and wiry, his hair reaching to the center of his back, his eyes a golden brown that practically glowed with anger or lust. He had a way of moving that made it impossible not to think of sex.

Alder had broad shoulders, a nice build, but not like a man who obsessively worked out. Or carried around band equipment every day. He wasn't as muscular as Jesse, but he had the roundest fucking ass.

Off limits. Both of them. But after a few drinks, shit happened. He'd made out with Alder once when the bus broke down in the middle of nowhere in Kentucky and they had to walk to get cell reception to call for repairs. Alder had been plastered and Jesse was a little stoned. And they were tired and the side of the road looked like a good place to lie down for a few minutes.

Alder's phone had rung just as Jesse began seriously considering fucking his best friend in the dirt. Thankfully, things weren't weird between Jesse and Alder after. He'd have hated to fuck up their friendship because he'd been stupid.

But it was different with Brave. Whenever they were alone, Brave would do or say something that made it almost impossible to care what Cole thought.

Like right now.

Cole had gone ahead to the next venue in South Dakota, which had been a late add to the tour, to check out the place and make sure security was tight. With him out of the way, Jesse had one less reason to keep his distance.

He lit the tip of the fresh joint, drawing in the smoke as Brave braced his hands on either side of him against the metal siding of the bus. With the joint between his lips, Jesse smiled, then took the blunt away from his mouth, letting out the smoke slowly.

"You have to sing tomorrow."

Brave shrugged. "That's why I wanna share. I'll be fine."

"*That's* not why you wanna share."

"Maybe not." Brave gave him a hooded look. "But you're playing hard to get."

Laughing, Jesse sucked on the joint, blowing the smoke off to the side. He hadn't gotten high enough to dull the effect Brave had on him, but he wouldn't let it show. Even though he could feel the length of Brave's dick against his thigh. And the thick stench of weed couldn't drown out the heady smell of sweat and faint cologne. Just having Brave close made him hard, but this wasn't a game to him. Brave would respect him more if he didn't give in.

"I'm not playing." Jesse slid his hand to the side of Brave's neck. He ran his thumb along Brave's tense jaw. "Open your mouth."

Brave's eyes drifted shut, his tongue running over his lips as they parted.

Taking a deep haul on the joint, Jesse brought his mouth close to Brave and breathed out the smoke. His lips were practically touching Brave's. Another inch and he could kiss the man. He wanted to, wanted to take all Brave could offer, but it wouldn't last. The fans and the fame had spoiled Brave. He'd grown arrogant. And distant.

The closed off man he was to everyone else wasn't good enough for Jesse. As he worked one hand into Brave's hair, offering another exhale of smoke, he met Brave's eyes.

Not a good idea.

Those fucking eyes had him ready to trash all the reasons his brain came up with to avoid becoming another of Brave's playthings.

Until they stopped seeing him at all. Brave glanced over his shoulder as footsteps approached, his lips slanting in a cold smile. "Need something, bro?"

"No." Alder looked ready to kill his brother. "Sorry to bother you."

Another fight. Nothing new. Jesse sighed and nudged Brave aside, looking from Alder to Tate. "You're not bothering me. What's up?"

"Forget it." Alder brushed Tate's hand away when the drummer tried to grab his arm, then headed back the way he'd come.

Not sure what was up with the man, Jesse handed Tate the rest of his joint and followed Alder, latching on to his wrist before he could climb back onto the bus. "Hey, you wanna chill out? Did you need something?"

Alder's jaw ticked. He squared his shoulders. "Tate needs cookies."

"Okay. You want me to go, or you just need a lift?"

Inhaling roughly, Alder leaned against the side of the bus. "Seriously? Right now, I don't give a shit about that. What the fuck are you doing? You know what Brave's like. Maybe it's none of my business, but—"

"You're worried." All right, that made sense. Jesse grinned as he put his hand on Alder's shoulder. He couldn't blame Alder for being protective. He was that kind of friend and Jesse would do the same if he saw Alder messing with the wrong guy. "I get it, and I love you for caring, man."

Alder snorted. "You're full of shit."

"I mean it. But I know what I'm doing, okay?" Jesse hooked his arm around Alder's neck. He grinned when Alder relaxed at his side, keeping pace as Jesse returned to the back of the bus to fetch Tate.

Malakai had joined Tate and Brave, taking over the joint— and not sharing much if Tate's pout was anything to go by. All the guys looked out for the young drummer, but Malakai tended to treat him like a kid brother, with more affection and watchfulness than the Trousseau brothers shared. He'd also known the boy the longest, so he'd been around when Tate had dealt with some serious addictions as a teen.

As far as Jesse knew, other than him, only Malakai and Cole had any idea how bad his drug addictions had been. Tate's grandmother checked in with Cole regularly, having gotten Tate away from his sister's guardianship when he was fifteen. She was the one who got her grandson clean and interested in playing drums rather than shooting up.

Cole had explained the situation to Jesse so he could help keep an eye on Tate. Which was almost impossible on the road. So long as he didn't do anything stronger than pot, Jesse wasn't too concerned, but Malakai tended to pull an intervention even with mild drugs.

The cold look he shot Jesse as he approached made him rethink his stance. He'd have to be more careful lighting up around Tate if he wanted to stay on the bassist's good side.

"You heading to the store?" Malakai asked as he dropped the joint and crushed it under his heel. He arched a brow at Tate when the younger man cursed under his breath. Running his hand over his close shaved head, he smiled tightly when Jesse nodded. "Good. Let's go."

Oh, this is gonna be fun. Jesse pulled out the keys to the van and glanced over at Brave. "Coming?"

"Naw, just pick me up some orange juice and a few snacks. You know what I like." Brave smirked as he passed his brother, who'd gone still at Jesse's side. Their shoulders slammed together and Jesse was almost positive one of them growled.

Be good to separate them for a bit. Connor was usually the one that pulled them apart when they came to blows, but he was hanging out with one of the other bands this morning, probably working out. Out of all the guys, Connor was the most down to earth, the calming presence that kept the others sane. Bringing him along would make the shopping trip easier, but Jesse hated to admit he hated dealing with the guys in public.

Inside the van, Tate claimed shotgun, practically bouncing in his seat. "We should go to Walmart. Stock up."

Shoot me now. Jesse met Alder's eyes in the rearview mirror.

Alder shrugged as though to say "What's the worse that could happen?"

You want a list? Jesse sighed and pulled out of the parking lot behind the venue. The Walmart was only about a five-minute drive without traffic, and there was none since all the people who earned money doing sane office jobs were sitting behind their desks. Then again, Jesse didn't have much to complain about. He loved the guys, and even though he didn't make a ton of money, he'd be miserable at a job that didn't revolve around music.

Besides, Alder and Malakai were easy to manage when they were sober. So the only one he really had to keep an eye on was Tate.

Who bolted from the van the second Jesse parked.

"What's the rush?" Malakai shouted after the drummer, who was dodging strollers and old ladies.

Tate spun around for a split second, face red, and held up two fingers. Then he was gone.

Fair enough. There were some things you couldn't do on the bus. Even Tate couldn't get in trouble in the bathroom. He wasn't a child.

But Jesse still hesitated when they passed the entrance, feeling like a parent not quite ready to let their kid out of their sight.

Alder laughed and punched him in the arm. "He'll be fine. Come on, this will go twice as fast if we get his cookies for him before he gets to browsing."

"Very true." Jesse grabbed a cart, following Alder and Malakai to the food section. Halfway there, both men made a detour and grabbed some socks. A bit further and a display of DVDs caught Malakai's eye. He stopped to check them out, picking a few new ones to kill some time on the road.

The book section was what grabbed Alder. He picked up two true crime novels; his literary drug of choice, then paused with his eye on a Game of Thrones box set. Not his style. As far as Jesse knew, only Brave had read any of the books. Just the first one actually. He'd mentioned wanting to get the others, but he hadn't had time.

Brow furrowed, Alder picked up the set. He put it down, then picked it up again, shaking his head before tossing it in the cart.

Neither Jesse, nor Malakai, said a word. Alder and Brave had the most fucked up relationship of any siblings Jesse had ever met. He could tell they cared about one another, but it was like they were afraid to let it show.

Safest thing was to pretend not to notice.

They finally hit the snack aisle. Malakai took off to get some "Real food", leaving Jesse and Alder to fill the cart with chips and cookies and cereal. The cookies, which were the priority, took the longest. Alder had all Tate's favorites memorized, but the aisle was crowded. He waited patiently behind a family of seven, a tired looking mother with children ranging from newborn to thirteen. The teenage girl was the first person to recognize him, and let out a piercing scream.

Her mother looked ready to cry as her daughter leapt on Alder, babbling about how much she loved him.

"Wendy, please!" The woman grabbed her daughter's wrist. The baby strapped up in a car seat attached to the cart began to cry. Two of the toddlers climbed onto the shelf, knocking over a dozen packages of cookies. The woman gave Jesse a helpless look. "I'm so sorry."

"That's quite all right." Jesse caught one of the toddlers as he slipped off the shelf. He bent down to the kid's level. "Wanna help me pick these up, buddy? I'll give you a dollar?"

The little boy nodded. His—twin?—joined in while their mother picked up the hollering baby and scolded her eldest child.

To his credit, Alder had managed to gently pry Wendy's hands off him, all while chatting with her about the band's latest album and offering to sign something for the girl if she promised to help her mother.

Naturally, Alder didn't have anything on him to give the girl. Or a pen.

Jesse laughed when Alder opened his wallet, looking totally lost. He took pity on the guitarist and plucked a guitar pick out of his pocket, handing it over.

Wendy took it with a big smile. She squealed when her mother found a pen in her purse. "Can you sign my bra?"

"No!" Both her mother and Alder exclaimed in unison.

"Hey, what's going on?" Malakai asked as he ambled over, his arms full of frozen fruits and vegetables.

The scream the girl let out drew the attention of every shopper in the area.

Likely the entire store.

"Is Brave here? Please tell me Brave is here too!" Wendy latched on to Malakai's shirt, her eyes wide. "I would do *anything* to meet him."

Malakai tried to back away from her. "Letting me go would be a great start."

"Excuse me, ma'am. Are they bothering you?" A heavyset man who looked like he'd walked straight out of 'The Worst of Walmart' strode up behind the woman, glaring at Malakai as though the bassist was some kind of predator.

Jesse wasn't sure if he should laugh or save his boys. When Malakai's eyes narrowed and the woman didn't answer—not her fault, her baby was screaming again and Jesse was pretty sure she'd lost a kid—Jesse decided they'd had enough 'fun' for one day.

He put his hand on Malakai's arm, nudged him toward the cart, and smiled at the big guy with the pizza sauce stains on his shirt. "Just a little issue with an avalanche of cookies. Wendy was about to help us pick up the rest of them." He glanced over at the teen. "Weren't you, sweetie?"

Her lips parted, her cheeks went red, and then she knelt beside her brothers to pick up the rest of the boxes. Pizza man grunted, grabbing a few boxes of sugar free cookies before storming down the aisle.

During the distraction, Alder had managed to get all Tate's favorite cookies. The woman retrieved her children, apologizing again before doing a quick head count. She went white.

"Where's Bobby?"

Jesse patted her hand. "What does he look like?"

She held up her hand to chest level, tears spilling down her cheeks. Malakai headed to the toy aisle. Alder headed to the electronics.

And Jesse stayed where he was as the woman ditched the carriage, taking only the baby as she began calling for her son and darting through the food section.

One of the kids was playing on a phone, another was sitting on the floor, talking to himself, so Jesse focused on the twins and the teen. Wendy chattered happily about everything she knew about the band. The twins tore open a box of cookies and started chowing down. He considered stopping them, but they were staying put and he had no idea of the protocol on telling someone else's kids what to do.

His phone buzzed in his pocket. He checked the text.

TATE: 911

"Are you fucking serious?" He looked at the kids. He couldn't just leave them. So he quickly replied.

JESSE: WHAT'S WRONG???

No answer. His blood went cold. Tate was a lot of things, but he wasn't a drama queen. He wouldn't text something like that for nothing.

"Can you watch them?" Jesse groaned when Wendy stared at him like he was completely fucking insane. "My friend needs me."

Her face brightened. "Brave?"

"No."

"So he's not here?"

"No. But you're a big girl, right? You must help your mom sometimes?"

Wendy blinked at him as if he must be stupid. "Hell no. They're not my kids."

Great. Jesse texted Brave.

> **JESSE: CAN YOU COME TO WALMART? TATE'S IN TROUBLE. I'M STUCK WITH A BUNCH OF KIDS.**

He held his breath, waiting for the reply.

BRAVE: ALREADY HERE.

All right, at least Tate wasn't alone. Jesse hated not being able to help him, but what was he supposed to do? He put his hands on the handle of the shopping cart, tightening his grip until his knuckles went white.

He held his breath, waiting for the reply.

Seemed like forever before the mother returned. He inclined his head, acknowledging her thanks quickly before half running to the front of the store. With the cart. Which he left by the cash when he saw flashing red and blue lights outside.

Both Brave and Tate were sitting on the curb. Bleeding.

Jesse cursed and knelt in front of Tate, ignoring the cops who were arresting three men off to the side. "What happened?"

Tate shook his head, his whole body trembling. "I came out to bum a smoke. This dude was all like 'You were checking out my ass!'. So I said, 'Well yes, you're a good looking guy.'" He wiped a trail of blood off his bottom lip. "I started going back in when he called me a fucking fag. He followed me with his buddies, so I sent a text out to you guys. He dragged me back out here and him and his friends started hitting me."

One of Tate's eyes was already swollen shut. He had an arm pressed to his side like he was in pain.

Jesse glanced over at the men being helped into the back of the cop car, wondering if he could make it there before the doors closed and kill the fuckers. No matter how stupid Tate had been, he didn't deserve this.

"Hey." Brave put his hand over the one Jesse had braced on his bent knee. "He's gonna be all right. I handled it."

"I shouldn't have—"

"Jesse." Brave's tone dropped to the one that went straight to Jesse balls. Which was messed up, considering everything, but he had a way of bulldozing over all Jesse's defenses. "Shit happens. Where's Alder and Malakai?"

"Probably still looking for that kid." Jesse ran a hand over his face. "Neither of them keep their phones on. They don't know—"

"Go get them. Tate and I've gotta talk to the cops." Brave's lips twisted into a wry grin. "Thankfully, there are witnesses. I'm hoping we don't get delayed. I want to bring Tate to the hospital to get checked out, but—"

"I'm fine!" Tate scowled. "I hate hospitals."

"I know." Brave put his arm over Tate's shoulders. "And I don't care. You're going."

Fuck, I love this man.

"I'll get the guys back to the bus. Give me a call when he gets checked out?" Jesse smiled at Brave's nod. A lot of people thought Brave was a complete asshole, but they didn't see this side of him. The leader who took care of the band. Who was aware of everything going on with the guys, whether they were sick or depressed or just having an off day. He didn't know all of Tate's past, but he still kept an eye on the kid, treating him like a little brother. More so then his *actual* brother.

But the reasons for that were complicated and Jesse stayed out of it. Alder clearly didn't need anyone, so Brave gave him space. Yeah, Alder worried about Jesse lusting after his brother, but that was because he didn't really know the man. There was five years between them. Brave was closer to Jesse's age at thirty, so they'd both lived enough to show the younger members of the band a few things. While Alder had been in college, getting a degree in early childhood education, Brave had been on the road with his first band, Live on Satan's Time. Brave had once confessed he'd been a lot closer to the oldest brother in the Trousseau clan, Valor, and all his hopes and dream had ridden on LOST making it big.

Valor's death had been tough on the whole family. Alder and Brave probably wouldn't even speak now if they hadn't figured out how fucking good they sounded together.

Jesse found Alder and Malakai, gave them the news, and then had to calm them down. The checkout lines were insane and by the time they got outside, the cops and Brave and Tate were gone. Jesse loaded up the groceries in the back of the van while telling the story of what had gone down in as few words as possible.

Malakai, predictably, looked like he wanted to hunt down the assholes who'd jumped Tate and dismember them. Alder didn't say much, but he was tense the whole way back to the bus. Once all the bags were unpacked and put away, he disappeared into his bunk with the curtain closed.

The crew was all done packing up the open tent and folding chairs, drivers picked for the van and the bus, and everything running right on schedule. All they had to do was wait to hear from Brave on Tate's condition.

A few hours passed. The other bands left the lot and the quiet was oppressive as night fell. Jesse perched on the edge of a picnic table behind the venue, waving the rest of the crew off when they asked if they should wait up with him. Whether it was twenty minutes or a full night, they had to grab whatever sleep they could. It was gonna be a long drive, either to the next show or back home to Detroit if they had to cut the tour short.

A cab pulled up and Jesse let out a sigh of relief as Tate stepped out of the backseat. Brave rose from the other side and his gaze locked on Jesse. Pulse stuttering at Brave's broad smile, Jesse pulled out another cigarette, knowing full well he'd regret all this chain-smoking tomorrow. He let the smoke out slowly, staring up at the clear night sky and the scattered stars that shone brightly for being so close to the city. He heard Brave approach, but didn't look at him. He needed a few seconds to raise his defenses before he faced the man.

He could deal with Brave being seductive—wasn't easy, but he'd managed for a while. But the man who'd rescued Tate was harder to resist.

"He's got a couple bruised ribs and the doctor wants him to take it easy, but Tate's got his go ahead to do whatever he wants so long as the pain's bearable."

Jesse winced, glancing over to see Brave was probably thinking the same thing he was. "Tate's got a pretty high pain threshold. Does the doctor know he's a freakin' drummer?"

"Yep." Brave sat on the table beside him. "He's been told to breath normally and not lay around too much. But get plenty of rest." His lips slanted with amusement. "He asked if I was Tate's dad. Not sure if I should be insulted or flattered. Mom said I was born a ladies man, so who knows what I was getting into when I was nine."

Cuffing Brave shoulder with the back of his hand, Jesse made a face. "That's sick, man."

"It really is, isn't it?" Brave's brow furrowed slightly. "I don't want to cancel the show tomorrow, but I won't let the kid hurt himself worse. He might have trouble sleeping tonight. I'm gonna take a shift behind the wheel if that's all right?"

"That's fine." Jesse dropped his half smoked cigarette and crushed it under his heel. They might as well head out. He'd planned to drive the bus through the night, but sharing the duty would be a hell of a lot better. "I guess I can crash in one of the empty bunks."

Brave shook his head. "They're all full of junk. You can sleep in my bed."

"No." Jesse wet his lips, trying to keep his tone light as he turned to see Brave frowning at him. "I'm not up for this tonight, Brave. The kid got hurt on my watch. Even if I didn't give a shit about being used, I'm not in the mood."

Before he could reach the door, Brave fisted his hands in Jesse's shirt and pushed him against the side of the bus. He held him there, breathing hard, bringing his lips close to Jesse's.

"I don't know where you got the fucking idea in your head that I just want to use you." Brave pressed against him, brushing his scruffy cheek against Jesse's smooth one as he whispered. "Being around you drives me fucking insane."

Swallowing hard, Jesse nodded. "You're used to getting what you want."

"Yeah, I am. And you're a challenge." Brave rested his forehead on Jesse's shoulder. "But that's not why I can't stop thinking about you. I wanna prove you wrong. I wanna prove I can have something good and not fuck it up."

Defenses completely wrecked, Jesse fisted his hand in Brave's hair, jerking him back enough to look into his eyes. What

31

he saw there sealed his fate. He inhaled roughly and nodded. "Okay."

Brave blinked at him, his lips splitting into that heartbreaking smile he wore so well. "That mean you won't turn away if I try to kiss you?"

With a soft laugh, Jesse closed the distance between them, brushing Brave's lips with his own in a soft kiss. "That's what it means."

Claiming his lips, Brave tasted him with the same wild abandon he had for everything he was passionate about. The pressure of his lips, his grip on Jesse's shirt, the way he moved his body, all showed Jesse the lust he'd been holding back. His attempts at seduction had been cautious before, but now they'd come in full force.

Not ready to go all in, Jesse drew away, gentling the kiss as he cupped Brave's face in his hands, taking in the flavor of honey and ginger and smoke. Brave's lips were hot, but his cheeks were cool under Jesse's palms. The night was cold for October in Ohio. The last thing they needed was Brave getting sick on top of Tate being injured.

He could go on kissing Brave all night, but instead, he let his hands fall to his sides and grinned. "Don't hate me, but we gotta go."

"I couldn't." Brave gave his head a rough shake, then laughed. "Hate you I mean. But you're right. Do you want me to drive first, or—"

"You check on Tate. I've got this." Jesse hesitated, running his hand over Brave's tousled hair before forcing himself to move. He got on the bus and immediately noticed Alder, sitting at the table in the front lounge, ear buds in his ears and a pad of paper set up where he was jotting down music notes.

As Brave went to the bunks to check on Tate, Jesse stepped to Alder's side and waited until he looked up. He wasn't sure what to say. Wasn't sure if he should say anything.

But one glance at Jesse and it was like Alder knew everything. His lips thinned and he let out a heavy sigh.

"I'll be fine." Jesse wasn't sure why he needed to explain, but he did. And he was desperate for Alder to understand. "You can say 'I told you so' if I'm wrong. But I don't think you'll have to."

Alder set his black pencil down on the paper, rubbing at the graphite smeared on the side of his left hand. "I'd never say that, Jesse. If he can make you happy…" He pressed his eyes shut. "That's all I want for you. You deserve to be happy."

"I am." Jesse said it without thinking. And realized it was true. He'd been waiting to see if the risk was worth putting his heart in Brave's hands. Now, he truly believed it was.

Smiling, Alder took a firm hold of his hand. "Then go for it. But don't forget, I'm here."

Jesse turned his hand to squeeze Alder's. "I've never doubted that, man. I love you."

With a rough inhale, Alder nodded. "I love you too."

Chapter Two

Screaming and singing were very very different. Danica Tallien sat in her hotel room in Vegas, listening to the playlist her agent had sent her. Everything from hard rock to death metal. Some of the music was like a little man in leather and metal studs cracking the inside of her skull with a pickaxe, but she listened anyway. She couldn't very well dive into the metal culture if she'd never listened to the music. This was kind of like studying the guest list before a party attended by the most influential fashion designers in the industry.

Only, a bit more fun.

A couple of bands had her relaxing and bobbing her head, taking in the complicated riffs and the deep, tri-tones that made the hairs rise on the back of her neck. For these songs even the screams added another layer, like a different range of the instrument a voice was supposed to be. The way the lyrics were snarled and growled made the lead singer sound like an animal. A beast barely under control, restrained only by the message in the aggressive music.

She could picture herself in the pit, jumping and cheering and punching her fist in the air along with the crowds who worshiped these bands. The very idea of being caught in the middle of all those bodies slamming together was invigorating. And terrifying. But so was this whole insane plan to change her image for the media.

Bullet came on and Danica smiled. She'd loved them for a while, even though she tended to stick with lighter pop tunes. Singing along, she finished touching up her makeup. The threatening headache faded away and she was able to listen to the next song without wanting to throw her iPod across the room. She didn't know the words to this one, but it was good. She checked her iPod for the name of the band. Her pulse sped up and she nibbled on her bottom lip.

Winter's Wrath, one of the bands she'd be meeting at the after party tonight. She was excited to see them live on stage, but hanging out in the private area reserved for VIPs was a completely different story. And it wasn't like she could just show up and hang out.

She had to be noticed.

Tightening her jaw, she gave a firm nod and looked down at her tight black jeans, stylishly ripped, and her black 'Merete' Wornstar t-shirt which had cuts in the material of the arms, back, and along the bottom edge. More the type of shirt you'd see on stage than in the crowd, but she couldn't blend in too much. Her waist-length, dark brown hair fell in loose waves, tumbling over her shoulders, held away from her face on one side with three rows of tight braids. Not too revealing, but not cutesy.

She didn't look like the little girl who'd done commercials and modeled kid's clothes for companies like J Crew and DNKY. No one would recognize her as the child who'd had backup roles in a couple of shows.

Those accomplishments filled her portfolio. And the experiences were fond memories, but had ended up hurting her career as an adult. She didn't have the edgy appeal so many designers were looking for.

But that will change. Tonight.

After lacing up her beige heels, she grabbed her purse, double checked for her room key, and strode out. She had about two hours left before the concert started and she needed to grab a bite to eat. Probably takeout in her car, because she wasn't in the mood to be gawked at. One would figure there were enough hot women in Vegas that guys wouldn't even notice anymore, but they did. And many forgot their manners under the bright lights of sin city.

Halfway down Tropicana, on her way to the little In and Out burger joint on the edge of town, there was a loud *Pop!* The steering wheel jerked in her hands. She bit into her cheek, tightening her grip to hold the wheel steady as she accelerated slightly to regain control. She eased off the gas, cruised into the other lane, then pulled off the road in front of a closed office complex.

All those lessons and warnings from her grandfather when he'd taught her to drive when she was sixteen had seemed excessive at the time. Now? Damn, she loved that man. He'd be so proud.

Even more so if she used the other skills he'd taught her.

She'd changed tires for friends before—guys and girls—so it didn't take long before she had the spare secured in place. And aside from a bit of dust, she managed not to get dirty.

It wasn't until she had her food and was chewing a huge mouthful of the fully loaded burger—her agent would kill her if she caught her eating all this cheese and bacon—that she noticed one of her acrylic nails was broken.

Damn it! She stared at the stupid nail, which with it's one little flaw, screwed up her entire schedule.

When she was a kid, chicks freaking over a broken nail used to make her laugh. As she got older, and started modeling, she learned to treat her appearance like a valuable asset. Her grandfather hadn't had the money to put her through acting classes. He'd helped her pay for a modeling portfolio and she'd repaid him shortly after she'd done her first commercial. Then she got a small part in a TV movie, playing the Native American friend of a girl in an early settlement town in California.

Once she hit her late teens, both modeling jobs and even callbacks for commercial auditions lessened. Her grandfather had his first stroke when she was eighteen, so she'd ditched her plans to move out of Bay Mills, Michigan and head to New York where she'd thought all her dreams would come true.

She didn't regret not going though. Half the models in places like New York and Los Angeles ended up working as waitresses and barmaids. Staying home, she'd helped her grandfather get healthy, found a job at the local boutique, and built a pretty decent online platform. Between her job, and the money her grandfather made working part time at the casino, they hadn't done too bad at first.

Unexpected things, like her car breaking down, the roof of their house needing repairs, and a pipe bursting in the basement, threw them from living comfortably to struggling to pay for the barest necessities. Her grandfather wanted to take on more hours, but she was so afraid he'd push himself too hard again. She couldn't lose him; he was the only family she had left.

An offer of representation from the talent agency, Diverse Faces, came a few days after she turned twenty-one. Like some kind of angel, Sophie stepped in, finding her several high paying photo-shoots, which brought in enough to pay the bills. Danica had to quit her job to keep up with all the traveling, and she hated leaving her grandfather, but he wouldn't let her stay. He'd been almost as excited as she'd been at her getting back to doing what she loved.

Two years later and Danica had an amazing career. One she was proud of. But Sophie believed Danica could do even more. She wanted to get Danica in front of the 'right people'.

The contract she'd signed was very strict about maintaining her figure, as well as how polished and respectable she had to appear in public. Which was funny, considering what Sophie had asked her to do. Either way, Danica felt a little guilty about the burger, since she knew her dietitian wouldn't have approved this much red meat in a week, never mind one meal. And if she gained weight, there'd be some explaining to do. Sophie would question how serious she was about her future as a model.

So yeah, no way was she going anywhere with her nails messed up.

Finishing up the last, delicious bite, Danica Googled nail salons near the venue. The show was happening at the Hard Rock Hotel. There was a salon a couple of blocks away with great reviews.

She still had enough time if she hurried, so she headed out, pleased to find the salon was off the strip and not too busy. She had her nail fixed within twenty minutes and left a nice tip to the sweet lady who didn't speak a word of English.

Hitting the sidewalk outside, she smiled as the sun slipped behind a few of the taller hotels, giving her a break from the blinding light. It was still warm out, but nowhere as bad as she'd expected. Then again, it was almost November. Sophie, who'd been born and raised in Vegas, had told her it actually got cold here.

Danica would have to see it to believe it.

Turning to get back to her car, which she'd left in a small parking garage, she almost ran into a man that was standing in front of the salon, staring at it with the same dread one might have before going into the emergency room of a hospital. He looked down at something fisted in his hand, then sighed and took a step forward.

Then took a step back, spun around, almost slamming right into her.

"Shit." He put his hand on her arm to steady her. "Sorry about that."

She smiled at him, trying to see past the long, black hair falling over half of his face. "That's all right. Are you waiting for someone?"

He shook his head. "No, I…have to go in."

"*For…?*" She bit back a smile as he ducked his head. He was tall, with broad shoulders and a presence she'd noticed in some of the most talented actors she'd come across in the business. The ones the camera loved, who you wanted to be near, but whose art meant more to them than all the glamour, fame, and money.

His hands were rough for an actor though. She noticed them as he held one up, showing her nails with chipped black polish. His fingertips were strangely calloused. He worked hard, whatever he did.

He pushed enough hair away from his face for her to see his sheepish smile. "Tate usually does them for me—I suck at it. I'm kinda avoiding him today, so I got to find another way to fix 'em. They look like shit." His brow furrowed. "Sorry. I swear too much."

"You're fine." She noticed he had something clenched tight in his other hand. "Did you bring your own polish?"

"Paint." He laughed when she arched a brow at him. Opening his hand, he showed her the bottle, which had the words 'ManGlaze' and 'Matte is Murder' on the label. "My brother calls it 'nail paint'. Supposed to be more manly or something."

She shrugged. "So I'm guessing you're not comfortable going to a salon. Not manly?"

"It's not that, it's just…" He shook his head and grinned. Damn, he had a nice smile. A quick flash of white teeth, with warmth that reached all the way to his dark brown eyes. "Okay, it's that. My manager has these rules and I'm not sure if I'm breaking them by getting a manicure."

"I completely understand. How about you don't take a chance and come with me." She continued up the sidewalk, glancing over when he hurried to keep up. "I keep an emergency nail kit in my car. Not enough to help me with a broken acrylic wrap, but I can take care of your nails if you want."

He didn't speak until they reached her car. Bracing his hip on the hood, he waited while she fetched her small kit from the backseat. "I appreciate this, but it wasn't really smart of you to bring some strange guy to your car. What if I was dangerous?"

Chuckling, she hopped up on the hood and pulled at his hand until he let him set it on her knee. Pulling on a pair of disposable gloves to protect her nails, she wet a cotton ball with some acetone and went to work on cleaning the thick layer of polish.

"If you're a dangerous guy using your nails to get me alone, props for creativity." She laughed and peeked up at him. "I'm armed and my grandpa taught me how to defend myself. There's no way he'd let me come down to Vegas otherwise."

"So you're not from here?"

"No, I grew up near Bay Mills, Michigan." She held her tongue between her teeth as she finished with his pinkie. "My grandfather owns some land right off the reservation."

"Oh…" The man looked confused. "I didn't think many… Fuck, I don't know enough to say shit. Never mind."

She put the cotton balls in a small waste bag in her kit, then took the 'nail paint' from him. "He inherited it from a man he worked for since he was a teen. An opportunity not many have, but there are good people out there."

"I know." He held still as she began painting his nails. "You just hear a lot about land disputes with the…Native Americans?"

She cocked her head, not sure why she couldn't stop smiling at this guy. "You're really caught up in being PC, aren't you? Yes, you can call us that and there are issues. I'm luckier than most. My grandfather raised me, made sure I got a good education and still experienced traditional stuff. I even know some Ojibwe, but I'm not as fluent as I'd like to be. I take classes when I'm home long enough."

"He didn't teach you?"

"He couldn't. He went to boarding school." She swallowed as her throat tightened. They needed to change the subject. Grandpa's stories of his education weren't pleasant. "What about you? You mentioned a manager. Are you an actor?"

"Something like that." He watched her carefully stroking the brush over his nails. "Is it shitty of me to not want to tell you much? Talking to you like a normal person is kinda nice."

Letting out a soft laugh, she nodded. "I get it. I'm usually just a pretty face."

"*Really?*"

41

Her eyes widened. "What's that supposed to mean?"

Withdrawing his hands, he held them up. Which was funny considering how careful he was with them. "I'm not saying you're not pretty. You're gorgeous. Stunning. I've never met a more beautiful woman in—"

Smacking his arm, she reached for his wrist so she could get started on the second coat. "Shut up. I don't believe a fucking word."

"I meant you're easy to talk to. And nice. And smart." His smile was all charm now. "Forgive me?"

"I'll think about it." She realized they were smiling at each other like a couple of idiots and turned her focus back to his nails. Being near him, touching him, didn't trigger the instincts she had fine-tuned to men who were just looking to get laid. There was no stupid-making spark between them either, which would have brought her guard up. She felt light. Happy. She could imagine drawing out these moments with him to hours, even days, like it was the most natural thing in the world.

Except she was here for work and she didn't have days to make new friends. Or even hours today. Her last runway job had made her enough to buy her some time, but she needed to land a decent contract before she could allow for any distractions.

Finishing his last nail, she closed the bottle and handed it back to him, checking the time on her phone. "I've got tickets to a concert, so I have to go. Let your nails dry for about twenty minutes and you should be fine."

"Thanks." He leaned over to look at her phone. "Shit. The concert's in less than an hour?"

"Yeah?" She studied his face, which was drawn with worry. "Are you going too?"

"Yep."

"Hard Rock?"

He nodded. "And I kinda walked here. I'll never make it in time."

She smirked. "Need a lift?"

Exhaling noisily, he grinned at her. "I owe you. When my nails are dry, I'll give you my number. You can text me when you've got time to go out? Maybe get a coffee or something?"

"Maybe." She hopped off the hood and opened the passenger side door for him. Once she was behind the wheel, she caught him awkwardly trying to put on his seatbelt and chuckled. "Let me get that."

Leaning over him, she had to fight not to press closer. He was solid, all muscle under his black t-shirt. He held very, very still as she drew the strap over his chest. She forced herself to start the car without teasing him for acting all nervous. They were both in a hurry. If he was going to the same concert, maybe he'd be at the after party. She wasn't supposed to be 'seen with' actors—especially those she didn't recognize, putting them on the same undistinguished level as her—but she'd like to spend more time with him.

"You mind if I put on some music?" She cursed herself as the words left her mouth. Since when did she ask? Unless her grandfather was in the car, she played whatever she wanted. Which, for the longest time, was modern country music.

He lifted his shoulder in a distracted shrug. "Go ahead."

At a red light, she plugged in her iPod, starting over the last song she'd been listening to. She bopped her head to the music, checking once to see if the heavy sound bothered the man. His face reddened, and the second their eyes met, he turned to stare out the window.

As soon as she pulled into the parking by the hotel, the man reached for his pocket, then gave her a questioning look. She nodded. His nails should be dry.

"Damn it." As soon as he had his phone out, his face lost all color. "I gotta go, but…maybe I'll see you inside?"

"I hope so." Not at all what she'd wanted to say, but he'd already taken off running. She rested her hip on the side of her car, giving herself a minute to regain her composure.

She'd met hotter guys. Men who graced the covers of magazines. Fitness models with bulging muscles and athletes doing their first centerfold. Many of them had hit on her, but she rarely got involved because this was her career and she wasn't about to fuck it up with all the drama involved in relationships with men whose egos were their first love.

Come to think of it, she hadn't gone on a real date in almost two years. Which meant she hadn't been enjoying much down and dirty fun since…ugh, no way was she going to start thinking about her first boyfriend. They'd been high school sweethearts. He'd gotten a scholarship to play football. Been drafted before he graduated. Having a pretty girl on his arm—AKA *her*—had been great until he gained a few fans. Then Danica was in the way.

He'd been her first and her last. She'd been heartbroken for a while, but Grandpa had set her straight. No boy was worth losing all she'd worked for. The distraction had lost her a few auditions. She'd gotten drunk once and that was the only time Grandpa had ever lost patience with her.

Understandable, considering he'd lost his daughter, Danica's mother, to alcohol poisoning when Danica was just a baby. And it wasn't a secret that many on the reserve turned to alcohol when life seemed hopeless.

Not that Danica didn't drink, but never when she was stressed or depressed. And she refused to let herself forget all her grandfather had done for her. She wouldn't risk her future for anything or anyone.

About twenty minutes later, she handed over her ticket and made her way to the front of the stage. Since she had a VIP ticket, there was a gated off area that she had access to, but the pressing crowd made her nervous, so she stuck close to the edge where she could clearly see the security in their yellow shirts.

The first band didn't seem to excite anyone, even though she thought they were pretty good. A few feet away from her some teenage girls wearing Winter's Wrath t-shirts took selfies and flirted with security, each loudly trying to one-up the other with their knowledge of heavy metal bands. One pulled down the collar of her shirt to show off a tattooed signature. She swore

Randy Taylor had signed her boob after fucking her. Her exact words.

Randy Taylor was in his forties. The girl *might* be sixteen. Danica doubted very much the well-known singer and author would even go there. She'd seen some of his interviews while getting familiar with the metal scene and he seemed like a smart guy. Messed up, but smart.

Considering how many guys had claimed to have fucked *her*, Danica didn't give the girl's claims any credit. Actually, she felt a little sick listening to some of these chicks talk about the guys. Two of the teens mentioned wanting to 'rape' Brave Trousseau. Because, yeah, that was cool.

Danica had never felt more out of place. She moved closer to a group of ladies that looked to be in their thirties. They weren't that much more into the opening band than the rest of the crowd, but they seemed normal enough. One looked over at Danica and smiled.

"Hey, sweetie. Are you here alone?"

Danica nodded, her cheeks heating as the five older women surrounded her. "I was in the area, and I've heard some of Horizon's music, so I figured I'd check it out."

"Nice! And they put on an awesome show." The woman glanced around at the others. "Drinks on me! Hurry up, because I don't want to miss our boys!" She took orders from all the ladies, then turned to Danica. "Do you want something?"

"A rum and coke would be great." Danica reached into her purse for her wallet.

The woman shook her head. "It's on me. We're all authors, except for a couple of *amazing* readers that came to hang out." She pointed at two of the women. "After a few, we may start telling you crazy stories about the people in our heads. If you can put up with us, you deserve a drink or two."

Being around these women put Danica at ease. Her face was hot from blushing as the authors gave her a few details about their books when the band took a short break, but she'd taken a few names down in the notes on her phone to look up later.

She'd never read the kind of books these ladies wrote, but she had a feeling she was missing out.

The author buying all the drinks, whose name she learned was Melanie Marchande, wrote about sexy billionaires. She was wearing an emerald corset and a long black skirt and had such a confident presence Danica found herself hanging on to her every word.

Until Winter's Wrath took the stage. The first strum of the guitar and the screams around her became deafening. All chatter stopped. Every head turned to the stage.

Danica let herself be pushed in tight with the crowd. Everyone else was throwing up devil horns, so she followed their lead.

But once her eyes hit the stage, she dropped her arm and pressed a hand over her mouth. The guitarist, the one starting the riff for a song she'd listened to for the first time today, whipped his head back to throw his long black hair over one shoulder. His fingers, with freshly painted black nails, moved in a blur over the fret board.

No wonder they'd been such a mess.

The woman at her side nudged her. Melanie grinned and pointed at the guitarist, practically shouting to be heard over the music. "Alder Trousseau. One of the best guitarists in the business. I'm trying to get in touch with his people to get him on a cover."

Danica nodded, not sure what to say. She tried to let the music absorb her, but she couldn't take her eyes off Alder. He'd changed since they'd sat together on the hood of her car, now wearing tight black jeans and a black dress shirt with the sleeves ripped off. The buttons weren't going to make it through the show. The second he'd picked up his guitar, a few had popped open, baring half his chest.

She would have been fine with their encounter being nothing but a fond memory. Granted, she might have wondered what would have happened if she hadn't brushed him off. If she'd given him her number and told him to call. But life would have gone on.

This changed everything. He was one of the very people she was supposed to be seen with. There was no way she could avoid him at the after party. Not that she wanted to.

But she couldn't be all casual now. Flirting and hoping for a photo opp. He'd become a real person. He'd treated her like one. When she saw him at the after party, could she play fast and loose and treat him like a complete stranger? The alternative was letting the photographers catch her with him. Which she wouldn't do.

Not without telling him why she was really here.

He didn't tell you who he was. You don't owe him anything.

True.

Actually, he owes you.

Very true.

After a few songs, the lead singer picked up the microphone and stared out over the crowd. An evil smile spread across his lips. "I'd ask you how you're doing, but we're in fucking Vegas! Are we ready to go fucking wild?"

The crowd screamed. The teens Danica had escaped could be heard over the rest crying out to the singer—who Melanie told her was Brave Trousseau—about how much they wanted him. He blew the girls a kiss.

"I'm sure a few of you will recognize this song, but I need to see you moving!" He put down the mic and put his hands together before him, then spread them wide. The crowd parted like the red sea and the drummer began to pound out a familiar beat, joined by the bassist. "If you don't know what's going on, get the fuck out of the way!"

Several men stayed in the cleared out area, some pacing, some bouncing in place. One did a flip, then gestured like he wanted the surrounding crowd to come at him.

Melanie backed Danica right into the guardrail. Laughing, she looked over her shoulder. "Stay right there! Things might get a little rough!"

"Wait… Wait… Wait…" Brave growled into the mic. "Go!"

The song began and the throng ran to meet in the center, all those not joining in pressing back to avoid flailing bodies. Danica had to fight to tear her eyes away from the violent scene so she could watch the show on stage. Brave threw his body to the very edge of the stage, his gritty screams making the words of the song nearly incoherent, but that didn't seem to matter to anyone. The temperature rose as Danica found herself moving to the music, bobbing her head in time to the aggressive rhythm, and by the time the second song ended, her hair was sticking to the sweat on her skin.

The drumbeat stopped suddenly and both Brave and Alder turned their backs on the crowd. Silence spread around the venue as the bassist dropped his guitar and ran to the drum kit. A low thrum of unease spread around her, and she bit her bottom lip as the rhythm guitarist stepped up to Alder's side. Alder nodded and picked up the mic.

"Those of you who follow us online know some shit went down last week. At *Walmart*." He gave the crowd that same sheepish smile he'd given her earlier. A few people laughed, but the low murmurs were full of concern. "Tate's toughed it out for the last few shows, but now he needs to listen to the fucking doctor and get some rest. What do you think?"

The crowd roared and a chant started. "Tate! Tate! Tate!"

"That's what I thought." Alder glanced over as a roadie helped the drummer off the stage. The drummer gave the crowd a parting thumbs up. Alder inclined his head at his young band mate. "His buddy, Derrick, is the drum tech and he's got some mad skills. We'll probably lose him to another band before long, but you wanna see what he can do while we've still got him?"

By the deafening response, the crowd approved. From the side of the stage, a teen with messy, bleach blond hair wearing a black Winter's Wrath t-shirt ambled over to the drums, giving a shy wave halfway there.

Brave took the mic from his brother, a wicked smile on his lips. "That boy's so getting laid tonight. Am I right, ladies?"

All the women in the crowd screamed in accord.

The woman standing beside Danica, another author whose name she was pretty sure was Sasha White, leaned close. "Total sub. Not my type, but if I ever write a Domme, she could so teach that boy a few things."

Danica's cheeks were blazing. She ducked her head. "I swear, you all could find inspiration anywhere."

"Absolutely." Sasha grinned at her. "The way you're looking at the guitarist is definitely going in a book."

Thankfully, the band started playing before Danica had to make some lame-assed protest. The fans didn't seem to notice the new drummer didn't have the unique sound of the man he'd replaced. Then again, the guitarists were giving it their all, lengthening their solos and pulling off some crazy antics that drove the fans wild. The rhythm guitarist swung his guitar around his neck, never missing a note. The bassist dropped to his knees during Alder's solo, curving his hands around the back of Alder's thighs as Alder threw his head back and thrust his hips.

Of all the things Danica had fantasized about, two guys hadn't really hit her radar. But watching the men toss all sexual restraints aside changed that. She covered her mouth with her hand when Brave grabbed the bassist by his hair and bit the side of his neck.

Shoving Brave, Alder growled something his mic didn't catch. The bassist stood between them, smiling at the crowd as he continued to play. Brave didn't miss a beat as he roared into the mic, but Danica caught the absence of Alder's vicious riffs. They returned so quickly, she might have imagined the slip, but part of her wondered if the animosity was completely staged.

After Winter's Wrath finished their set, the group of authors and readers asked Danica to join them at the bar. She went, not as drawn to the music with the next band as she had been with 'their boys'. She chatted with the women for a while, downing a couple more rum and cokes before asking the bartender for a water so she didn't get wasted. As much fun as she was having, this was still part of her job and the night was only beginning.

The attention of the women around her shifted and she turned to see what they were all looking at. She took a gulp of her water as her mouth went dry. A door at the other end of the bar had swung open and several members of the band came out. First was the bassist, with the drummer who looked a little pale, and was moving slowly. He covered his mouth as he coughed and the bassist patted his back, gesturing to the bartender.

"Can you fix my boy a hot toddy?" He watched the drummer sit on a stool, then leaned on the bar. "One more night, Tate. If you're not better by tomorrow, you're going back to the hospital."

Tate muttered thanks to the bartender as a steaming mug was placed in front of him. "I'll be fine. Just lost my breath a bit." He took a sip and grimaced. "Ugh, this is nasty. Can't I just have a shot of whiskey?"

"Nope. Drink up."

The rest of the guys joined them, all focused on the youngest member of the band. Danica tried to follow the hushed conversation of the other women, but she couldn't shift her gaze from Alder. He looked so worried; she wanted to go hug him. And then hug Tate—very carefully, considering the way he pressed his hand to his side and cringed.

Handing out hugs. Yep, that would be the *perfect* way to approach them.

Alder put his arm over Tate's shoulders. "You need to get checked out. I'll go with you. Won't be that bad."

"Will you guys lay off already? Malakai's been on my case since you got off the damn stage. Bad enough I needed to be fucking replaced during the fucking show." He tipped the mug to his lips, his throat working as he swallowed fast. "I'm not missing the after party because you all wanna play mommy. Like it or not, I'm getting my freak on tonight. YOLO, bitches."

Brave groaned and waived the bartender over. "I need a drink. You promise to never say that again and you can do whatever you want."

Once they were all served, the guys changed the subject, discussing everything from their next album to how they planned to spend the next few days in Vegas. Danica found it easier to pay attention to the authors brainstorming than listen in on how many strippers the band planned to fuck. She did notice Alder wasn't taking part in the conversation, but there was no way she could casually go over and say 'Hi' now. There were groupies hovering, waiting for their chance to pounce, and Danica refused to be counted among them.

Did that make her stuck up? Maybe, but she'd been conditioned for years to focus on appearances, physical and otherwise. Kinda funny, considering how her perceived appearance would change if all went well tonight. Either way, her best bet would be to wait for the right opening.

"You're not gonna find what you want at the after party, Tate. And Cole would have your head." Alder exchanged a look with Malakai that Danica couldn't read. "Come on, there's a place not too far you might like."

A nod from Tate and Alder led the way out the exit by the bar.

Danica sighed. So much for that plan.

Looks like I'll be attending the after party all on my own.

Hitting on strange men and hoping they didn't expect too much. She'd been telling the truth about knowing how to defend herself, and she'd had to prove it in the past, but rather than worrying about fending off horny guys, she'd been looking forward to spending time with Alder.

She hadn't known him when this had all started though, so really, nothing had changed.

Except the twinge of disappointment that didn't fade as the headlining band finished their set and it was time for her to leave her new friends with a promise to connect online. She made her way to the Vanity Nightclub, which had been taken over by the bands, allowing entry to only those with special passes—like the one she had. After showing the bouncer her card, she slipped in, happy that she'd at least managed to get here before the crowds.

Choosing a corner booth so she could observe before she dove in, she ordered a stiff drink and settled in, doing her best to look relaxed.

She had a feeling if Alder had been here, she wouldn't have had to pretend.

Chapter Three

The Piranha Nightclub was definitely the most colorful club Alder had ever been to. Dropping the cash for the bottle service that would get them into the VIP section, he followed the server through the lounge lined, outdoor patio, up to their private table in the skyboxes with Tate on his heel. Theatre smoke drifted around them as they made their way up the stairs, heavy technopop pounding an irritating beat that made him wonder how long he could put up with being here.

A few drinks and five minutes of Tate doing his thing on the dance floor should give them some good prospects. If Tate hit it off with some guy, they could bring him to the after party. And then whatever Tate decided to do with the guy in his room was his business.

Maybe.

Unlikely.

Serving himself and Tate some rum and coke from the supplies on the table, Alder studied the younger man. Tate had been pretty open about wanting to experience all kinds of wild sex with men, women, and maybe a combination of the two. The kid wasn't a virgin, but how much of his talk was just that? Even now, he held his glass to his lips and stared at the crowd on the edge of the balcony overlooking the dance floor in horrified wonder. There was no telling if it was because of the blatant sexuality displayed between the men, or simple inexperience. Either way, he was in *way* over his head.

Good thing they weren't downstairs.

If Alder let Tate take off with some guy, Malakai would kill him. No doubt about it. The rest of the band might jokingly treat Tate like a little brother, but the bassist seriously considered him family.

Not that Alder would let anything happen to Tate, but it was hard to figure out how much supervision the kid needed. His brothers never gave two shits where he disappeared to when they used to hit the clubs together. Valor, the eldest, had always hooked up with some chick early in the night. Then kept her around to show off before taking her home. Brave liked a bit of a challenge, so he'd work the crowd, looking for the first guy or girl that wasn't tripping over themselves to get with him.

Alder had done all right, but he didn't have Tate's messed up past. What if someone offered Tate drugs? What if…?

Bringing him out was fucking brilliant. What was the plan again?

Well, avoiding fucking the kid himself just to shut him up was part of it. Rejecting Tate's teasing advances was starting to feel like kicking a puppy. Because he knew exactly why Tate reached out to him, why Tate had decided to open up to him about the urges that had become more than curiosity.

Tate slept around almost as much as Brave did, but he was sweet to the groupies he messed with. A few of them he'd actually met online and still kept in touch with. If anyone was getting used, it was Tate. But cute little college girls and cougars would only break Tate's heart.

Men could do some serious physical damage. Tate had spent the last three years with either the band, or venue security, shielding him from the rowdy metal fans. Safe behind his drum kit, he didn't even make contact with the nuts in the pit. Alder wasn't sure the drummer could even throw a punch.

"We don't have to stay if you don't want, Alder." Tate refilled his glass, staring at the ice floating around the fizzing Coke as he cleared his throat. "It was cool of you to bring me here, but I know you hate this kinda music, and there's too many people and—"

"Tate." Alder smiled when Tate looked up. The mix of eagerness and fear in the younger man's eyes made his mind up for him. "We're here for a few days. Maybe you meet someone, maybe you don't. You've got a better chance here than at a gig."

Tonguing his bottom lip, Tate eyed the group of men closest to their table. He blushed and dropped his gaze when several gave him appreciative glances. "Am I looking for someone just to fuck me though? Like, aren't I supposed to wear something special to make it obvious I'm…available?"

"First of all, I can't tell you what you're looking for, kid. Second, no one's gonna think you're available if you're sitting here next to me." Alder leaned back, propped his ankle on his knee, and made a dismissive gesture with his hand. "Go dance."

"You afraid people will think I'm yours?" The fear disappeared as Tate gave him a slow, provocative smile. "You know, this would be a whole lot simpler if you'd just—"

"No, Tate." Alder rolled his eyes, reaching out to snatch Tate's glass before the boy got *too much* liquid courage. "Keep it up and I'll tell the first guy that asks about you that you're a top."

"What if I *am* a top?"

Alder snorted.

Tate gave him the finger, but he managed to get to the railing without any more stalling. Resting his hands on the barrier of the skybox, he began to sway a little to the music, transfixed on what he saw below. According to what Alder had been told about the club, the Go-Go boys were probably down there. Yet another thing Tate hadn't experienced.

It didn't take long before Tate lost his uncharacteristic shyness and started moving in a way that was gonna get guys stuffing bills in his waistband. Shimmying low, he worked his hips in a slow thrust as he rose, lifting the bottom of his shirt to bare his tight abs, showing off the cut lines of his pelvis as he shoved his jeans down an extra inch. He ran one hand over the solid length pressing against his zipper and his eyes drifted shut.

A man slid onto the bench at Alder's side. Alder gave him a bored look.

"He's something else." The man, built like a bear with a shaved head and thick arms that could snap Tate like a twig, watched Tate with a dark, predatory look in his eyes. "If he was mine, there's no way I'd let him put on a show like that."

Pulling out a pack of smokes, Alder took his time lighting one, then shrugged. "He's happier when I don't keep him on a short leash."

"Yeah?" The man scratched his clean-shaven jaw. "So…do you let him play? I've got a boy. Cute like him. Wouldn't mind lending him to you for a couple hours."

The man pointed at a preppy young blond with pale skin and big eyes. He was cute, in a clean-cut, jean ironing kinda way. Brave would have taken the deal in a second, even though Tate wasn't his to trade off.

But Alder wasn't his brother.

"Sorry man, but I'm possessive." Alder let the smoke out between his lips slowly, hoping the dude didn't press the issue. As confident as he was in his fighting skills, this guy was built like a damn dump truck. He could run Alder down without breaking a sweat. And he'd have to, because Alder wasn't letting him anywhere near Tate if he was still standing.

The man simply grunted. "Not that I blame you, but…*damn*. You're one lucky man."

After the big guy left, another shortly took his place. Sleazy-looking creep. Tate wouldn't have liked him. Or the one after, who knocked over Alder's drink and smelled like tequila and ass.

Finally, a man that looked close to Tate's age approached Tate, rather than Alder. Alder sat forward as Tate stopped dancing and the two started chatting. The man was only a bit taller than Tate, wearing a snug grey tank top that showed off some damn tight arms. He probably played some kind of sport. He had an earnest smile and he wasn't being pushy, just showing interest.

So when Tate brought him back to the table, Alder decided not to scare him off. Or pretend Tate was already taken.

"This is Mitch." Tate practically bounced onto the padded bench, grinning like a moron when Mitch slid in beside him. "He only listens to country music and he plays baseball. He can't believe I never watched a game. He asked if I was from Canada."

Alder chuckled, holding out his hand to shake Mitch's. "Nice to meet you."

"Tate says you work together?" Mitch's brow rose, as though he was silently asking if there was more between them. "He was pretty vague."

"He would be, but yes. We're coworkers."

"And you're leaving here to go to a party?"

Really? Alder glanced over at Tate. The vagueness made sense, if Tate didn't want his new friend treating him like some kind of celebrity, but there was no way to keep that secret while schmoozing with some of the biggest names in the industry. Bands that had performed all week had hung around for the party, so the guest list was pretty impressive. One of the reasons Alder didn't want to miss it completely.

"Nothing much is happening now, but we could drop in after…" Tate bit his bottom lip. "Umm, well, Mitch invited us to his place for a couple of drinks."

Us? That was…unexpected. Alder arched a brow at Mitch, whose cheeks immediately went red. Was this Tate's idea? If it was, then Alder could provide some awkward backup until the kid was comfortable, then ghost out when things got hot and heavy.

Alder checked the time on his phone. "Yeah, I guess we could swing by. Have a drink and you can get changed if you want."

"Me?" Mitch looked down at his clothes, then at Tate and Alder, who were both wearing black jeans and black dress shirts, Tate's with the sleeves ripped off. "What's wrong with my clothes?"

"Nothing, Alder's being a fucking snob." Tate shot Alder a dirty look, leaning close to Mitch to whisper in his ear. "I think you're perfect."

I hope these two fuck quick. Alder suppressed the urge to gag as Mitch put his arm around Tate's waist and whispered something back to him. *Otherwise, I'm ditching the kid and telling Malakai there's no way someone this sappy can be a serial killer.*

"I brought my jeep—I haven't been drinking or anything." Mitch started walking, his hand on the small of Tate's back. "Usually I come here, watch the dancers for a bit, then go home alone. I think I got lucky tonight."

Hell, can we trade him for a serial killer?

Fifteen minutes later and they were all in Mitch's condo, a fancy place there was no way a man Mitch's age should be able to afford. Only, Mitch was apparently the son of a plastic surgeon. And played pro-baseball. He made more money than most rock stars.

Nursing his beer while the two made out, Alder checked his phone again. It couldn't have been just five freakin' minutes since they'd gotten here?

He really didn't *need* to be here at all. "Look, guys. It's been great and everything, but—"

"Wait." Mitch pulled away from Tate and shot to his feet. "Please stay. I'll make it worth your while."

Tate blinked up at Mitch like he'd never seen the man before. Unfortunately, Alder had a feeling he knew exactly what kind of man Mitch was. Rich, pro-athlete used to getting whatever the fuck he wanted.

"How are you gonna do that, Mitch?" Alder rose from the loveseat he'd been reclined on while the pair had been making out. "I only came for the drink."

"Let me suck your dick. You don't seem like the type that needs to be seduced. You want a good fuck? I can give you that." He approached Alder, dropping to his knees and reaching for his zipper. "I'll let you use me however you want. You fuck me, we'll both fuck him. It will be a wild night."

"You touch me and you'll have to give your daddy a call to fix your face, pretty boy." Alder couldn't even work up the energy to get mad. He should have figured something was up when Mitch was so damn nice.

What kind of guy picked up another guy and asked his friend to come back to his place? Fuck, if Alder hadn't been so worried about Tate, he would have been suspicious.

Letting out a tired sigh, Alder looked over at Tate. "Come on, let's get out of here."

Without a word, Tate turned his back on Mitch and made his way out the front door. Alder stiffened when Mitch put a hand on his arm before he could make his own exit.

"I handled this all wrong. Get him to come back." Mitch tightened his grip when Alder tried to pull away. "I didn't mean to be so blunt. I just thought you'd appreciate me being honest."

"Oh, I do." Alder peeled Mitch's fingers off his arm. "Good night, Mitch."

Mitch's eyes narrowed. "Seriously? You're going to give up a sure thing for that fucking twink?"

Hand on the man's neck before his brain had a chance to catch up; Alder held Mitch up against the wall and forced himself to breath slow and steady. He'd had a temper as a teen, but he'd outgrown that shit. Somewhat.

Five years ago, he'd have laid Mitch out on the floor in a bloody mess. Lucky for him, Alder had learned to restrain himself. This asshole wasn't worth the jail time.

"Lock up when I leave. Some of Tate's friends aren't as nice as I am." He released the man and took a step back. "If the boy isn't his usual, happy self, I have no problem giving them directions to your front door."

Out on the curb, Alder lit another cigarette, the thick taste of ash in his mouth making him reconsider the sponsorship he'd been offered by the e-cig company. Quitting while on tour never seemed like a good idea, but he was sick of feeling like shit every time he leaned on the addiction for relief from all the stress.

Tate bummed a cigarette and sat cross-legged beside him on the pretty white rocks lining the edge of the sidewalk. "Thank you."

"For what? Letting that dick play you?"

"No. For just being here." Tate rubbed a hand over his face. "I know I'm a pain in the ass. I just...the rest of you know what you're doing. You take what you want and you don't give a fuck. I want that, but...well, obviously, I'm the same loser I always was. People keep giving me chances, and I keep screwing up."

"Don't talk like that. You're doing just fine." Alder put his arm around Tate's shoulders. "Fucking a dude isn't going to change much."

"You don't know that. I'm...I don't know. Like, lost or something. I thought focusing on the music would be enough."

"The touring schedule is just getting to you. We all need a break." Alder palmed his phone. "Let me call a cab. We'll hit the party and have some fun. Get this shit out of your head."

"Don't bother." Tate pointed at a van cruising down the street toward them. "I called Jesse."

A small smile crept across Alder's lips as he stood, then grimaced the second he spotted who else was in the van. He quickly cut Malakai off on the passenger side before the fuming man could get too far.

Malakai slammed the heel of his palm into the center of Alder's chest. "I suggest you move, Trousseau."

"Drop it, Malakai."

"Are you fucking kidding me? You were bringing him to the club. What the fuck are you doing here?" Malakai motioned to the mixture of lavish condos and massive houses around them. "You think he needs to be messing with people like this?"

Tate tried to step between them. "Mal—"

Alder shoved him aside. "Like what? Am I suppose to screen his boyfriend's incomes before handing him a condom and saying 'Make me proud, son'?"

"He doesn't need you getting him laid."

The second time Tate tried to interrupt, Jesse pulled him back. "Don't bother. They're both too smart to keep this going for long. Give them a minute to figure out how ridiculous they're being."

How the fuck am I being ridiculous? Alder scowled at Jesse, then sighed. "I was his goddamn wingman for the night. Jesus, Malakai, he's not a fucking child." Screw good intensions. Alder could be at the after party, chilling with an ice-cold beer, talking music with some of his idols. Instead, he'd wasted his night, Tate felt like shit, and Malakai was flipping out.

And just to make things even more perfect, he was pretty sure he heard sirens in the distance. Getting closer.

"These people don't take guys like us seriously, Alder. He was slumming." Malakai's anger had lost some energy. He messaged his temples with his fingers. "Shit, I'm not even mad at you. Just...I promised his gran I'd take care of him."

"So did I, asshole." Alder grinned when Malakai's lips quirked up at the edges. "How about neither of us tell her about the rich dick. That way we still get brownies next time we visit."

Malakai inclined his head. "Deal."

They both turned to find Tate gapping at them and Jesse smirking like he wanted to say 'I told you so.' Alder shrugged. So, he wasn't babysitter of the year. He and Malakai were good. Despite how smart Jesse seemed to think Alder was, the plan to get Tate a random hookup had been stupid.

Oh, and the cops were coming. Maybe they should make themselves scarce.

Jesse climbed in behind the wheel, starting the van as the rest of them took their seats. They cleared the upscale district and reached the hotel parking not long after. Whatever Malakai had been chatting with Tate about seemed to have cheered the kid up, so maybe their fucked up little side trip hadn't ruined the night after all.

The music in the Vanity Nightclub sucked, but at least it wasn't the techno crap that grated at the inside of Alder's skull. He spotted Connor at a booth with another band and dragged a chair over to join them, Jesse, Tate and Malakai squeezing in at either side.

Connor, as usual, didn't waste any time. Or care who was there listening. He gestured at Tate with his bottle of Coors light. "So how sore are you?"

Malakai's jaw ticked. Alder braced himself to intercede if the bassist decided the band didn't need a rhythm guitarist. Or a conscious one anyway.

"What makes you think I'm the one who'd be sore?" Tate swiped a drink off the table, earning a dirty look from the lead singer of a local indie punk band. Taking a swig, Tate gave Connor a smug smile. "You want details?"

"Not really." Connor reached over to pat Tate on the shoulder like he was a proud daddy who'd just been told his son hit a game winning homerun. "You seem like you're in a good mood. Tell me you ain't gonna call him in the morning and I'll consider that some damn good progress."

"I didn't even get his name." Tate polished off the drink, then waved over a waitress to order another round. He was putting on such a good act, it wasn't hard to figure out why it had taken his grandmother so long to see the dangerous path he'd been headed when he was younger. If Tate didn't want you to worry, he'd convince you everything was unicorns pissing rainbows.

Alder knew better, but the kid seemed fine for the moment, so might as well leave him be and enjoy the rest of the night. He thanked the waitress when she brought him a fresh beer, then took a slow, refreshing drink of the rich microbrew. Not his favorite kind of beer, he was a simple man, but Tate had probably ordered Malakai's favorite to get the bassist in a better mood.

The conversation around him was relaxed, with the members of the punk band asking questions about the business and soaking up all the information they could. The lead singer asked Jesse if he'd consider sticking around and helping them hire some roadies.

Without taking his eyes off the dance floor, Jesse chuckled. "You don't need roadies yet, man. Do the work yourself for the first few years, at least until you start hitting bigger venues and have too much equipment to handle. No point in spreading your budget too thin before you're even close to a living wage."

"I wish we'd hit it as fast as you all. You must be swimming in dough."

The punk band wasn't gonna make it very far if that's what they believed. Alder exchanged a look with Malakai. Tate choked on his beer, he was laughing so hard. Malakai's firm pat on the back came off as less helpful, and more to shut him up.

Curious to see what Jesse couldn't seem to stop staring at, Alder glanced over at the dance floor. First, all he saw was Brave, dancing with some chick.

Then, *all* he saw was Brave, dancing with *the* chick. The girl he'd met in front of the nail salon. The one who'd painted his nails. He hadn't thought much about her since he'd rushed off to start the show, because he hadn't even gotten a chance to ask her name.

And now, here she was, with Brave.

Brave, who had a boyfriend.

That's what Jesse was to him, right? Alder could accept Jesse being in love with someone else. He could even accept that person being Brave. No accounting for taste, but most people didn't see his brother for the asshole he was. But Jesse didn't play Brave's games and he deserved better than to be passed over after less than a week for some...

Damn it, Alder refused to believe the girl was some groupie, just looking to get with as many rock stars as she could.

Jesse's fist slammed into his shoulder and he jumped.

"What the fuck, man?" Alder punched Jesse in the arm, hurting his fist on the man's thick arms and making him laugh. "Asshole."

Rubbing Alder's knuckles with his thumb, Jesse flashed one of those smiles that could soften even the hardest of hearts. "Stop glaring. Brave isn't interested in the woman. You've got to stop assuming he's gonna fuck me over."

"I'm not." Alder paused to take a sip of beer, wishing Jesse didn't know him so fucking well. "But how do you know he doesn't want her?"

"They've been dancing for too long."

"Maybe she's playing hard to get." Alder liked that idea. He could respect anyone making Brave work for so much as a dance. Be the challenge Brave enjoyed without giving an inch.

Placing his hand casually on the back of Alder's wrist, Jesse shook his head. "They're having fun. Talking and laughing this whole time, and he's not even trying to seduce her."

Now that was surprising. Alder leaned back in his chair, surveying the room, trying to find a single woman in the club hotter than the one in his brother's arms. Sure, a few were cute, but none had the same draw as the beauty with the long black hair.

A gorgeous woman, but he'd known plenty of those. And could fuck one every day of the week if he wanted to. He didn't because a chick riding his dick, then wanting a selfie with him in whatever bed—or more likely wall of a bathroom stall—they'd fucked on, wasn't one of his turn-ons.

The woman dancing with Brave had long legs, nice tits, and a laugh that went straight to Alder's balls. But there was something more to her that he couldn't quite put his finger on. Damn it, he wanted to though. She'd been kind and so easy to talk to he'd really wanted her to take him up on that coffee date. His crazy life had him missing out on a lot of opportunities, so he tried not to dwell on them.

This was a second chance. One he'd damn well seize.

He'd stepped aside for Brave once. For Jesse's sake. He wasn't doing it again.

Standing, he ignored Jesse's mumbled curse and the questions from the rest of the band. He crossed the dance floor, then stopped a few feet away from the woman and his brother. He wasn't usually so fucking indecisive, but what the hell was he gonna say to her? 'Don't mind me barging in on the fun you're having with my brother. I think you're…special? Damn hot? Really sweet because you painted my nails?'

Ugh. You've been out of the game too fucking long, Alder.

Yeah, but games weren't his thing. And cutting in on her and Brave would come off like a pissing contest, no matter how cool he played it.

So stand here like a loser. Much better plan.

Before he could turn around and go back to the table, where he'd only have to face the guys, she glanced over and trapped him with her brilliant green eyes. The color reminded him of the one time he'd seen the Northern lights, slashing across the night, leaving him breathlessly gazing into the mesmerizing glow.

He managed to suck in some air as she pulled away from Brave and came toward him.

"Hey you," she said. A pretty pink blush spread across her cheeks as he quickly ran his tongue over his bottom lip. She kept her eyes locked on his mouth as she cleared her throat. "I wasn't expecting to see you again."

"Neither was I." Okay, that was slightly better than what he'd considered saying. But that was it. He had nothing else.

Which was weird. He'd never had trouble talking to a woman before. And he hadn't had trouble talking to her earlier today. What had changed?

She let out a soft laugh and reached for his hand. Her touch had even more of an impact than her hypnotic gaze. His pulse picked up a notch, matching the rhythm reached during his most intense guitar solo.

Checking out his nails, she let out an exaggerated sigh. "You ruined them."

He looked down and grinned. She was right. As usual, shredding on the guitar had chipped half the polish. Cocking his head, he gave her a crooked smile. "Guess I'll need to beg you to fix them again."

"You don't need to beg. Or come up with excuses to spend time with me." Her lips slanted with amusement. "You still owe me a coffee."

"At the very least."

"Don't start with the lines. You'll ruin the nice guy image I have of you."

A snort tore her attention away from him and Alder couldn't help but tense as Brave stepped up to her side and casually hooked an arm around her shoulders. "Danica, sweetie, don't let him fool you. He's just as fucked up as the rest of us."

Arching a brow, Danica—now Alder had a name, which he'd been too slow to ask for—tipped her head up to Brave. "Right. That whole rock star image, huh? Don't worry, I won't tell anyone you're both 'nice'."

"I'm not worried about you telling anyone." Brave shot Alder a look cold enough to shatter glass. "I'm worried you'll believe it."

Alder wasn't sure how to respond to that little jab. Arguing with Brave wouldn't win him any points. Even when Alder was right, he came off as the asshole when they took cheap shots at one another. Brave was too smooth and he always said the right thing. Which meant he'd be all calm and reasonable while Alder lost his cool.

"And that answers that question." Danica laughed and slipped her small, soft hand into Alder's. "Being trapped on a bus together for so long must put a strain on you all. Alder, why don't we make it a beer instead of coffee? All that dancing made me thirsty." She flashed Brave the sweetest smile. "Thank you for making sure I didn't spend most of the night sitting in the corner by myself."

"My pleasure." Brave's brow furrowed, and his lips thinned. He probably wanted to say more, but Danica had efficiently put them in the position of either acting like adults, or looking really immature.

Not that they always acted like grown ups, but Brave liked people seeing him as the calm, collected leader of the band. That front was worth more to him than whatever pleasure he got out of tearing Alder down.

There was a short, awkward silence, and then Alder found himself being led to the bar. His brain finally caught up and he ordered them each a beer. Bud light, after asking Danica what she preferred.

They found an empty booth away from the crowd and settled in, Danica sitting across from him, her attention on tearing the wet label off her bottle.

She'd gone from being relaxed to completely distracted. There was something on her mind, but he didn't know her well enough to start digging. So he jumped on the first topic he could think of that he hoped would break the ice.

"Did you enjoy the show? I should have offered you a backstage pass."

"You were running late." She took a deep breath. "But, since you brought it up, maybe my request won't be too weird."

He tongued his bottom lip, not sure what she was getting at. "Our next show's in LA. Will you be there? I'm sure I could—"

"Damn it, you really are too nice. You're gonna hate me." She held up her hand before he could object. "My agent had this plan, and it seemed like it could work, but now I feel like an opportunistic bitch."

Okay, I'm not sure what to say to that. He couldn't see her asking for anything horrible. Maybe she needed a ride to the show? That wasn't opportunistic though. "Tell me what you need. I won't hate you."

"Mostly just to be seen. That's why I'm here." She dropped her gaze, as though she was ashamed to admit that. "My image is all wrong."

"Come again?"

Shaking her head, she bit her bottom lip. "I was a cute little girl playing a secondary character the last time I did anything really impressive to add to my portfolio. My agent wants me to get some edge. She put out some calls to journalists she knows, hinting that a photographer might snap a few 'interesting' shots of me at this show. From what she told me, several took the bait. Now it's up to me to be seen with someone unexpected."

Was it crazy that her agent's idea made sense to him? Maybe he'd been in the business too long. Their manager had set Brave up with a few models to give the band some publicity. Things working both ways wasn't so far fetched.

But Danica could do so much better than him. "Sweetie, you've got your pick of some pretty heavy hitters. Why me?"

"Did I forget to mention how freakin' dirty it makes me feel that I agreed to this? I like you. If I'd come here just to see the show, I'd have wanted to hang out with you, no strings attached." She hunched her shoulders when a camera flash suddenly hit them. "When I did your nails, I couldn't help but wish I didn't have a job to do. But I'm trying to build a career and that always comes first. The agency paid for me to come here because they think I'll get some good offers if I get my face in some damn tabloids. Once people start tweeting and talking shit about me online."

She sounded so disgusted with the very idea he couldn't help but turn his hand to give hers a little squeeze and grin at her. He doubted he was who her agent had in mind, but maybe they could make this work for them both. Cole was always nagging at him, and the rest of the band, to be seen with chicks to kill the rumors that they were all gay. Neither Alder nor Danica had the freedom to explore their first, uncomplicated encounter, but if it could work in their favor?

He wasn't seeing a downside.

"My manager would love to see me with a woman like you." He stroked his thumb lightly over the pulse at her wrist, his smile widening at her sharp inhale. "So how about I let you use me, while I use you?"

She stared at the table, nodding slowly. "Yeah. That works."

"Hey." He reached up and placed his hand on her cheek. "I get it. This all started as a way to gain exposure. But there's more. I like you too."

"How could you? I'm asking you to let the media make more of me being with you than—"

"Than what? If there were no cameras, and I asked you to leave with me, would you say no?"

"I don't know."

Damn, she didn't pull any punches. But he liked her honesty. He ran his fingers lightly down the length of her throat. "Forget your agent. Forget my manager. Finish your drink and then look at me. See the loser who sat on the hood of your car and tell me what you want to do with him."

Her throat worked as she tipped her beer to her lips, polishing it off in just a few gulps. She slammed it down on the table and focused on his hand, which still held hers. Pressing her eyes shut, she nodded slowly.

"I'm not as sweet as you think I am, but for a minute, I wasn't the actress or the model everyone sees me as. I want to be the woman you saw." She groaned and pulled away from him. "I want to be her, but I *need* to be the one asking you to smile for the cameras and pretend I'm a glorified groupie."

He chuckled and caught her hand again, bringing it to his lips. "Groupies get a bad rep, but they're an important part of our history. They've inspired some of the greats."

"That makes me feel *so* much better."

"You're making a big deal out of this for nothing, Danica. I'm giving you what you need." He stood and pulled her to her feet. He was pretty sure she'd relax once they got past all those pictures she needed. And he wanted to give her a chance to be the woman she really was. The one she didn't seem to believe she could be anymore. "Then, maybe I can give you what you want."

She grinned, moving close to him and speaking low. "I don't even know what that is anymore."

"I do." He lowered his head, brushing his lips against her cheek. The perfect photo opp for all those cameras. But his words weren't for show. They were all for her. "You want to be real. And you have been. Trust me to know the difference."

Chapter Four

The trek from the Hard Rock Hotel to the Tuscany where Danica was staying was short, so she didn't bother getting her car. She'd paid for extended parking anyway, not sure if she'd be crashing in someone's room for the night to pull off 'the plan'.

Alder had asked her where she'd be most comfortable, and she surprised herself by immediately answering with her room. The very idea of getting up in the morning and doing the walk of shame in front of any diligent photographers made her nauseous. Not that she'd be a bitch and force Alder to do it either, but if he turned out to be an asshole, better him than her.

Hopefully, she'd read him right and neither of them would end up giving the rag reporters any more to talk about than necessary. The whole way to the hotel, she'd caught flashes coming from parked cars and around the side of buildings. Sophie must have come up with one hell of a story. Either that or Alder was a lot more popular than he seemed to think.

Aside from the cameramen though, no one recognized either of them, so she was able to relax, and laugh at the odd comment Alder made about 'All the cockroaches' that were crawling around the city.

He didn't have a high opinion of the reporters, that was for sure.

Once they reached the hotel, the flashes stopped. Probably not for long, but the crowd around reception made getting a good shot impossible. Deciding the press had enough material for one night, Danica grabbed Alder's hand and sprinted toward the elevators.

His deep laugh spread through her like the heat from a fireplace. Cozy and warm, comforting enough to banish the chill that had clung to her from the second she agreed to the crazy scheme.

But in her room, the sensation of leaning too close to that nice, warm fireplace had her cheeks blazing. Her tongue didn't want to do its job and form words. With the door closed, alone with Alder, all she could do was stare at him.

When was the last time she'd been alone with a man? What was she supposed to do with him now? Would he expect something in return for helping her out?

"Hey." Alder reached out to take her hand in his, a soft smile on his lips. "Don't look at me like that. I'm not going to jump you."

"You're not?" She pressed her lips together, trying to sort out the warring thoughts in her head. Considering how nervous she was, that twinge of disappointment didn't make any damn sense.

He chuckled and shook his head, drawing her into the room and releasing her hand to grab the rolling chair in front of the desk. He set it at the foot of the bed and sat, waiting until she perched on the edge of the mattress before he spoke.

"We haven't even gone on a date yet. The cameras might need to catch you being wild and reckless with a 'rock star'." He wrinkled his nose, as if referring to himself that way was distasteful. Then he rolled his eyes and shook his head. "It's just us now. How about we make this our first date? I'll order some room service—on my dime—and we can watch a movie." He put his hand on the arms of the chair. "I'll even stick right here if it makes you more comfortable."

He was too much. And absolutely perfect. She'd been lucky, meeting him when she had. How many other guys in that club would have come back to her room with her and been happy just watching a movie? And unless he was a *damn* good actor, he really meant every word he'd said.

She couldn't help tease him a little though. "If you sit right there, I won't be able to see the TV."

"True." He turned the chair, pushing it backward and riding it to the other side of the bed. "Better?"

This man was adorable. Which she wouldn't usually find so appealing, but the combination of him being cute, and sweet, and intelligent made him irresistible. There was something intense about him too, but she'd only seen a glimpse of it when his brother was being a jerk. Brave had been nice enough at the club, chatting her up and asking her to dance, but she hadn't been impressed with his sudden shift in attitude when Alder came into the picture. She wouldn't judge him on that one encounter though. Some siblings didn't get along. The why of it wasn't any of her business. Yet.

More teasing would be better than letting her brain get carried away with when it would become her business. She reached over and tossed a small cushion at him. "Are you aware that you're a big dork?"

"A dork? No, I think that's one of the few things I haven't been called."

"You can sit on the bed. I'll hold you to your promise not to jump me." She let out a surprised yelp when he pushed off the chair and dropped onto the bed beside her, the pillow she'd thrown at him hitting her in the face. "Hey!"

Pushing up on his long, muscular arms, Alder slipped back to lean against the headboard. "What do you want to eat? We'll be waiting for awhile, so we might as well call, then start the movie."

Resting on her side, she held her hand out for the room service menu. Her mouth watered at the selection, but she'd had a couple of beers and couldn't afford any additional calories. Most guys that weren't in the business got annoyed at how rigid she was with her diet, claiming a girl with an appetite was sexy.

Her looks were part of her career, so she didn't eat to impress anyone.

Not a conversation she wanted to have on a first date.

She tugged at her bottom lip with her teeth. "The veggie platter would be great. And maybe a couple bottles of water?"

"Sounds good." He called and placed the order, studying her face as he hung up. His lips slanted to one side. "You look surprised. First year we were on the road, we ate nothing but junk food. We all learned to cook, so the quality of food is better, but I don't get the chance to have fresh vegetables very often. They'd go bad if I got a bunch just for myself."

"You could get the single servings. They cost a bit more, but I find them perfect for when it's just me. Or me and my grandpa." She smiled, thinking of how her grandfather used to grumble when she tried to make him eat anything besides meat and potatoes. "I figured you're in good shape because you have a good metabolism, not because you watch what you eat."

Patting his stomach, Alder laughed. "I wish. Maybe when I was younger, but now? A few beers and I need to call in all the roadies to help me squeeze into my jeans."

Tilting her head, she tried to picture that. The image came out a lot dirtier than he'd probably intended. "That's hot."

"Yeah?" He gave her one of those looks again, like he was trying to read her. "I guess watching Malakai feel me up didn't gross you out?"

"Hell no. You two were sexy and I was surrounded by writers who got me thinking things I'd never considered before." She probably shouldn't have just blurted that, but for some reason, she didn't think he'd be weirder out by her confession. "I come across things on Facebook, or even at modeling gigs, where there's two guys all over each other. And it never did anything for me, one way or another. But with the music, and you both all sweaty and…" Okay, being comfortable didn't mean over-share. She ducked her head. "Anyway, you put on a great show."

"I'm glad you enjoyed it. Cole won't be happy, but it got the attention off Tate and gave the kid a chance to take a break." Folding his arms behind his head, he nodded toward the TV. "Anything you feel like watching?"

"I don't know, let's see what's on." Flipping through the On Demand options, she tried to find anything that looked interesting. Or even vaguely familiar. She'd been at the gym two hours a day, five or six days a week, for the past few months, in between photo shoots and auditions. By the time she got home she was usually too tired to bother doing more than check out social media and crash. She'd watch the odd series, but all the ones she enjoyed she couldn't keep up with unless they were on Netflix.

Netflix was her one guilty pleasure. When she got a full day off, she'd binge watch for hours. The most recent show she'd gotten into was Doctor Who.

Which she'd be watching now if she was alone.

"Anything interest you?" She glanced over at Alder, who shrugged, not looking any more impressed with the options than she was.

"Honestly, I've seen all the good stuff. Being on a bus for twelve hours, you either read, play video games, or watch movies." He scratched his chin. "I'm good with a chick flick if that's what you're into. I'm not picky."

"Oh good, because I've been *dying* to watch the new Nicholas Sparks movie." She scrolled through the movies until she found it. "There we go."

The effort he made not to cringe was comical. He chewed on the edge of his bottom lip. "Seriously?"

"No, not really. I just wanted to see your reaction." She giggled when he pulled out the pillow from behind his head and swung it at her. "Honestly, I'd love to watch Doctor Who. Have you ever seen it?"

"Yes. And I officially love you for suggesting it." He flashed her a big grin. "The rest of the band thinks it's lame, so I'm a closet fan. Can we keep this between us?"

"Absolutely." She reached over the side of the bed to pull out her laptop. Signing into her Netflix account, she quickly found the last episode she'd finished, laying on her stomach and pointing at the screen as he settled beside her. "I actually started watching the whole season from the beginning again, but I don't mind going back a few episodes if you aren't caught up."

"I like this episode. And the next one. Let's start here."

A few episodes in and Danica was losing track of time. She realized she'd fallen asleep when she opened her eyes and found the room dark. The duvet was covering her—Alder had managed to pull it out from under her without waking her up.

The pillow cushioning her head was solid and warm. And not a pillow at all. Eyes half shut, she rested her arm over Alder's wide chest, sliding her head to the indent of his shoulder. She'd never been this comfortable sleeping with a man in her bed, but had she ever even tried? She wasn't sure she'd ever met a man she'd have trusted enough to fall asleep in his arms.

Her body had made the choice for her. She'd curled up next to him without conscious thought.

And it wasn't weird. Wasn't awkward.

The next morning, she didn't even worry that he'd take one look at her and wonder what the hell he'd been thinking. She made them both coffee and cuddled up to him to watch the last episode they both remembered, picturing every morning being just like this and how happy she would be if her days all began with his smile.

Only, neither of them were living the kind of life conductive to sweet and normal and simple. Which came as a harsh reminder when she checked her phone.

Ten messages from Sophie and about a dozen texts.

Just a few more hours. Then I'll go back to dealing with the real world. She tucked her phone under her pillow, grinning when Alder did the same. It was nice, not having to rush or worry about anything. Their 'date' had been so laid back, Danica didn't want it to end. She felt like she was spending time with one of her closest friends.

Not that she wanted to 'friend-zone' Alder.

Or…maybe she did? He was someone she wanted to keep. She'd have a better chance if she could have him as a precious friend, rather than risk the precarious relationship status.

They hadn't even kissed. Maybe they wouldn't have any real chemistry. And if they didn't, they would be safe. What the media assumed wouldn't matter. They could play their parts and know that the friendship built between them would never change.

But…she had to be sure.

Rolling onto her stomach, she put her hands on Alder's shoulders, rising above him. He grinned at her and a tiny dimple dented his cheek as he brushed his fingers into her hair. He relaxed under her, simply waiting, as though he knew this was a step she was afraid to take.

She eased down, brushing her lips over his, and her breath caught in her throat. The brief touch had her absorbing the heat of his lips as though he'd branded her. She watched his face, wondering if he felt the same. He held her gaze, leaning up to catch her bottom lip with a soft kiss, drawing her down to him as he gently slanted his lips against hers. One hand on the back of her head, he held her in place, not forcing her to accept more, but telling her, without words, that she wasn't taking this step alone.

Hands flat on his shoulders, she dug her fingers into the tight muscles, letting her tongue slip past his lips, demanding just a little more. He sat up, pulling her into his arms, and the spark was lit. Not a small one that could be snuffed out by a harsh gust of air, but one that had all the fuel to start an inferno. He'd given her control, but with the way he kissed her, the way he made her feel, she became completely unwound. She let out a soft whimper as she straddled him, not sure what she needed more. For him to keep kissing her or to take over completely. If he did, she wouldn't stop him.

With a rough sound in his throat, Alder lifted her in his arms, laying her on the bed, one hand tangled in her hair. He tasted like black coffee, sweetened with just enough sugar to take off the bitter edge, his mouth so fucking hot. His tongue and his teeth played at her lips, a kiss with just enough pressure to linger even when he brought his mouth to her throat.

She tugged at his shirt, needing more of him. She couldn't remember ever being so desperate for skin on skin, for movement and touch, but she refused to think beyond this moment. She had him now and she might not for long.

His shirt was on the floor. Hers followed.

And then she saw a strange man, standing in the doorway.

Alder looked over as she went still. Shielding her with his body, he glared at the man. "What the fuck are you doing here, Cole?"

"How did you get in? Who are you?" Danica tugged at the blanket, her pulse steadying a bit since Alder seemed to know the man. Which didn't explain how he'd gotten in, but at least she didn't have to go for her gun.

"I let him in, Danica. He's Alder's manager." Sophie squeezed by the man; giving him an irritated look as she smoothed her hand over her perfectly straightened caramel and chocolate colored hair. Her glossy, pouty lips curved slightly at the edges as she eyed Danica and Alder on the bed.

With the hint of mischief in her eyes, and her smooth, brown skin defying any affects of age, Danica could see why people mistook Sophie for Gabrielle Union, even though she was at least ten years older than the beautiful actress. The constant comparisons had actually gotten Sophie involved in some of Union's charities. Both women were amazing role models, admired for their work.

Danica didn't hold any ill will toward the actress, however, so that's where the similarities ended. At the moment, she very much wanted to strangle her agent.

"Oh don't look at me like that. I tried to call, and text. Answer your phone next time." Sophie folded her arms over her chest, coming off more like a corporate business woman in her navy power suit and white shirt, than an agent many of the models teasingly referred to as 'their pimp'. "Since neither of you felt the need to be out of bed before noon, Mr. Cole and I got together for coffee and discussed your agenda for the next month or so."

The woman's lost her mind! Danica stared at her. "The next *month?*"

"You've got to be shitting me." Alder reached over the side of the bed, picking up her shirt and handing it to her before grabbing his own. He tied his long black hair at the nape of his neck, scowling at his manager. "*Our* agenda is *not* up for discussion."

"Is that so?" Cole let out a cold laugh and shook his head. He reminded Danica a bit of what James Dean might have looked like if he'd lived another 20 years and kept his youthful figure. He was dressed just as sharply as Sophie. They'd both come prepared to make this all about business. "You didn't seem surprised that photographers were following you in any of the pictures flooding Facebook and Twitter this morning. I'm assuming she told you she needs to use you for her image?"

"I told him everything." Danica jerked her shirt on, internally wincing as she heard it tear, but keeping her face carefully neutral. Cole seemed like an asshole, but she'd had to work with assholes before. And Sophie wouldn't have brought him here without a damn good reason. "I'm not sure what you were hoping to prove, bursting in like this…" She glanced over at Sophie who, as expected, didn't look the least bit sorry. "Give us a minute to get straightened up and we'll meet you in the lobby."

Pressing her lips together, letting Danica know without words that she wasn't very happy with her, Sophie inclined her head. She met Cole's eyes and gave him a tight smile. "After you."

Cole shot Alder a warning look, then walked out with Sophie. A good sign at least. Whatever they'd discussed, the manager had clearly decided Danica wasn't beneath his guitarist.

Except, he caught me 'beneath' his guitarist.

Danica sighed, dropping back on the bed with her hands over her eyes. "I am so sorry about this. Sophie's name is always on my rooms and I should have considered she wouldn't think twice about getting a key card from the front desk."

Taking hold of her wrists, Alder pulled her hands away from her face and leaned down to kiss her. "Don't be sorry. Cole probably spent the night trying to figure out who you were, then got your agent on the phone. She was probably worried, but he's playing some angle."

"So am I."

"I happen to like your angle." He brushed his lips across her cheek to whisper in her ear. "There were no cameras here last night. None this morning. Don't you *dare* let anyone ruin this for you."

"Or what?"

He grinned, drawing back a little to meet her eyes. "It's little early in the relationship for me to spank you, but we haven't been conventional about anything else."

Fuck. She tugged her bottom lip between her teeth, holding his gaze, trying to figure out if he was joking. His smile hadn't slipped, but she had the strangest impression that he was testing her reaction. If she freaked, he'd laugh it off. If she didn't…

She *should* make it clear there was no way he'd ever spank her. Except, the idea had her cheeks blazing and sent heat spilling into her core. The subtle, erotic threat had her imagining all the other things he could do to her after he finished reddening her ass with his hand.

Nothing with him would be boring, that was for sure.

Unfortunately, staying in here to explore what he'd do next would only result in Sophie and Cole coming back to find them. Their best bet would be to get the meeting over with.

Fingers crossed that they had any free time once the pair were done with them.

She sighed again and Alder chuckled. "You don't have to say a word. Want me to go down and keep them busy while you jump in the shower?"

"No, that's all right. Sophie might keep things brief if she's worried about me being photographed looking like I just spent the day in bed."

Shoving his hands in his pockets as they stepped into the hall, he shrugged. "Considering how important tarnishing up your image is, I don't think you looking like you just crawled out of my bed will be a problem."

True, but he was missing one very important fact. She bumped his shoulder with hers as they stopped to wait for the elevator. "You forget, I brought you back to *my* room. All modern woman, claiming my man like a boss."

"Claiming me, huh?" He gave her a hooded look as the elevator doors opened and he pulled her inside. "Take a bit more than a few kisses to 'claim me', sweetheart."

"We don't have time for more."

"We have some."

The doors closed and he lifted her up, his kisses leaving her flushed and rumpled and damn giddy by the time they stepped off onto the main floor. She *seriously* hoped Sophie and Cole would make this quick.

They didn't. Actually, within minutes of dragging her and Alder to the hotel restaurant for sparkling water and salad— Alder's manager ordered for him right after Sophie ordered for Danica—their day was planned out. Alder had to go back to his hotel, make himself presentable, and then get the band together. And while he did, Danica was being dragged to a hairdresser Sophie had worked with in Vegas before.

And she didn't need to shower or get changed first. Of course not. After her hair appointment, she had a local casting call Sophie wanted her to check out. She could slip into one of the outfits Sophie had in her rental on the way.

There wasn't enough time to do more than eat and say a quick goodbye to Alder before Sophie towed her away. And Sophie had absolutely no sympathy when Danica pointed out how rude she'd been. She led the way to the parking garage, jotting down notes on her phone.

"He's busy. You're busy. Now stop pouting, you're creasing your forehead." Sophie's tone softened as Danica slid into the passenger seat. She patted Danica's cheek. "Honey, you need to slow down a little, okay? You were supposed to play to the cameras, not get involved with a dirty rock star."

"He's not a dirty rock star. Don't be a snob, Sophie."

"Fine, maybe he's a nice boy. And if he is, that's great." Sophie closed the door, heading around the car to get in behind the wheel. "You'll have plenty of time to find out exactly who he is."

Danica leaned back against the headrest and let out a dry laugh. "When? Did you schedule another date?"

"Of course not, you don't have *that* much time." Sophie shot her a wicked smile. "But you'll be together for long enough to figure out if you love him, or hate him."

"We will?"

"Absolutely. There's nothing like a road trip to define a relationship." Sophie's smile widened when Danica furrowed her brow with confusion. "You're going on tour with the band. Cole will give you all the details when we go meet the rest of his boys."

"On tour…" Danica's eyes widened. She'd considered maybe heading to LA with them, but this sounded like a lot more. "For how long?"

"That depends. Right now, Cole has proposed an arrangement that is beneficial to you and the band. No reason for you not to try for the gig here, you can meet them in LA if necessary. Then you can commit to working with them for the duration of our agreement." Her eyes hardened a little, reminding Danica that Sophie hadn't become as successful as she was by playing nice. "Until you get a better offer."

A better offer… Well, that told her one thing. Being sent on tour wasn't simply about her image anymore. Cole was looking to hire her. His 'proposal' wasn't up to Sophie's standards, but it was a job and it would get Danica some exposure.

If all went down like Sophie intended, the offers would come. And Danica would be doing photo shoots all over the world again. She might get casted for TV shows. Or even movies.

And it would happen fast. All she and Sophie had worked for.

Exactly what Danica wanted.

Except, it meant Sophie was wrong about one thing.

I don't have much time at all.

Bianca Sommerland

Chapter Five

The sloped, white screen canopy covering Fremont Street was blank at the moment, but it provided shelter from the glaring sun. Jesse dodged slow walking families of tourists as he made his way to the Golden Nugget, checking his phone to make sure he hadn't gotten a text from Malakai, telling him they'd switched machines.

He found the guys near the exit, Tate slumped, half asleep, against a slot machine, while Malakai stood behind Brave, arms folded, not looking too impressed.

Brave shook his head and pulled out his wallet, taking out a twenty. "Fucking chill out, Malakai. I set myself a limit. I haven't hit it yet."

"If your limit is over three hundred dollars, you're an idiot." Malakai grumbled, snatching the twenty out of Brave's hand. "But more importantly, you haven't slept."

"Neither have you." Brave glanced over at Tate and let out a sharp laugh. "Or the boy. Why are you riding my ass?"

"Because you're acting like a fucking child."

"Right. Well, I guess the sympathy didn't last long. No one asked you to stay with me."

Jesse met Malakai's eyes, jutting his chin toward the exit so he could have a moment alone with Brave. Once Malakai got Tate on his feet and started off, Jesse put his hand on Brave's shoulder.

"I shouldn't have hung out with the other roadies so late. I thought you'd crashed for the night." He squeezed the tense muscles under his hand. "What happened?"

Brave lowered his head to his hand and sighed. "We were all heading to bed, but Tate wanted to talk about some shit, and I have a few bottles of the good stuff in my room, so we headed there to wind down after the party. We didn't stay long. Someone left fucking white rose petals on my bed. In a puddle of what looked like blood. And there was a note."

"Damn it, why didn't you call me?" They were going to have to hire security if this kept up. Between Tate getting his ass kicked, and whoever the fuck was messing with Brave, Jesse couldn't protect the band on his own anymore. "What did the note say?"

Reaching into his pocket, Brave pulled out his phone, then showed Jesse a picture of a crumpled piece of paper.

'You'd be immortal if you'd died'.

Almost the exact same thing the man who'd attacked Brave onstage had said.

What the fuck is going on? He gnashed his teeth in frustration. *I should have been with him.*

"I didn't call you because Malakai insisted we call the cops. And they checked the room and filed a report. And that's it. The hotel offered me another room, but I was too wired to sleep." Brave shrugged. "If I'd called you, you would have flipped out. I just wanted to forget all this shit."

"By blowing all your money on the slots?"

"Something like that."

At a loss at what to say, Jesse moved his hand to the back of Brave's neck. The man was usually responsible with money, so there was no point to lecturing him. Malakai had covered that anyway. Sleep was another issue. Brave would go for days without slowing when something got to him. And some crazy fucker having broken into his room was definitely getting to him.

"I'm not tired." Lips slanting, as though Brave was aware of how childish he sounded; he pushed away from the slot machine and stood. "I could eat."

Considering how much they'd had to drink last night, food was a very good idea. Jesse put his arm over Brave's shoulder as they headed out to Fremont. They walked with Malakai and Tate, who looked ready to take a nap on the sidewalk, until they reached the end of the street. Then both he and Malakai called a cab.

Assured that Malakai would see to the young drummer, Jesse got Brave in the second cab, giving directions to the Motel 6 on Tropicana, where he was staying. In his room, he shoved a change of clothes at Brave, then directed him to the bathroom for a shower while he ordered some pizza.

It was close to noon. Pizza and chicken wings would suffice until after he got the man to bed.

Having Brave in his room would normally have him thinking with his dick, but he couldn't shake the heavy weight of unease in his gut at the idea of Brave having a fucking stalker.

He didn't have any control over how the band handled travel, or who they hired, but he managed the roadies. A few of them were big enough to double as security if Cole rejected the idea of hiring professionals. Two were ex-military and they might have some buddies looking for work if Cole would let him take on some new hires.

He'd tried to keep his relationship with Brave low-key, but fuck Cole's 'rules'. If nothing else, he'd be sharing a room with Brave when they weren't on the bus. And he'd be sleeping on the bus, even if it meant he had to sleep on the sofa because all the band's shit was filling the empty bunks.

Since Brave probably hadn't informed Cole about what had gone down last night, Jesse called him, cursing when he was redirected to voicemail. The manager wasn't a bad guy, but he saw the roadies as beneath him. If he talked to Jesse, it was because he needed something done. Otherwise, he figured Brave or Alder would deal with the crew.

Fuck him.

Jesse answered the door to the delivery boy, paid the kid, then set the pizzas with the drinks and box of chicken wings stacked on top on the desk at the other side of the room. He'd polished off two slices by the time Brave came out of the bathroom.

Wearing nothing but a towel.

Fucker.

Reclining on the bed, a sly smile on his lips, Brave held out a hand like he was some kind of goddamn prince, waiting to be served. His diva routine pissed off most of the crew, but Jesse just laughed, knowing the lead singer loved messing with people. Those who assumed he was full of himself, he didn't bother with. His real friends called him on his shit.

"If you're too tired to get your own food, you're eating it cold." Jesse grabbed a chicken wing and ripped a chunk of the delicious meat off with his teeth, grinning when Brave let out an irritated huff. "I'm your boyfriend, not your butler."

"I thought boyfriends were supposed to be sweet." Brave sucked his teeth at Jesse's shrug. He slid across the bed, leaning off the edge until he could almost reach the pizza box. He grunted his thanks as Jesse passed him a piece. After chewing for a bit, Brave swallowed and lifted his head. "Listen, I'm sorry Malakai dragged you into this. I didn't—"

"How about being sorry you didn't call me yourself?"

"That too."

The man had to be the worst boyfriend Jesse had ever had. Then again, he had a feeling he was Brave's *first* real boyfriend. Between LOST and Winter's Wrath, Brave had been living the 'rock star' life for almost ten years. Why bother with commitment when you had fans throwing themselves at you?

Grabbing his arm, Brave tugged Jesse down to lie beside him on the bed. "It really bothers you, doesn't it?"

"Yeah." Jesse lifted his shoulder dismissively. "But it's done. Right now, we're gonna get some rest. Then I'll have a chat with Cole about how to keep you safe."

The edge of Brave's lip twitched. His gaze focused on Jesse's mouth. "I'm feeling pretty damn safe at the moment."

Considering the man only wore a towel that was useless in covering his hardening erection, Jesse certainly hoped so. He smirked at Brave. "Is *that* what you're feeling?"

"Hmm." Brave moved closer, flicking his tongue over Jesse's lips. "Something like that."

Anyone who knew Brave would call Jesse a liar if he told them nothing had happened between them besides a few really hot, stolen kisses. Not just because they were on tour and privacy was a joke if you even managed to find a dark corner and an hour away from the entourage that trailed the band. Brave found ways to get what he wanted, but he hadn't pushed for more.

Jesse had made it damn clear he wanted to take his time. And Brave respected that. He'd been serious about proving himself and all Jesse's doubts had faded over the last week. Fine, Brave still hadn't opened up as much as he'd like him to, but that would come in time.

"Fuck this shit." Jesse shoved Brave onto his back, displacing the towel and claiming his mouth with bruising pressure as he fisted his hand around Brave's dick. He breathed in Brave's harsh exhale, curving his free hand around the back of Brave's neck.

Their bodies aligned as he moved over Brave, too lost in the moment to care that he was still fully dressed. He was careful to keep his full weight off the man, he knew he was much heavier, with all the muscles he'd gained from hauling around the band's equipment, refusing help whenever possible because he didn't trust anyone to be as careful as he was with the guitars and the drums and the amps.

Brave was one of those weird people that forgot to eat when they got wrapped up in their obsessions. He had a band that badgered him enough to keep him from getting too skinny, but the body writhing under Jesse was all muscle and bone. Strong and sleek, moving the same way he did on stage that made all the women scream like they would climax as they thrashed around to the music.

He moved down Brave's body, loving all the desperate, throaty sounds Brave was making. He'd been around Brave seducing both men and women for a quick fuck, and the man was always in control. There was something about Brave that oozed sex, but he collected lovers, not like notches on his belt, but more like they were brief reminders that he was *alive*. Maybe Jesse worried too much, and yet, he couldn't ignore the feeling that Brave still struggled to deal with the grief of the eldest Trousseau brother's death. It had been years, so most assumed he was over it. But they didn't know Brave.

Right now, Jesse doubted Brave was thinking about Valor. Or the psycho that was stalking him. Jesse had managed to get him out of his head for a little while.

Which was an amazing fucking accomplishment.

He ran his tongue over the salty, slick head of Brave's cock, pressing his hand down on Brave's hip when he tried to thrust into his mouth. He used the flat of his tongue along the length of Brave's dick to stimulate him, without giving in to his demands. As he worked his way down to Brave's balls, he held his cock in a loose grip, stroking him at a languid pace until the soft groans Brave let out grew louder.

"Fuck, Jesse. You're killing me here!" Brave gently placed his hand on the back of Jesse's head. "Please let me feel your fucking hot mouth. I've been thinking about it for the past week."

Jesse licked up the length of Brave's dick, then grinned at him. "Just think. If you'd just talk to me, I'd have done it already."

As Jesse circled the head of Brave's cock with his tongue, Brave's whole body jerked. "Shit. Okay, I promise to talk to you more. I'll talk your fucking ear off. And we can snuggle. And…damn it, name it and I'll give it to you."

Chuckling, Jesse fisted his hand at the base of Brave's dick. "If I didn't already love you, you'd be screwed pal. That's got to be the worst come on I've ever heard you use."

His whole body going still, Brave looked down at him. "You love me?"

"Yes. I have for a long time." Jesse smiled at Brave's shocked expression. Those three words might come as a shock to some, especially since the relationship was so new. But he'd loved Brave for years. They didn't have to be fucking for it to be real. "Don't panic. I don't expect you to say you love me too. Actually, if you try, I'm kicking you out of my bed." He resumed stroking Brave's dick so there was no question as to what he wanted to happen. "Say it when you mean it. For now, what we've got is good enough for me."

"What's we've got is good." Brave ran his hand over Jesse's hair, pressing his eyes shut as Jesse took him in his mouth. "So fucking good."

Cupping Brave's balls, one hand on Brave's thigh, Jesse slid his mouth down as far as he could go, swirling his tongue, all his focus on driving the man completely out of his mind. He wouldn't let the words he'd said distract him. He'd meant it when he'd said he didn't need to hear them in return. He'd gotten what he *needed* from Brave so far. All he'd promised. He didn't have to watch Brave leave the bus with random strangers. He didn't have to worry that the man he loved was burying his feelings in random hookups, blocking out reality because it was too hard to face.

Taking him deeper, faster, Jesse fought to ignore his own painful arousal. If Brave was any other man, he'd be fucking him by now, but he was feeling particularly selfless. He could jerk off in the shower later. This was all for Brave.

"Stop." Brave shuddered, so close to release, Jesse sensed the tension in his balls and along his throbbing dick. Inhaling roughly, Brave eased himself out of Jesse's mouth and rose from the bed. "Don't move."

Brave stood and grabbed something out of the pocket of his jeans. He moved behind Jesse, leaning over him as he unzipped his jeans. "I can't wait anymore."

Tensing, Jesse fisted his hands on the mattress, not sure exactly how he should voice his objections. Brave's hand wrapping around his dick made it hard to think at all, but the slick pressure against his back hole brought some clarity.

He gritted his teeth, fighting the urge to pull away. "I don't bottom, Brave."

Pressing his lips to the back of Jesse's neck, Brave spoke softly. "Have you ever?"

"Yeah. And it was bad and we're not discussing that now." Jesse groaned as Brave continued jerking him off. "Fuck, don't stop."

"Give me this, Jesse. I swear, you won't regret it. I couldn't fucking stop if I tried. You've got me so wrapped up in you, You're all I can think about." Brave's finger pressed in deep, stretching Jesse in a way none had in a very long time. "I'm sorry if someone hurt you."

"Don't…" Hell, Jesse wasn't even sure what he was asking. He didn't want to talk about the fucked up shit in his past. Which was bad. He couldn't expect Brave to open up to him without doing the same. He moaned as Brave pushed in even further. "I don't know if I can do this."

"You can." Brave replaced his fingers with his dick. The thick head pushed in, and it wasn't the pain that had Jesse bowing his head and resisting the urge to strike out. He was trapped in a time when he had been young and stupid. When he'd trusted the wrong people.

Moans and deep thrusts. Hands on him that felt so good, he'd be stupid to object. Everything had been fuzzy then, but it wasn't now. This was Brave. Brave cared about him and he was here by choice.

His jaw hardened at Brave pounded into him. He could tell Brave knew what he was doing. He angled his dick to hit the right spot. He bit into Jesse's shoulder while stroking his dick, holding back for so long, Jesse sensed he was waiting until Jesse joined him in the mind-numbing peak of climax.

Holding him close, Brave whispered in his ear. "You're not the only one who knows when someone is fucked up. Forget everything, Jesse. Feel what I'm doing to you. You're fucking mine. And I won't give up until you know it."

The grip on his dick tightened. Brave twisted his hand in Jesse's hair and Jesse panted as all his senses turned to the surge of pleasure rushing through him. He pressed his face into the mattress to muffle a shout as he came.

Brave let out a soft, satisfied moan, picking up speed until the sound of flesh slapping flesh filled the room. Both their bodies were slick with sweat. Fingers digging into Jesse's hips, Brave let out a low growl and slammed in one last time.

After he pulled out, Jesse straightened and headed to the bathroom. He wasn't ready to 'cuddle'. He started the shower and let the hot water hit him. But unlike the last time he'd let someone do this to him, he stayed on his goddamn feet. And he didn't shed one fucking tear.

By the time he returned to the bedroom, he was feeling like himself again. But he still didn't want to talk. And thankfully, Brave looked too tired for a conversation anyway. When he dropped onto the bed, Brave took off to clean up.

He wasn't sure when Brave got in bed, because he was already asleep. But when he woke up, Brave was pressed up against him, one arm over his chest, with his head on Jesse's shoulder.

With a sleepy smile on his lips, Jesse pressed a soft kiss on Brave's temple. Yeah, things had been a little weird for him for a minute, but that would pass. He'd managed to pull Brave in a little closer. If things between them were gonna work out, they'd both have to work through some shit.

Hopefully Brave would start sharing more of his issues so Jesse could help him get past them. And at some point, maybe Jesse would be able to do the same.

Closing his eyes, he heard his phone buzz. Tempted to ignore it, he stared at the ceiling, loving how comfortable this was. They wouldn't get a lot of time to just relax together. The band was still on tour.

And Jesse was still technically working.

He quietly moved to the rolling chair in front of the desk, then answered his phone.

"Do you know where Brave is? Malakai told me what happened last night." Cole sounded more irritated than usual. Or maybe it was concern. It was hard to tell. "I went to the police station, but they have nothing. One actually told me I should make sure it wasn't a fucking prank. If he's not with you, then we need to find him. If something happened—"

"He's with me." Jesse wasn't going to dissect Cole's motives. He might just be keeping track of his investment, but maybe not. "He didn't sleep. No one knows where I'm staying, so he was able to crash for a bit."

"Good idea. He awake yet?"

"No, he *just* fell asleep. Why?"

There was silence on the other line. Then a heavy sigh. "Band meeting. I figured we could all get together for a late lunch. Then take off for LA tonight."

One look at Brave and Jesse shook his head, even though Cole couldn't see him. None of the guys slept very well on the road and they hadn't even had one full day without a goddamn show yet. Cole might be a great manager, but he was going to burn them all out if he didn't give them some downtime.

"The crew's scattered today, Cole. We've been on the road for weeks and they were looking forward to Vegas. How about breaking the news to them that we're cutting their downtime short early tomorrow?"

"Not a single one of them will be up before noon." Cole cursed softly. "Get the bus gassed up and ready to go right after the meeting. And tell your boys if they're not ready to roll out by 2:00, we're leaving without them and I ain't paying for shit."

"Sounds like a plan, Boss." Jesse ended the call, then sent out a text to the rest of the stage crew. His men weren't slackers, so they'd be at the fucking bus on time. Cole even suggesting they'd flake out pissed him off. He kept the tone of the text simple. Plans changed. Extra work meant extra cash. They still got their per diem on days off, for food and stuff, but it was nothing compared to the wage on a workday.

Yeah, some roadies blew their money on booze, drugs, and women, but the ones he kept around had family back home—ex-wives and kids sometimes—or shit they were saving up for. Point was, they'd appreciate the extra money.

But Brave wasn't the only one who needed more sleep. Putting his guys on the road after they'd been partying all night would be dangerous.

Cole had probably figured that, which was why he hadn't bitched too much. Him putting off the meeting was interesting though. He usually just talked to Brave about the schedule, or any crazy way he'd come up to promote them. Jesse could count on one hand the amount of times he'd gotten the whole band together to discuss anything besides them completely screwing the pooch.

So this was important. Not important enough to rush, but maybe he should ask around and see if Brave needed to go have a chat with his manager sooner rather than later.

If anyone would know, it would be Alder. Jesse hadn't heard from him since he'd taken off with that girl. The man wouldn't bother answering his phone if he was busy, but he always got back to his texts. Within an hour or so.

Unless it was Jesse.

Jesse sent the text, keeping it light so Alder wouldn't think the worst.

JESSE: HEY, KID. GOT A MINUTE?

Less than a minute passed before the little dots formed in the green bubble. Alder was typing.

ALDER: NOT IF YOU'RE GONNA CALL ME 'KID', ASSHOLE.

Snorting, Jesse continued typing.

> **JESSE: SORRY, HONEY. YOU STILL WITH THAT CHICK? SHE WAS REALLY INTO YOU.**
>
> **ALDER: NO...SHE HAD STUFF TO TAKE CARE OF. BUT SHE'S COOL.**
>
> **JESSE: JUST COOL? SHE BLEW OFF BRAVE TO BE WITH YOU. THAT MUST HAVE FELT GOOD.**

The little dots started moving. Then stopped, like Alder had suddenly changed his mind about whatever he'd started to say. There was nothing for a few minutes.

> **ALDER: I KINDA HATE YOU WHEN YOU SAY SHIT LIKE THAT. YOU THINK I WANT WHAT BRAVE HAS? BY THE TIME HE'S DONE WITH HIS TOYS, THEY'RE BROKEN. BEEN LIKE THAT SINCE WE WERE KIDS.**

Ouch. Jesse was pretty sure Alder didn't mean to include him as one of Brave's 'toys', but he couldn't help wondering. Alder always assumed the worst of his brother.

His phone buzzed as another text came in.

> **ALDER: THAT CAME OUT WRONG. SORRY.**
>
> **JESSE: SO YOU DON'T THINK HE'S PLAYING ME?**

Another long pause.

> **ALDER: SO, ABOUT THE GIRL. DON'T TELL ANYONE, BUT SHE'S COMING ON TOUR WITH US. FUCKING MEDIA IS CREAMING OVER PICTURES OF US. COLE WAS GONNA HAVE A MEETING TO TALK TO THE BAND ABOUT HER.**
>
> **JESSE: HE MENTIONED A MEETING. I ASKED IF WE COULD DO IT TOMORROW.**
>
> **ALDER: LOL. YEAH, AND I BET HE GOT BITCHY, BUT AGREED, RIGHT?**
>
> **JESSE: YEP**
>
> **ALDER: SHE HAS A PHOTO SHOOT. HER AGENT WANTS HER THERE FOR THE MEETING. COLE WAS GOING TO DO IT WITHOUT HER, BUT NOW HE HAS NO CHOICE.**

Well, that explained that. Jesse grinned at the thought of Cole dealing with a model's agent. The agent seemed like the type of woman who wouldn't take his shit. And if Jesse could get that impression after just a text from Alder, he couldn't wait to meet her.

Cole delaying a band meeting for *anyone* was huge.

> **JESSE: SO ARE YOU GONNA SEE HER TONIGHT?**
> **ALDER: NO. COLE'S GOT ME DOING TWO INTERVIEWS WITH SOME BLOGGERS. AND HER AGENT HAS ALL KINDS OF STUFF FOR DANICA TO DO BEFORE WE HEAD OUT. I SWEAR, IT'S LIKE THEY'RE TRYING TO KEEP US APART UNTIL WE'RE ON THE DAMN BUS.**

Could be. Jesse tapped his fingers on his knee, thinking over how he could help Alder with the cock-blocking duo. He wasn't sure what the agent's angle was, but Cole probably considered the woman a distraction. Yeah, he wanted the guys seen with girls, but that was for public appeal. Relationships didn't last long on the road, whether the chick trailed after her man or waited for him at home.

Getting to know someone while trapped on a bus for hours could put a strain on the best of friends. It could tear a band apart if they didn't make time for themselves. Unless Danica was of a special breed of women, she would get tired of the guys after the first few hours.

> **JESSE: DID YOU TELL HER HE'S PROBABLY TRYING TO SCARE HER OFF?**
> **ALDER: WHY THE FUCK WOULD HE DO THAT? HE'S GOT ALL KINDS OF PLANS FOR HER!**
> **JESSE: FOR HER. BUT NOT FOR THE TWO OF YOU.**
> **ALDER: SHIT. I GOTTA TALK TO HER. HER AGENT IS SOME KIND OF DRAGON LADY. JUST AS BAD AS COLE, SO I'M SURE SHE'LL GET IT.**
> **JESSE: I'LL LEAVE YOU ALONE SO YOU CAN CALL HER THEN. GOOD LUCK.**

Moving to set aside his phone and check the area for somewhere he could get decent coffee, Jesse was surprised when his phone buzzed again. He frowned as he picked it up and read Alder's last text.

ALDER: I FORGOT TO GET HER PHONE NUMBER.

Loser. Jesse shook his head, grinning as he called Alder, tired of typing. "Are you serious?"

"Yeah. Shit, I gotta go. Cole just came out and gave me a dirty look. I'm supposed to start the interview. Not sure why he doesn't have Brave doing this. I'm not that interesting."

"It's your handsome mug that gave the media a hard-on, pal." Jesse leaned back in the desk chair, picturing how red Alder's face must be with all the attention he was getting. He was fine with fans, cool on stage, but reporters annoyed the hell out of him. Whatever answers they managed to squeeze out of him were usually delivered with a scowl. Good thing Cole was just parading him in front of bloggers. For now.

"I guess I'll have to wait until tomorrow to see her." Alder let out a rough, frustrated groan. "With the guys. And her agent and Cole not giving us a fucking minute alone."

Poor kid. Jesse sat forward, lowering his voice when he saw Brave stir in the bed. "*Or* you tell me where she's staying and I give her your number. You two should have breakfast and show up at the meeting together. That will throw everyone off."

"You wouldn't mind?"

"Wouldn't have offered if I did." Jesse grabbed the pen and pad on the desk and quickly jotted down the girl's name and room number. Her hotel wasn't far. He could be there and back in less than an hour, but just in case he wrote Brave a short note saying he'd be back soon with coffee. "And Alder, can you do me a favor?"

"Sure, man. Anything."

"Smile for at least *one* picture?" He didn't see that happening, but Cole might get off Alder's case if he played nice. "Even a sarcastic smile. It won't hurt, I promise."

Alder snorted. Then hung up.

I'll take that as a no. Jesse chuckled, then shoved his feet into his worn, black Vans and headed out. He took the band's van, hoping it wouldn't be too hard to find parking at the hotel. As luck would have it, there was a sign up restricting hotel parking to guests only. And those waiting for valet clogged up both lanes.

Squeezing past the congestion, Jesse maneuvered back onto a side street, finding a place to park about a block away. By the time he'd reached the hotel, he felt like he'd aged ten years. Running on just a few hours sleep wasn't as easy as it had been in his twenties.

If this doesn't prove I love the man... Jesse quickly made his way across the casino floor, toward the elevators for the North tower.

When he reached the right room, he knocked on the door, hoping the girl wouldn't be too weirded out if he asked he for a glass of water. If she was even *here.*

A thought that hadn't occurred to him until right this moment. Damn it, Alder had mentioned a photo shoot. This whole trip was probably a waste of time.

"Damn it, Sophie, I asked for fifteen minutes! It's been five!" The door swung open and an angry young woman in a bathrobe stepped right in his face. Her eyes went wide. "Oh shit, I'm sorry, I thought—"

"You should really check who's at the door before you answer." Jesse tried to keep his eyes on her face and not let them drift down the where the huge robe was gaping over the swell of her breasts. He gave her his friendliest smile. "Are you Danica?"

She backed up, partially closing the door, her eyes narrowing. "Yes. Can I help you?"

"Jesse Vaughn. I'm one of the roadies with Winter's Wrath." That didn't get her opening the door. Smart chick. "Alder mentioned you guys didn't exchange phone numbers. I offered to come give you his so you can meet for breakfast or something."

Her face brightened and she let out a light laugh. "He's such a dork. Give me a minute to get dressed? I…uh…" She tugged at her bottom lip with her teeth. "Would you think I was a bitch if I asked you to stay there?"

"Not at all. Can you bring me some water when you come back though? It's dusty outside and I had to park down the street."

"Sure thing. I swear, I won't take long." And with that, she shut the door in his face.

Leaning against the wall, Jesse took out his phone, figuring he'd kill some time playing Candy Crush. But before the game had even loaded, the girl was back. Fully dressed, with her hair in a ponytail.

She was fucking cute. Jesse tried not to stare, but he couldn't help notice her incredibly long legs in those painted on jeans and the way she filled out that modified Slayer T-shirt. The shirt was cut just high enough to show off her belly button and fell off one slender shoulder. Her black hair was long and thick, and she had nice lush lips and high, sculpted cheekbones. And the biggest, most alluring pair of green eyes he'd ever seen.

She smiled at him and held out a cold bottle of water.

The woman was a goddess.

Alder's a lucky man. Jesse took the bottle and uncapped it, thanking her before gulping down the cool liquid. "Ah, that's good."

"I bet." She tucked her thumbs into the pockets of her jeans. "It was nice of you to come just for a phone number. The guys make you do stuff like this often?"

"No, they don't ask me for much really. The beer runs go to the new guys. And I'm doing this as a favor for a friend." His brow furrowed as she avoided his gaze. "There a problem with that?"

"No, it's just…did Alder tell you how we met?"

"I assume it was before the party?" He'd thought Alder was worried about Brave hitting on anything with a pulse, while in a relationship, but when he'd approached the girl they hadn't acted like strangers. "Not sure why it matters."

She nodded slowly. "Maybe it doesn't. He's okay with it and if he tells you and you hate me later, we can work it out then."

Chicks are weird. Jesse shrugged, not sure what else to say. Alder was a big boy. If he was dating a guy, Jesse might give the dude the third degree and warn him not to hurt his best friend. He couldn't do that with a girl. They were all fragile and shit. One of the reasons Jesse had never dated one, even though he found them attractive. He'd slept with a few when he was younger, but he'd been a mess back then and didn't remember any details.

As far as anyone knew, he was gay. And he was far enough on that side of the spectrum that any inclination he had toward the fairer sex was irrelevant.

Point was, he didn't have the first clue how to deal with women.

He was just here for a phone number, so it didn't matter.

"Let me get a pen. Sophie should be here any minute." Danica ducked her head and skittered back into the room, leaving the door open, likely trusting that he'd stay put. Which he did.

"Excuse me, can I help you?"

Jesse spun away from the door and faced the tall woman standing there, glaring at him. He put his hands up, figuring it was safe to assume this was Danica's agent. "I'm with the band."

One black brow raised, the woman looked him over. Then nodded. "All right, but Danica is very busy. Cole should have contacted me if there were any issues."

"I'm not here because of Cole."

"Then why *are* you here?"

Danica burst through the door, shoving something into Jesse's hand as she smiled at her agent. "He was just leaving, Sophie. I'm ready."

"That's good, but I'm afraid the photo shoot was delayed. We have enough time to grab something to eat if you're hungry?" Sophie's features softened as she reached up to tuck a loose strand of hair behind Danica's ear. "I know I threw a lot at you without warning. And I doubt those boys will have any good meals on the tour."

Jesse scowled as he stuffed the crumpled paper Danica had given him into his pocket. Granted, the guys ate more junk food than he liked, but he'd personally taught a few to cook. He'd actually planned to get up early and stock the fridge with some fresh meat and fruits and vegetables. After LA they wouldn't stop for almost two weeks. And with the girl coming along, he'd make sure she was well fed.

Maybe it was stupid to be offended, but he did his best to take care of his boys.

"Ma'am, I apologize for butting in, but there will be a lot of good meals. If Danica has any preferences, please let me know." He folded his arms over his chest as Sophie gave him an amused look. "I'm sure a model has a special diet, but even if you want her eating vegan shit and tofu, I can make that happen."

"Danica will no doubt enjoy whatever is available. I'd love it if she would eat tofu, but the girl loves her meat." The edge of Sophie's lips quirked. "I can provide you with a menu from her dietitian since you're being so accommodating."

"That's fine with me." Jesse forced a smile, fighting the urge to cringe at the idea of following a model's diet plan. Alder was so taking turn cooking. His girl was turning out to be a lot of work. "Bring a list of food requirements or anything else she needs to the meeting tomorrow."

Danica slammed the side of her fist into the open door. "Hello? Danica is right here and quite capable of feeding herself. She will not need special treatment, thank you very-fucking-much."

Sophie's eye widened. "Sweetheart, we've discussed your language. Travelling with a band shouldn't change how you behave."

"Oh, it won't." Danica inhaled slowly. Then she grinned at Jesse. "If you don't want to get away as fast as you can, would you like to have an early dinner with us? My agent has just reminded me of my manners."

I like this girl. Jesse stuffed his hands in his pockets and grinned at her. "I'd love to!"

Smile tight, Sophie nodded and led the way to the elevators. Jesse waited while Danica closed her door and walked with her down the hall.

"Please don't get the wrong impression of her. Or me." Danica kept her voice low, slowing her pace before they got within hearing of her agent. "She knows the band will be good for my career, but she's worried. And I'm not some diva. I might have to exercise more, but I'll eat anything."

Jesse leaned close to her, speaking low. "I get her being protective. And since Alder likes you, I'll give you the benefit of the doubt."

"Thank you."

"If you were a guy, I'd tell you if you hurt him, I'll destroy you. But since you're not, I'll just ask you nicely not to. He's a good guy."

Danica cocked her head, looking up at him. "If I was a guy? That's an odd thing to say."

Shit. It is, isn't it? Alder hadn't known the girl long enough to tell her he was bisexual. Knowing the man, it wouldn't be long, but Alder wouldn't appreciate Jesse blurting that out like an idiot.

So Jesse just laughed and waved it off. "I spend too much time with other men. Don't mind me."

Arching a brow, Danica inclined her head. "I don't think I'll mind you at all. You seem like a good guy, Jesse. And you're a great friend."

"We'll see if you still think that when you hear me yelling at you all to get your asses out of bed the day of a show."

"I will. I've been yelled at a time or two." She smiled when Sophie let out an amused snort. "Don't forget, Jesse. My lifestyle isn't all that different. I can do this."

Jesse put his hand on her arm as they stepped onto the elevator. He met her eyes, somehow feeling like she was someone he could become comfortable with in no time at all. Which would be good for them both on the road.

"I believe you can."

This was guilt food. Danica took a big bite of fried chicken, resisting the urge to moan in pleasure as the tender meat and savory breading filled her mouth. She'd chatted with Sophie and Jesse while waiting for their orders, but once the plate was in front of her, she was entirely focused on enjoying every single bite.

Sophie was trying to make up for something. Whether it was the original, crazy plan or what she'd come up with since, she knew Danica wasn't happy.

Using a delicious meal to put a model in a good mood might not be the smartest plan, but Danica wasn't about to complain. She knew Sophie trusted her to keep in good shape. Granted, it would take days to burn off these calories, but workouts were just another part of Danica's job. The guys were pretty much all slim and toned, so they must exercise. Whenever she had a chance, she would do her aerobics and the yoga routine she had memorized. No way would she let Sophie regret giving her this treat.

Sometimes, Danica envied the models who could eat whatever they wanted, and drink every night, and still keep their lithe bodies. But then she opened her eyes and faced the fact that she was damn lucky to still be part of this industry in her mid-twenties. Most of those girls were still in their teens. If they continued the way they were going, they'd be washed out by the time they hit twenty.

Danica had managed to avoid the status quo, because diversity was becoming more and more in high demand. Sophie had found a niche in the market, which was growing more popular every day. Different ages and ethnicities. She had one model who was making more money in her forties than she had in her twenties, an Asian woman whose smile could light up a room and who had men of all ages begging for her attention. She had contracts with some of the highest-end clothing lines, all trying to keep with the times and prove they were open-minded.

Danica's goal was to follow in her footsteps. And with Sophie, the dream could become a reality.

So she wouldn't hold any crazy schemes the woman came up with against her.

"Can you give us an idea of what Danica should expect on the road?" Sophie asked, setting down her glass of red wine. She'd lost the stuffy attitude she usually showed strangers and had been chatting with Jesse about sports, of all things. He seemed impressed with her knowledge of football and they'd been debating recent rule changes, a discussion Danica couldn't take part in. The only thing she knew about football was that the players had a hard time holding a smile for the camera during a photo shoot.

Jesse set down his fork and relaxed back into his chair. "We don't have women on tour very often. Once in awhile, one of the guys will drag a groupie along that he's enjoyed, but they usually leave at the next stop. It's not an easy life." He picked up his napkin and wiped his mouth, pausing as though he was carefully thinking over his answer. "The guys are successful enough to have a nice bus. I'll head over to it early tomorrow to clean out one of the bunks, get the sheets washed and everything. Brave gets moody when things are messy, so she won't have to deal with slobs."

"But the men she'll be dealing with. Will they respect her?" Sophie leaned forward, resting her forearms on the table. "She is capable of defending herself, but I'd rather her not have to."

Jaw hardening, Jesse met Sophie's eyes. "She won't have to. I wouldn't be with the band if they treated women badly. Yes, sometimes they spend time with wild groupies, but one thing I've noticed is they rarely…they don't go off with fans alone. It might seem crude, but as the band becomes more popular, there's no avoiding the opportunists."

Danica hugged herself, hating that Jesse might soon see her as one of them. Yes, her presence might be good for the band, but she'd come here for an opportunity.

What if he found out? He was close to Alder, he wouldn't have shown up to bring her his number otherwise. She didn't need to share all the sordid details, but she did want to see where he stood on her presence.

"Why do you think Cole wants me touring with the band? I'll be honest, being seen with the guys will be good for my career, but I have no idea what it will do for them." She tugged her bottom lip with her teeth. "There are plenty of pictures out there after last night."

Jesse shrugged. "I'm not sure what he's up to, but I can guarantee he'll put you to work. He's all about contracts, so he'll probably have one for you tomorrow at the meeting. He wants the band to reach the next level. And Sophie, I assume, wants the same for you. I'm guessing, whatever the plan, it will be good for everyone."

"Yeah." Danica took a sip of her water. She was a little surprised that Sophie hadn't ordered her wine as well, but she probably had her reasons. Among them being the temptation to drink with the band. Danica would be juggling calories if she ended up having beer with the guys, but she knew her limits. "To go back to Sophie's question, is there anything I need to know? One of the guys I need to avoid before he has his coffee, or—"

"If any of the boys are up before noon, you should be fine. It doesn't happen often, but once in a blue moon Tate gets up and wants practice. So if you want to sleep in, he'll drive you nuts. Connor is usually the first one up, and he does chin-ups on the bar set up in the doorway of the back lounge. Brave takes over the back lounge for a few hours to write songs. Alder spends a few hours in the front lounge with his guitar, sometimes jamming with Malakai. The two of them get wrapped up in writing the music for the band." Jesse smiled, seeming lost in thought. "I wouldn't bug them when they're bent over the notes, but it's cool to watch them. One thing I can say is the guys are serious about what they're doing. Yeah, they can be a hot mess, but for the most part, they're all artists. If you keep that in mind, you won't have any issues."

Danica couldn't help but smile as she reached out to touch Jesse's hand. "Thank you. I was afraid I'd be stuck for hours with a bunch of drunk, obnoxious men who still acted like little boys. But now I'm thinking it won't be so bad."

Jesse patted the back of her hand and chuckled. "Oh, don't get me wrong. There will be times that you wonder if any of them are adults. They tussle and argue and when they're playing video games? Damn, I've been tempted to leave every one of them at a rest stop. But for the most part, they're good guys. And the band means everything to them. If Cole thinks you'll be an asset, they'll treat you like a queen."

"That's good." She wrinkled her nose, considering one of the things he'd mentioned. "I don't play video games. Will they mind if I keep to myself and read?"

"Not at all. Brave doesn't play. Both he and Alder constantly have their noses stuck in a book." Jesse winked at her. "The guys take that as a sign that you want to be left the fuck alone."

She nodded, feeling more at ease about the whole thing. She was looking forward to spending time with Alder, but she didn't want the band to see her as a burden. She had no problem entertaining herself. So long as the guys didn't think she was being unsocial.

"What about the media? I've noticed you haven't had as much exposure as you could." Sophie brought the conversation right back to business. No surprise there. "Cole mentioned getting the band more press. Will the band be comfortable with that?"

Jesse reached for his glass of water, his brow creasing slightly. "There's a reason Cole has been with us for so long. I can't say the guys love the press, but they'll go along with whatever he comes up with."

"Good." Sophie smiled. "I've done my research, and Cole knows what he's doing. I'm looking forward to working with him."

You are? Danica brought her glass to her lips to hide her frown. Other models with Sophie's label saw her as a money hungry bitch, but those girls were newbies and didn't appreciate everything Sophie did for them. They hated waking up early in the morning for a photo shoot. They got pissed when Sophie kept them away from the parties and the wild lifestyle.

Danica had worked with Sophie long enough to understand her narrow-minded, determination to give every one of her models a career that would last. But Cole didn't seem to have the same vision. He'd seemed very cold with Alder. He'd assumed Danica hadn't been honest with him. Just a mention of the man had her guard up.

But maybe that wasn't fair. Cole was dealing with a bunch of young men and trying to bring them to the next level as a whole. He had every reason to question Danica's worth.

After they finished eating, she waited outside for Jesse, waving Sophie on so she could speak to him alone. "I don't have a pen, but please tell Alder to call me."

"I will."

"I've never done anything like this before."

"I know." Jesse pulled her in for a hug and kissed her cheek. "Don't worry, sweetie. Things move fast in this life, but that's not a bad thing. Alder will look out for you. And so will I."

She let out a light laugh. "You don't even know me."

"I don't need to. He likes you already. And he's got good fucking taste in people." Jesse cupped her cheek and winked at her. "I'm one of his favorites, and I'm pretty awesome. So that says a lot about you."

She snickered and held his steady gaze. "I'm happy I got to meet you. You've made this whole thing a lot less scary."

"Good. Don't forget that when your agent and Cole are hashing out the details."

"I won't."

He stepped away, paused. "I've decided it doesn't matter that you're a chick. Don't hurt him. If you decide you're not interested, or you've got to take off, let him down easy. He doesn't play games with people. If you fuck him over, I'll find a way to hurt you."

The hesitant way Jesse spoke assured Danica he wasn't physically threatening her. He wouldn't resort to that. He'd find another way. One she wouldn't enjoy, but regardless, it proved he cared about Alder very much.

And she respected that.

"I won't hurt him. I don't know where things will go from here, but I'm a straightforward kinda girl." She reached out to squeeze his hand. "Don't worry. Even though I'm all kinds of hot stuff, I'm still wondering why he's interested when he could have anyone."

"And that's what makes you the perfect choice." Jesse brought her hand up to his lips to kiss her knuckles. "From what he's said, he thinks the same thing when he looks at you."

She waited in front of the restaurant while Jesse grabbed a cab, then got in Sophie's rental. They were going straight to the photo shoot, so she had to pull it together, but she couldn't help wonder how much her life would change on tour with the band. Whatever this would do for her career, she had a feeling it would go beyond all the new interest the media would have in her.

Every time she thought of Alder, she couldn't help but smile. Even in the short time she'd known him, he made her happy. She wanted that to last.

It was too soon for her to get invested in him, but her heart didn't seem to care.

Seeing him in her future was far too easy. There were so many obstacles that could keep that from happening, but she believed, together, they could overcome them all.

Things *did* move fast in this lifestyle. But the opportunity they had could last beyond the short time they had in the spotlight. Maybe it was too soon to hope for more. But she couldn't recall the last time she'd considered what tomorrow might bring.

But right now, she was looking forward, and she couldn't help but believe she'd found someone who she could hold on to. Someone real.

Her life consisted of fake smiles and Photoshop making her into nothing more than a perfect picture on a page. An idealistic face and body meant to sell makeup and clothes, not a person anyone could be close to. But Alder had seen *her*. The real woman.

So she might be making more of what they had than was actually there, but Jesse's warning stuck with her. He wouldn't have said a word if Alder wasn't thinking about her. Wondering what they could have.

Being on tour would force them to put it all on the line. And if their newborn relationship could survive this, it could survive anything.

She needed to get some sleep though. Because tomorrow would be the ultimate test.

Chapter Six

I should have rented a limo.

Alder checked the time on the dashboard of the SUV he'd borrowed from one of the roadies. And wondered if he'd planned the breakfast too early. They'd be on the road in a few hours and maybe Danica should have the chance to enjoy a real bed while she could. He didn't want to rush breakfast though, and she had seemed excited about going out together before the meeting with the band.

He just wanted the date to be perfect. Not that he had the first idea what a 'perfect' date was like. Or even a really good one.

The passenger side door swung open and Danica bounced onto the seat, flashing him a brilliant smile as her high ponytail swung over her shoulder. "Oh good, you've got the AC going. It's nasty here when it's windy."

And just like that, all his uncertainty vanished. The woman was like a shot of espresso the morning after a crazy party when too many drinks fogged his brain. He grinned as she pushed up onto her knees and leaned over him like she'd completely forgotten she was wearing a sexy little summer dress. Either that or she didn't care about being all proper. Which would be pretty damn awesome.

"Sorry, I'm nuts in the morning. It's great to see you." She placed a hand on his chest to brace herself as she kissed him.

"Thank you for sending Jesse to get my number. He's pretty awesome."

"He really is." Alder curved his hand around the back of her neck, savoring her lips, which tasted like coffee and raspberries. A horn sounded and he chuckled as she drew away quickly and plopped onto her seat. "Ready to go?"

She nodded, glancing in the rearview. "Yeah. I'm starved and I think the guy behind us is about to get out and come yell at you. Really, Alder. So thoughtless of you to hold up traffic."

With a snort, Alder pulled out of the hotel entrance, starting the GPS on the dashboard as they left the strip. One of the bellhops at the Hard Rock Hotel had recommended a place in Henderson called The Black Bear Diner. He swore he'd never had a bad meal there and their breakfasts were amazing.

Alder had checked out the menu before leaving to pick up Danica, and was relieved to find they had low cal options. Which she might appreciate, but he absolutely needed. Cole had gotten a call from a British men's apparel company who wanted to use the band in a few commercials. When Alder had given Cole his measurements, the man had practically snarled at him. Brave had the long, slender body type they were looking for, but Alder was too bulky.

Of course, Brave would have turned down the offer—he didn't mind the sponsors they had so far, one for shoes and another that owned a huge portion of the candy market—but he didn't want the band going 'commercial'.

So actual commercials were out for him. But Alder still felt like a loser after the chat with Cole. He had some nice definition, but his jeans were getting snug.

"You missed your turn." Danica put her hand on his knee. "I was enjoying the sights, but you're awfully quiet. Are you worried about the meeting?"

Alder blinked, took the next turn as the GPS instructed, then shook his head. "No. It's really stupid actually."

"'It's'? Well, that was vague as hell." She cocked her head and gave his knee a little squeeze. "You're a dork, but I don't think you're stupid."

He laughed and put his hand over hers. "I appreciate that."

"Good. So talk, Mister."

Pushy little thing, isn't she? He glanced over at her and shrugged. "Cole was bitching about my gut getting too big. I'm thinking he's right and I should lay off the beer."

Sitting back, Danica sighed. "Yes, because *that's* not something I could possibly understand."

"I know you do."

"Good. So let's put it this way. I think you're fucking perfect, but if it's an issue for you, lay off the beer and workout more." She gave his shoulder a light punch as he pulled into the diner parking. "I'm going to need a yoga buddy anyway, so it works for both of us."

"Yoga?" He put the SUV in reverse, backing into one of the few available spots. "Umm...not sure I can do yoga. I'm not that bendy."

"You will be. And I'm hoping to reap all the benefits!" She undid her seatbelt, arched up to kiss his cheek, then got out.

He stared after her, needing a minute to adjust after her admission. All his blood had vacated his brain, surging right down to his dick, making his already snug jeans uncomfortably tight.

She was absolutely incredible. Guy or girl, he wouldn't have opened up like that with anyone he'd dated in the past. But Danica made it easy to be himself.

After they were seated, he reached for the menu, but Danica pulled it out of reach, flipping hers open and grinning at him over it. "Do you trust me?"

"Yes." He relaxed against the back of the booth, curious to see what she'd order for him. He wasn't loving the idea of egg whites and whole wheat bread, but just by looking at her, he could tell she knew how to keep her body in perfect shape. And if he was going to get back in Cole's good graces, he'd take any advice she had to give.

Actually, once Cole saw what a good influence she was, he'd probably leave the two of them alone. If Jesse was right, Alder needed to avoid any attempts Cole might make to sabotage their relationship.

The waitress came over, a smile tugging at her lips as she noticed Danica hogging the menus. "What can I get you, sweetie?"

Danica picked up the menus and handed them to the waitress. "Two orders of The Mini Volcano, with coffee—do you like coffee?"

"Yes, thank you." Alder frowned when the waitress patted his shoulder in passing. He could be completely off, but he'd sensed some pity coming from her. *What the fuck?*

"Stop scowling. She probably thinks I have your balls in my purse." Danica set her purse on the table and peeked inside. "They're not in here, so no worries."

Rolling his eyes, he leaned his forearms on the edge of the table. "Is that where you want them?"

"Absolutely not. I like them right where they are." She winked at him, reaching across the table to take his hands. "I'm going to make sure you're well fed, but you get the bill. Next meal we share, you pick what we eat and I pay."

That sounded fair. Not that he'd let her pay if they were at a restaurant, but he planned to have their next meal be one he cooked for her. On the bus.

Sending her on a grocery run with Jesse would fulfill his end of the bargain.

Thinking of Jesse, he met her eyes. "So I heard you had supper with Jesse and your agent last night? Sounds like she was decent to him?"

Danica's shoulders lifted slightly. "I guess. She gave him the third degree about the tour, but it wasn't too bad. He made it clear I would be fine. Actually, he made the bus sound better than a hotel."

"He did?"

"Clean sheets? Meals on-the-go? This is going to be awesome!" The twinkle in her green eyes told him she was teasing. He let out a sigh of relief and she laughed. "I don't expect a luxurious ride, but he did tell us enough that Sophie isn't worried and I'm pretty sure I can tough it out. I've never seen the inside of a tour bus, so who knows? But my grandfather had a mobile home for the first few years after he got his property, so I grew up in small spaces. He built a nice little house now, so I've been spoiled for a bit, but I'm used to finding my own space when I need it."

"Did you need it a lot?" Alder moved his hands so the waitress could set down the coffee. "I mean, you sound like you love your grandfather very much, but was it tough when you were a teen? Just you and him?"

"Sometimes? I mean, he's got some interesting ideas about how the world should work. He hates any music after the sixties and he can be a slob. I used to do chores just so I could listen to my iPod without him complaining that I'd shut myself off from the world." She fixed her coffee with cream. And no sugar. There was a fond smile on her lips as she told him about her childhood. "He hated all my clothes, but he wanted me to fit in, so he'd bring me shopping and point out clothes he'd seen on other girls at my school. I went through a long hippie phase and dragged him to vintage stores. Which he complained about constantly, but now he shops there all the time. He taught me how to manage money. I think we learned a lot from one another."

"Sounds like it." Alder hoped he'd get to meet the man one day. He must be one of a kind to have raised a woman like Danica. She wasn't like any of the models he'd ever come across in the business. "Does he know you're going on tour with us?"

She wrinkled her nose. "Not yet. But I'll give him one thing. He has a lot of respect for Sophie, so he probably won't be thrilled, but he'll expect me to do whatever's best for my career."

"I hope it works out then."

"Me too."

Taking a sip of his coffee, black, Alder did his best to school his features. He usually took his coffee with five packs of sugar and a lot of cream, but he needed to cut back.

"You're adorable." Danica put her hand over his cup before he could lift it again. "Some cream and a bit of sugar won't stack on the pounds. I'm seriously thinking the beer is the biggest issue, but we'll work on it, okay? No huge changes unless I say so, got it?"

"Yes, ma'am." Alder added enough cream to give his coffee a nice, light color, then dumped in three packets of sugar. He took a sip and let out a soft sound of pleasure. "Much better."

"I bet." She tipped her own mug to her lips, studying him over the rim. She placed her mug on the table and straightened a little "Your turn. Tell me about the band. Or your family. Or your favorite subject. Jesse."

Alder inhaled sharply. As he was sipping. And choked.

Rushing around the table, Danica firmly patted his back until he stopped coughing and could breathe again.

"So much for a safe subject." She rubbed his back for a moment, then returned to her side of the booth. "Is it horrible that my mind is going to all kinds of places you might think are totally off base? I mean, it wouldn't have if I hadn't seen you and your band guy all over each other, but—"

"I'm bisexual."

Shit.

He hadn't just blurted that out.

You really did, asshole.

"Shit. I'm sorry, I didn't mean to—" He bit his tongue when Danica put her hand up. Then leaned out of the way as the waitress set their plates in front of them. Once the waitress moved out of hearing, Danica motioned for him to go on. "I hadn't planned to tell you like that. I *did* plan to tell you though."

She nodded slowly, holding her bottom lip between her teeth as she poked the egg topping the two pancakes on her plate with her fork. Squaring her shoulders, she met his eyes. "So you like both guys and girls. Have you ever been with a girl?"

"Yes."

"Not because you had to, but because you wanted to? I'm sorry, that was rude. And it didn't feel like you were forcing anything while we were making out, but... I like you a lot, Alder." She twisted her fork into the pancakes. "If I'm just here to cover for something, I need to know before you break my heart."

He pressed his eyes shut and rubbed his temples. "You're not a cover. I like you too and I want to see where this goes. But I won't lie to you. I won't practically drown on a sip of coffee and pretend you mentioning Jesse wasn't the reason."

She pressed her tongue against her top lip thoughtfully. "Well, you have good taste."

Letting out a rough laugh, he reached for her hand. "Jesse is dating my brother. Yes, I had feelings for him, but he's not interested in me. So I'm cool with being friends."

"And I'm the rebound?"

"No, you're unexpected. I've known for a while that me and Jesse weren't going to happen. Hell, he's in love with my brother, and me and Brave couldn't be more different." He stroked the back of her hand with his thumb. "I wasn't looking for a relationship. The band has taken up so much of my life; I think part of me just focused on the person I was closest to. I've had the opportunity to date different guys and girls, but none of them appealed to me."

"So you slept around while lusting after your roadie?" Her face went beat red. "Okay, that was mean. My grandpa says I should count to ten before I let any of my thoughts spill out of my mouth, but I've lost that skill with you."

"And I am totally cool with that." He picked up his fork and cut a piece of pancake. After slowly chewing a mouthful of rich, syrup covered goodness, he licked his lips and cleared his throat. "If you ask Brave, he'll tell you I am the worst 'rock star' ever. I don't sleep with groupies. I don't sign boobs. Or dicks."

She let out a laugh that was almost a snort. "Damn. I'd have liked to see that."

"You're a kinky little thing, aren't you?"

"Maybe a little. But I'm glad we're talking about this. I would have been all paranoid about the groupies, but now I can add the roadies, and the security, and all the hot guys on tour as potential competition. I may have to start up kickboxing if I want to keep my man."

"No. I'm loyal, Danica. I give what I expect to receive from whoever I'm with." He cut another piece of pancake, dipped it in his egg yolk. "You're around male models all the time. Do I have to worry about them?"

"Point taken. We'll save the jealousy for later." She took a big bite of pancake with a folded slice of bacon and let out a moan of pleasure. "Damn, this is good. Over half of what we can eat today, but so worth it!"

"*Half?*" Alder stared at his plate. It was a good helping of food, but he fixed himself meals like this at least twice a day on the road. When they had enough food in the fridge anyway. Connor ate three times as much as the rest of the band, but he had a crazy metabolism and was addicted to exercising.

Danica nodded as she took another bite. She cleaned her mouth with a gulp of coffee. "That may change after I see how much you workout. I'm going to call my dietitian before we hit the road. So rather than have any more awkward chats about our sexual preferences, you'll have to give me your height and weight and a share of your soul."

"Sounds good." Sounded horrible. But he had to get serious about getting in shape. Cole wanted him and Malakai to take off their shirts more often during shows. Sell the sex a bit.

Thankfully, he felt comfortable taking off his shirt in front of Danica. He wasn't a total dog. But cameras could be cruel and if Cole had his way, the entire band would be half naked between the pages of the biggest alternative rock magazines by the end of the year.

Getting to a place where he'd be okay with that would be a lot easier with Danica's encouragement.

But he was getting tired of talking about, or even *thinking* about, his body.

"Did Sophie have any more insight about what Cole expects from you on the tour?"

Danica shook her head. "I think Cole's waiting to see how the band reacts. He's worked out most of the details of the contract with Sophie, but it was basic stuff. Less than what I'd make for a runway show, but a bit more than I'd get for a photoshoot. The band will own any pictures I take with you all, but if it's used for promo, I get a bonus. I think it's fair."

"And Sophie?"

"She won't be happy with anything less than a magazine cover or a movie deal."

"Ah." Alder finished the last bite of his pancakes and eggs. He picked up his bacon with his fingers, then put it down, wondering if Danica would question his table manners. But she picked up her last bit with her fingers and popped it in her mouth, so he did the same. After polishing off his coffee, he used a napkin to clean the grease from his lips. "So she'll be shopping around while you're on tour with us?"

"Probably. But I do have a say and I won't leave until I've done what I can with you and the guys. I can't wait to see what I can possibly do to help you." She reached into her purse and pulled out a CD, pointing to the cover which had a woman reclined on a red sofa. "Something like this? I'd love it! I don't think I need to be on tour to model for one of your album covers, but I hope it's being considered."

"If it isn't, I'll suggest it."

Her eyes went wide. "Please don't. Cole knows we're into each other. I don't want that affecting anything he offers. I want to know everything I do with you guys is because of my looks and my skills."

With an attitude like that, Alder wasn't sure how she'd ever seen herself as opportunistic. He grinned and nodded.

"You've got it. I won't use what little influence I have to get you a better deal." He cupped her cheek. "You have a Sophie. Nothing I could manage even compares to what she'll come up with."

"Very true." She put her hand over his, and they continued to chat about lighter subjects as they had another cup of coffee. They shared a few favorite bands and had been to a few of the same venues in Detroit to see them live as teens. They got into a short debate about gun control after hearing a heated discussion at a nearby table, but agreed to disagree. They had similar views on religion and politics, meeting somewhere in the middle.

And they both loved animals, which Danica insisted was the only thing that mattered. Her grandfather had a cat that he shared the house with and he loved more than he'd admit. He'd gotten the kitten for Danica right after she got home from a runway show in Finland when she was seventeen. Knowing full well she wouldn't be home long enough to take care of him.

He'd named the scruffy black cat Ninja, because he said the little rescue kitten was sneaky. Whenever she went home, she'd find the cat cuddled up on her grandfather's lap.

Alder told her about the stray dogs he and Brave had been bringing home for years. Their parents were great with the dogs, but limited the ones they kept to three. The others were given good homes with neighbors. At this point, he knew every dog on the block.

He missed his two girls, Ink and Ebony, whenever he went on tour. Brave's dog, Ewok, had spent a few months on the bus their last tour, because he was smaller than Alder's German Shepard mixed mutts, but he'd gotten a bad ear infection and had to go home for treatment.

They'd be back in Detroit in two weeks, and he was doing much better, so he might be joining them again. Except for Jesse, the roadies hated having Ewok around, since they needed to watch him while the band was on stage and he was an energetic little thing.

Danica offered to help with him.

And Alder was pretty sure he'd fall in love with her before long if she didn't stop being so freakin' awesome.

His phone buzzed. A text from Jesse, letting him know the band was waiting for him and Danica. And Cole was getting pissy.

Alder sighed and gestured for the waitress. They'd been here almost three hours. He left a big tip to make up for them hogging the table.

And he took Danica's hand as they made their way back to the SUV.

"I'm glad we got to do this." He opened the passenger side door for her. "This tour will be tough. The band is being pushed to another level, and you're part of it, but since you haven't been through any of this before, you might get overwhelmed. I hope you know you can come to me. About anything."

"I will." She curved her fingers into the collar of his T-shirt and drew him close, claiming his lips. "And you've shown me I *can.*"

He felt much better about bringing her to the meeting and letting her face the guys with that assurance, but that didn't last long.

Standing behind the bus, under the frame tent, they'd been talking for about ten minutes before Cole made his announcement.

"I've hired a choreographer in LA. Danica will be on stage for the show." He didn't seem to notice every member of the band staring at him. Or care if he did. "Performing 'SLUT'."

Danica wasn't sure who she should grab first. Both Sophie and Alder looked ready to rip Cole's head off. But then Jesse put his hand on Alder's shoulder. So she brought her attention to Sophie.

Who stepped up to Cole and jabbed her finger into the center of his chest. "Her contract specifically states that she will not be asked to do anything demeaning. I suggest you explain yourself before I negate this whole deal!"

"Sophie—" Danica sighed as Sophie continued her diatribe about legal terms and respect. There was no talking her down when she thought one of her girls was being mistreated.

And the fact that Cole was simply nodding, completely unaffected by a single word, was just making the situation worse.

Danica wasn't offended, because she'd heard the song. But Sophie clearly hadn't.

Brave slammed his fist into the side of the bus. "Enough!"

Sophie pressed her lips together and glared at him. Cole folded his arms and his brow furrowed as he turned to his lead singer.

The band, all but Alder, looked like they were trying not to laugh as Brave stepped up to the manager and the man took a step back.

"You're being an asshole. And I get why, in your twisted mind, you'd want to see if the chick knew what she was signing on for." He pointed at Danica. "She's not freaking out, so she gets it. So what if her agent doesn't listen to our fucking music?"

"The song is still very sexual. The last thing we need is a hard core feminist dragging her girl off the stage in the middle of a show." Cole's tone was steady, but he didn't seem as confident now that Brave had called him on his shit. "And what about you? Will you be comfortable performing with a woman?"

Brave's jaw ticked. "Don't fucking start that shit with me, Cole. I'll play nice in public and follow your goddamn rules. You think me feeling up a chick on stage will be good for the band? I'll do it. Otherwise, it's none of your business what I do with my dick."

"Fair enough." Cole took a deep breath as Brave backed off. His expression changed so abruptly, Danica wondered if he had any experience as a model. The cameras must love him. That fake smile was more genuine than anything she'd ever manage to pull off. "Now that we've gotten past the unpleasantness, please let me clarify. SLUT is a song Brave wrote to disregard all the negativity behind the word. It's actually quite empowering."

"Is that so?" Sophie looked at Danica, relaxing when Danica nodded. "Very well. But I would like to hear from the band. Are you all comfortable with Danica joining you on tour? I expect you will have to make some drastic changes in your lifestyle. She's not one of your groupies and—"

"Sophie, I don't need them changing anything for me." Danica's face heated as the men's eyes locked on her. Then she felt a strong hand take hers and the weight on her chest lifted as Alder smiled at her.

"She might dress better than the women we know." He looked pointedly at her jeans and T-shirt, as though he wanted to make sure no one missed his sarcasm. "But she's not as high maintenance as she seems."

One of the men she'd seen sitting with Alder at the after party let out a dry laugh. "She wears a bit *more* clothes than the women I hang out with. Honestly, I don't see a problem with having her on the bus, but I can't say how I feel about the whole act until I see it."

"I'm with Connor." The man who'd been protective of the drummer—she was pretty sure his name was Malakai—rested his forearm on the youngest member's shoulder. "Why don't we call LA a test run? See if we like that act. And how the fans respond."

Tate nodded, tilting his head to one side as he looked from Danica to Alder. "Are you guys together? I saw some stuff online and some of the female fans are freaking out. Won't seeing her all over Brave make it worse?"

"That's a very good question, Tate." Cole rubbed his chin in thought. "The photos being spread around are bringing some positive attention to the band, but I think it would be good for Danica to have her own title. She's a paid performer, so we could add her to the website and make it official. Let the fans have fun speculating who she's with."

"Why is it such a big deal if they know she's with me?" Alder shook his head when Jesse whispered something to him from his other side, but the tension left him when Danica squeezed his hand. "I'm sorry, but this is getting ridiculous. Fine, she's not coming along just as my girlfriend. But we *are* together."

Cole's smile changed, making him look a bit like a shark, even though Danica was pretty sure he was going for sympathetic. "Alder, I know this relationship is new and it's very sweet you want to tell the world. But what looks better on her resume? Performing on stage with Winter's Wrath, posing for album covers and other marketing material? Or spending some time on the bus following her boyfriend around?"

Damn it, he's right. She didn't want to have to choose between her career and Alder, but if she was forced to...she really hoped *he* wouldn't be the one putting her in that position.

"Maybe the question should be whether *you* will have an issue with her performing with me, Alder." Brave's tone was cold, but at least he was being direct. And not playing Cole's games. "Is it more important to claim her than it is for this opportunity to benefit everyone?"

Alder dropped his gaze as his brother continued to stare him down. "No."

Danica released the breath she hadn't realized she'd been holding. She hoped this didn't mess up their budding relationship, but they could figure that out on their own. The most important thing was her presence not causing a rift with the band.

Which her silence didn't help. She needed to stop letting Sophie and Alder speak for her.

"I'm sure you'd all like me a lot more if I gushed about how much I love your music, but I only starting listening to it a few days ago. I enjoy most of the songs, but not enough to ask any of you to sign my boobs. You'll need new material." She grinned when Tate barked out a laugh. The other guys smiled. Even Alder. "This is an amazing opportunity and I'm happy Sophie and Cole set it up. I'm serious about my career and I can tell you're just as serious about bringing this band to the top. I think we're gonna have a great partnership."

Brave clapped slowly and stepped toward her. "Diplomatic and smart." He lifted her hand to his lips, brushing her knuckles with a soft kiss. "I look forward to dancing with you again, sweetheart."

She caught his amused gaze flick past her before he headed to the front of the bus and had no doubt he was goading Alder. She refused to acknowledge the childish rivalry he and Alder seemed to have going on. But when she turned and saw Jesse with his hands on both of Alder's shoulders, speaking low, she couldn't help but wonder if there was more to it than she'd first assumed. She hadn't seen any jealousy in Brave's eyes, even though he'd tried to provoke it in his brother.

He obviously knew Alder and Jesse were close, but did he have any clue that his brother had been in love with the man? Did he love Jesse too much to care?

Not really any of her business, but she had a feeling, if anything was going to put a strain on the band, it wouldn't be her presence.

The band wouldn't have lasted this long with so much animosity between the brothers.

Which meant it was getting worse.

Chapter Seven

"You wanna cookie?"

Danica started and looked up from where she'd stretched out to read a science fiction novel she'd found, Xenogenisis. Not the type of book she'd normally read, but she'd quickly become completely engrossed in the story. So much so that she hadn't heard that the band had stopped practicing in the back lounge.

She sat up and shook her head, smiling at Tate as he withdrew the box of cookies. "No thank you."

"I guess you're not really allowed to eat stuff like this. The rest of the guys aren't either. Well, Brave could, but I'm pretty sure he's not human." Tate stuffed the cookie into his mouth, then swung open the fridge in the kitchen area. "You want some carrots?"

Laughing, Danica shook her head again. "I'm good. I am curious why cookies are forbidden. Is Cole really that strict?"

"Not really, but he can make you feel like an ass if you do something he doesn't like. Gain weight, wear the wrong clothes, shave your head." He gave her a sheepish smile as he ran his hand over his semi-mohawk. "I thought he was gonna kick me to the curb when I gave myself a buzz cut a few months after joining the band. He said it 'ruined my signature look'. I wore a beanie until my hair grew back—even when it was crazy hot out."

"I know what that's like. I put blue streaks in my hair once and Sophie wanted to strangle me. She wasn't shy about telling me. Was a bit easier to fix than a shaved head though."

"Yeah…but I'm lucky. As a drummer, I need as many calories as I can get. And it's the cookies or coke, so Cole doesn't get on my case." He took another cookie out and grinned as he took a bite. "He doesn't know I'm more scared of what my Grandma will do if I start up again. Don't tell him though. He'll stop being so nice."

'Nice' didn't seem like a word anyone could use to describe Cole, but Danica kept that thought to herself. She was relieved when he'd told them he'd be driving up to LA on his own, rather than in the bus. Alder had mentioned Cole usually rode with them—his bunk was the only one never used for storage—but on this tour he'd been taking his car more often. Something about making detours when the band didn't need him so he could set up new opportunities.

"I won't say a word." She placed the book cover flap between the pages to save her spot as the rest of the band came into the front lounge. Malakai and Alder sat on the sofa across from the one she was sitting on, setting a notebook on their knees as they began to jot down what looked like notes.

Connor dropped down on the floor and started doing pushups. "Is it just me or is this drive taking forever? I need to move!"

"You're such a freak, Con." Brave stepped over Connor and sat beside Danica, propping his feet up on Connor's back. "It's been about two hours. You want me to ask Jesse to pull over at a rest stop so you can jog for a bit?"

Nodding, without pausing his steady up and down motion, Connor nodded. "That would be awesome, man."

"I'll talk to him, but you're gonna have to chill out a bit on our next trip. It's only a four hour drive and we shouldn't be stopping at all." Brave pushed off the sofa and ruffled Connor's hair. "But we're ahead of schedule, so it's fine.

Another situation Danica wasn't sure she had any right to comment on, but there was something familiar about Jesse's mention of Connor constantly working out, and the almost desperate way Connor talked about moving. She'd met a few models, of both sexes, that shared that particular obsession.

"Have you ever had an eating problem, Connor?" She bit her lip when Alder and Malakai stopped writing notes and Tate stared at her. "I'm sorry, that was blunt. It's just…obsessive exercising can be a symptom. We're told to look for signs at the agency and I just wondered if you…" *Real smooth, Danica. You can shut up now.*

The men's attention had all turned to Connor as he rose to a crouch. "I exercise enough to be able to eat whatever I want. And hey, it's cool, I'm not offended that you asked. There's usually a guy from one of the bands we tour with that asks at least once. They've diagnosed me with everything from OCD to bulimia. My doctor says I'm just hyperactive."

"And he gets prescriptions for the good stuff!" Tate blurted, taking Brave's spot beside Danica, still holding on to the cookies. "Medicated marijuana. But he won't share."

"*Your* doctor doesn't like the idea of you taking any drugs."

"Not that it stops you from bumming from anyone who's soft for your puppy dog looks."

Alder and Malakai spoke almost at once, shaking their heads as they both gave Tate disapproving frowns.

Tate rolled his eyes, hopping up as the bus rolled to a stop. "Speaking of which, I'm gonna see what Jesse's up to. If Brave's not all up on him, maybe *he'll* share."

"He better not!" Malakai called out, but Tate was already gone, with Connor trailing after him.

Grumbling to himself, Malakai followed them out.

And Danica took the opportunity to cover her face with her hands and call herself a few creative names. Including one her Ojibwe teacher often used. "*Ningiiwanaadiz!*"

Eyes wide, Alder crouched down in front of her and pulled her hands away from her face. "What does that mean?"

"I am crazy. There's no insults in Ojibwe, but it's fitting. I'm screwing this up so badly!"

"No you're not. If I know Connor, and I do, he thinks you're sweet for caring." He circled her palm with his thumb. "Stop second guessing yourself. We're stuck on this bus together, all seven of us, for days at a time. At some point you might say or do something, or one of the guys will, and shit will hit the fan. But right now they're getting to know you and they like what they see."

He rubbed her knees and held her gaze while she considered his words. And she realized he was right. This trip was going to be a lot more strained if she didn't speak her mind. Honesty, concern, and complete openness were all parts of who she was.

"Okay. I get it." She wrapped her arms around his neck. "You want to get some fresh air, or take advantage of our precious seconds of privacy?"

Alder ran his hands up her thighs. "Seconds aren't enough for all that I want to do to you. And I'm tempted to be selfish, but you need to get used to taking every opportunity to get off the bus. Have you ever been down this highway?"

"No, I usually fly to LA."

"Come on then. The view is pretty sweet if we are where I think we are."

As they headed for the door, two older men Danica didn't recognize ambled onto the bus. She spotted Tate's young drum tech behind them and figured these must be the roadies.

One of the men, with a shiny bald head and a face covered in scars and tattoos, greeted Alder, inclined his head to Danica, then collapsed onto the sofa they'd just left.

"Like fucking chewing on dirt in the van—had to keep the windows open. Malakai's trying to fix the AC, and Jesse told us to come grab a beer and chill in here for a bit." Without rising, the man held his hand out to Danica. "Forgive me for not getting up, but I need to rest my old bones. I keep telling the guys I won't do tours in the South anymore, but I'm full of shit. You can call me Skull."

"Nice to meet you, Skull." She was tempted to ask for his real name, but he'd have told her if he wanted to be called anything else. "I'm Danica."

"And you really are as gorgeous as the boys keep saying." He chuckled and dropped his arm over his eyes. "Treat her good, Alder. Jesse's already told everyone he'd personally break kneecaps if anyone messes with her. I think, after hearing that her agent assumes we're all scum, the rest of the boys will want in on that."

"Not gonna be an issue, Skull." Alder rubbed Skull's head, patted the shoulder of the drum tech who was raiding the fridge, then gave the last man, who looked like he'd stepped straight off a tank—and was about the size of one—a hand-clasping, man-hug.

Outside, Alder waited for her, quickly taking her hand to lead her away from the bus. They walked across the dry terrain for a bit, climbing up one of the smaller hills that surrounded both sides of the highway. It didn't take long to reach the highest point, but Danica's mouth was dry and her throat felt caked with dust.

The man was crazy. The sun beat down on them unmercifully and red dirt rose in a gritty haze around their feet, with just enough of a breeze for her to taste it in her mouth and feel it in her eyes. At least she was wearing running shoes, but Sophie would throw a fit if she saw Danica exposed to the elements like this.

Stop whining. Five minutes in the sun won't ruin you for life.

Probably not, but why had he brought her up here?

Standing behind her, he put his hands on her shoulders and turned her to look over the horizon. Then he brought his lips close to her ear. "When you travel as much as we do, you can forget to appreciate not many get the chance we've been given to see the world. Look."

And she did. And she forgot the heat and all the worrying and pretty much everything else.

The view was incredible. Through the deep slope of mountains crested in rich foliage, she could make out the city. A thin sheen of fog wrapped around the base of the skyscrapers, giving them a surreal, majestic aura. She leaned back against Alder, taking in the sight and realizing she'd never really stopped and seen anything in any of the places she'd been.

Of course, she'd paused in Paris to see the Eiffel Tower. In Rome they'd driven by the Colosseum. In every city she'd ever visited, there had been attractions that she wished she could just stand there and stare at, even if only for a few minutes. But she was always rushing off somewhere.

She'd been to many places without experiencing any of them.

"Thank you." She held his hands against her chest and kissed the side of his wrist. "I needed this. I didn't expect to get many more chances to explore with the tour than I do when I travel for runway shows or photo shoots."

"Ah, well, that's where things are a bit different. Not all the guys are into doing the touristy thing, but I'd rather lose a little sleep than miss out." He pressed his lips to her hair. "But I can go on stage with dark circles under my eyes. I could play the guitar in my sleep. You need to be all bright eyed and cheerful."

She absolutely loved that he understood that she hadn't been neglecting the opportunities. Sophie was strict, and while it limited Danica's free time, it was the only way she'd ever be successful.

Considering what would be expected from her on the tour, she sighed. "I still have to be all bright eyed and cheerful."

"That depends. You really want to sell that you're living the 'rock star' life?"

"Ha! There's selling it, and there's having pictures of me too drunk to remember I decided panties ruin the lines of my dress."

He let out a soft groan. "You cannot expect me to continue being a gentleman if you talk like that."

With out a soft laugh, she turned and poked him in the center of his solid chest. "When have I *ever* asked you to be a gentleman?"

"Very true. Would you prefer I throw you over my shoulder and toss you into my bunk?"

She pictured that, not sure whether or not she should object. He'd make a hot caveman, but…

"If you tossed me into your bunk, you'd give me a concussion."

"True."

"And would you be comfortable with your brother a few feet away?" Her mind was running wild again. She was sure she was blushing, but now that she'd been on the bus, all she could think of was making love, surrounded by virtual strangers, and trying to keep quiet. And she couldn't imagine being quiet with Alder. By the time they finally got a moment alone, she was pretty sure both of them would combust. "He'll be listening and picturing what you're doing to me and—"

Alder put his hand over her mouth and let out a rough laugh. "Well, with that disturbing thought in my head, no, I wouldn't be comfortable. And I'd rather not give the rest of the guys something to jack off to."

"You say the sweetest things!" She gave him a little shove, shaking her head as they started back down the hill. "And you've ruined my fantasy of rock stars having orgies on their bus every single night."

Tripping over a rock, Alder almost went face first into a straggly little tree. He landed on one knee, his shoulders shaking.

Shit! Danica hurried to his side. Was he hurt?

He was laughing.

She smacked his shoulder. "You scared me, you asshole!"

He put his hands up and rose to his feet. Sweat trickled down his face, and he had a smear of red dirt on his dimpled cheek. "I'm sorry, I just wasn't sure whether to be shocked if you *wanted* the orgies, or just laugh at the fact that you thought we had them. Then I pictured the looks on *all* the guys faces if I suggested it and I was a goner."

"So no orgies at all?" She reached out to wipe some of the dirt off his cheek. "It's supposed to be sex, drugs, and rock and roll. You can't just skip the sex."

"We don't, we're just not...I mean, maybe some bands do it, but my *brother* is part of this band. And I'm really starting to hate this conversation. Are you into one of the other guys? I mean, I could probably... It's Connor, isn't it?"

"Nope." She continued walking, curious to see how many guesses he'd make before he figured out she was messing with him.

"Malakai?" He jogged to keep up with her. "It must be Malakai. After seeing me and him on stage... Honey, you don't want to mess with him. He's almost as bad as my brother. He doesn't fuck anyone he cares about. He'd be a dick to you after and I'd have to—"

"Okay, stop." She spun around, putting her finger to his lips as he halted in front of her. "I haven't slept with *you* yet. I wouldn't mind watching you and Malakai grope each other again, but I think I should watch some gay porn to see how I'll react to more. Would you watch it with me?"

His lips parted. He swallowed. "Umm...sure?"

"Good. Now that's settled and I'm glad we didn't get to Tate. He's adorable, but I'm more likely to hug him and bake him cookies than get naked for him."

Alder made a face, his gaze locking on something behind her.

She pressed her teeth into her bottom lip. "Tate's there, isn't he?"

"Yep. And I'm very sad." Tate stepped up to her side and gave her the most pitiful look. "Can I get that hug now?"

She pulled him into her arms, pulling his head down to kiss his forehead. "Will cookies help too?"

"Absolutely." He squeezed her tight, then handed her a bottle of water. "Jesse sent me to look for you guys. He thought you might need this."

"Mmm." Danica quickly uncapped the bottle and took a few gulps. The cool liquid was like a balm in her dry mouth and throat. "You're amazing."

"But not amazing enough to get naked for. It's okay, your boyfriend feels the same." Tate winked at her before spinning around and sprinting back to the bus.

She arched a brow at Alder.

He shrugged. "You may not be the only one who's considered orgies on the bus."

"I bet." She finished her water and took his hand. "Hotel in LA. My treat. I still need to make up for breakfast this morning."

His brow furrowed. "A fifteen dollar breakfast doesn't equal a freakin' hotel. Anywhere. Especially not in LA."

"Maybe not. But what I'll make you do once we get there?" She rose up on her tiptoes, fisting her hand in his hair and nipping his ear. "That'll make us even."

Chapter Eight

Sex is addicting
Love that you're giving
Understanding that all I need is your
Trust

The frustration, and sheer exhaustion of the band hung heavy in the humid air, but Alder sensed Danica was having a harder time than the others. The fact that the choreographer wouldn't get off her case didn't help. When they'd first stepped into the rented warehouse space—less than an hour after they reached Los Angeles—and Cole gave them the 'good news' that the lady was available today, Danica had been raring to go.

Her energy actually got the whole band pumped up. She was used to having very little time to prepare before hitting the runway.

But this wasn't a runway, and the choreographer, Madame Croissant—or something like that—had humiliated her more than once, even asking if Danica knew how to do anything besides gracefully walk in a straight line.

Dismissing the band, Madame Croissant had made Danica go through the simple dance moves alone for about fifty minutes before deeming her 'passible'. And Alder had stood just out of sight the whole time, grinding his teeth, with Jesse at his side.

"This isn't a fucking Broadway show. What's this woman's deal?"

"I don't know. Our girl seemed fine after she saw the routine a couple times." Jesse folded his arms over his chest. *"Not sure she will be after this. And honestly, the whole thing seems fake as fuck."*

"I agree."

"We can't afford security, but Cole can throw money into this shit? Dude, you guys need a new manager."

"Brave won't fire him. He was the manager for LOST." Alder rubbed his hand over his face. *"And Valor hired him. Which means we can't even discuss the subject."*

"Maybe you can't talk to him. But I can."

Alder had a feeling Jesse was overestimating his influence on Brave, but he'd just nodded, relieved that the band was called back in before he was tempted to invite Danica to get the hell out of here.

Maybe he should anyway.

One look at the determined set to her jaw and he trashed the idea. She would hate him thinking she couldn't hack it. Being her boyfriend, while working with her, meant there were some lines he couldn't cross.

She wouldn't drag him off stage if he played until his fingers bled—which, thankfully hadn't happened in years—so he would show her the same respect.

He did step straight up to her and pull her into his arms for a hug though. She looked like she needed it.

"Thank you." She laughed, tipping her head up and blinking fast. "I'm good. Let's get this over with."

He kissed her forehead, then took his place and lifted his guitar from the mock Ego-Rizer of stacked mats. He slung the guitar strap over his neck, letting it settle on his shoulder as Tate began the beat on the drums. SLUT had been controversial because the opening beat reminded a lot of people of the Foo Fighters *Hero*. But besides the brief familiarity, the quickening breakdown, and the guitars coming in with a dark tri-tone, gave the song an enduring quality that was unique. The loving words might come out brutal for the most part, but the chorus was sensual, in a way that worshiped the woman being tagged with the dubious endearment.

Weaving between them all, Danica walked tall and proud, then spun around to drop to her knees in front of Connor. She threw her head back as he ran his hand between her breasts. On the next beat she rose and put her palms flat on the drums. She matched a break in the steady beat to avoid Tate snapping his drumsticks onto her hands.

Then she came up behind Alder and he wasn't supposed to react. She slid a hand over his chest, then ran both down his back. His pulse raced at her touch and he inhaled roughly to fight the surge of lust. The heat of her lingered when she slipped away. After seeing her twist and spin between them all in practice, again and again, he could picture her strutting across the stage, slowing her pace as she reached Malakai.

On her knees again, she whipped her head back and forth, risking getting her hair tangled in the strings, but Malakai strummed rapidly, lifting his hand with every long chord, giving her a chance to snap her head back before his hand came down.

She moved to the front of the stage, gyrating, dragging her hands through her hair as she bent her body backwards. So strong, elegant and powerful, he knew the crowd would be reaching for her. Showing her as much love as they showed every member of the band, trapped in the thrall of the music.

Losing himself into the familiar, jagged rhythm, Alder inhaled evenly as he transitioned into the softer tones. He whispered into the mic along with Malakai.

"Slut. Slut. Slut."

Brave pulled the mic to his lips, growling the first words of the chorus. "A word that means you're wild, free, and *mine*!"

Alder and Malakai snarled into their mics. "S.L.U.T. S.L.U.T."

And then Brave sang sweetly, so seductive all the ladies in the crowd usually sighed rather than sang. "Sex is addictive. Love that you're giving. Understanding that all I need is your... *Trust*."

All together they shouted. "*Slut!*"

Only the last time that the chorus hit did Danica approach Brave. He wrapped her loose hair around his hand, dropped the mic, and bowed her over his arm.

He ran his hand up her thigh, between her breasts, then along the curve of her throat.

Only, this time, rather than stop right before their lips touched, he ran his tongue over her bottom lip.

And she slapped him before shoving so hard he couldn't hold her, and she fell.

Hard.

Alder reacted without thinking. He saw his fist swinging towards Brave's face, the distance between them crossed in a blink, so blacked out in rage time passed in a blur. And then he was tackled to the ground, his guitar digging into his chest, Jesse holding his wrists.

And as he inhaled roughly to calm the fuck down, he heard Danica and Brave and the choreographer yelling.

"What is this? I won't deal with territorial men! They almost had the act down pat if she hadn't ruined it with her little fit!" Madame Croissant threw her hands up in the air, and Alder could see her striding up to Cole as she lost her damn mind. "And the fighting? I instructed them *not* to react! You told me they were professionals!"

Meanwhile, Danica was shoving Brave while screaming in his face. "Why would you do that? You're not supposed to kiss me, never mind try to stick your tongue in my mouth!"

Brave, as usual, was sickeningly calm. "Danica, I—"

"No! You're fucking with my career! You heard her; I'm horrible at this! And I was trying, but you—" Her voice broke and she took a step back. "I don't know why you thought that was okay, but now I'll probably lose the gig and this will all be for nothing."

Alder nudged Jesse's shoulder to get the other man off him. He got why Jesse had stopped him from punching Brave, but he needed to go to Danica. He had to fix this.

Holding his hands up, Brave nodded slowly. "I went too far and I'm sorry. I just couldn't bear her saying you had no passion. That you looked too stiff on stage. I thought it would help you relax. I was wrong."

"Yes, you were." Danica covered her face with her hands, her shoulders bowed. But as Alder approached her, she held a hand up and shook her head. "Can we try it again? Just one last time? Please? I can do this!"

Cole, who was trying to talk Madame Croissant down, paused and looked over at Danica. And smiled.

"Danica, I can see the effort you've made. You've lost nothing. And I respect the fact that you're willing to try again." He ran his hands through his hair and took a deep breath. "Let's take a short break, and then we'll give it another go." His eyes narrowed as he focused on Alder. "Work this out. This will *not* happen in front of a crowd."

Inclining his head, Alder moved toward Danica, but stopped when he saw Brave draw her over to a stack of mats and kneel in front of her.

Those lines that couldn't be crossed between their relationship and their careers were looking like fucking walls at the moment. As much as he wanted to comfort Danica, the issue was between her and Brave. And Alder couldn't fix this for her.

Not if he wanted to prove he respected the work she was doing with the band.

Off to the side of the mock stage, Jesse was smoking a joint. And sharing it with the other three members of the band. Malakai didn't even comment on Tate taking a few tokes.

He couldn't join them. All his protective instincts were on high alert, but they wouldn't be welcome now. He headed to the closest exit and slid down the wall, right outside the door, and pressed his head to his knees.

The band was worth whatever he had to sacrifice. Which might be his damn sanity, now that Danica was with them. But at this point, he had some promises to keep.

A promise that he wouldn't react to Brave touching her. Unless she needed him to step in.

But how the fuck would he know? Any other man would have pushed Jesse aside and made it clear that no one could treat his woman like that.

Only, he'd seen how Danica had reacted to his question of why they couldn't be open about their relationship. Whatever her feelings for him, her career came first. And she wouldn't bother with a man who didn't respect that.

He wasn't sure what was worse. Wondering if he'd gone too far, or if Brave had.

In a normal lifestyle, the answer would be obvious, but that wasn't the life they were living.

He jumped as someone touched his shoulder.

"Hey, kid. It's just me." Skull crouched down in front of him. "Here, have a drink. And don't get all worried about drinking too much, or that damn diet Cole's pressured you to be on. I'm a smart old man, and I wouldn't put this drink in your hand if you didn't need it."

Alder took the flask Skull handed him and took a few, deep swallows. "I *shouldn't* need it."

"Maybe not, but you care about that girl." Skull rubbed his hand over his close shaved head. "And I think she's worth it, but I'm going to tell you something I've held back for way too long. You're a good man, Alder. Some may think you're a fucking pushover, but I see what you've sacrificed for this band. What you put up with from your brother. If Winter's Wrath ever gets anywhere, it will be because of all the work you've done. How you kept all the guys together."

"Brave's done a lot too." The praise stuck in Alder's throat. He knew Brave would never appreciate any credit coming from him, but it didn't change the fact that his brother had earned it.

"Stop with that shit. I get he's your big brother, but if he was mine? I'd have told him to go fuck himself a long time ago. He's pushing with Danica because he knows you won't do shit."

"She's working with the band, Skull. I don't think she'll appreciate me staking my claim against my brother."

"Maybe not, but if she's as smart as I think she is, she'll put up some fucking boundaries. What happened up there wasn't fucking cool." Skull ground his teeth. "Brave reminded me of Valor right there. And that's not a compliment."

Okay, that's enough. Alder shoved the flask into Skull's hands. "I appreciate your concern, but Valor fucking saved Brave. And he was my brother too. You don't get to talk shit about him."

Skull let out a rough laugh. "Right. Valor, the fucking hero. I think you all forget I worked for Brave before Jesse came around. I remember you as the kid who always got left behind. And I knew Valor for the man he was. And know Brave, probably better than you."

"Cool, but you know Cole will fire you if he hears you talking like this."

"I know, but I'm not talking to him. I'm talking to you." Skull put his hand on Alder's shoulder. "I haven't ever seen you into anyone like you are with this girl. Except for Jesse—yeah, I know about him, but no one else does." Skull's words slightly eased the tension from Alder's chest. "I love Jesse like family, but he was a fool for choosing Brave. He's gonna get hurt, but let him. He deserves it. Danica doesn't."

"Brave isn't interested in Danica." Alder played the scene over in his head, the way he should have before going after his brother. With all the pressure the choreographer had put on her, maybe it made sense. Brave was an asshole, but at that moment he'd probably just wanted Danica to relax. "He's just putting on a show."

"That he is. And if it hurts you, all the better." Skull drew away, then shrugged. "I'm just an old man, telling you what I see. And I see you trying to let your girl do her thing. But Brave will use that, so don't step back so much that it looks like you don't care."

"How do I show I care without fucking this up for her?"

"That's a very good question, boy." Skull gave him a sad smile. "And I wish I had an answer for you."

When shit went to hell, Danica had so many thoughts going through her head, she wasn't sure what she wanted to do more. Scream or cry.

If Alder hadn't let her deal with Brave alone, she probably would have punched *him*. And then she would have felt horrible, because could she really expect him not to react when a man tried to take advantage of her?

She wasn't even sure she'd be half as cool as he'd been watching her on stage with his band mates if the situation was reversed. And it would be soon. She'd have to see him with groupies and resist the temptation to wrap her hands around their necks.

Especially since many of his fans were teenaged girls.

After the rehearsal was done, she'd escaped to the bathroom. And she was still here, with the door locked, hands on the sink, head bowed as she tried to slow her racing pulse and hold back tears. Last thing she needed was to face the band with her face all blotchy.

"You're fine. Get back out there before someone comes looking for you. That will be just as bad as you acting like a fucking baby about one stupid kiss." She glared at her reflection. Fine, Brave touching her lips with his tongue had startled her, but it was no different than having to kiss another model, male or female, for a sensual magazine spread.

Only, with those, she knew what to expect.

Brave apologized. Let it go.

She nodded at herself, then turned on the cold water and wet her fingertips, sliding them over the back of her neck as she took a few slow, calming breaths.

She could do this.

But stepping past that door and playing like everything was normal would be a challenge. A challenge that had her hesitating with her hand on the doorknob for much longer than necessary.

Maybe everything isn't all right yet. Fake it until it's real.

Now *that* she could do. She'd been an actress, after all. And hoped to be one again.

Stepping out of the bathroom, she looked around, spotting Jesse leaning against the wall at the end of the short hallway. The rest of the band was nowhere to be seen.

"You get the job of making sure the female wasn't losing her damn mind?" She asked, keeping her tone light.

Jesse chuckled, stepping up to her side as she made her way to the main floor of the warehouse. "No. I think Alder feels like an asshole for flipping the way he did, so he's giving you some space. I'm not dating you, so I don't have to be all careful."

"I almost wish he didn't read me so well. If he'd been the one standing here, I would have let him have it."

"Really?" Jesse glanced over, one brow lifted. "I guess I can't read you at all. You don't strike me as the kinda girl who expects her man to be perfect. Or made of fucking stone."

"I don't, but he has to understand the situation." She slowed her pace as she heard the guys outside, laughing and chatting like nothing had changed. That was good. She might not be completely screwed. Yet. "He can't be my knight in shining armor. We both have a job to do."

Letting out an irritated huff, Jesse shook his head. "That wasn't part of the job *either* of you should have to put up with."

Danica cocked her head and put her hand on Jesse's arm, stopping him before he could step out onto the loading dock. "Are you pissed at Brave?"

He laughed, dropping his gaze, his jaw ticking slightly as he clenched his teeth. Then he sighed. "Being pissed won't get me anywhere with Brave. My situation isn't that different from yours, sweetie. Only, I'm Brave's employee and I don't just have to keep a lid on our relationship in public. I have to make sure Cole doesn't suspect anything."

"Is it really a big deal if he finds out? He must know Brave's gay?"

"Brave's as…relaxed with his sexuality as Alder is. Maybe more. Most of the guys in the band are, just so you don't end up shocked if you walk in on anything." He lifted his head and winked at her. "I think that's part of why they get along so well."

Made sense. Any guy who was strictly straight would probably be uncomfortable trapped on a bus for days at a time with men as sexually fluid as the band seemed to be. He wouldn't even have to be homophobic or anything. Just some of the teasing on stage might be too much.

She arched a brow at Jesse. "That doesn't answer my question. Why would Cole care if you and Brave are together?"

"Why does he care that you and Alder are? You've got the right parts for the image he wants for the band, which is why he's adding you to the performance. But the guys should seem available. It keeps the fantasy alive for all the female fans."

"Brave clearly has no problem playing on that fantasy."

"True, but Cole might see me as a threat to Brave's focus on the band. And I'm easy to replace." His lips curved into a small smile. "But you aren't. So I suggest you pick your battles, but don't let him walk all over you."

She smiled back, biting her lip as she realized her hand was still on his arm. She let it fall to her side. "Are you talking about Brave, or Cole?"

"Either of them." Jesse turned like he was going to head out, then paused and glanced over his shoulder at her. "And don't be too hard on Alder. What Brave did was fucked up. If I hadn't been running interference, I might have gone after Brave myself."

"But you love him."

"I do. But I keep my promises, Danica. I said I'd look out for you."

"I can take care of myself."

"Clearly." He reached out, tucking a strand of hair behind her ear, his fingers lingering for a moment as he met her eyes.

"But it would suck if you had to do it alone all the time. When I stopped Alder from going after Brave, part of me was worried you'd think no one cared. That Brave could do whatever he wanted and you'd just have to deal. But you don't."

She closed her eyes, that very moment flashing through her mind, all the anger and frustration coming back to her. Jesse was right. For a moment she'd wondered if she should have just finished the stupid routine. Pretended Brave's actions were exactly what she'd signed on for.

But they weren't.

She didn't think Brave had meant to disrespect her, but he had. And Jesse's words made her confident in the fact that she could set some limits. She'd have his support.

And she had no doubt that she had Alder's as well.

"I appreciate that, Jesse. I don't know how I'm going to handle this yet, but I'm guessing me and Brave should have another chat." She rolled her eyes and shook her head. "Most of our talk after it happened was telling each other that it was no big deal. And it wasn't, really. I just…I need a head's up, you know?"

"And you should have one. That way, you can either give consent, or say 'Hell no!'."

"Exactly." And damn, he'd really hit the nail on the head. That was why she'd freaked. Her choices had been taken from her in a way she'd never experienced before. Not that her life had been all unicorns and rainbows, but her grandfather had insisted on her always having options. He'd even gone to her school when she was a little girl and she complained about a book assignment.

After seeing the movie, *Lord of the Flies*, she'd been so upset, then horrified to find the book on the list of required reading in sixth grade. She didn't like math either, but she still had to do that. She'd figured her grandfather would take the same approach with the book.

Instead, he'd sent a note to her teacher, asking for another book she could read instead. When her teacher replied that she would lose marks if she didn't read the book, her grandfather brought the issue to the principal.

Such a silly thing to remember now, especially since she ended up reading *Tess Of The D'Urbervilles* instead, and it was even more upsetting, but she could still remember her grandfather grumbling about how narrow-minded the education system could be.

"Sometimes, you only have two choices, and neither of them seem good. But the options give you some power, my girl." He'd taken out a cigar then, *lighting it as he stared out the window of their little trailer house. "Never let anyone take that power away from you. Because once they take that, you've given them everything."*

Jesse touched her arm, drawing her from her memories, back to the present. "You okay, kid?"

"I am." She'd been so worried she'd have to pretend to be okay, but she really was, now that she'd gotten a chance to talk to Jesse. He'd made everything that had bothered her seem acceptable. Like she didn't have to put up with everything thrown at her just because she'd been given an amazing opportunity. "And I'm so happy you came to talk to me. Alder could have said exactly what you did, but he kinda has to take my side, because we're a thing. You're neutral."

"I have to be." He drew away from her, his brow furrowing slightly. "But before you start thinking I'm completely detached from the whole situation, I need to be honest with you. Before me and Brave got serious, me and Alder fooled around. Nothing big, but I've kissed your man. I've thought about fucking him."

Whoa! Her mouth went dry and for a moment, all she could do was stare at Jesse and try not to picture him and Alder together. If Jesse was a girl, she might feel threatened. Since Alder had admitted to liking guys too, she probably still should be.

Her cheeks heated, because threatened was the *last* thing she was feeling.

"But you didn't?" She cleared her throat. "I mean, you two haven't…"

Jesse ducked his head and let out an awkward laugh. "No. Alder's not someone you have a fling with. I decided our friendship was more important, and I had this thing for his brother. You may have noticed, they're not the most loving of siblings."

"Yeah… Any clue as to why?"

"After meeting their parents, I'm thinking it's because Alder is the baby and they turned all their focus to him after their first born died. Please don't repeat that, though. It's just a guess and it would hurt them both to know their parents have favorites." Jesse ran his hand through his hair. "Damn it, I don't know why I'm even telling you this. Except…when it comes to the band, to Cole, to the fans, Brave is the star. And I need to know Alder doesn't feel alone, you know?"

She inclined her head. "I get that, but Brave—"

"Brave isn't the arrogant asshole he pretends to be." Jesse rubbed a hand over his lips. "When he goes home, he's living in Valor's shadow—Valor was their older brother. The one who dragged the rest of them into this world. He was the golden boy and even some fans still judge the band against the music he made. He was something else."

"And Brave is still trying to step out of his shadow?" Everything Jesse was telling her sounded complicated, but it explained a lot. Including the tension between Brave and Alder.

Jesse nodded. "And Alder is eclipsed by them both. And I don't think he cares. He's close to his parents. To everyone else in the band. He's accepted that he'll never take Valor's place with Brave, but…I don't know, it's kinda sad. It's like Valor's death created a great big gap in the family. Alder and his parents are on one side. Brave is on the other."

"It is sad, but I appreciate you telling me. It makes Brave seem like less of a jerk." She looked out over the loading dock, to where Alder stood with the roadies, not speaking to any of them, lost in thought. And then to Brave, who had his arm over Tate's shoulder and was laughing at something Connor said, while Malakai stood apart, observing everything much like she was. "He's made the band his family. Because he's not part of his own."

"Yes."

"But Alder is part of the band. And they accept him, but Brave can't help holding him at arm's length." Damn, she wanted to go hug Alder. He might have his parents when he went home, but with how much time the band spent on the road... Brave made him pay for their parent's mistakes every fucking day. And that wasn't fair.

Hopefully, one day, the brothers could meet in the middle. But until then, she and Jesse were stuck in limbo. Jesse was still Alder's friend, but he had to stand by his man. And if she was forced to choose, she'd do the same.

But she did have one last question, while Jesse was in such a sharing mood.

"What happened to Valor?"

Jesse swallowed hard, leaning against the side of the truck entrance, his arms crossed tight against his chest. "LOST only had a van. They weren't big enough for a bus, but they were getting there. They had an insane tour schedule, but they were a hit with the fans even opening for bigger bands. So they toughed it out." He leaned his head back against the cement wall. "A few days before Christmas, the van broke down. They were on their way back to Detroit, on a road in the middle of nowhere. They couldn't get cell reception, so Valor headed out to call a tow truck. Brave and the rest of his band stayed in the van, trying to keep warm. They figured he'd walk for a bit, then make the call. Another car ended up finding them and they were all brought to the hospital in bad shape. It took two days to find Valor. He'd ended up lost in the woods and...well, I'm sure you can figure out the rest. The media had a field day with the tragedy. I think Brave still blames himself for what happened."

"Jesus." Danica's throat was tight. Her eyes teared as she imagined Brave in the hospital, being treated for exposure to the cold with the rest of his band, not sure whether his older brother was all right. Then finding out he'd never found help. That he was gone.

And then to have his own parents distance themselves? Maybe connect him to the loss, while holding Alder close?

She couldn't be mad at Brave anymore. The band was all he really had. And she had become a way to help the band breakout.

Sure, he was using her, but in the same way she was using him and everything he'd built. She had a plan. So did he.

They could achieve their goals by working together. Much more easily now that she understood his motives. He wasn't trying to disrespect her in any way. Cole's whole scheme probably made sense to him and he just wanted it to play out as intended.

She'd keep everything Jesse had told her in mind when she approached Brave about what had gone down at the rehearsal. Which was probably exactly why he'd told her all he had.

"I'll be nice. I mean, I still expect him to be clear about what he'll do to me on stage, but I get why he didn't hold back."

"Don't be too nice, he won't take you seriously." Jesse gave her hair a little tug, his teasing smile lightening the mood. "And talk to Alder first."

"I suppose that's a good idea. And I'm guessing this conversation stays between us?" She hopped off the loading dock, walking backwards to grin at Jesse as he followed. "I'll warn you in advance, I'll probably be kissing your boyfriend. On my terms this time."

"Fair enough." Jesse chuckled. "I've kissed yours."

"Shall we compare notes?"

"While braiding each other's hair and painting our nails? Are you looking for a gay best friend, Danica?"

She shook her head. "Just a friend, Jesse. And I'm happy I found one. Thanks again for sticking around."

"Anytime, kid."

As she made her way over to Alder, all the roadies simultaneously found somewhere else they needed to be. Braced against the bumper of the bus, Alder held what looked like a black cigarette between his lips. He watched her while letting out a trail of white smoke.

Smoking definitely wasn't her favorite of dirty habits for a guy to have, but she hadn't seen him smoke before now, so maybe it wasn't something he did often? He didn't smell like a smoker. Or taste like one.

He caught her staring at the cigarette and his lips tipped up on one side. "It's an e-cig. I'm trying to quite smoking and this vape company sent me a trial kit after asking me to do some promo for them. Cole just left it on my bunk. It's not that bad."

"I know a few models that vape. It's supposed to be healthier."

"Supposed to be, but we'll see." He gave the e-cig a skeptical look. "Fucking rush of nicotine is making me high."

Leaning against him, her thighs on either side of one of his, she curved her hand around the back of his neck. "Does that mean you're in a good mood?"

He touched his forehead to hers. "I'm more concerned about the mood you're in. And surprised that you're speaking to me."

"Ha! I ain't even mad." She flicked her tongue over his bottom lip. "But there's something I need to do, and I'm hoping you won't say no."

"I don't think I could ever say no to you."

She really hoped that wasn't true, but in this case, she'd hold him to his word.

Because he wasn't going to like this. At *all*.

Hand curved under Brave's jaw, Jesse let the smooth smoke pass from his lips into the other man's mouth. Telling Danica about all the shit in Brave's past reminded him of how his own opinion of the lead singer had changed after Alder had told him the same story.

"Why do you put up with his shit?" Jesse demanded after the show, sickened by how Brave had torn into Alder over a delay from a goddamn string breaking on his guitar. Right up on stage too, he'd mocked Alder for using a metal pick.

Jesse had replaced the string as quickly as possible, but not before the whole crowd was laughing at the lead guitarist.

But Alder just shrugged. *"He's been through a lot of shit. Hear me out. Once you know what happened, maybe you'll get it."*

Snapping his fingers in Jesse's face, Brave jerked him from his thoughts. "If you're going to bitch at me about that whole thing with Danica, just do it. You piss me off when you go all quiet."

Jesse's lips thinned. "Is there any point? You don't think you did anything wrong."

"This is between me and her. It's got nothing to do with you."

"Clearly."

Brave snorted and snatched the joint right out of Jesse's hand. "*'Clearly'*. Who the fuck do you think you are, man?" He leaned close, his tone going cold as he spoke low enough that only Jesse could hear him. "We fuck. I promised I wouldn't screw around on you, but all this sensitive, judgy stuff you pull is too much."

"I'm not judging you, Brave." Jesse pulled out a cigarette, because the weed wasn't doing a damn thing to calm his nerves. He fucking *knew* Brave put his guard up when he felt his control over any situation slip, but that didn't make being pushed away any easier.

If he took anything Brave was saying personally, he might as well call their relationship quits now. But he wasn't ready to do that. Not yet.

So he'd do his best not to react and hope Brave would get over the foul mood he was in.

From the corner of his eye, he spotted Danica striding toward them, Alder by her side. He straightened, not sure what was up, but positive nothing good would come of it.

153

Alder stopped a few paces away from Brave, but Danica stepped right up to him. Rising up on her tiptoes, she fisted her hands in his hair and drew his lips to hers. When Brave went still, she simply held him, kissing his passive lips until he let out a low growl and wrapped his arms around her, returning the kiss with barely contained passion.

At which point, she drew away, framing his face with her hands. "This is what I consent to. And nothing more. If I pull away, you stop. And we'll figure out a way to make it look good on stage. Okay?"

Brave stared at her. His lips parted. "You bitch."

"Maybe I *am* a bitch, but we've got to work together, right?" Danica smiled sweetly, holding a hand up as if she sensed Alder was about to get involved. But her man had his hands fisted at his sides, his stolid expression making it obvious they'd discussed this beforehand. She patted Brave's cheek. "Like it or not, I'm setting some limits. Deal with it."

And with that, she turned and walked away.

Alder didn't move, so naturally, Brave lashed out at him. Latching on to the collar of Alder's T-shirt, Brave practically snarled in his face. "You put her up to this, didn't you?"

"You think I want my girlfriend kissing you? I know how hateful you can be, and I told her this would set you off." Alder pried Brave's hand from his shirt. "But you own that stage, *brother*. The band revolves around you, and Cole will always bend over backwards to give you everything you want. He might pressure her to do more than she's comfortable with, but if you try, she's done."

"Then why isn't she done already?" Brave held his arms out wide and let out a cold laugh. "If I'm such a fucking asshole, why doesn't she just quit?"

Lips cutting into a thin smile, Alder gave his brother a level look. "Because, for some reason, she believes you're the kind of man who can show her some respect. That you're more dedicated to the band than to your fucking ego. I'm curious to see if she's right."

Jesse watched Alder leave, then held his breath as Brave paced back and forth along the side of the bus.

Brave slammed his fist into the side of the bus. "Fuck this! Fuck her! Fuck you all!"

As Brave stormed off, Tate tried to approach him and ended up on his ass, shoved aside without so much as a backward glance.

The poor kid looked completely lost as Jesse ran over to pull him to his feet.

"This is it." Tate ran a hand over his hair and bowed his head. "We're done."

You might be right, boy. Jesse squeezed Tate's shoulder, not sure what to say. Maybe he'd fucked up telling Danica all he had. Suggesting she not be 'too nice' probably hadn't helped either.

He understood why she'd confronted Brave the way she had. Hell, there was no way she could have predicted his reaction. From the little he knew of her, she'd probably expected Brave to laugh and agree to her terms. When he hadn't, she'd done the only thing she could. She left the ball in his court.

What Brave would do now? Fuck if Jesse had the slightest clue.

Chapter Nine

Danica didn't have to pay for a hotel that night. Or she *hoped* she didn't have to. When the cab pulled to the hotel where Sophie had gotten a reservation for her, she had to double-check the address. Then she peered up at the opulent, Sofitel Hotel on Beverly Boulevard, not sure if she even wanted to get out of the car.

She'd been to nice hotels in the past, but always on the modest end of the spectrum. She wasn't an A-lister.

Getting out before the cabbie could, Alder came around to open her door and held out his hand. He frowned when she hesitated. "What's wrong, Danica?"

Taking his hand, she stepped onto the curb. "This is just too much. Sophie knows I don't expect to stay anywhere fancy."

"If you're not comfortable here, we can go somewhere else." He cupped her cheek, sliding his thumb over her bottom lip. "We can go sleep on the beach if you'd like. Tonight is ours and I've decided we're doing anything that will make you happy."

"I don't want to have to think about where else to stay." She pressed her eyes shut and sighed. "One night won't be too bad. I'll have to talk to Sophie about showing off money I don't have. Most of my travel expenses are covered, but I'm paying for this on my own dime."

"Not if you let me pay for it."

"Nope."

"Half?"

"Stop." She tugged at his hand, thanking the cabbie and laughing when Alder took out a few bills for the tip before she could even open her purse. Their two small suitcases were picked up by the bellhop, who led the way into the hotel, moving off to the side to wait for them by the front desk.

A pretty young Asian receptionist smiled brightly at them. "We've been expecting you. Sam will bring your bags up to your room now. If you'll give me just a moment, the manager would like to speak to you."

"The manager?" Danica glanced over at Alder, squeezing his hand when she noticed him watching the other guests of the hotel walk by. He didn't appear intimidated, and no one was looking down on him, but for all she knew, he was just playing it cool.

Or, more likely, she was projecting her own unease. He didn't have to live in the world of the rich and famous, facing people who judged according to labels and connections.

She did, but she usually had Sophie's people with her, making sure she was perfectly polished. Right now her hair was a mess, she was wearing the same jeans and T-shirt she'd traveled and rehearsed in, and she didn't have a list of names memorized and an approved list of topics to discuss.

"Miss Tallien, a pleasure to meet you." A lean, black skinned man with a trim, full beard, wearing a tailored, navy blue suit, stepped up to her with his hand out. "My name is Langston Wright, the manager and, as Sophie insisted I tell you as quickly as possible, Sophie's cousin."

"You have a beautiful hotel, Mr. Wright." Danica shook his hand, feeling a bit more relaxed about Sophie's choice. She smiled over at Alder. "This is my boyfriend, Alder Trousseau, the lead guitarist for Winter's Wrath."

Mr. Wright shook Alder's hand, the flesh around his eyes creasing slightly as he grinned. "I can't say your music is my style, but my eldest daughter is a huge fan. I would have known you without an introduction, considering your poster is on her wall."

Alder laughed. "I'm not sure if I should apologize or not."

"No need to apologize, I'm honored to have both you and Miss Tallien as guests." He motioned for them to follow. "My dear cousin called in one of the many favors I owe her. I would have welcomed you regardless, but she was concerned that you'd be too focused on the expense to truly enjoy yourself. This is not costing you, or her, a thing."

Danica inclined her head as they stepped onto the elevator. She bit her lip as Mr. Wright swiped a keycard over the scanner to access the penthouse floor. "Thank you, but I still don't understand. Why did she need to call in a favor at all?"

"She mentioned you'd had a long day and you deserved a little treat." He handed her the key card. "Please don't hesitate to call the front desk if there's anything you need. I hope you have a very pleasant stay."

She and Alder stepped off the elevator, heading down the hall while Mr. Wright went back down. As soon as the elevator doors closed, she quickened her pace.

"Excited?" Alder lengthened his strides, easily keeping up.

"A little? I don't usually stay at hotels just for the fun of it. And I'm usually alone."

Alder spun her around, his smile wide as he led her in a dizzy-making dance down the hall. "Well, you have no choice but to have fun."

She giggled, clinging to his neck as he swooped her up in his arms when she tipped off balance.

He brought his lips to hers, speaking softly, trapping her in his dark, passionate gaze. "And you've been alone too long. Which might intimidate some, because you don't really need anyone, do you?"

"I find it better when I don't. Then I know everyone who's in my life is there because I want them to be." Her lips curved up as she met his eyes. "But you don't find that intimidating?"

"No, I find it sexy as hell."

A swipe of the card and he swing the door open. Before it had fully closed, he had her up against the wall. His lips slanted over hers and she gasped at the surge of pleasure from just the pressure of his body and his mouth. She raked her fingers into his hair, pulling it loose from the leather tie. The long, ebony strands were as soft as her own and she loved how wild he looked with it spilling free around his broad shoulders.

His lips moved to her throat and her back bowed at the rush of heat lashing straight down her nerves. He ran his teeth over the same spot and she clenched her thighs, whimpering as he played at one of her most sensitive trigger points. Most men missed the signals until she was holding them still and saying 'Yes! Right there!', but she always sensed Alder was intently focused on her. Like he'd never miss a thing.

If he could do this with his lips on her neck, what would he do with the rest of her?

She needed to know, but she wanted more of him. Now, while there would be no interruptions and she could take everything. She tugged at his shirt, and his lips left her just long enough for her to yank it up over his head.

Then he was kissing her again, and she pulled herself to him, breathing in his every exhale, a rough laugh escaping her as he wrapped her legs around his hips and ground against her.

Even through his jeans, and hers, his solid length had her so aroused the friction alone almost set her off. She sucked on his bottom lip, clenching her thighs to bring him closer, her fingers digging into the thick muscles of his back. Touching his bare skin had her even more needy. Greedy. The clothes that remained were driving her insane. She wanted them gone, but she didn't think she could let him go for long enough to manage to shed another piece.

He didn't give her a choice. Sliding her down his body, he latched on to the base of her shirt, peeling it off her in one smooth motion. One hand on the back of her neck, he claimed her lips again while his free hand came between them to snap open the button of her jeans and draw the zipper down.

His fingers reached her clit and she dug her nails into his back, pressing against him, the jolt of pleasure stealing her breath. His skin was calloused and rough, but he touched her with just enough pressure to tease the tiny bundle of nerves. She usually needed so much stimulation to get off that she'd shamelessly pretended in the past so she wouldn't discourage the man she was with.

There was no reason to fake anything with Alder. He hit all the right triggers so easily, she surrendered control of her body without a moment's hesitation. His fingers dipped into her and her lips parted as her core clenched around the thick, stretching press of them.

"Fuck, you're so hot and wet." He sucked lightly on her throat, letting out a low growl. "I need to feel this—" He thrust his fingers in deeper, forcing her jeans down with his wrist for easier access. "You." His teeth grazed her neck. "*Now.*"

She rested her forehead on his shoulder, lost in just feeling him inside her, driving her up to the edge of climax already. Just a little longer and she would come, but she refused to take the quick release when she could have so much more. When she could have all of him.

Clasping his face between her hands, she drew him down to her breasts, whimpering when he caught one nipple between his lips and circled the tip with his tongue. She latched onto his belt, hoping he'd understand what she wanted, because she couldn't do more then make unintelligible sounds as the arousal stole any coherent words from her lips.

He cupped her breast with one hand as the fingers from the other left her. She hissed at the ache of emptiness threw her off balance, but then she felt him undoing his belt. His jeans opened and her hand found him.

For a moment, they were tangled together, her stroking him while she pushed her jeans the rest of the way down. But she was still wearing shoes, so he pulled away from her, dropping to his knees to pull one foot free of her jeans and her sneaker.

Without warning, he hooked her leg over his shoulder, cupped her ass in his hands, and brought her pussy to his lips. The rush of pleasure slammed into her as his tongue dipped into her and she threw her head back.

Her whole body tensed as she cried out, both from the climax that sent a white-hot spill of heat right to her core, and from the crack of pain in her skull.

His mouth left her. He straightened, gently placing his hand on the back of her head. "Are you all right?"

"Yes, but…" Damn it, the orgasm had come and gone so quickly, she'd ended up even more needy then she'd been before. But she could speak. So she could tell him. "Fuck me, Alder. Please just fuck me!"

A slight tilt to the edges of his lips and his eyes darkened with passion. Then he bent down again. And she decided she might have to kill him.

Until she saw what he'd taken out of the pocket of his jeans. She swallowed hard as he tore the condom wrapper open with his teeth. For some reason, the right man doing that was the sexiest fucking thing she'd ever seen. The way he held her gaze told her very clearly 'I will have you.'

After rolling the condom over his long, thick dick, he lifted her up against the wall, spreading her thighs with his hips. With one arm around her waist to hold her up, he guided himself into her, pressing in until the head of him penetrated her fully, but no more. She braced for him to thrust in, but he waited, bringing his hand up to smooth her hair away from her sweat slicked cheeks.

"Look at me, Danica."

She held her breath as she met his eyes. They were such a rich, dark brown, like a soft deer hide tanning in the sun. She ran her tongue over her bottom lip, tangling her hands in his hair as she tipped her lips up to meet his.

And he drove into her, stealing her breath as she cried out, his tongue meeting hers in a passionate kiss as his body moved against her. Into her.

Hooking his hands under her knees, he spread her open, finding a rhythm that had her mindlessly digging her nails into the back of his neck and his shoulders. The friction as all her inner muscles tightened around him set her off like a lick of flame over a pool of gasoline.

The fire spread, then exploded with a deep thrust that spread fuel over the hungry blaze. All the oxygen around her fed into the inferno and her core undulated around him until she couldn't hold back her screams. She clenched down as he pulled almost out of her, then he slammed in hard.

Her whole body jerked as she felt him pulsing within and she clung to him as her oversensitive center hit another sharp climax.

Heart pounding, she rested her head on his shoulder, hoping he'd hold her for just a little longer. Her whole body was shaking and she wasn't sure if she could stand yet. He had one hand braced against the wall above her head, and he was breathing hard, but his arm around her waist was strong and steady. She willed her pulse to slow, trying to remember how to breathe normally.

As the heated rush gradually diminished, the air cooled her damp flesh. She kissed his shoulder, tasting the salt on his slick skin, smiling as he lifted his head.

"I think my legs might work now." She bit her bottom lip when he pushed away from the wall, wrapping his other arm around her. She could still feel him inside her, growing soft. Her tender body was comfortable holding him, but he must be tired from holding her so long? "You can put me down if you want."

Or keep holding me. I'm not sure I'm ready for you to let me go.

He shook his head as though he'd read her thoughts. "You feel good, right here in my arms. If you'll let me, I'll keep you here all night."

They were standing a few feet away from the door.

She looked over at it and grinned. "Not *here*?"

He chuckled. "No, not here."

163

Easing out of her, he scooped her up in his arms, cradling her against his chest.

Then he kissed her cheek. "Right here."

She was partially aware of him carrying her to the bed, but after that, all she knew was warmth in his embrace. Halfway through the night she opened her eyes, having kicked the blanket off in her attempt to remove the one sock that was still on her foot. He'd taken her remaining shoe and her jeans off at one point, but had missed that little, beige ankle sock.

Before she even had to get up to pull the damn thing off, he was leaning over, slipping it off her foot and tossing it over the side of the bed.

Then he adjusted the blankets over her and laid her head on his shoulder.

"Better?"

"Mmm." She flatted her hand on the center of his bare chest, eyes closed, wondering what higher power she had to thank for finally giving her something wonderful that she hadn't had to earn through years of hard work. "Much."

Alder was almost too perfect. He was a good man, an amazing lover, and all she could have ever wanted. What she might have with him had come almost too easy, and if she wasn't so worn out, she might try to analyze it. To figure out what she had to do to make it last.

But tonight was good. And maybe perfect couldn't be real, but she could accept good.

Looking her gift horse in the mouth could wait until tomorrow.

Chapter Ten

The manager hadn't been kidding about providing *anything* they might need. Alder smiled as he looked over the breakfast spread he'd laid out on the table with the man from room service. He'd tried to pay with his credit card when he'd called, so Danica's agent wouldn't get the charge, but apparently there was a note in the room's file that had all charges covered, complementary of the hotel.

He'd kept in mind both his and Danica's diets, so there was a lot of fruit, but the lady at the front desk had laughed when he'd struggled to order and told him Sophie had everything handled. The receptionist had given him a list of options and agreed that one of everything would be fine between the two of them.

There were scrambled egg whites, rye bread, buttermilk pancakes, and even some bacon. A fresh fruit salad bowl sat in the middle of the table with a silver ladle. Three other bowls held different kinds of berries. There was a bottle of champagne and orange juice, and a carafe of coffee.

Healthy, but not boring. Maybe this wouldn't be so bad after all.

With the table all set up, Alder padded across the room in his socked feet, wearing the plain, black pajama pants he'd packed in case the night had ended differently. He hadn't planned to rush things, if Danica hadn't been ready. Granted, they'd both been at the breaking point by the time they stepped into the room, but he hadn't assumed anything when he'd grabbed his stuff.

Which had worked out, since he wasn't ready to get dressed yet, but didn't want to have breakfast in his boxers.

He grabbed one of the white bathrobes from the bedroom closet before approaching the bed. Danica looked so peaceful, sleeping with the pillow he'd used held against her chest, he hated to wake her up, but they both had to meet with the band in a few hours. Another band meeting, then the last rehearsal before the show tomorrow night.

The meeting was at 11:00am. Which meant she had two hours to have something to eat, get dressed, and get her head in the game.

Her long, sleek black-brown hair spilled over the white sheets, covering the side of the bed she'd abandoned as she'd curled up right in the center. She looked so beautiful and vulnerable with her features all softened in sleep. Her long black lashes rested on her golden cheeks, her eyelids stirring slightly, as though she was dreaming.

He sat on the edge of the bed, waiting until she sighed and hugged the pillow a little tighter. Hopefully she'd been having a good dream. And it was over now. She probably didn't get to sleep in often, and he wasn't sure if 9:00am counted—it didn't for him—but he really wanted the day to start off pleasant for her.

He had no idea what the rest of the day would hold.

Brushing his hand down her arm, he spoke softly. "Hey, beautiful. You ready to get up?"

She wrinkled her nose, flopping onto her back with her eyes still closed. "Do you have coffee?"

I'm an idiot.

He let out a quiet laugh. "I can bring you some?"

"Oh, would you? That will make you even more perfect. Which is scary, but coffee makes everything okay."

"This is true."

Scary? He wasn't sure how to take that. Maybe he should ease off a bit.

Or, better yet, he should prove she didn't have anything to be afraid of.

He pushed off the bed, heading to the breakfast spread to fix her a cup of coffee. He added just enough cream to make it the color he'd seen it when she'd fixed her own at the diner. When he returned to the bedroom, she was sitting up with the sheet pulled over her breasts.

And the way she smiled at him when he held out the coffee sent a spill of warmth from his chest straight down to his groin.

She took a sip and pressed her eyes shut with a sigh of pleasure. "I'm not sure I've ever been this spoiled. When I'm home, I make sure the coffee is ready before Grandpa gets up. He's grumpy in the morning, but I learned when I was little that a cup of coffee and a cigar gets him to stop grumbling. He used to work late at the casino, but he always wanted to be up with me before I headed off to school."

"Then why did he grumble?" Alder tried to picture Danica, a sweet little kid rushing to fix coffee every morning with an old man scowling and cursing under his breath. But Danica didn't sound upset when she talked about her grandfather, so maybe he had it all wrong.

His father had always been gone before he got up for school. His mother was still asleep, because she'd worked late nights for most of his childhood as a photojournalist. Sometimes she traveled for work and was gone for weeks at a time.

Valor and Brave had made sure he had his lunch packed and had breakfast for as long as he could remember. His eldest brother, Valor, had always been sharp with him, but back then, Brave seemed to like him. They'd had a fun little routine of Alder forgetting to grab a piece of fruit for his lunch. Brave would yell 'Heads up!' before tossing an apple or an orange to him on his way out.

Danica touched the back of his hand. "Okay, I don't know what mornings were like for you, but maybe I said that wrong.

My grandfather would get up before me, he'd tap on my door to make sure I was up, and he'd go make my lunch. He's old, so he'd have the odd ache in his back and mutter about it bugging him. When I fixed his coffee he'd sit down to enjoy it while I ate my cereal. Now that I'm older, I try to take care of him like he used to take care of me. I make sure he doesn't have to do *anything* before he has his coffee."

The picture he'd painted in his head shifted, and he smiled. He liked the idea of Danica having a good childhood. "Sorry, I didn't mean to assume the worst. From what you've told me about your grandfather, he sounds like a good guy."

"But there's a reason you assumed the worst. You don't talk about your parents. What were they like?"

His smile slipped. He dropped his gaze as she took another sip of coffee. "Umm…well, they both worked a lot? My father was a mechanic. He owns his own shop and I think he hoped at least *one* of his sons would take on the family business. He took over for his father."

"But you all got into music."

"Yeah…well, Valor did. Me playing the guitar wasn't a big deal, because Brave is good with cars and while Valor was learning the piano and the guitar and singing, at least he had one son doing something productive. I was too young for anyone to worry about."

Neither of his parents had known about his music teachers thinking he had a worthy talent. He'd begged them not to say a word. He'd seen his father and Valor fighting too often to even dare letting his parents know he dreamed of being like all the guitarist he'd worshiped since he was old enough to pick a CD out of his father's collection and play along with the classic rock songs.

Valor had refused to pick up a single tool. When he was sixteen and their father had pressured him to learn to drive, he'd laughed and said he'd be so rich and famous, he'd never have to drive himself anywhere.

Alder had been about seven at the time. Brave was eleven. And while their father was cursing Valor out, telling him he'd end up playing on a street corner for loose change, Brave had been picking up all the tools both had thrown around the garage, trying to distract Dad by asking about an old engine their father was restoring.

Years later, when Valor started LOST, and Brave proved to be an even better singer than he was and joined the band…well, Alder was pretty sure his father gave up on the lot of them.

"So…did your father even ask you if you wanted to take over? I mean, did you ever work on cars?" Danica took his hand, stroking his knuckles with her thumb, watching his face with concern in her eyes, as though she'd seen something that had her worried about his place in his family.

He forced a smile and shrugged. "I think when Brave put down his tools and picked up a mic, my father gave up. He mentored this kid straight out of trade school and he trained him to help him manage the shop. By the time I was old enough to learn, he'd seen me with a guitar."

"And he wasn't proud of you?"

"Valor and Brave had a band that was doing well. And he never went to see them once. So no, he didn't think much of me following in their footsteps." Not that Alder really blamed him. Alder had started off his own career playing with local cover bands in bars. He'd gone to university part time for a while, planning to teach music for a living, but his dream had been to start a band like his brothers.

If Valor had lived, he'd still be playing at weddings for young couples, and small outdoor summer events that couldn't afford a 'real' band. Maybe he'd be teaching, but he'd never have let go of the dream that had been impossible until Brave had let LOST fall apart and started over.

Danica's brow furrowed. She didn't seem to understand his twisted family dynamics. Not that he could blame her. Her grandfather had supported her pursuing modeling and acting. His dream probably didn't seem outrageous to her.

169

"What about your mother?"

He let out a bitter laugh. "Those photographers that followed us the other night? Well, my mother would have been one of them back then. Now, she covers bigger stories, but before she made a name for herself, she was always chasing the next big thing. I think she saw LOST once. She sold pictures of her own son doing coke. Mom of the year right there."

"Brave?"

"No. Brave's never done anything real hard-core, as far as I know. But Valor lived the lifestyle to the fullest. She never submitted the photos under her real name, but I found copies a few years ago." Bile flooded his throat as he remembered Valor tearing up the tabloid magazines with his pictures, cursing whatever 'bitch' he'd given a backstage pass to that had taken advantage of him. He'd died without knowing it had been his own mother.

Danica shook her head. "Damn it, Alder, I'm sorry. I didn't mean to dig, but with how worried you were...I figured that had to come from somewhere. Neither you or Brave had it easy."

Frowning, he looked up at her. "Or Valor. I mean, I didn't know him well. He was nine years older than me, but I still remember him having it out with my dad all the time. And whenever my mom was home, he'd do nice things for her. He'd play her songs and sit there and listen to her talk about her latest big story. He loved her so much."

"And you loved them both." She shook her head and took another sip of coffee. "Your parents sound like they were—and *are*—very ambitious people. It's clear they passed that down to you and Brave."

"I guess they did." He hated how bitter he felt talking about his parents. When he went back home, things were pleasant, and he'd developed a better relationship with them as an adult then he'd had as a child or a teen. Which was the side of his parents the rest of the band knew from the handful of times Winter's Wrath had played back home in Detroit.

But Danica asking him about his parents was different. He wanted to be completely honest with her; he knew she wouldn't accept anything less.

But this wasn't how he wanted to start their day. Their food was getting cold. "You up to leaving the bed? I have a Sophie approved breakfast waiting for you."

"Should I be afraid?"

"Nope. There's real food."

"And you were surprised." She giggled as she slipped from the bed naked, holding out her arms as he glanced down at the robe in his hands.

Damn, being all sweet kinda sucked sometimes. She was fucking gorgeous and he hadn't gotten much time to admire her sleek, sexy body. He wanted to run his hands over her curves. Lick and suck every soft inch of her while she writhed under him, begging him to take her.

"I'm gonna jump you if you keep giving me that look." Danica brought her hands up to his shoulders, moving closer to lace her fingers behind his neck. "Will you feel totally used if I do?"

This woman is an angel. A naughty, sexy, fucking perfect angel.

He grinned and dropped the robe somewhere to his left. "Not at all."

A wicked smile spread across her lips as she put her hands on the center of his chest and shoved him onto the bed, straddling him and kissing him as though she was starving.

Maybe a cold breakfast wasn't so bad after all.

An hour later and Danica sat on Alder's knee, wearing the robe he'd brought her, snacking on berries while checking her messages on her phone. She had one long email from Sophie, which she'd put off until she'd finished another cup of coffee, but when she finally got to it, her faith in her agent was restored.

Reading it over again, she snickered and glanced over at Alder.

Who was scowling at his own phone.

"Uh oh. What's wrong?" She'd let him give her the bad news first, then cheer him up with Sophie's latest plan.

Alder shook his head. "I get that me and Brave aren't close, but I'm hearing about him getting another message from some sicko in a mass text from Cole. Apparently everyone else knows about it, and Cole would like to discuss the new security measures Jesse's suggested."

"Did this happen last night?"

"No, back in Vegas. I'm not surprised Brave didn't say anything to me, and the rest of the band stays out of shit between me and him." He ran a hand over his face and shook his head. "But Jesse... I guess I didn't expect things to change so much with me and him. I should have."

"*Or*...maybe I've just been stealing you away too often. You're still friends, Alder." She worried her bottom lip between her teeth, studying his irritated expression. "Is that enough for you?"

"Yes, but I just wish..." He dropped his phone onto the table and pulled her closer to his chest, wrapping his arms around her. "I wish things between me and Brave were different. I'm gonna try to talk to him—shit, this is dangerous and I'm allowed to fucking care."

She inclined her head. They both knew Brave might not react well, especially after the way she'd confronted him yesterday, but no matter how pissy the lead singer got, he'd appreciate his brother's concern.

She refused to believe he wouldn't feel the same if it was Alder's life at risk. They'd both lost a brother already. But maybe something good would come out of Brave having to constantly look over his shoulder.

Maybe he'd finally accept that his brother had his back.

Looking over the breakfast they'd only just started lazily munching at, Danica considered her options. Her whole body was aching in all the right places and she really wanted to savor the last bit of time she had alone with Alder before they went back to their responsibilities with the band. But she'd have him tonight. The big show wasn't until tomorrow, so really, all they had today was another meeting and a rehearsal.

If they left now, Alder would have some time to talk to his brother. And she might have a few minutes to make peace with Brave herself.

"You want to head over to the warehouse early? Is that where we're meeting again?"

Alder cocked his head, his brow lifted. "Yeah, we're meeting there, but I figured you wouldn't be in a hurry to be around our lovely Madame Croissant."

Croissant? Danica snorted. "That's Madame Courchesne. Not sure how you got 'Croissant' out of that."

His lips tipped into a sheepish smile. "I may have stopped listening to her when she started being a bitch to you. I heard Tate call her that a few times, so I thought that was her name. Might be that he's not a fan of our choreographer either."

"Probably not. Did you hear her lecture him about how he should be sitting straighter behind the drums? If it wouldn't have screwed with the sound, he'd probably have laid his head right on the snare."

Alder laughed. "There's still time. I wouldn't put it past him to mess with her today."

"After we almost got all the moves perfect yesterday? No way." Danica hopped to her feet, popping one last blackberry in her mouth before heading to the bedroom to get dressed. "I bet he'll be on his best behavior."

Joining her in the bedroom, Alder tugged on a fresh shirt, then gave her a challenging smile. "What are you willing to wager?"

She touched her tongue to her bottom lip and smirked at him. "I think I might enjoy having you as a slave for the day."

"I think you get whatever you want from me either way, so winning won't mean much." His words were sweet, but there was a cockiness to his tone that had her arching a brow at him as he bent down to lace up his black sneakers. "And you'll be pissed when you lose if I demand the same thing."

"I will not."

"No? All right then, you've got yourself a bet." He straightened and pulled his long hair into a low ponytail, his dark brown eyes sparkling with amusement. "I'll even be nice when I win and not make it too obvious to the guys that you're my little slave girl. Though, I think you'd look cute dressed like Leia from Star Wars. You know that gold bikini?"

Putting her hands on her hips, she stared at him. "In private, I'd have no issue wearing that for you, but don't even *think* of making me dress up in front of the band unless you want me to consider some slave boy outfits for you when you lose."

He made a face, then nodded. "Fair enough."

She grabbed her purse, looking over her outfit one last time. Cole had some special outfit coming in tomorrow for her to wear at the show, which she was more than a little anxious about, but for rehearsal, she'd gone with plain black skinny jeans and a snug, black Guns and Roses tank top. She'd be wearing heels on stage, so she'd decided on wearing her boots with four-inch heels to practice in.

Thankfully, she had enough experience strutting around in footwear of any style; she could probably run just as fast as that chick in Jurassic World while being chased by dinosaurs. In stilettos if she had to.

Not that she'd tell Cole about that particular skill. He might come up with some crazy plan to make her play damsel in distress, escaping some kind of monster.

Thinking of plans reminded her of Sophie's. She waited until Alder joined her in the hall, pulled the door to their room shut, and took his hand, lacing their fingers together. "You know the whole issue about keeping our relationship low key so I'm not just seen as your girlfriend?"

Alder's smile faded. He inclined his head.

"Well, Sophie was approached by a perfume company that wants us to do a commercial together. She's still working out the details, but apparently our pictures online that first night inspired them." She laughed at the play of emotions on his face, everything from uncertainty—probably at the idea of doing a perfume commercial—to cautious interest. He was so easy to read. "She wasn't happy about the whole thing with Brave—seems like Cole called her to do damage control, probably expecting me to go crying to her about the whole thing."

"Did you tell her anything?"

"Not yet. I'll shoot her an email on the drive to the warehouse, but she's done a complete 180 on the idea of you and me being together." She squeezed his hand as the enthusiasm from reading Sophie's message returned. "The offer probably helped, but she asked if you liked the hotel and she wants to know your size."

Alder blinked, glancing over at her as they stepped onto the elevator. "My size?"

"She's probably gonna buy you something. She's big on presents." Danica wasn't sure how to explain to him how much a gift from Sophie meant. But she'd try. "She grew up poor, but she's built a very successful company with Diverse Faces, so she's rich, but very careful with her money. She gives a lot to charity, and has all kinds of investments, but when she wants to show one of her models, or someone she's worked with, that she appreciates them, she's very generous."

"But I haven't done anything."

"Yes, you have. Cole mentioned you going after Brave, but he apologized for your behavior, and said it wouldn't happen again. Sophie loves that you wanted to defend me." She let out a soft laugh as she considered Sophie's exact words. "She knows me, so she insisted I shouldn't be mad at you."

"But you were." He scratched at the bit of scruff on his cheek, his lips curving up a little. "And you had every right to be. I can't be losing it like that."

"True, but after it happened I was wondering what I would have done in your place. Like, if some chick randomly kissed you."

He chuckled, like he already knew the answer. "I don't think Jesse would have been able to hold you back."

She grinned as they stepped off the elevator and made their way across the lobby. "If he's as smart as I think he is, he won't even try."

"After yesterday, I think everyone knows not to fuck with you." Alder let her pass ahead of him, nodding to the bellhop who asked if they needed a cab. "I wasn't sure about letting you confront Brave like that, but seriously? It's better you put him in his place now then have it be another thing for me and him to fight about."

"I agree. The two of you need to work out whatever this bullshit between you is."

"If that's even possible. Either way, I'm happy Sophie's on our side." A cab rolled up to the curb and Alder got the door for her. "I'm not sure how Cole's going to react, but he'll love the idea of a commercial."

She waited until he climbed in on the other side of the backseat, excitement making it hard to sit still. "So you'll do it? I mean, it's not a sure thing, but Sophie could represent you for this one time. She'll get you a great offer."

"I'll do it." He laughed when she strained against her seatbelt to hug him. "Hopefully, I won't disappoint you. The only times I've ever been in front of a camera is on stage or during interviews. If this commercial is anything like the ones I've seen…?"

She put her hand on his thigh and rested her head on his shoulder. "You'll do fine. You'll have me."

He leaned over, pressing his lips to her hair. "That's the only reason I said yes."

She smiled, relaxing against him. Their whole relationship had started with a crazy plan to further her career, then continued as a way to bring exposure to both her and the band.

She'd been so afraid there'd come a point when she had to choose between him and her ambitions, but so far, life seemed willing to give her both.

There was no way to know how long that would last, but for now, she'd enjoy every single moment she was allowed to just be happy.

Jesse pulled off his T-shirt and used it to wipe the sweat from his face, looking over the drum kit Derrick had just finished setting up, nudging Tate's small black stool over with his foot before nodding with satisfaction and waving the kid off to take a break. If this was an actual show, they'd be dealing with all kinds of audio equipment, but they were sticking with the basics, so now the band was good to go.

The rest of his men were outside, cracking open a few cold ones, enjoying their last slow day before the band resumed their tour tomorrow, starting with the venue in LA. At least they didn't have far to go, just the other side of town, but it was a sold out show.

With twice the press of any they'd done so far, which Cole had warned him about just an hour ago. Everything had to run smoothly.

The man was annoying the fuck out of him with his micro-managing, but part of that was probably because Jesse was already in a foul mood. He'd brought Brave to a random motel, away from the rest of the band so whoever was fucking with him wouldn't have any way to find him. Passionate fans often tracked where the guys were staying and posted online. Which didn't explain how the crazy son of a bitch leaving sick gifts for Brave had found his damn room, unless he—or *she*?—was following him.

Coming to Los Angeles early might have thrown the freak off their trail, but Jesse was still keeping an eye out.

To the point that he'd slept in the van parked in front of the motel when Brave kicked him out of the damn room.

He tossed his soaked shirt onto a stack of crates by the loading dock and joined the other roadies, muttering thanks when Skull handed him a cold beer.

Skull's eyes narrowed as he studied Jesse's face. "Trouble in paradise?"

Jesse snorted, taking a few gulps of beer before wiping his mouth with the back of his hand. "If you mean we might all be looking for new jobs by the end of this tour? I'd say that's a good possibility."

The older man just laughed. "That bad, is it?"

Before Jesse could answer, Tate and Malakai ambled over. Malakai hefted himself up onto the edge of the loading dock, while Tate sat right on the asphalt beside the case of the beer, tossing one up to Malakai before helping himself to another.

Tate looked about as miserable as Jesse felt. He tore the label on his beer to pieces and scowled. "Couldn't you do something to cheer Brave up, Jesse? Fuck, you had all night."

Damn it, Tate. Jesse rolled his eyes as the other roadies looked over at him, all curious. They didn't know about him and Brave.

And he really didn't need them finding out. Skull wouldn't tell Cole, but the others might.

"I don't think he'd appreciate me calling him a hooker, Tate." Jesse prayed Tate would play along. Or at least keep his mouth shut. "But you're right. Getting his dick sucked might put him in a better mood. Why don't you go offer?"

Tate blinked. Glanced over at Malakai, who shook his head. Then bit his bottom lip. "Brave wouldn't let me suck his dick. I've asked."

Two of the roadies choked on their beer and Skull threw his head back, laughing before he leaned over and ruffled Tate's hair.

"I love you, kid." Skull took another swig of beer. "You all need to stop worrying about Brave. He'll get over it." The amusement in his eyes grew even brighter as he looked out across the parking lot. "One way or another. Looks like the younger Trousseau brother is on a mission."

Jesse tipped his beer to his lips, taking a sip as he watched Alder put his hand out for Danica. Alder glanced over to where Brave was stepping down from the steps of the bus, but he didn't head in that direction.

Instead, his gaze locked on Jesse. And he looked fucking pissed.

Jesse straightened as Alder came toward him. "So let's hear it. What are your suggestions for security? I'm guessing we're hiring some more guys? I hope you'll keep them more informed then you've kept me."

Ah…okay, that explains it. He held his hand up, shaking his head. "Alder, there's been a lot going on. I figured Brave would tell you…" He pressed his eyes shut, dropping his head when Alder scowled. He'd known very well Brave wouldn't tell him shit. "I'm sorry."

"Don't worry about it." Alder folded his arms over his chest. "Will security be with us before the show tomorrow?"

"No." Jesse exchanged a look with Skull, who simply shrugged. Helpful bastard, wasn't he? "Tank and Skull will be working with me to keep you guys safe. I'm still trying to talk Cole into hiring someone, but he thinks we can manage."

"Fuck that. Is he here yet?" Alder's expression softened as Brave joined them. He turned to his brother. "Look, man, I know things aren't great between us, but this is different. You're my brother and I don't want anything to happen to you."

Brave let out a cold laugh. "Isn't that sweet. I'm fine, little brother. But it looks like your girl has something to say to me." He glanced over at Danica. "What's it going to be today, darlin'? You wanna kiss me, or slap me?"

Her lips parted. She inhaled a slow, even breath, then hiked her chin up. "Neither. I think we understand one another now. And it's obvious you're a complete asshole to anyone who's not willing to kiss your ass, so how about we just agree to be civil?"

"Civil?" Brave's eyes narrowed. "You call me an asshole, and you expect me to be civil?"

She gave him a tight smile. "You called me a bitch. I'd say we're even."

Another car pulled up. Cole stepped out, followed by Madame Courchesne. Both were all smiles.

"We ready to get started?" Cole asked as if he didn't notice the obvious tension.

With a sound of disgust, Brave turned his back on them all and started into the warehouse with Malakai and Tate trailing behind. "Let's get this over with."

Cole shrugged and moved to follow them, but Alder cut him off, meeting the manager's eyes with a steady gaze.

"You sent us all a message about security. That still hasn't been discussed."

Glancing over at Jesse, Cole arched a brow as though he was confused. "Jesse, didn't you tell him our plans?"

"I did."

"Good. Then it's settled." Cole moved to step around Alder.

Alder put his hand on Cole's arm. "No, it's not. The roadies have enough to do. You're going to hire professionals."

The pleasant smile on the manager's lips slipped. He shoved Alder's hand off his arm. "The band might be doing well, Alder, but you can't handle the expenses of hiring extra people. I understand your concern, but—"

"I don't think you do, but either way, I wasn't asking Cole. I'm telling you to hire someone." Alder's tone was hard, but not like he was angry. There was a determination to his every word. A confidence Jesse had never seen him display before. "With the money I'll be bringing in doing that commercial with Danica, we can afford it."

"I haven't agreed to—"

"You don't have to agree, Cole. You work for *us*." Alder's lips slid into a hard smile. "You might want to remember that."

180

Cole hesitated, staring at Alder like he'd never seen the man before. Then he nodded. "Of course. I'll make a few phone calls while you guys are rehearsing."

"Good." Alder watched Cole walk away, pulled Danica close to give her a quick kiss, then jumped up onto the loading dock to join the band.

Danica stood at Jesse's side, pride in her eyes and she looked over, grinning. She put her hand under Jesse's chin and he realized his mouth had been open through the whole exchange.

His cheeks heated.

She giggled. "Is it just me or is he fucking hot when he's all take charge?"

"I'm not sure how to answer that." He had to admit, he liked this side of Alder. Brave usually gave Cole free reign, but if Alder started calling the manager on his shit?

The band was at a crossroads. With the stress of the tour and the strain between the brothers, there was no telling whether Winter's Wrath would survive all the success they'd worked so hard for.

But Alder stepping up to the plate might be the deciding factor.

And Danica was right. He *had* been fucking hot, standing up to Cole like that.

Jesse chuckled and bumped Danica's shoulder with his own. "I could say you're lucky he never pulled anything like that before. And that I'm with Brave. Otherwise, you might have some competition."

"Don't I know it!" She gave him a playful shove. "All right, help me up. And wish me luck. With the mood your man's in, this should be even more fun then it was yesterday."

He put his hands on her hips to lift her up on the loading dock. Then he paused, trying to find a way to make this a little easier on her. He'd been dealing with these guys for a long time and they still managed to catch him off guard.

She needed some kind of advantage.

"You know, Brave might be a jerk sometimes, but he's proud of the band. He loves the music." He leaned close, speaking low as the roadies stepped around them to climb up on the dock, probably getting ready to watch the show. "If you let him know you appreciate what he's doing, he'll probably be nicer to you."

Danica nodded, putting her hands on his shoulders as he picked her up. Standing on the dock, she looked down at him, a tiny smile on her lips. "Thank you, Jesse. I'm not sure I've told you how much you being here for me while I'm trying to figure this out means to me."

He smiled back at her. "You're the best thing to happen to Alder in a long time, sweetie. I'm happy he has you."

Holding his gaze, Danica's cheeks reddened. She nodded, then ducked into the warehouse.

He shook his head, not sure what to make of her acting all shy all of a sudden.

Chicks are weird.

As he joined the rest of his men, he caught Danica pulling Brave aside. They talked for a bit, Brave's expression closed off at first. But then she said something that cracked through his cold detachment and his expression warmed. He asked her something and she nodded enthusiastically.

Brave strode up to his mic, holding it loosely in his hand before turning to face the rest of the band. "Things have been a bit tense, so let's do something fun to warm up, all right? We've got a request from our beautiful little dancer. A song I don't even think most of our fans remember we covered on our first tour."

He frowned suddenly, looking at the unmanned guitar propped up on the stack of mats between Alder and Malakai.

"Where the fuck is Connor?"

"I'm here!" Connor shouted from the parking lot, leaping up onto the loading dock and sprinting across the warehouse. "Sorry, I went for a jog figuring I had plenty of time, but someone put the word out that we're practicing here and there's fans blocking the fucking street! Had to sign a few boobs."

"Poor baby." Brave gave the rhythm guitarist a wry grin, shaking his head. "Let's do this!"

And just like that, the mood had shifted. Alder started the intro to Hoobastank's, Crawling in the Dark, letting the notes drift off as he waited for a nod from Brave to tell him he had the right song. As he continued, cutting the notes into a heavier riff with the band's unique sound, Tate broke in with a wild beat that seemed almost out of control, but as Connor came in with the rhythm and Malakai filled in the bass, the rough, gritty sound came together.

The cover played homage to the original, but added a depth of emotion leaning more towards rage than pain.

Together, the band let their anger and frustration out with the music. Hopefully leaving it where it belonged.

Chapter Eleven

Standing in the center of the stage, Danica looked out at the expanse of the Wiltern Theater, the pounding of her heart loud enough to fill the silence. Excitement and fear swirled together in her stomach, making her damn happy she'd skipped lunch. She wasn't sure if she was going to be sick or pass out.

Strong arms came around her from behind, and her whole body reacted to the comforting presence like she'd just been given a warm injection of tranquility. She didn't even have to look to know it was Alder holding her. He made her feel like no one else ever had. Desired, safe, and precious. And other things she had no words for, but they were…well, as he would put it, "Fucking amazing."

When they'd gotten to the venue, he'd kept an eye on her, but she'd managed to play off her apprehension for the most part, and the band had stepped off the bus and gotten straight to work. Security had arrived—not the ones from Horizon that kept the crowd under control during the show, the new ones Cole had hired—and the head of security had taken the guys aside to explain the new policies he was implementing to keep them safe.

Danica had been dragged off by the stylist Sophie had called in to have her hair and makeup done, so that had given her a break from freaking out about the show. Being plucked and primped and painted were familiar. Even the discomfort of being laced into the red satin and black leather over bust corset

Sophie had sent over for her was nothing new. The micro-mini leather skirt looked more suitable for a lingerie runway than a heavy metal show, but the stylist had been equipped with Youtube videos of other band's live performances from Sophie to silence any objections Danica might have.

So she didn't bother protesting, but as soon as the stylist was done with her, she'd made her way to the stage to get her bearings.

And until Alder had joined her, she'd been terrified.

He pressed his lips against the side of her throat, holding her close to his solid chest. "Tell me what you're thinking."

She took a deep breath and closed her eyes. "I'm picturing thousands of people out there, wondering what the fuck I'm doing on stage with their favorite band. Cole wants me to come out for two other songs and improvise. I'm going to make a mess of this. I'll trip over the electrical cords, or fall off the stage, or—"

"Or you'll be just as graceful as you are on a runway. You'll feel the music and you'll forget all those people out there." He turned her to face him and the tenderness in his eyes made her racing heart skip a few beats. "With all the lights shining down on us, we can hardly see them through most of the show. I've never been to a fashion show, but I've seen them on TV. You have celebrities and photographers and all kinds of rich people all around you, staring at you. Now *that* looks fucking scary."

She let out a soft laugh, not surprised that he'd see it that way. To her, the catwalk was easy. She kept her head high, her expression blank, and took the same measured steps she had a thousand times before. No one was really looking at *her*, they were admiring the talent of the designers, catching up on the latest trends, and deciding where to spend their money.

"I've been walking the runway since I was fourteen. I don't even really remember what it's like to be nervous in front of a camera. But being on stage in front of a thousand of your screaming fans...?" She shook her head; pretty sure she was only going to make herself more nervous if she didn't stop visualizing the crowd. And all the ways she *might* mess up. "Let's change the subject. This theater is beautiful. It's easier to picture people sitting out there to watch the opera with glasses of champagne than it is to imagine metalheads in a mosh pit."

Alder nodded, looking out at the balconies and the high ceiling, with gold accents, and what looked like half a sun artistically reaching out between the rafters, the architecture of the whole theater designed with heavy ancient Egyptian influences.

The seating above was elegant, with rich red seats and fancy banisters, but the area in front of the stage ruined the sophistication. All the seating had been removed and there were crates that still hadn't been stashed away from all the bands' audio and lighting equipment. About half an hour ago, VIP fans had been brought in for the sound check, but they hadn't been allowed to take pictures because—as Jesse had told them while acting as the host—they didn't need everyone online to see the mess.

"We do venues like this all the time, so I'm used to it." He shifted her hair over one shoulder and bent down to kiss her neck again. His tone deepened in a way that heated her blood and made it very difficult to focus on anything he was saying. "Churches are still a little weird though."

She tipped her head to the side, enjoying the distraction of his lips moving down her throat, even though she was so turned on her panties weren't going to survive the night. They were already a little damp.

Maybe he could help her with that.

"How much time do we have?" She hooked her fingers to the belt of his distressed, black jeans so he'd have no doubt as to why she was asking. "I have an idea of how you can help me relax."

He gave her a hooded look and took her hand to draw her backstage. "Enough for me to take care of you."

All five bands had retreated to their busses, or headed out to local restaurants, to chill out before the show started. The crewmembers were still around, adjusting the lighting and setting up the merch tables. Backstage was surprisingly empty, but she knew a roadie could show up any minute.

Alder didn't seem at all concerned, so she took his lead, moaning into his mouth as he pushed her up against the wall behind the heavy, red stage curtains. He cupped her pussy under her skirt, shifting aside the lace covering her and dipping a thick, calloused finger inside her with a soft groan.

"I love how wet you get for me." He dragged his finger out, spreading the moisture over her clit, circling the tiny bud until she had to bite her lip to keep from crying out at the sharp spark of pleasure. His hot breath brushed her throat as he leaned closer to her, easing his finger in and moving over her clit in a deliciously, torturous rhythm. "Feeling you like this, I can't help thinking about how you taste. I could spend hours with your legs wrapped around my neck and my mouth on your sweet pussy."

Oh, I like that idea. Her core tightened as he pressed another finger into her alongside the first. She was so aroused, she knew he'd set her off before long, but she needed to see him as out of control as she was. He always paid close attention to her, giving her anything she could want or need.

Right now, what she needed was to return the favor.

Curving her hand around the back of his neck, she drew him down so she could whisper in his ear. "I still don't know what you taste like. That's about to change."

Tugging his belt open, she maneuvered him around so his back was braced against the wall. When his hand left her she grabbed his wrist and sucked his fingers, enjoying both the flavor of herself on his skin and the way he sucked in a sharp breath as he watched her.

She opened his jeans, freeing his long, hard dick which she'd felt inside her more than once, but still hadn't had a chance to admire.

Stroking him, she ran her tongue over the swollen head, which had darkened with his arousal. Along his length were thick veins and his pulse beat against her tongue as she ran it up the underside of his dick. Teasing him with a flick of her tongue, she tasted the bead of precum slicking the slit of his cock.

"Baby, that feels so fucking good." Alder cupped her cheek, shifting his hips slightly as she wrapped her lips around him. "God, you're beautiful."

Cupping his balls in her hand, she let her saliva slick his whole length, moving faster, watching his face until he tipped his head back, muttering what sounded like a prayer.

From the corner of her eye, there was movement. She slowed, not sure if she should stop and warn Alder.

But then she saw who it was and a naughty little voice in her head told her to keep going. She still remembered those teasing words about how she "Might have had competition."

They wouldn't get in trouble for getting caught. Not by him.

He can either leave, or he can stay and watch.

And for some strange reason, she kinda hoped he'd stay.

Jesse swallowed hard as he stood in the shadows behind the stage, his cock swelling as Danica circled the head of Alder's dick with her tongue. She had a wicked smile on her lips and he knew she'd seen him.

He pressed his fist to his lips to hold back a groan as she took Alder deep into her throat. Damn it, he wasn't sure what turned him on more. The idea of her using her mouth like that on him, or taking her place and putting that look of absolute mindless pleasure on Alder's face himself.

Maybe he shouldn't have told her about fooling around with Alder in the past. This might be her way of staking her claim. She didn't seem the spiteful sort though, and aside from holding his gaze for a few seconds, she was entirely focused on Alder.

The brat is getting off on being watched. He inhaled roughly, stifling a laugh as he quietly backed away. Living on a tour bus for weeks on end, being a bit of an exhibitionist would serve her well. He wasn't sure if he'd be able to act as voyeur very often though.

Not when the only play he'd been getting lately was his own fucking hand.

Hell, he'd even gone to the bus, figuring Brave might want to relieve some pressure before hitting the stage, but Cole seemed to be reasserting his position with the band and was taking every opportunity to talk to Brave alone.

Alder showing more interest in the management of the band clearly made Cole nervous. The man took advantage of the distance between the brothers and loved the fact that Brave usually gave him complete control over running the band.

He was scrambling now to make sure that didn't change.

With Brave constantly isolating himself, Cole might get his way. Jesse tried not to meddle in band politics, but his relationship with Brave was falling apart along with everything else. Rehearsal yesterday had lightened the mood, but Brave had still asked to spend the night alone.

He refused to discuss what was bothering him, but maybe it was time for Jesse to stop giving him a choice.

Thinking over Cole's routine, Jesse figured he should probably be somewhere in the venue, dealing with last minute shit with the organizers. Malakai and Tate would be grabbing a bite to eat, and Connor…well, they crazy fucker was either running around the block or screwing a groupie in the alley.

If he wanted any time with Brave, he'd finally have the opportunity.

Not for long, but he'd take it.

Climbing onto the bus, he found Brave sitting in the front lounge, earbuds in his ears and a thick book open against his knee. His long black hair spilled over his shoulders, framing his face. His features were relaxed as his gaze remained locked on the pages and Jesse took a moment to admire the handsome man he'd considered untouchable for so long.

Brave possessed the presence and looks of a rock god, but there were times when his dark eyes reminded Jesse of something even wilder. Like a predator hunting down anything he desired, from the way he paced the stage like a sleek panther, trapping the audience in a mesmerizing thrall, to the seductive smile that so many men and women couldn't resist.

Most saw either the god or the predator, but Jesse saw the man. The protective leader, the passionate artist, the man who tempered kindness with harsh words because he couldn't bear to be seen as weak. When Jesse looked at Brave, he sensed that Brave needed someone who wouldn't let him push them away.

So far, though, he hadn't figured out how to get past the barricades Brave had built around himself. When Brave had said he wanted to prove so much to Jesse, there'd been a moment when Jesse thought he'd found a way in.

He'd only made it as far as Brave's bed. And after that one time, he couldn't even manage that anymore.

"You gonna keep staring at me, or you gonna tell me what you want?" Brave didn't look up from his book. He turned the page, his jaw hardening as though he was irritated.

Jesse took a deep breath, then moved to crouch down in front of the other man. "How about you tell me what I did to piss you off?"

Brave's eyes narrowed. He stuck a ripped piece of paper between the pages of his book, then set it aside. "You didn't do anything. Actually, I'm curious how much you'll put up with. Do you enjoy being treated like shit?"

"Do you want me to give up?"

"I don't know." Brave's brow furrowed. He brought his hand to his face and rubbed his eyes. "You should. I was wrong, Jess. I'm going to fuck this up and you will get hurt."

"Why, because you're not easy to be with? Don't you think I fucking knew that already?" Jesse put his hands on Brave's knees, waiting until Brave met his eyes before he continued. "You're dealing with a lot. I get that, but I'm here for you, Brave."

"And what do you want from me? I'm not going to start talking about my feelings. I don't need you to hold me and tell me everything will be okay." Brave leaned forward, raking his hands into Jesse's hair. "The only thing you can do for me is let me use you. And not hate me when I'm done."

Jesse wet his lips with his tongue, not sure whether or not he should consider this progress. What Brave was asking for was entirely physical, but it was a start. He wouldn't back down now that he had his foot in the door.

"I won't hate you." Jesse rose up on his knees, swiftly undoing the button fly of Brave's jeans. The man might pretend to be completely detached, but his dick was hard, straining against his boxers. When Jesse fisted a hand around his dick, he let out a low sound of pleasure that edged on pain.

"You crazy fucker." Brave groaned as Jesse dropped down to swallow him whole. "If you were smart, you'd stay away from me. I've given you every opportunity to make a clean break."

Whatever Brave said, his actions told a completely different story. His grip on Jesse's hair was painful, like he needed find a way to hold on to him, even as he pushed him away with every word. He thrust in deep and Jesse relaxed his jaw, letting Brave use him, hoping the man would finally accept that he wasn't going anywhere.

Letting out rough growl, Brave pulled Jesse away, dragging him to his feet even as he stood. He moved behind Jesse, reaching around to undo Jesse's jeans.

"This is gonna be fast, but next time will be all about you." Brave's wallet dropped onto the sofa. His fingers, slicked with lube, stretched Jesse as he bit into Jesse's shoulder, right through his shirt. His dick replaced his fingers and drove in hard. "Damn it, I don't know how I managed to stay away from you so long."

"Don't." Jesse latched onto the back of the sofa, breathing through the pain of being taken so roughly, knowing that they'd had to get to this point before things could get better. Brave was finally with him. Really with him. And he wasn't holding back anymore. "Don't stay away from me, Brave. I'm tougher than you seem to think."

Barring an arm across his chest, digging his fingers into

Jesse's hair, Brave spoke with his lips against Jesse's throat. "I believe you, but I can't help wondering—" He rammed in, grinding deep, then pulling out almost all the way. "—how much—" His pelvis slapped against Jesse's ass as he picked up the pace. "—you're willing to take."

"Everything." The pain shifted with the friction and Jesse panted as his cock throbbed. He wouldn't come without his dick being stimulated. He needed Brave's hand on him. "Fuck, Brave. Please touch me."

Slamming into him so hard, Jesse's arms almost gave out, Brave found his release. He leaned over Jesse with a cold laugh. "I like hearing you beg. You say you're willing to take anything? Good. Then you'll wait until I'm ready to give you more."

Jesse rested his head on the back of the sofa, wincing as Brave drew away from him. His throat tightened as he heard Brave's steady footsteps retreating. Water running in the bathroom.

Shoving up to stand straight, Jesse adjusted his boxers and jeans to cover himself, waiting for Brave to finish in the bathroom so he could go clean himself up. He'd been warned that he'd be used, but he hadn't listened, had he?

You still willing to take everything, Jesse? The voice in his head was cruel. Bitter.

When Brave came out of the bathroom, he met Jesse's eyes for a split second before heading out. And there was some regret in those golden depths before Brave had looked away.

He still didn't believe Jesse. He hadn't meant to hurt him, but he couldn't help testing him. Almost as though he was convinced Jesse would give up and was willing to sabotage what they had to prove it.

Showing him how fucking wrong he was wouldn't be easy, but Jesse loved him. And he wouldn't give up until Brave understood exactly what that meant.

Am I willing to take everything?

The answer was simple.

Yes.

Chapter Twelve

When the blazing sun is gone,
So very long before the dawn
Your tiny light comes from on high,
We whisper wishes as you die.

Alder's bones vibrated as the music flowed through him, and he grinned as Danica skipped across the stage while he strummed a minor-key breakdown of Twinkle Twinkle Little Star, followed by a recording of creepy sounding kids singing along. Danica smiled sweetly at the crowd, mouthing the words to the children's song as they all screamed and chanted along.

Fallen Star, was one of Winter's Wraths' most popular songs. And also one of the most hardcore.

Brave growled into the mic. "Let's open up this fucking pit!"

The crowd parted, leaving a circle in the center, a few rows back from the stage. Young men, and a few women who looked like they could take any of the guys in a fight, spilled into the center. Those that weren't smashing into one another ran around and around, as if the music had given them so much energy, they couldn't stop moving, they had to find a way to burn it off.

Around the circle pit, those who weren't joining in gave the runners little shoves, partly to keep them going, partly to keep from getting rammed into.

There were bands that went their entire careers trying to get the crowd worked up like this, but never really pulled it off. Fan interaction could make or break anyone who stepped up on this stage. Not only with what they did out on the floor, but if they responded to what the singer told them to do.

And Brave had them all in the palm of his hand. At the chorus, he held up the mic and a thousand voices sang the words he'd written. When he set the mic in the stand and raised his hands to clap the beat, everyone began clapping along with him.

This was the second song in their set of six, and as soon as it finished, Brave grabbed the mic and stepped to the edge of the stage.

"Hey, Los Angeles, how the fuck are you tonight?"

Screams were his only answer. The throng pressed against the barrier and security, the three new ones Cole had hired, and the five that worked for Horizon, moved forward to shove back the few crazies that tried to climb over.

"You might have noticed, we brought something sweet for you all to enjoy." Brave motioned to Danica, who was standing just out of sight side-stage, and she sauntered up to his side, waving at the crowd.

Alder's heart swelled as he took in her easy smile, the confidence in the way she moved. Brave might own the crowd, but if Danica kept putting on such an amazing performance, bringing everything the fans were feeling right up on stage with every thrash of her body and thrust of her fist in the air, they were going to fall in love with her.

"She's been teasing you so far, but now, it's time for her to give you a little more." Brave wrapped Danica's hair around his hand. Whispered something to her away from the mic.

She gave him a slight nod.

Jaw clenched, Alder braced himself for what he knew was coming. Yeah, they had the routine, but Brave would use this as an opportunity to get the fans all riled up. As he kissed Danica, the volume in the theater rose to a deafening level.

Even more when Brave jerked away from Danica and began whispering in the mic. "S.L.U.T. S.L.U.T."

Louder and louder. And the crowd joined in.

Danica smirked at Brave, Tate thrummed out the beat, and she spun away to begin the dance that she'd been criticized for by Madame Croissant—fuck whatever her name was, she was an evil bitch—for days.

And Danica fucking nailed it. He had to fight to focus on playing, because her allure had even more fans than usual trying to get past security. The crowd surfers got a bit further, and shouted out to her as the guards dragged them to the side of the barrier to push them back into the crowd.

As the last chorus began, Danica approached Brave, but before he could dip her back over his arm, she wiggled free, blew him a kiss, and strutted up to Alder. He stared at her, hitting the wrong note as she held out her hand.

Letting his guitar hang on its strap, he latched on to her wrist, pulling her into his arms and taking her lips in a rough, wild kiss, tasting his own blood as she tugged his bottom lip between her teeth.

The crowd was chanting again. "Slut! Slut! Slut!"

He smiled as Danica trembled in his arms, her eyes wide as she stared up at him. "You were fucking incredible."

"Brave is going to hate me."

Alder glanced over at his brother.

Brave gave him a mock salute, then went back to chatting with the crowd. He had their attention back on him, so he was happy. What he would say or do after the show was a completely different story, but Alder wasn't too worried.

His brother's ambition trumped even his ego. Clips of the performance would be online within minutes. By the time they left the venue, they would have plenty of feedback.

If it was good, Brave would be very happy with Danica being spontaneous.

It will *be good.*

"He won't hate you." Alder kissed her cheek, which got a few of the fans closest to his side of the stage shouting out crude suggestions. He ignored them. "Let's finish this. I want to get you back to the hotel for a bit before we've got to hit the road."

Danica grinned at him, squeezing his ass before slipping off backstage. She came out again briefly for the last song, one of their most militaristic, with the lyrics following the drum beat, while the guitar rhythm cut in at the pace of marching soldiers. *Center Mass*, was a song about breaking free despite all odds, and every member of the band had gotten fan mail about how the song had changed—or sometimes *saved*—someone's life.

All Danica really had to do was throw her fist in the air, while Brave belted out the refrain, then join them in screaming the chorus.

"Reload! Fire! Reload! Fire!"

When Winter's Wrath left the stage, fans called for an encore. Standing on the sidelines, the lead singer of Horizon clapped Brave's shoulder as they passed.

"That's a tough act to follow, man. Keep that up and we'll be opening for you all next year!"

"Just say the word and the spot is yours!" Brave called back to him. He led the way to the back exit, as usual, but instead of disappearing into the bus to snag the shower first, he waited by the door, grabbing Danica as soon as she stepped outside.

Alder resisted the urge to pull her out of his brother's arms as Brave swung her up above his head, letting her slide down his body before kissing her forehead.

"Thank you, sweetheart. You just turned a damn good show into a fucking masterpiece. Having you up there raises the bar and we needed that." Brave put his hands on her shoulders. "Tell me what you want and it's yours."

At first, Danica looked too stunned to reply, but then she poked Brave in the center of his chest. "You have to be nice from now on. To everyone."

Brave smile looked a little strained. "Nice?"

Danica cocked her head, as though considering. "Pleasant?"

Brave sighed.

Shaking her head, Danica laughed. "Not quite so much of a dick?"

"That I can do." He put his arm over her shoulders, directing her toward the bus. "Let's have a beer. I think one of the roadies got Bud Light, just for you. You've burned enough calories for a real drink though."

"Is the great Brave Trousseau offering to fix me a drink?"

"Name your poison, my sweet girl."

All right, Alder knew it was good for the band to have Brave and Danica getting along, but did he have to touch her so much? And why was she letting him?

It doesn't mean anything, Alder. She fucking kisses him onstage. He's just being affectionate.

Yeah, Brave didn't do affectionate. Not even with people he was fucking.

Though, sometimes he made the effort for people he *wanted* to fuck.

A heavy hand settled on his arm. He glanced over his shoulder to see Malakai. "Relax, Alder. Brave hasn't been in this good of a mood for months. Don't ruin it."

"I won't."

Tate trotted up to his other side, his bare chest glistening with sweat, walking so close Alder had to slow his pace. "Dude, you're practically growling."

Connor joined them. A strange, and rare occurrence right there. He jogged up, looping his arms around Tate's neck and cutting in front of Alder, forcing them all to stop in the middle of the lot as Danica and Brave disappeared onto the bus.

What is this, a fucking intervention?

"Let me be the only one who'll be straight with you, buddy." Connor swept his wet hair off his forehead with one hand, then pulled off his own shirt to wipe the droplets of sweat from running into his eyes. "Give them a few minutes to make nice. He's not gonna fuck her."

"No, he's not. But I don't trust him not to try something."

"Do you trust her?"

"Of course I trust her!" Alder decided he liked Connor a lot more when he was more focused on pumping iron and running laps than with what was going on with the band. "Why the fuck would you even—"

"She'll have his balls if he tries anything. She's made that clear." Connor folded his arms over his chest, like he had no intention of moving anytime soon. "Hang out here with us, have a smoke, and don't give Brave a reason to fuck with you."

"Since when do you care what goes on between me and Brave?"

Malakai let out a bitter laugh. "Since it became obvious the shit between you and him is going to tear this band apart."

Tate nodded, stuffing his hands in his pockets and shuffling his sneakers. "We liked you calling Cole on the shit with security. Hell, it's about time someone put him in his place. He's fucking pushy and we're tired of his crap and—"

"Get to the point, Tate," Malakai said, his lips slanting with amusement. "This is about Brave and Alder."

"Right." Tate nodded. "You guys are brothers. You don't have to like each other, but you have to try."

I have to try? Have any of you fucking met my brother? Alder shook his head, stepping away from the three of them, wanting to demand what they expected him to do. He'd given up on getting along with Brave. If it wasn't for the band, they wouldn't have any contact at all.

But they did have the band.

And with Danica joining them on the tour, with all the guys working so hard to make this their breakthrough year, maybe his relationship with Brave had to change. That he hadn't even been told about someone breaking into Brave's room attested to how bad things actually were.

Jesse, of all people, hadn't considered telling him.

For all Alder knew, Brave would laugh at any attempt he made to regain what they'd had when they were young. He was good at making Alder feel stupid and worthless, but Alder wasn't a child anymore, looking for his big brother's approval.

He'd do what was best for the band. Which might be exactly what helped them reach some common ground.

Because like it or not, they'd built Winter's Wrath together.

The band that the fans loved.

Creating music they would be remembered for.

He turned back to his band mates, men he'd spent three years with, who were more like family than his own parents and brothers had ever been.

Doing this for Brave would be tough, but for them?

He shook his head, tugging Tate away from Connor to rub his knuckles into the kid's skull. "Fine. I'll try. But someone better get me a damn beer. My brother needs time alone on the bus with my girlfriend. I wouldn't want to interrupt."

Danica sipped the cocktail Brave had made for her with a mix of juices and alcohol from the well stocked bar and fridge. She was a bit surprised a bus full of guys kept drinks like peach schnapps handy, but maybe they had a lot of groupies on the bus.

Not since she'd been with them, for which she was grateful. She still didn't know how she'd react to random chicks climbing all over Alder. And with how often he had to see her in the arms of his brother, she knew she couldn't flip out to him catering to his fans.

She glanced over as Brave perched on the seat beside her, taking a few gulps of beer while watching the door with his brow furrowed.

"I think they're giving us some time to ourselves." Danica took another sip, letting out a happy sigh at the sweet burst of citrus, sharpened slightly by the vodka. She wouldn't be having many of these. Brave had made it strong and it would hit her hard if she overindulged.

Brave rested his arm on the back of the sofa, shaking his head. "And I thought my brother was a smart man."

"He is."

"Not if he's giving me an opportunity to seduce you." Brave gave her a hooded look as he licked a drop of beer from his bottom lip. "With a women like you, a man needs to set very clear boundaries. And he hasn't."

"He doesn't need to. I'm capable of setting my own." Danica relaxed back into the sofa, trying to play off like Brave's suggestive remarks didn't bother her in the least. Her acting skills came in handy with him, but it was hard not to let her frustrations show.

Would he really come on to her, just to hurt his brother?

Leaning forward, Brave set his beer on the side table, then rested his elbows on his knees. "Do you think you're the first girl to come on this bus, convinced she was completely devoted to one of the guys, who ended up making the rounds? The guys like you, and they're treating you differently because you're working with us, but I'm willing to bet one night, you'll have a bit too much to drink and ditch uptight professionalism."

"You think I'm uptight?"

"I think you're pretending to be." Brave stood and picked up his beer. "But maybe I'm wrong. Maybe you'll make Alder happy. You're already good for the band, and that's the only reason I haven't fucked you yet."

The arrogance of the man was mind-blowing. How did he *ever* get laid...no, she knew the answer to that. Groupies played into a rock star's ego, they didn't expect him to be a decent human being. But she did wonder how he'd managed to hook up with a guy like Jesse.

She shook her head, deciding she was finished with her drink. And the conversation. "You promised you wouldn't be a dick anymore."

"I did, didn't I?" Brave stepped up in front of her, taking her hand as she sat forward, and bending down to press a soft kiss on her knuckles. "Maybe I need more practice."

"Ya think?"

He chuckled, releasing her hand and backing away. "Tonight went well. You'll get all kinds of offers, which is exactly what you want. But let me ask you this. How long are you planning to stick around? Your contract ends in a month and then you're free to leave."

"Is this your way of asking me to stick around?"

"No, this is my way of asking you if getting serious with Alder is even fair to him. Your career will always come before him. Right now, being seen with him has its advantage, but what if next month, being on the arm of an athlete suits you better?" Brave folded his arms over his chest and leaned against the cupboards at the end of the kitchenette. "Your lifestyle is all about appearance. Ours is all about moving on to the next show. They won't align for long."

All right, maybe she *did* understand what Jesse saw in Brave. He had to be looking very *very* hard to see beyond the cold, calculating asshole Brave tended to present as a default, but just beneath the surface, there seemed to be a man who cared very much. She'd seen that man a little with the band—mostly with Tate, who all the guys were protective of—but most of the time he focused on what was best for Winter's Wrath.

This time, he seemed to be looking out for Alder. And doing his best not to make it obvious. "So what are you suggesting?"

"Absolutely nothing. I want us to be friends. Friends are honest with one another."

"True." She polished off the last of her drink and stood. "So as your friend, let me be honest with you. I think you care about your brother more than you let off. I think, in some twisted way, you're trying to protect him."

"Is that so?" Brave's whole expression changed. There was a flash of anger in his eyes, but it was gone so fast, she might have imagined it. His brow rose slightly as his lips slanted with amusement. "Would you still believe that if I told you I knew he was in love with Jesse?"

Danica's lips parted. She inhaled slowly, shaking her head. "But that's not why you—"

"Shh." Brave came toward her, putting one finger over her lips. "It's our little secret. As friends."

She scowled at him, shoving his hand away from her face. "We're not friends. And if you actually did that to your brother, you're an even bigger asshole then I thought you were."

"So long as you're aware of that, you'll do just fine."

Feeling sick to her stomach, she turned her back on him, rushing off the bus, not even sure where she was going. She didn't see Alder or the other guys until she heard him calling out, then running to catch up with her.

"What did he do?" Alder's eyes were hard, and she could tell he was ready to go after his brother. All she had to do was give the word. "Danica, I can tell you're upset. If he touched you—"

"He didn't." She shook her head, blinking fast and thinking even faster. If she told Alder about Jesse, he'd be furious. And all the progress the band had made would be ruined.

You have to tell him something.

A partial truth might be enough. "He brought up my contract ending in a month. He's convinced me and you won't last if I decide to take another offer."

Alder snorted. "Babe, he's never had a real relationship. I'm not even sure how he's kept things going with Jesse for as long as he has. Don't let him get to you."

Nodding, she let Alder pull her into his arms. She pressed her forehead against his chest, her mind racing as she considered how she could fix this without Brave's actions tearing the band apart.

Or worse, letting him destroy Alder. And break Jesse's heart.

Chapter Thirteen

During the night, Alder woke to the sound of soft footsteps padding away from the bunks, toward the front lounge. The bus had turned onto a rough road, and Danica must have been jolted awake. Two days out of Los Angeles, two nights on the bus, and he was pretty sure she hadn't had a decent night's sleep.

Sliding out of his bunk, he went to check on her, keeping quiet so he wouldn't bother the other guys.

He spotted Danica at the front of the bus, whispering to Jesse, who was driving.

"Aren't you tired?"

"Naw, I took a nap while Skull was driving." Jesse sounded alert, as he always was behind the wheel. The scent of coffee filled the bus, so he'd probably had a travel mug filled up, sitting in the cup holder beside him. "You must be exhausted though. Still not used to sleeping in the bunk?"

She shrugged. "It's not that. I just…I got spoiled, sleeping beside Alder for a few nights. I've never had trouble sleeping alone, but now even the tiny space on the bed beside me feels so empty. You know what that's like?"

"Unfortunately, no. I've never had a guy willing to stick around that long."

Alder swallowed hard, not sure why Jesse's admission felt like a fist to the gut. At one time, he would have been more than happy to rest his head on Jesse's shoulder while they slept. Or let Jesse use him as a pillow.

Once he'd let Jesse go, accepting his relationship with Brave, he hadn't looked back at what might have been. And he'd been lucky enough to find Danica. There was nothing missing in his life, so why dwell on the past?

But he'd assumed Jesse was doing fine with Brave.

He doesn't sound fine.

Not that Jesse would come to him about problems with his brother. *Obviously.* But he seemed comfortable talking to Danica, which was good.

He stood back in the shadows, loving that Danica had found a way to be there for his best friend when he couldn't.

She put her hand on Jesse's shoulder. "Can I ask you something?"

"Sure."

"Why?" She bowed her head and sighed. "Wait. Don't answer that. It's none of my business."

"What isn't? Why I chose Brave?" Jesse had lowered his voice so Alder had to strain to hear him. Even if any of the other guys were awake, there was no way they'd catch a single word. "Why I didn't see what an amazing man Alder is? Our friendship means *everything* to me. And maybe that could have lead to more, but I was too fucking scared to risk it."

Fuck. Alder pressed his eyes shut, backing up a few paces. He couldn't listen to this anymore. He was with Danica. He was falling in love with her, even though he wasn't ready to tell her so. Whether or not things worked out between Jesse and Brave had nothing to do with him.

Yeah, he wished he could fix this for Jesse. Even though he'd let him go, the man still owned a piece of his heart. And that piece was fucking hurting for him. He wanted to drag Brave out of bed and tell him to smarten up. But that would only make things worse for Jesse.

There was absolutely nothing Alder could do to improve the situation.

Danica could be there for Jesse in ways he couldn't though. Which was the only thing that made it possible for him to climb back into his bunk and close his eyes. The bumpy rhythm of the bus lulled him into a restless sleep.

Because, no matter how hard he tried to convince himself otherwise, he knew there had to be more he could do.

Anything.

Fuck, even a single word he could say.

Or even... *I'm sorry.*

Jesse expected Danica to head back to bed after he'd blurted out way too much in response to her one word question. He wasn't even sure why he'd opened his damn mouth. The girl was *with* Alder and she was going to see him as a threat.

"How Alder can make a person feel *is* scary." Danica moved her hand to the side of his neck. Stroking lightly with her thumb and sending a pleasant little chill down his spine. "He scares me sometimes. And I've known him for about a week. But from the moment I met him, I felt comfortable. Like he belonged in my life."

Jesse nodded, not taking his eyes off the road. "I felt the same way."

"Does it bother you? Talking to me about him?" Danica pulled away. "I could change the subject if it makes you uncomfortable."

With a rough laugh, Jesse glanced over at her. "It doesn't bother me, but I don't get why *you're* okay with it. I mean, I told you we fooled around. And we're still close. Isn't that weird for you?"

"Not at all. Picturing you and him together bugs me less than the idea of groupies."

"Me and him *together*?"

"Yeah. It's kinda hot, actually." She had a wicked little smile on her lips. "Would it be bad of me to ask for details?"

The girl is killing me! Jesse shifted in his seat, staring out at the dark road. He wasn't sure how to answer that. His dick was getting hard just thinking about laying in the dirt, holding Alder, their hard bodies grinding together.

But he was dating Brave. Kinda.

If being used and discarded constantly could be given any kind of label.

At least Brave was a heavy sleeper, so he didn't have to worry about the man overhearing the conversation. Alder and Tate were the light sleepers, but Tate would be banging around the kitchen if he was awake. And Alder would probably come see why Danica wasn't sleeping, so the only concern was whether or not he was comfortable being open with the woman.

He hadn't known her very long either, but he already considered her a friend.

And he needed one. Now more than ever.

"If I give you details, you have to swear you won't get all bitchy with me after. Alder isn't a cheater and dudes that are in a relationship aren't my thing." His lips thinned. Apparently, his 'thing' was guys that treated him like shit. He seriously needed to figure out where he and Brave were going with their 'relationship'. If anywhere.

Brave needs you.

He had to believe that. If not, he'd have to face that he was wasting his time.

But every time he wondered if he was, he heard Brave, telling him all the things he'd waited so long to hear.

"I wanna prove you wrong. I wanna prove I can have something good and not fuck it up."

Whatever Brave did to him, he couldn't stop caring.

Why?

He wasn't even sure he could answer that question. He'd been silent for a long time, and he was surprised Danica hadn't given him a little nudge to keep talking, but when he looked at her, she was staring out at the road, lost in her own thoughts.

So he let his own drift.

A couple of years ago, long after Alder had given him plenty of reason to not judge Brave for the ice cold front he put up for anyone he didn't give a shit about—which tended to include his own brother—Jesse had gone to the Trousseau household to pick up the guys before another long tour.

Their mother had let him in, looking way too young to have adult sons. She was actually wearing the band's latest T-shirt and a pair of black skinny jeans. She'd invited Jesse in and sat with him while her sons finished packing. Drinking beer and talking about travelling, he'd felt welcome.

Until her husband joined them.

"Brave will never learn. You're drinking? Before driving my sons?" Gallant Trousseau—the family had a history of weird names—sat at the other end of the table, glaring at Jesse. "I'm sure it's expected in the 'lifestyle', but is it possible for you to make sure both my remaining sons make it back alive?"

Jesse set down his beer, feeling like an idiot for accepting the drink, even though the man's wife had insisted. He cleared his throat. "Uh...Alder likes driving. I brought my car, because my sister will pick it up after work so we don't pay for parking. I won't drink again today."

"Right. But you're all driving around the country in a fucking van."

"Brave told me you're a mechanic. And that he learned from you." Jesse forced a smile, hoping their father would find some assurance in his next words. "He keeps the van in good shape. You've taught him well."

"If he listened to anything I've taught him, he would be home, working with me." The man snorted. "But he gets all kinds of pussy and dick on the road, doesn't he? Which matters more than a respectable career."

This sounded too much like the conversation with his own parents. Right before his father had told him to get the fuck out. Jesse ground his teeth, hoping Alder and Brave would hurry up so he didn't have to deal with their father any more.

He'd had more than enough dealing with his own after a wild party ended up with him drugged up on Rohypnol, and in the hospital, getting tested for STDs. Since he was gay, he'd asked for everything that had happened to him.

According to his father, anyway.

"Your sons are very talented. I imagine you're proud of them." Jesse held his stiff smile as he met the man's eyes. "If you're not, well, that's your problem."

While Gallant grumbled, his wife took Jesse's hand. Her eyes flooded with tears. "Please understand, we just want what's best for our boys. Brave is obsessed. That same obsession is what took Valor from us. We know Brave is too far gone, but Alder… Can you promise me you will bring him home? Maybe you can convince him to give up this crazy dream of his. We can't lose him too."

As if Brave was already lost. As if they'd given up on him.

Jesse stood and inclined his head. "I'll make sure both your sons make it home in one piece. Thanks for the beer."

As he'd turned away to go tell the guys to hurry up, he'd seen Brave, standing in the doorway, looking absolutely crushed.

Brave had headed to the car with his bag, not even saying goodbye to his parents. Jesse waited while Alder got hugs and kisses and supportive words from them both.

Whenever they were in Detroit, and Mr. and Mrs. Trousseau came around, it was the same thing, all over again. They missed Valor. They worried about Alder.

Brave might be harder to love, but he didn't deserve it any less.

Danica had asked him about his time with Alder though, and for some reason, the idea of her getting all hot and bothered, imagining them together, amused him.

If he was a nice guy, he'd make it seem like nothing.

Only, he wasn't feeling particularly 'nice' at the moment.

"You still want details, or you thinking it would be a bad idea to know just how easily I could get your man off if I tried?"

Eyes wide, Danica stared at him. "I wasn't sure you wanted to tell me."

"Not sure I do. I like us being friends." *One last chance to let it go, sweetheart.*

She simply nodded. "This won't change anything. I like being friends with you too."

Jesse tightened his grip on the steering wheel, focusing on the road as he took a wide turn. "All right, so we finally had a bus. Was the middle of the summer and I swear, we hit almost every fucking state in three months. And we were heading up to Canada in a couple of weeks. We're still dealing with the same rental company, but they'd warned us to get the bus checked after a certain mileage. Our bad that we didn't. The bus died in the middle of the night. I pulled off on the side of the road in Kentucky and checked it out, but I'm no mechanic. I had no fucking clue what was wrong with it. The engine light went off, then the whole thing just gave out."

He really wanted a cigarette. Or a joint.

That night he'd felt the same. And he'd gone outside to light up, smoking two cigarettes and a joint, not wanting to wake any of the guys up since they'd been up for half the night at a crazy after party. Every single one of them was plastered.

Since he knew he'd be driving, he hadn't had a drink—he never did before heading out, because fuck that. He expected his men to be smart drivers and he wouldn't mess with the lives of the band. Or the people they might pass on the road.

Anyway, for some reason, that night, the bus breaking down messed him up. Maybe it was because his mom had left him a message, telling him his dad had a stroke. And he'd spent the whole drive thinking about how he couldn't go home. His dad had made that pretty fucking clear.

Skull had pulled up in the van a few minutes later. He'd looked ready to strangle Jesse for getting stoned. Told him they needed a tow.

When Alder came out, stumbling and squinting in the headlights, Skull pointed up the road and told them to walk until they got cell reception.

So they'd started walking.

Danica's laugh pulled him from his detached recount of that night. "I've never seen either of you that out of it."

He smirked. "We learned from our mistakes. I'm not sure who was holding who up. For me, everything was blurry. I never smoke that much anymore, but that night, I had rolled up a fatty and finished most of it before Skull showed up and tore me a new one."

"Now *that* I can see. Skull is awesome."

"He really is." Jesse smiled, even though, at the time, Skull had made him feel like a stupid kid.

He let himself drift back into the memories as he continued telling Danica about that night.

Tired from the show, and the party, Alder had made it over the next hill, then decided he needed to sit down for a minute.

Right on the side of the road.

And he was hot, so of course he took off his shirt.

Spreading it out on the gravel by the road, Alder laid down, laughing when Jesse tried to pull him to his feet.

"Give me a minute. I'm about to pass out."

Jesse sat down beside him, scowling. "You're gonna get me fucking fired. If Brave wakes up and sees you gone, he'll—"

"He won't give a shit." Alder dropped his arm over his eyes. "Go back and tell him I'm dead. You'll see. He'll be relieved."

"Fuck, Alder. Don't talk like that. You know it's not true."

"I'm not Valor. He loved Valor." Alder pressed his lips together, turning away from Jesse. "Fuck, I'm drunk. Don't listen to me. Just leave me here and keep walking. I'm gonna say something I'll regret."

"I'm not leaving you. And you'll forget it all in the morning, so no worries, okay?" He wasn't sure why he wanted to touch Alder, but he did. He put his hand on the side of Alder's face, leaning down as he spoke, completely focused on Alder's lips. They looked so soft. And Alder wasn't the determined, career obsessed man he'd come to know. He was vulnerable and hurting and Jesse wanted to make it all better.

Alder had stared up at him. "What are you doing, Jesse? You have to know I won't forget you?"

"Won't forget me what?" Jesse bent down, kissing Alder, not seeing a single thing wrong with how fucking good the man's mouth tasted. How the little sounds of pleasure Alder let out made him feel. He tasted like smoke and whiskey; a combination that Jesse didn't usually go for, but on Alder's lips was fucking addictive. "Taking advantage of you?"

Fisting his hand in Jesse shirt, Alder ground up against him. "You can't take advantage of the willing."

"Fuck." Jesse ran his hand down the hard chest beneath him, loving how those tight muscles jumped at his touch as he worked his way down to the belt of Alder's jeans. "The things I want to do to you…"

"What's stopping you?"

Shaking his head, Jesse kissed Alder again so he didn't have to answer. Alder was too fucking young, living a crazy life on the road, and rarely this impulsive. Jesse liked the kid too much to risk hurting him, but maybe he didn't have to stop. Not yet.

"Jesse…"

"Jesse?" Danica chuckled when he looked up at her and blinked. "So you were making out on the side of the road? That's it?"

"Yeah…pretty much." Was that all he'd told her? At some point, he'd stopped recounting the whole encounter and started reliving it in his head. He had a feeling he'd stopped talking somewhere around Alder's shirt coming off. "My phone started going off in my pocket and Cole flipping out ruined the mood. We sobered up real quick and that was it."

She nodded slowly, not looking convinced. "All right, well no reason at all for me to feel threatened then. You don't know if you could get Alder off if you tried. You never have."

Jesse arched a brow at her. "Should I have fucked him in the dirt? He would've let me, but even stoned, I had—and *have*—too much respect for him."

"And your friendship was too important for you to ever go there again."

"Exactly."

"And now?"

He tightened his grip on the steering wheel, his lips curving slightly. "He happens to have a very sweet girlfriend. Lucky for her, I'm not looking to steal him away."

She sighed, as if that hadn't been at all what she'd wanted to hear.

Have I mentioned lately that I don't get chicks?

Thrumming her fingers on his shoulder, she caught his eye in the reflection of the black windshield. "Maybe I shouldn't have asked for more details about you and Alder."

"Yeah?"

"Maybe I should have just asked you to show me." Danica giggled when he playfully cuffed her arm with the back of his hand. "G'night, Jesse."

"G'night, Danica."

He heard her pad back to the bunks, hopefully to finally get some sleep. The girl needed to get used to the bus if she was going to be doing this for a month.

Not that he minded the company.

The conversation though…he wasn't sure what to make of that. She was lucky he was with Brave. If not?

Show you? Sweetie, you have no idea what you're asking for.

One day, she might find out.

Chapter Fourteen

After they'd been on the bus for at least a year—all right, just a week, but Danica felt like it had been *much* longer—Danica found herself falling into a comfortable new routine. Most of which consisted of reading, then moving around the bus, then reading some more. She hadn't had this much time to read in her entire life, and she'd already finished a few books. One from each of the authors she'd met.

All of which she loved, but left her in a very uncomfortable position on a bus surrounded by men she couldn't help compare to the heroes in the books. Watching Connor lift weights outside the bus, his muscles swelling with each rep as sweat dripping down his bare chest got her staring, appreciating how an athlete could be perfect eye candy.

Then, when Alder joined him and Connor helped him adjust his position, one hand on his hip as he reached around Alder's body to show him just how far to lower the weight as he bents down…damn it, she was tempted to take some time to herself in her bunk.

Malakai had the protective, nurturing qualities down pat. At a signing in Arizona, he'd stuck close to her and Tate while Alder and Brave were dragged off to have lunch with a few locals that had won a contest. The bassist spent the whole signing pacing between them like a bear watching over his cubs. His hard stare had the more enthusiastic fans behaving themselves, which helped both her and Tate relax. Tate had no trouble flirting with his band mates, and he was fine with his older female fans, but his teenage admirers seemed to make him nervous.

He didn't have to deal with them for long with Malakai hovering and the new security guards watching over the guys. Two had gone with Alder and Brave, but the one that stuck with the remainder of the band strictly enforced the 'hands-off' rule.

Tate himself didn't get her all hot and bothered, though his teasing could make her blush. She still had the urge to hug him whenever he looked upset or uncomfortable. He'd taught her to play a few of his favorite video games and she loved how riled up he got when she started beating him. He pretended to be a sore loser, but he'd goaded the other guys to play against her and bet on her every time.

He used the money to fan himself once in awhile. Which got shoes, pizza crusts, and the odd dirty sock tossed at his head. She definitely never got bored with him around.

Out of all the guys, Brave was the only one she still wasn't sure about. She could kind of see him as one of the arrogant, billionaire heroes that were trendy right now, but even the worst of those had moments when they were approachable.

Of course, she knew very well that was partially her fault. The first few days, she'd been standoffish with him. Which was stupid. She'd had to play nice with both male and female models who were despicable people. Whether she liked it or not, she had to develop a working relationship with Brave.

Thankfully, she hadn't been needed onstage for the small shows they'd done in Flagstaff and Tucson. The band's next big show would be in Dallas.

Cole had shown up this morning with the *great* news that he'd rented rehearsal space for them in Albuquerque, where they'd be stopping for the night. He was still in his own car, so at least he wouldn't be staying on the bus with them. She couldn't relax with him around.

And she wasn't the only one.

He'd gone into town with Jesse and Tate to do a grocery run—which all the guys seemed to think was weird, but no one objected. Alder and Malakai were working on some new solos, and Connor had gone hiking in the desert, so she took advantage of the privacy and gave her grandfather a call.

She'd called him every morning since their first day on the road. Which was different, since he wasn't fond of chatting on the phone, but once she'd told him she was touring with a band, he'd insisted.

He answered on the first ring. "How's my beautiful girl?"

Danica smiled and leaned against the wall at the head of her bunk. "Good. Doing my best to keep busy, but it's nice not to be rushing around from one photo shoot to the next."

"I bet." He laughed. "You always seemed happier when you were doing that TV show. More time to make friends, scripts to read, and constant change of pace."

She snorted. "You hated that show. You said they had our culture all wrong."

"They certainly did, but I let you do it and ignored all my 'friends' who spoke badly of you. I knew my girl was making something of herself." His voice warmed with pride. Then he paused. "I can't say performing with a bunch of screaming, dirty rock stars is what I had in mind, but Sophie assured me they're treating you well."

"They're not dirty rock stars, Grandpa." She shook her head, grinning at the image he'd probably painted of Winter's Wrath in his head. "Have you listened to any of their music?"

"Don't ask me to do that, *ikwesens*." He cleared his throat. "Your language teacher told me it's not horrible."

Sitting forward, Danica's eyes widened. "You've seen Ms. Nitsch?"

"Yes. She's a nice lady. She convinced me to go to the sweat lodge when I told her I was worried about you." He made a soft '*humph*' sound. "Pushy woman. She's trying to get me to be more active in the community. It hasn't been horrible."

Cheeks sore from smiling so wide, Danica tried to contain her enthusiasm. Grandpa hated when she made a big deal about him socializing. Since she'd gone off on her own, he'd been content with only Ninja as company, rarely leaving the house unless he needed something.

As much as she loved their cat, the feline could only do so much.

She'd have to bring Ms. Nitsch a gift for taking care of her Grandpa while she was gone.

"Are you less worried?"

"A little. I would like to meet this boy you seem so fond of, but I know he must be a good man if he's caught your interest." His voice was calm, as though he truly believed what he was saying. "You've been alone for too long. I'll decide if he's good enough for you, but he can entertain you for now."

She rolled her eyes. "He's not 'entertaining me', Grandpa."

Grandpa chuckled. "Then what use is he?"

"Grandpa!"

"I love you, my girl. And I hope you're happy, whatever you're doing," he said, quietly. "Don't worry about calling me every day anymore. I've been going to Ms. Nitsch's classes, talking to her students about my childhood. She thinks they can learn from me—I'm not sure why. Those times weren't good."

Her throat tightened. "I know. But I don't mind calling you. This is the longest we've talked in a few days."

"Because we are both busy. But that's good. Let a few days pass and we'll have plenty to tell one another." He sounded distracted. "This time, I have to be the one to let you go. But I need to know that you're really doing well. You're eating properly? Sleeping?"

Eating, yes. Sleeping? She was working on that. "I'm fine, Grandpa. And you?"

"Yes. Mary wouldn't have it any other way. I love you."

"I love you too."

She hung up the phone, wondering what exactly was going on between her grandfather and her teacher. Mary Nitsch was almost Grandpa's age, so they were a good match, but he'd been uncomfortable with her at first because he had a jaded view of education in general.

Not that she could blame him, but if he ever gave love a chance again, Ms. Nitsch would be very good for him. She was active within the tribe and one of the strongest people Danica knew. She'd known Danica's mother and had told her stories about when her mother was younger.

And she was one of the few people, besides Grandpa, who hadn't resented Danica's ambitions. At times, within the tribe, there was a rift between traditional and modern life. Danica had been raised very modern, coming back to her roots more as an adult. She did what she could, but in following her own path, she'd gone against what many in the tribe believed in.

They still welcomed her when she returned for ceremonies, but she couldn't completely ignore the underlying resentment. Or blame anyone for it.

Too many hadn't been given her opportunities. And her presence was a reminder of what they'd never have.

Which was part of the reason why she returned less and less.

Taking a deep breath, she shook off the melancholy trying to take hold and pushed out of her bunk. She heard singing and hesitated. The only one still on the bus was Brave, since Alder and Malakai had gone outside with their notepad. She didn't want to bug him, but his voice was alluring, making it impossible to walk away.

Silently, she moved closer to the curtain that separated the back lounge from the sleeping area. She brushed aside the curtain, holding her breath as she spotted Brave, his back to her, singing as though the words flowed out from his very soul.

The song was familiar, but she'd never heard it sung like this before. *Come as you are*, by Nirvana. He wasn't even singing in the rough, wild style of Winter's Wrath. Every note was deep and clear, beginning with a quiet tone that hinted at so much more passion, until his voice reached a crescendo, leaving no doubt as to the pain and anguish pouring out.

As he hit the final chorus, he brought his hand to his hair, the chord ringing out in a way that brought tears to her eyes. A man could break down in tears and show less emotion than

Brave did when he was singing. His talents were unmatched, but it was all the darkness within that truly made him stand apart from the rest.

She wanted to tell him how amazing he was. Fuck, she wanted to hug him. To figure out a way to forget how hateful he could be and find the source of that pain.

The sound of clapping came from behind her, cutting through the moment of silence.

"That was incredible, Brave." Cole stepped around her. "I wouldn't normally recommend you doing covers on stage, but some bands have success with them. We could record it in Detroit, get it up on Youtube in a few weeks. Draw in some new fans."

"No." Brave glanced over at her, inclining his head in a way that made her feel like he'd known she was there and hadn't minded her listening. Then his expression hardened as he turned to Cole. "I wrote a song for the new album. We can record that if you want and release it as a single."

"Fine, but I still think—"

"I'm starting to think my brother's right." Brave pulled a black elastic off his wrist and flipped his hair into a messy bun, looking more put together with that simple updo than Danica could ever manage. "You've lost touch with your position as our manager. You're good at what you do, but know your limits."

Cole's eyes narrowed. "Can you excuse us, Danica?"

Before she could answer, Brave shook his head. "She's fine where she is. This conversation is over, Cole."

"It's not over! I am completely devoted to this band and you know it. Do you have any ideas how many offers I've gotten?" Cole shook his head. "You know what, it doesn't matter. I wanted to discuss LOST."

Brave went white. He fisted his hands at his sides. "LOST has been disbanded for almost four years."

"Exactly. The anniversary of your brother's death would be the perfect time to release a song in his memory. It will appeal to fans of LOST and we may be able to use some of your old material." Cole sounded excited. "Think about it. Winter's Wrath, recording the songs Valor wrote."

At first, Danica was sure Brave was going to punch the manager. Then, she wasn't sure he would be satisfied with anything that left the man breathing. Maybe she should go find Alder or Jesse. The murderous rage in Brave's eyes might be more than either of them could handle.

An icy cold smile sliced across Brave's lips. "Mention LOST, or Valor, to me again and I will fire you, Cole. This is your *last* warning."

"Got it." Cole stormed out.

Before Danica could do the smart thing and follow him, Brave was at her side, blocking the curtained doorway with his arm. "For someone who doesn't like me very much, you sure do spend a lot of time watching me."

"I never said I didn't like you."

"You didn't have to." He moved a little closer, dropping his tone in a way that made her shiver. But not in a good way. "Was there something you wanted?"

She shook her head. One thing she *had* learned about Brave, which became even clearer with his abrupt shift in demeanor, was he could be the biggest asshole when anything set him off. Most of the time, he just got quiet, but then there were moments like this when he was downright scary.

He let out a bitter laugh. "Then get the fuck out of here."

As soon as he moved his arm, she bolted. Running away from him chaffed her pride, but confronting him would accomplish nothing. He hadn't really *done* anything, he just rubbed her the wrong way when he was in this mood. As though he could shut off any emotion and stop giving a fuck.

How do you even talk to someone like that?

The sun shone brightly outside the bus, practically baking anything it touched, but the chill lingered.

Until Alder stepped out from under the frame tent the roadies had set up. He walked right up to her and took her in his arms. "Hey, angel. Are you all right?"

"Yeah, I'm just tired of being inside." She smiled up at him.

He frowned, clearly not buying it. "You might be a great actress, but you're a horrible liar."

"Fine. Can we not talk about it though?"

"If you answer one question." He rubbed her arms, watching her face as she nodded. "Who upset you? Cole or Brave?"

She cupped his face in her hands. "Either way, I need to handle my own issues with the guys. *All* of them."

"Understood, but you can still tell me. I swear, I won't go breaking anyone."

A few feet away, still lounging in one of the camp chairs set up under the tent, Malakai chuckled. "You might want to lead off with something better than a promise not to break anyone, pal. I wouldn't tell you shit either."

"Thanks, Malakai," Alder said, dryly. "That's very helpful."

"Maybe not to *you*, but anything that will get you to drop the subject." Malakai's tone became serious. "She doesn't want to come whining to you every time someone hurts her feelings. I can respect that. You should too."

Alder's eyes widened. "I do."

Damn it, he was trying so hard, she couldn't help but kiss him and laugh. "I love you guys. And no worries, I know I can talk to you. But Malakai's right. So let's talk about something else."

Taking her hand, Alder drew her back to the green camp chair he'd abandoned, plopping down, then lifting her up to sit on his lap.

One of her very favorite places to sit. She snuggled up to him, resting her head on his chest.

"Any particular topic?" He asked, idly stroking her hair.

She lifted her shoulders and smiled. "Tell me what you guys were working on."

"Well, we've pretty much got the solos for three of our news songs perfected, along with a new melody we think will sound great with the right lyrics." She could hear the satisfaction in his voice, as though he felt he'd accomplished something great. He grinned when Malakai nodded and lifted his beer like he was cheering their efforts. "Once we finished that, we were just messing around. Playing old songs."

Glancing over, she saw his guitar case. Which was closed. Malakai's guitar was propped up against the side of his chair. "You play another instrument?"

"Ah...no."

"Then...?"

Malakai snorted. "You two are so fucking adorable, it makes me sick. Alder, she's impressed with you already. You can tell by the way she looks at you. She's not going to dump you when she finds out you're a mediocre singer."

Alder's face reddened.

Danica shot Malakai a dirty look. "And here I was, thinking you were the sweet one of the group."

Hands up in the air, Malakai shook his head. "His words, not mine. I think he should sing more than the odd background verse, but he's decided if he doesn't sound like Brave, he's not good enough."

"We've actually never had that conversation." Alder picked up a beer cap from the cup holder and chucked it at the bassist. "I said I'd rather play guitar when it was brought up. That was it."

Tipping her head back, Danica gazed up at Alder. "So you have no problem singing for me?"

He pressed the tip of his tongue into his bottom lip and took a deep breath. "No, I don't mind."

Malakai sat up. "Well fuck, I think the man's in love with you, Danica."

Her lips parted. "Why?"

"Because he usually only sings when me and him are alone. Not sure if I should be jealous." Malakai winked at her. "Lucky for you, I'm willing to share."

She stared at him, her cheeks heating. Her plans so far leaned more toward getting Jesse and Alder closer, but she couldn't forget how much chemistry her man had with Malakai on stage.

This could get very very complicated.

"The look on your face." Malakai snorted. "If you two ever want a threesome, let me know. But you have to promise not to get attached. Which is the only reason I haven't tried to get into Alder's pants before. Maybe, now that he's got you, he won't expect commitment from anyone else."

Holy shit, does everyone want a piece of my man? Danica wrinkled her nose, deciding, right there and then, that Malakai was the *last* person she'd ever consider letting into her and Alder's bed.

"I can't make that promise, Malakai." She stroked her hand down Alder's chest as she noticed him glaring at the other man. "I'm big on commitment too. If you want to join us, you'll have to give up any other guy *or* girl that catches your interest." She batted her eyelashes at him. "Actually, I think the van's empty if you want to—"

"*Fuck* no." Malakai actually scooted his chair back, holding his guitar in front of him like a shield. "I'm allergic to relationships. You two can keep those particular shackles to yourself."

A soft laugh had them all looking over to the side of the tent, where Jesse had come up at some point and stood leaning against the tent frame, arms folded over his chest. "I'm not sure why Sophie was worried about you being able to handle yourself with the band. Everyone always considers Brave the dangerous one, since Malakai's such a sweet, caring guy, you wouldn't expect him to be just as much of a player."

"The only player lately." Malakai pointed out, retrieving his beer and grinning at Jesse. "You've ruined Brave. Congratulations."

Jesse arched a brow. "Thanks?"

"I mean it. He always snagged the hottest piece of ass. Now my only competition is Connor."

"And Tate?" Danica nodded her thanks when Jesse grabbed a couple of beers from the cooler and handed her one. She hadn't had a drink in a few days, so she could indulge a little.

Alder shook his head, idly toying with a strand of her hair. "Tate goes for more experienced women. The type that can teach him a thing or two. The other guys take their pick of groupies."

"Not always groupies. We've had our fair share of models and actresses." Malakai grinned at Danica. "Those girls are fun to unwrap. They look so perfect until you get them in the bedroom. Or the closest bathroom stall. Then they're the dirtiest—"

Jesse cuffed Malakai upside the head. "Enough beer for you. You're acting like a fucking pig. I think Danica gets the point. You're not her type."

Malakai smirked. "Glad that's cleared up." He stood and handed Jesse his guitar. "She wants to hear Alder sing. You play for the lovesick puppies. I'm gonna go make sure Connor isn't sharing his medical grade with our little drummer boy. Last I heard, Tate was offering to suck his dick for a few puffs. A few days without any and Connor might go for it."

"If he did, don't kill him!" Alder called out as Malakai ambled off toward the other buses.

Waving dismissively, Malakai shouted back, "I make no promises!"

These guys were too much. Danica slid off Alder's lap, snagging another chair so she could face both him and Jesse. She was even more eager to hear them together than she had been when Malakai had been sitting where Jesse was now. She had a feeling Malakai had spotted Jesse before any of them. Which meant all his talk had been to get Jesse to take his place.

Strumming the guitar, as though re-familiarizing himself with the instrument, Jesse ran his tongue over his bottom lip. "I don't think I've ever heard you sing, Alder."

"Yeah, I only do it around Malakai. Not for any special reason." Alder curved a hand around the back of his neck, digging his fingers into the muscles. "Helps when we're putting all the pieces of the songs together."

"Does Brave know?"

"No. Everyone leaves us alone when we're composing." Alder rolled his shoulders. "Look, don't make a big deal about this. Brave wants three songs ready to start recording in Detroit. Otherwise, we wouldn't have been doing this out in the open."

Jesse inclined his head. "So he's gotten more lyrics written?"

"Nope. Just the one song. But it's ready."

"Cool." Jesse glanced over at Danica, an apologetic smile on his lips. "I'd play that for you—give you an exclusive preview of the next album, but I'm a little rusty. Mind hearing something I've played before so I don't completely embarrass myself?"

She reached out and patted his knee, giving him a crooked grin. "The two hottest guys on this tour are about to perform for me. I'll take whatever you give me."

Crimson spread over the tops of Jesse's cheeks. "That sounded suggestive as hell."

Alder looked from Jesse to her, his brow furrowed. "What?"

"Nothing, hot stuff." Danica took Alder's hand, lacing their fingers together. One of the things she loved about the man was how clueless he was about his own appeal. "Just the usual. Everyone wants you."

He snorted, casting an amused look at Jesse, as though he expect his best friend to laugh as well. When Jesse didn't, he cleared his throat. "All right, how about music? Do you know '*A Tous Le Monde*'?"

"Megadeth? Fuck, of course I know it." Jesse played a few unfamiliar notes on the guitar. Apparently the right ones, because Alder nodded. "Let's do this, 'hot stuff.'"

Both men were blushing a little, and Danica wanted to pat herself on the back. Fine, this didn't mean anything serious, but they were closer than she'd ever seen them. What happened later today, or tomorrow, didn't matter. Brave couldn't use Jesse to lash out at Alder, while carelessly trampling on Jesse's feelings, if he wasn't coming between them.

But you're *between them.*

Only, she didn't think she was. Not that she had the first idea how things would work out if Brave cut the act and moved on, but she believed in what she had with Alder. His connection with Jesse could be…well, like what their friendship was. Only, a bit more physical.

Or nothing of all might come of it. Jesse had chosen Brave when Alder was available. They might be friends and that's it. Either way, she wanted Alder to have the choice.

The idea shouldn't make so much sense to her, but it did. She couldn't stand by and watch Alder fool around with all kinds of fangirls, but by all accounts, he didn't do flings. Whatever happened between him and Jesse would mean something.

As Jesse played the guitar, and Alder began to sing, the beauty of the music tightened her throat. They were both too damn modest. Jesse had a natural talent and his fingers moved over the strings as if he'd been born to hold that guitar in his hands.

But even that didn't compare to the sound of Alder's voice. He didn't have the immeasurable power Brave possessed, but his tone was deep and soulful, drawing emotion into every word, the raw expression of longing he brought out making goose bumps rise all over her flesh.

Listening to them was an experience she wouldn't have missed for the world, but she had to face one very obvious fact she'd missed while plotting out all her ideal plans for them. Her eyes teared as she forced herself to accept the one thing she hadn't considered.

They didn't need her for the music. She was only here on the sidelines as they created it, together.

They might not need her if they finally passed all the obstacles standing in their way.

Would she be willing to step aside, so she didn't end up being yet another one for them to deal with?

She wiped under her eye, grateful both were too into the song to see her struggling with thoughts that hadn't even occurred to them yet. In such a short time, she'd come to care about them both so much.

If she did nothing, there was no risk of losing Alder, right? Maybe Brave would smarten up and be the man Jesse deserved. Maybe he'd been lying about getting with Jesse because he knew his brother loved the man.

And maybe she'd get that unicorn she'd begged Santa for from the time she was three until she stopped believing at him at eight.

She loved Alder.

Her own admission surprised her, even though she'd suspected as much. The knowledge made her heart swell, and her chest ache, all at once.

I love him.

Which meant absolutely nothing if she was too selfish to let him go.

Chapter Fifteen

Alder combed his hair straight, eying Danica through the mirror in the changing room, wishing he could figure out why she'd been so quiet lately. For the past few days, actually. Not that anyone else noticed. She still smiled and laughed with the guys. Teased Jesse and avoided Brave.

But Alder saw something different in her eyes. A hardened set to her jaw. As if she was very determined. For what, he had no idea.

The shadows under her eyes had faded, so at least she was sleeping better. He'd finally gotten her to admit she missed sleeping with him. They'd even made love in his bunk—very quietly—and for a while after, she'd seemed happier.

That hadn't lasted for long. He needed to find out what had happened to make her so sad.

Looking back, he tried to place the exact moment things had changed. All he came up with was when she'd been on the bus alone with Brave and Cole that one day, but she'd insisted she was all right.

What else could it be?

"Are you ready?" Danica asked, crossing the dressing room to stand behind him. Her hair was still wet from her shower. She'd be getting her hair and makeup done with the stylist while the band did sound check.

Alder turned and picked her up, spinning around to sit her by the sink. "Not quite. I need to ask you something."

Her bottom lip quivered. She bit it hard, then inclined her head. "Okay."

"But first, you're going to tell me something. Are you leaving me?"

Her eyes went wide. "What?"

"You're upset. You're not telling me why, so I have to guess." He bowed his head, curving his hands over the top of her bare knees. She was wearing a little, pale blue terrycloth robe, and her skin was still damp from her shower. His dick took notice of all that bare flesh, so easily accessible, but he made himself focus on getting the right words out. "You've still got over two weeks on your contract with the band, but Sophie has been looking for other opportunities, right?"

"Yes, but I haven't agreed to anything."

"So she's found you another job?" He fought not to sound disappointed. Their relationship wouldn't last if she felt bad every time she had to take off. Sure, the first time would be tough, but if what they had was as strong as he believed, the distance wouldn't matter. What counted was when they were together. "Danica, I want you to take it. Your career means so much to you, which makes it important to me too. If you have to do a runway in Milan, or go back to LA for a casting call, or…hell, even up to the cold North for whatever they do up there…"

"I've done runways in Montreal." She released a small, breathless laugh, staring at his hands. "Actually, I do have one booked in a couple months."

"Then bring a coat."

"I always do when I'm up there in the middle of winter." She cocked her head. "I'm happy you're cool with me having to leave for work."

"Good."

"But I won't be for awhile. Cole's trying to extend my contract. I'll be doing a few music videos with the band *and* an album cover."

"That's awesome!" All right, so she wasn't upset about having to leave. Which meant he didn't have the first clue what was wrong. Unless… "Fuck, I'm an idiot. Is it that time of— *Ow!*"

Damn, the girl is stronger than she looks. He rubbed the center of his chest. Coming away with blood.

She covered her mouth with her hand. "Oh my god, I'm so sorry! Sophie sent me a ring for my birthday and I forgot to take it off!"

He glanced down at the trail of blood and chuckled. "Remind me not to ask about your period ever again."

"You jerk. You shouldn't ask—not like *that* anyway." She rolled her eyes as she grabbed a towel off the edge of the sink and pressed it to his chest. "I'm not on my period. If I was, you'd be in a lot more pain."

"I believe you."

She peeked under the towel. "This is deep. Do you know if there's a doctor here?"

"It's a little cut. Give it a few minutes, I'll be fine." He took the towel from her, holding it to his chest himself. One of the guys probably had glue or tape. Good news was, Cole probably wouldn't make him strip on stage. "Happy birthday, by the way. I wish I'd known."

"It's not until Saturday. Sophie sent the gift early because she's heading to Paris tomorrow and she'll be really busy. We did a video chat while I opened the present." Danica smiled at the beautiful ring, which had two delicate wings in white gold framing her yellow birthstone. "She wanted to see my reaction."

"Do you have any intention of telling me what's actually up with you?"

She bit the tip of her tongue, her brow creasing as though she was thinking hard. "All right, if you must know, it's Brave."

I fucking knew it. Me and my big brother are gonna have a fucking talk.

"Stop scowling, he didn't do anything." She dropped her gaze to the towel. "Cole brought up Valor. Brave didn't react well. He got all cold and asked me to leave. I know there's nothing I can do for him, but I see how divided the band is and I hate it. He pushes everyone away and it's not right, because you all let him."

All right, now he felt like an asshole.

Except, he knew his brother a bit better than she did.

"The only thing I can do is make sure Cole backs off. Do you know how the subject came up?"

She nodded. "Cole wants him to write a tribute song. And he wants the band to cover some of LOST"s music."

Alder cringed. "That would do it. Brave will get even more pissed off if I mention anything to him, but if he had it out with Cole, one of two things will happen. Cole will come to me—in which case, I'll make it clear the topic is closed—or he'll wait a little while and ask Brave a different way."

"I think heading him off would be a good idea."

"Consider it done." He smoothed her hair away from her face. "You know, I've always been so excited to climb up on stage, to give in to the music and enjoy every fucking second of worship from the fans for what we've created. But then I met you and what I feel with them screaming my name is nothing compared to when I hear it from your lips, even in a whisper."

She gave him a hooded look, drawing him close and whispering in his ear. "Alder."

He shuddered, cupping the back of her head and setting his teeth lightly into her throat.

"You're horrible." She moaned, shoving against his chest, gasping when the towel shifted and fresh blood soaked into the white fabric. She placed her hands on her red cheeks. "I'm all turned on and you have to go. Get that taken care of. And I have to get ready."

"I'm sorry." But only a little. He'd willingly go on stage with a hardon, knowing she was as eager as he was to ditch the crowd after the show and find somewhere private. Unless… "How long do you really need with the stylist? I think you look perfect already."

"You think?" She glanced down at the robe. "I guess I can dance like this. The crowd certainly won't mind."

Yeah, the band probably won't mind either. One wrong move and she'd be flashing them all.

"Not happening." He latched onto one lapel of the robe and tugged it over the swell of her breasts. "I'm not crazy about you walking around backstage like this either. I get that you trust us, but there's other bands and they—"

"My stylist is down the hall. And Jesse has one of your security guys trailing me."

"We hardly know them!"

"He's Skull's brother, Alder." Danica shook her head. "I'll be fine. You're the one *still* bleeding."

"Let me walk you to the other dressing room. Then I'll get this taken care of."

"No. You're heading in the other direction."

"It'll take me a minute to get you there."

"Damn it, Alder!" She sighed, then hopped off the counter. "Fine, but since you're not in a hurry, tell me what you were gonna ask when I came in."

Damn, he'd completely forgotten about that. He scratched his jaw, studying her face, not sure now was the right time to bring up the subject. It was a big step. One she might not be ready for.

He got the door for her, carefully considering his next words. The security guard fell into step behind them silently.

"You've got that look again. Stop second guessing yourself with me." She walked backwards down the hall, frowning at him. "What is it?"

He inhaled roughly and met her eyes. "I want you to live with me."

She stumbled and he reached out to grab her wrist, dropping the towel. Warmth trailed down the center of his chest.

Danica paled. "Oh, Alder. That looks bad. Please go get it fixed?"

"I will, but—"

"Jesse!" Danica grabbed the towel, her gaze going passed him as she pressed it to his chest. "Will you talk to him please?"

Quick footsteps came up to his side. Jesse cursed as he took the towel from Danica and checked the stupid cut on his chest. "What the fuck, Alder?"

"It's nothing." Alder tried to pull away from him, but Jesse took a firm hold on his arm. "Danica, that came out wrong. I don't mean permanently. Unless you want—"

"Danica?" A short, plump woman came out of a room at the other end of the hall. "You're late!"

"I have to go." Danica gave him a quick kiss on the cheek. There was a flash of pain in her eyes as she turned to Jesse. "Take care of him?"

"I will." Jesse tugged him in the other direction. He glanced over at the security guard. "Stay with her. I've got him."

With a curt nod, the man in the yellow shirt hurried after Danica.

There was a walky-talky stuck to Jesse's belt, which he only used when they played big arenas. It went off and Jesse snatched it up.

"Yeah, I've got him, but I'm bringing him to the greenroom. Have the EMT meet us. He got a nasty cut on his chest." He held the walky-talky to his ear, rolling his eyes. "No, I have no fucking clue how it happened. I'll get him there as soon as I can."

Shit, it's just a little fucking cut. Alder jerked away from Jesse, grinding his teeth. "Dude, chill out."

"Chill out? There's fucking dried blood on that towel. How long have you been bleeding?"

"Maybe fifteen minutes?"

"And it hasn't stopped? Fuck this, I'm bringing you to the hospital."

Like hell you are. "If there's an EMT here, they can tape it or something. It's not that bad."

"I could fucking strangle you, do you know that?" Jesse kept the pressure on Alder's chest, putting his other hand on the small of Alder's back as he quickened his pace. "You gonna tell me if me or Danica were bleeding like this, you'd say 'It's not that bad'?"

A strange jolt of emotion hit Alder right in the center of his chest at the mention of either of them getting hurt. No, he wouldn't be all cool. He wouldn't care about the concert, or anything but making sure they were okay.

If he had no choice, he'd have trusted Jesse with Danica.

Which was a little weird. Yeah, the man was his best friend, but Danica owned his fucking heart. He loved the woman.

You love Jesse too.

Not the same.

You sure about that?

He stopped in his tracks as it hit him. What if Danica thought his relationship with Jesse went beyond friendship? He'd admitted to her that he'd loved Jesse once. Saying that was in the past might not be enough. Jesse and Brave's relationship didn't seem all that stable. Jesse clearly wasn't happy.

"Come on, Alder. Don't tell me you're afraid of the EMT." Jesse met his eyes. And took a step back at whatever he saw there. "Shit man, what's going on?"

"It's you. That's why Danica's been so quiet and sad lately." Alder groaned and rubbed a hand over his face. "She thinks she'll lose me to you."

"Well, she's wrong. I'm with your brother." Jesse nudged Alder toward the greenroom. "Make that clear to her and she won't need to worry."

"I thought I had." Alder's shoulder dropped as he let Jesse shove him toward the table in the center of the room, where an old, bald guy was sitting with some kind of forms laid out before him and a huge first aid kit by his elbow.

He sat down, half listening to the old man as he explained that Alder had to sign a waiver to get the cut taken care of. He glanced over the forms and signed at the bottom of each page.

Then he leaned back while the EMT tossed the towel aside and began cleaning the cut. He winced at the sting, but his mind was racing and he really needed to figure out how he'd fucked up so badly.

"Alder, listen to me." Jesse put his hand on Alder's shoulder. "That girl is in love with you. And I think you love her too."

"I do." Alder pressed his eyes shut. "But I've done a shitty job proving that if she thinks I want someone else."

Jesse sat back and his lips thinned. "You didn't do anything wrong. This is all on me."

"You? How is any of this on you?"

"She's noticed things aren't great with me and Brave. And she's asked about me and you." Jesse dropped his hand to his knees, staring at the floor as he tightened his grip. "I told her stuff."

"*Stuff?*" Alder held still as the EMT began placing butterfly stitches along the cut. He tried to figure out what the hell Jesse could have said to make Danica question their relationship. "What stuff?"

"Nothing much. Just about us making out that once." Jesse's lips twitched up slightly. "We were joking around. I figured it was no big deal."

"Our friendship means everything to me. And maybe that could have lead to more, but I was too fucking scared to risk it."

That was what Jesse had said to Danica.

Alder had fallen asleep and pretty much forgotten the whole thing, because he'd figured it was no big deal too.

Jesse had never acted like he wanted more. Their friendship was enough.

Apparently, Danica didn't agree.

"Tell the guys I'll be there in a bit." This wasn't right. Of all the things to go wrong in their relationship, lack of communication was *not* going to be one of them. "I'm going to work this out."

As he stood, Jesse pressed down on his shoulder. "You're already running late. Work it out after the show."

He stayed put as the doctor put a dressing over the cut. "Don't you think she's been upset long enough?"

"I think she's going to be fucking pissed if a misunderstanding affects either of your jobs."

Very true.

He waited to be dismissed by the doctor, then headed for backstage, doing up his sleeveless black dress shirt on the way to save time.

Only to find Brave wasn't even there yet.

"He's on his way." Malakai said in response to his questioning glance, while tuning his guitar. "Cole brought in a journalist to do an exclusive with Brave. He suggested the rest of us get started without him."

"Sounds good." *Sounds like I could have taken a minute to clear things up with Danica.*

Malakai jerked his chin at Alder, his eyes on Alder's chest. "You good?"

"Yeah. Just paid for opening my stupid mouth." He clenched his teeth as Jesse handed him his guitar. He wasn't thrilled with how Jesse had handled the situation either. "About several things."

Cocking his head, Malakai nodded slowly. Then abruptly smiled. "I think you're forgiven."

Danica sprinted onto the stage, stopping short in front of him and catching her breath. He handed his guitar back to Jesse and pulled her in his arms.

She flattened her hands against his shoulders to keep herself away from his chest. "Careful."

"I will be." He tucked a strand of hair behind her ear. "That was quick?"

She licked her dark red stained lips and nodded. "I asked her to hurry. She was nice about it—I told her I needed to talk to you before the show or I'd be worried and mess up the dance or something."

"Is it about me asking you to live with me? I only meant—"

"Yes." Danica giggled, tugging his hair when he dropped his gaze. She pressed her forehead to his. "I mean yes, I'll stay with you. I know you're not asking for forever. Just while we're in Detroit for now, right?"

"Yeah." He inhaled, his chest expanding with relief. "I'm serious about us, Danica. I need you to understand. Nothing— no *one*—will change that. You're the only one I want."

She pressed her lips together. "That's something we can discuss some other time. Tonight we put on a great show, we enjoy the after party, and then I'm stealing you for the rest of the night. After the conversation with Malakai, I'm thinking the van could be useful."

A discordant tone rang out. Malakai straightened. "Did I hear my name?"

"Yes." Danica shot him a crooked grin. "We're plotting to seduce you."

The bassist rubbed a hand over his close shaved head. "Very funny. I'm gonna start calling you *Trouble*. And have a word with Alder about keeping you in line." He gave Alder a hard look, but his eyes were shining with mirth. "After I make several girls at the after party extremely happy. Maybe a few guys too. And toast my fucking freedom."

"Cheers to that!" Connor called out as one of the roadies hooked up his guitar. "Can we get the sappy off the stage already? It's killing my mojo."

Tate hit his drum with a *Ba Bum Bang Ching!* "Ignore him, Danica. He's just jealous. I think you're both adorable."

Connor snorted. "Great. You broke him."

Danica blushed and ducked her head. She ran her hand carefully down the side of Alder's chest, avoiding the patched up cut under his shirt. "I'm on a roll with that tonight. You sure you're all right?"

Alder nodded, taking her head between his hands to kiss her artfully tussled hair. "Golden. You gonna stay and watch us?"

"Nope. I'm going to head to the greenroom and relax for a bit. This is your thing." She skipped out of reach. "I just needed to know things were good between us."

"I promise, I'd tell you if they weren't."

"Same here."

As soon as Danica was out of sight, one of the roadies led the VIP ticket holders into the arena. Their excited chatter drew Alder's attention, and he left his guitar with Jesse so the man could tune it and set up the audio signals with the front of house engineer.

Pandering to the fans before shows was usually Brave's job, but when the lead singer ran late, the task fell on the rest of them. Starting with Alder.

He didn't mind small groups like this though, so he hopped off the stage, nodding and smiling as the fans, about fifty of them ranging in ages from about thirteen to forty-five, called out his name and started asking questions all at once.

"Hey, guys. Thanks for coming down to see us." As he began to speak, they quieted, almost as though they were afraid he'd say something profound and they'd miss it. "You all ready for the show?"

There were some shouts and fist pumps from the young men in the crowd. The rest cheered and clapped. The youngest girls giggled and stared at him.

He avoided the gaze of one of the younger chicks who mouthed 'I love you' to him.

"Before we get started with the private warm-up show, are there any questions?"

A young lady with thick, black-framed glasses, pink hair, and a dozen piercings all over her face, stuck her hand up in the air. Her pale cheeks went red when he nodded to her. "Where's Brave? Not that I don't love you too. I love you and I have your picture, like, everywhere in my apartment, but he's a *god*."

"He's probably getting his dick sucked!" A boy in the back shouted.

"OMG, I would *sooo* suck his dick!" The girl who shouted ducked behind her friends. Who all looked way too young to be making that kind of offer.

But Alder had heard worse, so he simply chuckled. "If we could avoid the topic of my brother's dick, that would be awesome."

The crowd laughed.

"Brave is doing an interview, but he should be out here soon." Alder pulled out his phone to check the time. Brave better hurry up. Bored, restless VIPs would be a shitty way to start the night. But he had an idea on how to entertain them. "For now, how about you all line up on the side of the stage. We'll bring you up, five at a time, and you can take pics with the band and talk to all of us."

The fans *loved* that idea.

The one member of the band's security detail that was present? Not so much. As Alder climbed back on stage, Skull's brother—whose name was probably not Ballz, but that's what everyone called him—approached Alder, his rugged face drawn with aggravation.

"We've got two guys on your brother. This many people on stage with just me watching you? Not smart." Ballz watched the fans line up, all nice and orderly, but didn't seem impressed. "Things could get out of hand."

Thankfully, Jesse came to the rescue. He waved the other roadies over then patted Ballz's shoulder. "I couldn't agree more, but it won't be just you. Take care of the line while my men stick close to the boys."

With a curt nod, Ballz headed to the floor to keep the fans from getting 'out of hand'.

Alder bumped shoulders with Jesse. "Thanks. The 'boys' appreciate it."

"You'd better." Jesse glanced over to the side stage, his brow creasing slightly. "This was a good idea, but if Brave doesn't show up, we're gonna have a problem."

Following Jesse's gaze, Alder nodded. The fans might love the whole band, but that girl had said it best.

Brave was their god.

They wouldn't be satisfied without him. And then Ballz's might have a real reason to worry.

In the greenroom, Danica tried to keep out of the way as the police interviewed Brave and the band's two security guards. She held the mug of coffee she'd poured before everything had gone to hell in her cold hands, chewing on her bottom lip, struggling to hold back nausea as one of the cops bagged the evidence.

Brave hadn't even been able to wash his hands after opening 'the gift'.

And he looked just as sick as she felt.

When she'd come into the room, Brave was posing for pictures for the journalist, a bored expression on his face. He'd given Danica a rare smile, but kept his focus on the tall blond woman who spoke at him endlessly, only pausing to breathe when she shot questions at him.

Extremely personal questions. Some about Valor, which seemed to please Cole, who'd stood behind the cameraman, a smug smile on his lips.

Just when Brave looked ready to cut the interview short, one of the arena's young staff members bolted into the room, holding a black, heart-shaped box with a red ribbon wrapped around it.

He stuttered something unintelligible as he held the box out to Brave.

Brave gave the harried young man an indulgent smile. "Thanks, kid. I love chocolate."

"N-not from m-me." The boy's cheeks went beat-red. "Some guy d-dropped it o-o-off for y-you."

"Well, thanks for bringing it then." Brave turned away from the journalist and undid the ribbon.

The box hit the floor.

"What the fuck!" Brave backed away from it.

Danica put her hand over her mouth as her lips parted. Sitting in the center of the box was a heart.

A real heart.

The boy burst out crying, tripping away from Brave when he tried to grab him. "I-I d-didn't—"

One of the security guards was already on the phone with the police. The other quickly dragged the boy out of the room. Not too roughly at least, but Danica felt so bad for the kid. She didn't believe for a second that he'd known what was in that box. He'd just been doing his job.

And now, the journalist was showing the same sickening glee as Cole while the police finished their report. She was getting a much better story than Brave would have given her.

Ignoring them both, Brave approached the cop who was bagging the card that had been in the box with the heart.

He cleared his throat as the cop looked over at him. "What does it say?"

The cop made a face. "You sure you want to know?"

"Yeah."

"It says 'The day he became immortal is coming. And you will join him. With all my heart, your biggest fan.'"

Brave's pale face took on a green cast. He took off toward the bathroom.

The other cop touched Danica's arm before she could follow him. She gave Danica a card. "If you or Mr. Trousseau think of anything else, please give us a call."

"We will. Thank you." Danica took the card and slid it into the back pocket of her uber-short, cut-off jean shorts. "Do you think he's in danger?"

"Between this and prior incidents, I would advise he take every possible precaution. I don't want to speculate, but he seems to have a very determined stalker." The female cop's lips thinned. "Unfortunately, situations like this tend to escalate."

"But we won't have to cancel the show?" Cole came up beside the cop, looking alarmed for the first time. "With the security in the arena—"

"You should tighten security, but between your men and the police presence, I imagine the suspect will make himself scarce." The cop shot Cole an icy glare. "But I appreciate your concern."

"Concern is all well and good, but as they say, the show must go on," Cole said, with a charming smile for the cop.

Needing to get away from Cole before she ended up slapping him, Danica quickly made her way to the bathroom.

On his knees by a toilet, head against the wall of the stall, Brave looked so fucking vulnerable, she didn't hesitate to walk straight up to him and bend down to give him a hug. She wasn't sure whether he would welcome comfort from her, or if he'd lash out, but she had to let him to know she was here if he needed her.

He wrapped his arms around her waist, releasing a shaky laugh. "I'm fucking pathetic. Wasn't even a human heart. A goddamn cow heart from a butcher or something."

"Which makes it okay?"

"No, but I can't be freaking out. Shit like this happens." He tipped his head back, eyes closed. "Just…why now? No, don't bother answering. I know why now. But it's fucked up, you know?"

"I know." She smoothed the damp hair sticking to his forehead away from his face. "Tell me what you want to do. If you want to cancel the show, you know the band will stand behind you. Fuck what Cole wants."

Brave snorted, shaking his head as he rose to his feet. "Naw, I need to be on stage. Show that fucker he didn't get to me."

"I totally get that. But you do know *no one* is gonna leave you alone for a fucking second, right?" She cupped his cheek in her hand as she looked up at him. "Be careful until this sick freak is caught."

He nodded, dropping his gaze to the thigh high boots covering his snug black jeans. "I'll be careful, but promise me something?"

She had a bad feeling about this. "Okay…?"

"Don't tell anyone. Not before the show. They'll be too distracted and this is one of the biggest crowds we've ever played for. We need to put on the best performance of our careers."

Damn it, he was right. But Alder and Jesse would not be very happy when they learned she'd kept this from them.

Not only that, but were her acting skills up to the task? The bit of coffee she'd drank churned in her stomach every time she remembered that pale heart, sitting in that pretty box.

"Please, Danica? Look, I'll owe you one. I'll even break things off with Jesse." Brave's lips twitched when she gaped at him. "I was gonna do it anyway. I'm aware I've been a complete dick, hanging on to him."

"Yes, you have."

"But, if you think about it, would you and Alder be together if I hadn't hooked up with Jesse? Really, you should thank me."

All right, apparently he was feeling better. She sighed and shook her head. "I'm not thanking you. But I won't say anything to the guys."

"Good."

"*You* are telling them after the show though." She folded her arms over her chest, biting back a smile as Brave rolled his eyes and went to wash his hands. "You want the band to succeed? Start acting like you're in this together."

He snorted. "Next thing you're gonna ask me to be nicer to my brother."

"Is that really unreasonable?"

"No." He shrugged, looking at himself in the mirror as he carefully schooled his features. "I'd say I'd try, but I don't want to lie to you."

She threw her hands up in the air, groaning with frustration. "Damn it, Brave, why is it so fucking hard for you to be close to him? Alder loves you!"

"I know." Brave faced her, a stiff smile on his lips. "But it would be better for him if he didn't."

Jesse tensed as the crowd that had been calm and orderly for almost half an hour suddenly lost their damn minds. Those still waiting in line lost it first. Then the ones on stage caught sight of whatever was causing the commotion and began flocking toward the side stage.

Standing way over on the other end with Alder, he couldn't see what was going on, but it didn't take long to figure out when he spotted one of Brave's security guards forcibly pressing through the throng.

"Back off or everyone will be forced to leave!" Ballz shouted as he tried to block the line that was now a jumbled mass of bodies. "I won't tell you twice!"

"Brave, I love you!" A woman screamed.

Once his guards got him past the fervent mob, and Jesse and his crew helped security herd the fans off the stage, Brave picked up the mic. His gruff laugh filled the arena. "I don't want you all to have to go, since I just got here. You wanna play nice so security won't haul you out?"

The fans cheered and spread out behind the barrier. They still reached out for Brave, but none tried to get closer.

Security took their places on the other side of the barrier and Jesse motioned for the crew to head backstage.

Brave smiled broadly. "Sorry I'm late. Had to do a fucking interview, but since I'm here now, you ready to rock?"

Screams and cheers gave him his answer.

He picked up the mic and sauntered across the stage. "We have this pre-show routine we do to get warmed up that we've never let anyone see before. So no recording. This is just for you." He paused as the fans got noisy again and put up his hand to quiet them. "Each of the guys will start up a song—has to be classic rock. Or at least old shit." He grinned. "The rest of us have to guess what the fuck he's playing and join in. It's a hot mess when we all guess wrong, but it's fun."

"No cheating!" Connor shouted into his own mic. "You all can't give us hints."

"Fuck that!" Brave countered. "Cheat to win, motherfuckers!"

Hollering and holding up devil horns, the fans clearly agreed with Brave. Jesse shook his head as security shifted a bit closer to the barrier like they were expecting trouble. All three of them were good men, retired soldiers Skull had called in when Cole had given the green light to hire protection for the band, but they had no experience with metal fans.

If they were nervous already, he couldn't wait to see how they'd handle the show. They'd done fine at smaller venues, but an arena was a completely different beast.

"You probably all know our drummer, Tate, was fucked up for a bit. He's still sore—poor baby—but he's been splitting shows with his drum tech and taking his meds like a good boy—"

"We love you Tate!" A few girls called out.

"Aww, aren't you sweet?" Brave winked at the girls. "Anyway, he's gonna tough out the whole show tonight, so how about we let him go first?"

As the enthusiastic ruckus died down, Tate began a steady thump on the bass drum. Every other member of the band bowed their head, listening closely. When he tapped his sticks together to the same beat, Jesse was pretty sure he knew the song, but it wasn't until Tate added the symbols that he was sure.

Alder joined in with the guitar part and then it couldn't be more obvious.

Black Betty, by Ram Jam.

Which had come out before most of their audience was born, but they still managed to sing along with Brave as he started his own gritty rendition of the oldie.

Next up was Connor. He didn't challenge anyone when he strummed the first few chords of *When I Come Around,* by Greenday.

The audience shouted out the lyrics before any of the band bothered joining in.

When the last note trailed off, Brave sighed loudly into the mic. "You guys aren't even trying! Malakai, don't disappoint me."

Malakai smirked. The notes he played sounded repetitive. Familiar, but some songs were tough to nail down without the other instruments. When Tate guessed and came in with a beat, Malakai stopped, held up his hand, and shook his head.

Then continued with those same notes.

Damn it, I know this song. Jesse's brow furrowed. He was pretty sure he'd *played* this song before.

But for the life of him, he couldn't figure it out.

"Ah, fuck me!" Alder laughed and came in with an entirely different set of notes.

Laughing, Malakai leaned close to his mic. "He's got it."

Old Time Rock 'N Roll, by Bob Segar. Which should have been obvious, but Malakai hadn't started with the part usually covered by the piano, which Alder had just played.

As the song came together, Brave gave Malakai a thumbs up.

When it ended, he turned to Alder. "You're up, bro."

Alder stared at Brave like he'd spoken some foreign language. Probably because Brave never called him 'bro' without being cold or sarcastic.

Rubbing his fist over his lips, Alder shook his head. "You never get to have fun with this. Let's see what you got."

They held each other's gaze for a few seconds before Brave inclined his head. Something was up, but Jesse wasn't sure what. It had to be big if Brave was suddenly being decent to his brother.

But as the professional he was, Brave didn't let the silence last long. He cleared his throat and looked at Jesse. "Can I have some water? Fucking dry in here."

247

From the side of the stage, the drum tech, Derrick, scampered over with a bottle of water. He rushed off the stage before Brave could even thank him.

Drinking half the water, Brave's gaze trailed over the crowd. He held up the bottle.

Predictably, all the fans' hands shot up, shouting for his leftovers. Which happened at every single show. Jesse still thought it was weird.

Brave tossed the open bottle into the crowd, spraying half of them before a girl snatched it out of the air and poured it over her thin white T-shirt. She wasn't wearing a bra and all the guys around her cheered.

"Very nice, sweetheart." Brave licked his bottom lip provocatively. "Come see me after the show."

Jesse pressed his eyes shut, refusing to let the invitation bother him. Brave wouldn't fuck the girl. She was too easy.

He ain't fucking you much either, loser.

Grinding his teeth, Jesse leaned against the barrier, hoping the band would finish up with the pre-show soon so he could get their shit out of the way for the opening band.

Mic in hand, Brave stepped up to the edge of the stage. "All right, bear with me. I haven't done this in a long time."

He wet his lips again, whistling softly, the notes coming out clearer as he gained the confidence he usually showed in everything he did. But Jesse didn't think it was the whistling that threw him off.

The song showed a different emotion than Brave ever brought on stage. Sadness and regret. Both feelings he tended to mock as too emo for any of Winter's Wrath's music.

And he still hadn't sung a single lyric.

Coming in with a muted trill on the symbols, Tate swayed a little, as though hearing the rest of the music even before Alder joined with the opening chords, strumming softly.

Patience, wasn't one of Guns N' Roses most popular songs, so very few of the fans knew it, but as Brave sang, they took out their phones, holding them up like people had once done with lighters.

Skull stepped up to Jesse's side. "He's got them calm. We need to talk."

Backstage, Skull told him why Brave had really been so late. The band wasn't to be told anything, but since he and Jesse were working so closely with the new security, he'd thought it was important to give Jesse all the details.

Pacing between the empty guitar cases and crates of audio equipment, Jesse laced his fingers behind his neck, trying to fucking remember how to breathe. If he got his hands on the psychopath stalking Brave, he'd kill him. Beat him to a lifeless, bloody pulp. He didn't even care if it would land him back in jail. The fucker was a dead man.

But the cops hadn't found him yet and the son of a bitch had followed them halfway across the goddamn country. Not that difficult, since their tour was posted online.

"We're canceling the rest of the shows." Jesse stopped pacing and turned to Skull. "If this could happen in Vegas, and at a huge place like this, what's next? Even with security, keeping Brave safe at the smaller venues is gonna be impossible."

Skull shook his head. "Cole will never—"

"Fuck Cole!" Jesse slammed his fist into the closest solid object he could find. A huge metal support bar. Which sliced his knuckles open. The pain steadied him as he stared down at the blood dripping onto the floor. "Singers don't live very long working with him, now do they?"

"You can't blame Cole for what happened to Valor, Jesse." Skull glanced disapprovingly at Jesse's bloody hand, but didn't comment on it. "That boy dug his own grave long before he died."

That was an odd thing to say about a man who was regarded as a hero by the entire fucking music world. Jesse frowned at Skull. "What are you talking about? He thought the whole band would freeze to death if he didn't go for help."

"That's the story," Skull said with a nod.

"But not the truth?" Jesse wasn't sure why he bothered asking Skull. If the man hadn't shared the information in the three years they'd worked together, he wasn't going to do so now.

"Not my truth to tell. Ask your man." Skull shrugged when Jesse arched a brow at him. "Maybe he'll be ready to talk about it. Maybe not. Either way, go get that fucking hand patched up. You're making a mess."

Saluting with his undamaged hand, Jesse went to find the EMT. Who wasn't happy to see him. He cleaned and bandaged Jesse's hand, grumbling the whole time.

The show went well. The after party was wild, as usual, but all the guys—and their one girl, who didn't touch a single drink—made it out in one piece.

He got everyone to the hotel and dragged both his and Brave's suitcases to the room he was sharing with the man, whether Brave liked it or not.

Brave didn't protest. He simply collapsed on the bed and dropped his arm over his eyes.

Jesse sat beside him, considering whether it would be underhanded to dig while Brave was piss drunk. If he was honest with himself, this was probably the *only* time Brave would speak openly about anything he considered unpleasant.

"Brave?" He figured he should make sure the man hadn't passed out. He'd lost track of the amount of whiskey Brave had tossed back while pretending to have fun with members of the other bands. He'd done a good job of avoiding his own band mates once they left the stage.

Brave grunted, squinting at him with his hand shielding his eyes. "What the fuck do you want?"

"What happened tonight? Before the VIP show?"

"If you're bringing it up, you already know." Brave covered his eyes again. "If you're staying in here, turn off the fucking light and go to sleep."

So much for that. Jesse sighed, figuring he'd try again tomorrow. After pouring a few pots worth of coffee down his boyfriend's throat. He stood and started toward the light switch.

"Wait. Actually, we do need to talk." Brave forced himself to a sitting position with a groan. "This thing with you and me? It's not working. Sorry."

Hand hovering over the light switch, Jesse went still. Then let out a rough laugh. "Go to sleep, Brave. You're not dumping me while you're drunk."

Brave shrugged, pushing off the bed and stumbling across the room to grab the ten-dollar water bottle off the minibar. "Fine. I'll do it again in the morning."

Jesse switched off the light and went over to the second bed. He shed his clothes, climbed under the covers, and closed his eyes. Brave would forget the whole conversation in the morning. Then maybe he'd get some answers.

Only, Brave didn't forget. He was cold the next morning when he told Jesse it really was over. They'd had fun and all, but he missed his freedom.

To make things even better, Cole didn't have to argue to keep the tour going.

Brave wouldn't even consider canceling a single show. Even if it killed him.

Which he informed the entire band when the subject was brought up by his brother.

If Jesse thought Brave had been heartless with him, it was nothing compared to his words to Alder, when the youngest Trousseau brother dared imply it wasn't worth the risk.

"What are you worried about, Alder? No one's after you. With me out of the way, you can have your perfect fucking life. Use that fancy degree; teach little assholes how to play music. Have a dozen kids with your sweet bitch." Brave sneered at Danica as he spoke. He managed to block the punch Alder threw at him. *"Actually, either way, I think you better start considering what you want. You can be replaced, you know."*

"Cut it out, Brave. We're doing the shows." Malakai stepped between the brothers. *"No one's being replaced."*

"You all can be, you know." Brave shook with rage, glaring at the men who'd been at his side for years as if none of them meant a thing to him. *"Anyone else have anything to say?"*

No one did. Not that Jesse blamed them.

One thing was very clear. To Brave, the music, the fans, and what he'd created was all that mattered. From what Jesse had heard of Valor, he'd been the exact same way.

And if Brave continued the way he was going, he'd meet the same fate as his older brother. Without being remembered as a hero.

Despite how hurt and angry he was, Jesse would still do everything in his power to protect Brave. He just had to figure out how the hell he was going to shield the man from his worst enemy, which wasn't the stalker.

The biggest threat to Brave was Brave himself.

Chapter Fifteen

Saturday morning, Danica was jolted awake with her phone buzzing against her cheek. She lifted her arm to reach for it and groaned as all the muscles in her body seized up on her. For some reason, she'd had a restless night, tossing and turning in Alder's bunk, feeling every single bump in the road. Alder had been up with Malakai for a while, working on a new song they were writing. She wouldn't blame his absence for how sore and tired she was, but damn it, she liked it a lot more when she could.

Squinting at the phone, she smiled, relaxing back onto her pillow as she answered. "Good morning, Grandpa."

"Morning? Are you sick, Danica?" Her grandfather huffed, speaking softly to someone before bringing his attention back to her. "I'm sorry, I've been told you're allowed to sleep in on your birthday and I shouldn't fuss over you. But you would tell me if you were sick?"

"I would, I promise."

"Good girl. Oh, and happy birthday. From Mary too." His voice softened, like just talking about the woman made him smile.

Danica loved hearing him like this. She always worried about him being alone, but he wasn't anymore. "Thank you, Grandpa. It's weird that I slept in. What time is it?"

"Almost noon. And why would it be weird?" His tone went hard. "Those boys don't bother you, do they?"

"They try not to, but there's only so much space on the bus." She also wasn't a heavy sleeper. Since either one of the band members, or the roadies, often drove through the night, there was almost always someone sleeping in the bunks. The guys tried to be considerate, but the odd laugh or cupboard doors opening and closing or…well, anytime Tate decided to pick up his sticks, took pure exhaustion to ignore.

She hadn't reached that point until last night. As much fun as dancing was, she'd had to start working new muscles and they weren't happy with her at the moment. Slacking on her yoga routine had been a bad idea.

"Well, I hope you have a great day, my girl," her grandfather said, sounding happy again. "Mary made you a pair of mittens and a hat. I bought you some proper winter boots so you—why are you glaring at me, woman?" He went silent. Then snorted. "She's not happy that I told you about your presents. You haven't seen them, so act surprised."

Danica laughed, her throat tightening a little, because she missed him. She'd see him again soon, but all her birthdays for the past two years had been spent traveling somewhere. His habit of telling her what her presents were before she opened them hadn't changed since she was a kid, which was nice and familiar. The gifts were always practical and he liked telling her how useful they would be.

She swallowed hard, taking a moment to make sure her voice sounded normal so he wouldn't worry. "I'll be surprised. And I'm sure I'll love everything. I'll see you in a few days?"

"I'm looking forward to you coming home. Your damn cat keeps perching himself on Mary's shoulder like he has a right to be there. She doesn't mind, but he gives me this look when I try to move him." Her grandfather snorted. "He's claimed her and we have to put him in his place."

"If he's claimed her, you know she's an amazing person. Cat approval is the only approval that counts."

"I suppose so. Not that I needed him to tell me how amazing she is."

Awww! She couldn't wait to see her grandfather with Mary. He sounded like he was falling fast and hard.

"Give her a hug for me. I love you!"

"Love you too, *ikwesens.*"

Once she'd hung up, Danica grabbed the sweater she'd stuffed under her pillow—actually, one of Alder's hoodies that she'd claimed—and pulled it on. With all the zigzagging across the states, she was never sure about the temperature. Some days were warm, while others dipped close to freezing. The one time she'd wondered out to the front lounge in a tank top and boxers in the middle of Nebraska had taught her a hard lesson.

Leaning over the side of the bunk, she listened, surprised she still didn't hear anyone.

The bus was *very* quiet. Unnaturally so.

Then she heard Tate. "Can we get her up *now?*"

They know how to whisper? She grinned as she lowered herself to the floor. Well, that was sweet of them. She'd tried not to let how tired she was show, but not much got by Alder.

She hopped off the bunk and stepped into the lounge.

The entire band and all the roadies were crowded in there. Black and gold streamers were strung everywhere and someone had hung up a pink banner that read 'Happy Birthday'.

Tate spotted her first and a huge smile spread across his lips. "Happy birthday! I made you breakfast!"

He gestured to the table where there was a *huge* stack of pancakes, all different colors, with icing drizzled over them and two sparklers, which Tate quickly lit.

"Happy birthday!" All the men in the room shouted.

She bit her lip as it began to quiver and Alder came toward her. He held out his arms and she leaned into him, struggling to compose herself. Her eyes watered and she shook her head, not sure why she was suddenly so emotional. Her birthday had usually been a quiet day with her grandfather when she was younger. She'd seen the other kids with cupcakes their mothers brought to class, or went to parties where two loving parents brought out a big cake and sang to their little boy or girl. And for awhile, she'd wanted what they had.

So Grandpa had thrown her a party when she was eleven. He'd been so uncomfortable, trying to stay out of the way as well-meaning women from the tribe took over organizing the food, drinks, and games. Danica had found him away from all the noise, working on a piece of deer pelt he'd bought from a local hunter. His mother had taught him to make moccasins when he was a boy, and he usually made them each, and the few people he liked, a pair every fall.

Until then, she'd never been interested in learning. But that day, she wanted to.

"Can you teach me, Grandpa?"

He frowned, not looking up from the pelt he was cutting. "You should be with your friends."

"But I want to learn." She cocked her head, using the one reason she knew he'd understand. "Shouldn't I have a choice?"

He looked at her then. "Don't you want *to play with your friends?"*

"They're only my friends today. They don't usually like me because I get paid to smile at a camera." She realized then that she didn't like pretending to like people. And neither did her grandfather. "They say I'm not even pretty. I don't want to share my cake with them."

Letting out a surprised laugh, he leaned over and hugged her. "All right, you don't have to play with them. But you will share your cake, they're our guests."

"Fine." She let out a dramatic sigh. "But will you teach me?"

"Yes." He picked up a needle, already strung with sinew from the same deer that the pelt had come from. "Do you know how to sew?"

"No. You haven't taught me that either."

"Then that's where we'll begin."

She never asked for a party after that. To her, all the presents weren't worth pretending to have friends for one day. She didn't have parents, but she had her grandfather. And the time she spent with him was special. Because he truly loved her. Every gift from him meant something.

Sophie kept her birthdays simple as well. She'd brought Danica out to lunch once in Paris and given her a new purse. She'd remembered Danica's stories about her grandfather's useful gifts, and she'd decided Danica needed a fancy purse worth more than most people's entire wardrobe.

"You'd never buy it for yourself, but people see you, Danica. They see you, and something as insignificant as a purse or a pair of shoes will mark you as one of the elite." Sophie laughed and shook her head. "It's pretentious, I know. But don't think of the cost. Know that I want people to look at you and see what I do. A woman who can have the most expensive, stylish things in the world, but remains the same, strong, beautiful person she was raised to be. I know you miss your grandfather, but he tells me all the time that you'll keep shining as bright as you do now. And I believe him."

Rubbing her back, Alder leaned close, speaking softly. "Tell me what you're thinking. Is this too much?"

"No, it's perfect." She moved to wipe the one tear that fell down her cheek, but Alder used his sleeve to dry it, his eyes never leaving her face. "I've always hated fake parties and meaningless gifts. I don't feel like that about what you guys have done for me. No matter how many issues there may be, when you care about something, or someone, it's real."

She considered the tension between Alder and Brave, and corrected her claim, but only to herself. Brave pretended not to care *very* well. But if he ever stopped hiding behind whatever made him afraid to love his brother, she had a feeling nothing would come between them.

Hopefully, he'd see that too. Before it was too late.

His broody, false front didn't matter now though.

Those pancakes looked damn good. And Sophie had told her several times that birthday calories didn't count, so she could have as much as she wanted. Maybe Alder would share. Her birthday rules applied to him too, because she said so.

"You good now?" Alder was still watching her. And she could feel him relax even before she nodded. He could tell she was ready to enjoy her party. Fuck, she loved how he paid attention to every little detail, reading her body language and her face and doing his best to give her what she needed.

He wouldn't always be right, but the effort? It meant more than she could say.

"I'm good." She held his hand as she made her way through the crowded bus lounge, hugging Connor, then Malakai, and finally Tate. Brave was standing in the back, behind the roadies, a stiff smile planted on his lips.

No hug for him.

"Wait!" Tate pulled something out of his pocket as she sat at the table and picked up the fork. "I have candles for you to blow out. They looked stupid with the sparklers, so I took them off, but you gotta make a wish."

"You're so right. Thank you, Tate." She grinned at him as he put the candles on the cake. Then she wrinkled her nose. "Twenty six?"

"Umm...yeah?" He glanced over at Alder, who shook his head. "Shit. Okay, don't freak. I don't think you're old or anything, but—"

Jesse, who was sitting on the sofa other side of the bus, snorted. "You think twenty-six is old?"

"No!" Tate slapped a hand over his face. "I just...Danica isn't like a teenager. She's cool, but mature, so—"

Malakai draped his arm over Tate's shoulder. "Stop talking, kid."

"Okay." Tate bit his bottom lip and gave Danica the most adorable, apologetic look. "You want me to light them anyway?"

"Yes, please." She snickered. "Just remind me, in two years, that I already used up that wish."

The flames flickered once both candles were lit, but Danica couldn't think of a wish. Not for herself anyway. She had so much and she still couldn't believe how lucky she was. Her career was flourishing, her grandfather wasn't alone, and she'd fallen in love with the most amazing man in the world.

So she gave her wish to him. She wished that Alder could have the one thing he'd missed out on for too long. A brother that loved him. And showed it.

Closing her eyes, she blew out the candles.

"Time for gifts!" Tate reached under the table, coming up with an armful of presents wrapped in newspaper. "Open mine first."

He dumped the presents on the table and handed her one that looked like it had been carefully wrapped with the comics section of the morning paper. *This* morning's actually. The gift was thin and bent slightly. There was a solid, rectangular lump in the middle.

She shook it and he laughed. When she tore the wrapper, he folded his arms over his chest, rocking in his sneakers.

"I know coloring books are a kid thing, but I see chicks talking about it on Facebook all the time and they find it fun and I thought you'd like it." His face went red. "Maybe it's stupid."

"Goof, it's not stupid." She flipped through the coloring book, which had intricate pictures of mystical creatures on every page. He'd also gotten her a small box of pencil crayons. "I love it. It will keep me busy on tour when I get bored of video games."

"But you can't get too bored. You're good at them!" He looked like he was reconsidering giving her an alternative source of entertainment, so she tucked the book and the crayon box behind her.

The rest of the gifts were all band merchandise. She now had two hoodies, several T-shirts, key chains, posters, and two different beanies with the Winter's Wrath logo. It might seem to some like the guys had taken the easy way out of finding gifts for her, but she'd learned that selling merch at shows actually covered a lot of the band's income.

None of the guys had just grabbed the stuff to give her. They'd have paid for it so it didn't cut into the band's earnings. Which made each gift special.

Alder's gift came last, but he didn't give it to her right away. Moving away from her, he stood next to Jesse. Malakai handed Jesse his acoustic guitar.

"I've spent the last two days working on this. And driving both Jesse and Malakai nuts by changing my mind every other fucking minute because it seemed so cliché and stupid." He cleared his throat. "But then I thought of how often we do this. Write songs, hoping they'll mean something to the fans. Knowing they mean something to us. And if I was going to give you anything, it should be what means the most to me. Besides you." He smiled as she put her hands to her hot cheeks. "The music."

Jesse strummed a few notes, long and soft, with a dark tone.

Alder bowed his head, nodding a little to the beat of the music. All the men on the bus went quiet.

And Alder began to sing.

"Surrounded by the roar,
of a surf-tormented shore.
Where the melody is bittersweet
And love's only a four-letter word.

You remind me this is a dream.
Won't be long before I wake.
Northern lights in your eyes,
Too fucking good to be real.

This dream within a dream."

His voice swept over her, deep and strong, rising like a tide crashing against the shore, like the words in the song, wearing away any doubts, leaving behind nothing too weak to survive the storm.

She didn't try to hide the tears as the song ended. If the guys didn't get how much this meant to her, too damn bad. They had a chick on the bus. And her wonderful man had given her the most amazing gift. One that would last long after everything she owned, everything worth holding on to, was sitting in the attic of one of her grandchildren's homes.

Because his music was art. And true art could never be forgotten.

"Please tell me you're going to record that song." She pushed out of her seat and took his hands in hers, the crimson blush spreading high on his cheeks making the gift even more precious. He didn't sing in front of many people, and he'd sung in front of the entire band and crew for her. "Alder, that was beautiful."

Alder's lips quirked slightly and he lifted his shoulders. "Winter's Wrath doesn't do ballads. But I'm happy you liked it."

"She's right though, bro." Brave strode through the small space between the band and crew in the lounge, reaching into the fridge for a beer. He took a few sips, then held the beer up as though in cheers. "I didn't know you could write lyrics. Or sing so good. A few more years and you can take my place. Make the band soft rock and go mainstream. Good job."

Slamming the fridge door, Brave stormed past all the stunned members of his band and off the bus.

Alder's jaw ticked. He framed her face with his hands. "Do not let him ruin this for you."

She inhaled quickly and smiled at him. "No fucking way. I'm ready to dig into those pancakes. Wanna share? It's not cheating on your diet because today is special."

"It's not? Really?" Alder let her lead him back to the table. He pulled away abruptly. "Almost forgot. Here."

The box. Unlike the other gifts, it was wrapped in pretty, emerald green wrapping paper with a crooked bow on top.

"I guessed your favorite color. Or…ok, that's a lie. After the first time I looked into your eyes, green became *my* favorite color." He gave her a small smile. "They're fucking cool though."

"Thank you, but you don't need to use lines on me. I'm yours, Alder."

"The day I stop trying to win you is the day I don't deserve to have you." He pressed the box into her hand. "I hope you like it."

She unwrapped it slowly, because the paper was pretty and she didn't want to rip it. Not that she had a clue what she could save it for, but she'd think of something.

Inside was a silver cuff. With the lyrics of Alder's song stamped into it.

"The bassist of Horizon makes these. I thought he was gonna lay me out when I asked if he could make one in two days. But he pulled it off." Alder ran his thumb over the carefully pressed words in the metal. "I owe him. Likely a body part, but it was worth it."

Slipping the cuff onto her wrist, she read over each lyric, not wanting to look at Alder because she couldn't blink back the tears. "I don't know what to say."

"You don't have to say a word. I wanted to make your birthday special, even though you're stuck with us." He pressed his lips to her forehead and wrapped his arms around her. "You look happy. You're crying, but I think they're happy tears."

"They are."

"Good. I plan to make you happy for a long time, Danica. As long as you'll let me. I don't write lyrics. I've never been in love. But you make me believe I can have anything. Do anything." He kissed her, softly, and whispered. "But all I want to do is love you."

"There's so much you can do. And I'm saying I love you first." She laced her hands behind his neck. "Not today though. You surprised me. When I say those words, you won't see them coming because there's no taking them back. I mean them now, but when I say them? I'm saying forever. I'm giving you all I am. And that scares me, because you're wonderful and I'm still convinced I'll wake up tomorrow and you won't be there."

"That I'm just a dream?"

"Exactly."

"Good. Because that's exactly how I feel about you. But it's the way I felt when I first stepped up on a stage holding my guitar. That it couldn't be real. But it's real." He gave her a hooded look. "When you hear my voice. When I touch you. When you feel me inside you…it's all real. You're wide awake, Danica. Every morning when you wake up, I'll be right here." He placed his hand over her breast, where her heart was beating faster with his every word. "And I'm not going anywhere."

"Good, because that's exactly where I need you."

A dream within a dream. His song fit them perfectly. His dream had been for his band to succeed. Hers to be a face people would remember. To become a woman that, years from now, girls back home would look up to. They wouldn't hate her for being different. They would know they could reach for what they wanted out of life and still find love.

Because that was the dream within the dream.

To reach for your own stars.

And find you aren't alone.

Chapter Seventeen

Late November and Chicago was covered in snow. Probably wouldn't last, it had been a warm fall, but Alder had enjoyed walking with Danica along the Lakefront Trail in Jackson Park, snuggling together against the cold as they looked out at Lake Michigan.

Danica hadn't packed a coat since she'd started the tour with them in Vegas, but Tate's thick bomber jacket wasn't too big on her. She'd worn a Blackhawks toque, ignoring his allegiance to the Red Wings, and catching fat snowflakes in her bare hands.

So adorable, with her cheeks all red and her eyes wide as she took in the sights. For a little while he'd been able to enjoy watching her and forget that she'd be leaving him for a few days.

But Sophie had found her a casting call that was too great an opportunity to pass up. In Detroit, so she'd headed there ahead of them. It wouldn't mess with her obligations to the band. The only reason she'd hesitated was because she hated the idea of leaving him alone to deal with his brother.

"We talked about this, angel." Alder framed her cold cheeks with his hands as she insisted she would try to talk to Brave again. That she would feel much better about leaving if the band wasn't falling apart. "You have your job. I have mine. Part of mine happens to be dealing with Brave acting like a complete asshole."

"He wants you to hate him."

"I don't hate him. I want to punch him sometimes. I don't understand him." Alder sighed and shook his head. "But I don't hate him."

"Well, he acts like he hates you, but you have to know he doesn't." She hiked her chin up, meeting his eyes. "Not that it matters, because I love you."

Even now, staring out at the snow covered streets as Jesse pulled the van up beside the bus that had been left in the Walmart parking lot during the last show, Alder could hear her saying those words so clearly, it was like she was right here with him. He'd been speechless at first. Danica wasn't the type of woman to say she loved someone if she didn't mean it.

Combing his fingers into her hair, he tipped her head back and claimed her lips. There were so many thing he needed to tell her, but first, he had to show her what her words meant to him. He kissed her as though he couldn't breathe without her. As though her touch was all he lived for.

Because he'd given her his heart and his soul and when she wasn't with him, she took a piece of both.

"I love you. I love waking up and seeing you sleeping beside me. I love how you make the music and the stage your own with every move you make. I love how just your smile can kill all the fucking demons that haunt me." Nothing he was saying was enough, so he kept going. "I love how much you care about everyone and how fucking fierce you are protecting those you claim. And that you've claimed me, you amazing woman. I love that most of all."

Her eyes teared and she inhaled roughly. "Have I? Because I don't know if that's a good thing. There's so much that you haven't seen yet. So much more I want to give you."

"What more could you possibly give me?"

"Just...more. And I would tell you, but I still haven't figured out how." She let out a broken laugh. "I will though. And when I do, know it's because I love you. Okay?"

He'd agreed. He wasn't sure what exactly he'd agreed to, but she'd smiled, so it couldn't be a bad thing.

The next morning she'd rented a car and driven to Detroit. The bed beside him was cold and empty, but her pillow on the bus still held her scent. Which helped him sleep.

And between the influx of interviews, practice, and the show, he was too busy to dwell on the fact that he'd grown used to having her close. They talked on the phone and texted throughout the day, so that helped when he missed her. Most importantly though, he reminded himself that if their relationship was going to last, he had to learn to deal with days—and at some point weeks—apart.

I can do this. He told himself again and again.

Jesse elbowed him in the side. "You ever plan on getting out of the car?"

"Yeah." Alder forced a smile, grabbing the case of beer he'd set at his feet. He'd taken to going on beer runs with Jesse so he'd have an excuse not to stay on the bus. Come to think of it, Danica getting a break from the tension between all the members of the band was good. Hopefully, by the time they got to Detroit, they'd have made peace.

Would probably help if they weren't avoiding one another. He glanced over his shoulder at Malakai, who'd been sitting in the backseat, so quiet he'd almost forgotten the man was there.

"You got the whiskey?"

Malakai held up the bottle with a snort. "Like I'd forget the one thing that makes Brave bearable? Gotta tell you man, I think making him walk to South Bend might do us all some good."

Walk in the fucking cold? Are you fucking serious? As frustrated as he was with his brother's attitude, Alder wouldn't even consider leaving Brave anywhere. What if something happened to him?

Pretty sure that's not what Malakai meant. Relax.

Right. Normal people didn't freak out at the idea of someone getting a little chilly. The snow on the ground was already turning into slush. And no one would actually kick Brave off the bus.

As Jesse open the door and a cloud of noxious smelling smoke spilled out, Alder reconsidered that last thought.

If Brave and Connor were smoking up with Tate, Malakai might very well make them both walk to South Bend, Indiana. On crutches.

There goes our fucking security deposit. Alder sighed as he climbed the steps and walked into the front lounge, depositing the beer on the sofa.

A loud groan came from the back of the bus. "Fuck, you're tight."

Alder froze.

Jesse growled and strode to the back of the bus.

Malakai almost knocked Alder over as he took off after Jesse.

What the fuck? Alder was pretty sure that had been his brother's voice. And that he didn't want to go back there.

If he was right about what was going on though, he had to. Or his brother was a dead man.

The sound of flesh slapping flesh filled the bus as Jesse shoved the curtain to the back lounge aside.

Alder took one look and then grabbed Malakai.

"You son of a bitch!" Malakai twisted in Alder's grip, his eyes blazing with murderous rage. "I'm going to fucking kill you! He's a kid!"

Dragging deep on the joint between his lips, Brave continued to thrust into Tate, one hand on the back of the young man's neck as Tate's lips slid over Connor's dick.

Brave let out a cloud of smoke and laughed, his glazed eyes fixed on Malakai. "Does he remind you of your brother? Is that why you're always looking out for him? Take mine and we'll call it even."

Shoving Alder aside, Malakai spun around and stormed off the bus.

Jesse stood there, his throat working as he backed up, shaking his head. "Damn you, Brave."

Alder tugged Jesse away, putting his hands on Jesse's shoulders. Jesse was shaking and his face was deathly pale. He and Brave had broken up days ago, but that hadn't suddenly erased what Jesse felt for his brother.

Not that Brave cared. About Jesse. Or the band. Or anything at all.

He seemed to be determined to self-destruct. And take anyone stupid enough to stick around down with him.

"Go after Malakai." Alder gave Jesse a little shake when the man simply stared at him. "Let me deal with this."

"I'll get Skull to—"

"Skull doesn't know Malakai as well as you do. Jesse, he's pissed. He'll find the closest bar and pick a fight just to let off some steam." Alder hoped he was wrong. Malakai hadn't done that in years, but he hadn't been this angry in years either. The man could take pretty much anything, but Brave was good at finding a person's weakness and exploiting it.

He'd have done less damage if he'd driven a knife right into the center of Malakai's chest.

Nodding, Jesse ran his hands through his hair. He shook his head and laughed.

"You know, no matter what the rest of us do, it's always been Brave that can make, or break us." He blinked fast, his teeth cutting into his bottom lip. "We're fucking broken."

"No, we're not." Alder fisted his hand in Jesse's hair, pulling him close. "I'm not giving him that kind of power and neither will you. Get Malakai. And let me prove we have something worth fighting for. Because I'm not ready to give up."

Not looking convinced, Jesse headed off the bus. He slammed the door behind him.

And Alder stood there, leaning against the side of the bunks, waiting for the steady sound of fucking to stop.

He didn't have to wait long. He heard the sound of a zipper.

Then Connor, speaking softly. "I don't know what the fuck I was thinking. Malakai's right. He's a kid. I don't know why I let you talk me into this."

"Stop being such a pussy." Brave snarled. "He was begging for it."

"He's right here." Tate whispered. "And I didn't know they'd care."

Brave laughed. "Really? They'd have flipped out at us letting you get stoned."

"Then why did you let him?" Connor asked.

"Because life is short. Because I really don't give a fuck what anyone thinks." A fresh wave of smoke spilled out of the back lounge. Cigarette smoke. Brave hadn't smoked in years because it fucked with his voice, but he'd clearly stopped caring about that too. "I thought you two were the only ones who still knew how to have a good time. Guess I was wrong."

"You think this is a good time?" Connor let out an incredulous laugh. "Jesus, Brave. This band is all I have. I've given everything to you, to *this*. Yeah, I love living it up, but not to the point that everything we've built will be worthless. We have to talk to them. Tell them…I don't know. Something."

"Why? Are you sorry you sucked my dick? That Tate had your dick in his mouth a few seconds ago?" Brave's laugh was cruel. "Because you looked like you were enjoying yourself."

"I was, but I wasn't trying to hurt anyone. It's obvious you were."

Connor came out, looking startled when he saw Alder. He immediately dropped his gaze, raising a shaky hand to his face.

"I fucked up." He sank down to sit on the edge of Tate's bunk, speaking softly. "Things have been…well, fucked up. But we were chilling and laughing and I…I don't know. I guess I just needed a break from all the tension, you know? It's not an excuse. I just need you to know I can't lose the band. We have to figure out what the hell went wrong."

"We will." Alder was tempted to tell Connor to take a walk, but him running across Malakai right now would be very very bad. "Go sit in the front lounge. I'll send Tate out in a minute, but for fuck's sakes, keep your hands off him."

"No problem there." Connor ambled wearily out to the front lounge. Minutes later, Tate shuffled by Alder and went to join the rhythm guitarist.

Hoping Brave had put some clothes on, Alder stepped into the back lounge. Tate's favorite quilt covering his brother after all that was a little messed up, but better than nothing.

Sinking into the seat on the sectional across from Brave. Alder considered his words carefully. Looking at his brother was difficult. The smirk on Brave's lips made crossing the room and laying him out seem like a much better idea than trying to reason with him.

"Come on, Alder." Brave tapped his cigarette into the empty whiskey bottle he was using as an ashtray. "I can't wait to hear what you've got to say."

Nothing that will change a damn thing. Brave wasn't listening to anyone. He certainly wouldn't listen to Alder.

But he might smarten up if he had to face the damage he'd done.

"I'm leaving tonight." Alder didn't get any satisfaction from the way Brave's lips parted as the cold detachment gave way to shock. He hated what he was being forced to do, but desperate times called for desperate measures. "I'm taking the van and any of the guys that want to come with me are welcome. You aren't. Security will stay with you, along with any of the roadies who aren't sick of your shit."

Brave's brow creased. "We have a show tomorrow afternoon."

"I'm aware of that. But we can all be replaced, right?"

Shooting off the sofa—thank fucking god, he was wearing boxers—Brave closed the distance between them and grabbed the collar of Alder's jacket, jerking him to his feet. "I don't know what you're playing at, Alder, but I warn you, if you do this—"

"What? I'm out? You used that threat already. I got it." Alder pried his brother's fingers from his collar and pushed him back a few feet. "You've gone too fucking far. When you're ready to work *with* us, we might have something worth saving. I believe we do, but as things stand? I'm done."

Turning around and leaning his hands on the back of the sofa, Brave nodded slowly. "Then go."

Alder didn't want to leave. He wanted to force Brave to tell him why things had gotten so bad. If they'd had any kind of relationship as siblings, maybe the kind of relationship Brave had with Valor before he died, maybe Alder could reach him.

But they didn't. And Alder's final words would mean nothing if he didn't follow through.

So he left.

And the entire band came with him. Leaving Brave with the three security guards and Skull.

Skull's decision to stay surprised Alder, but he was grateful when the man pulled him aside to explain why.

"You're doing the right thing, son." Skull squeezed his shoulder as they stood by the driver's side of the van. "I want to tell you something I'm not sure you've ever heard from anyone. I'm proud of you. He needs a serious wake up call, and you're the only one capable of giving it to him." A rueful smile crossed his lips. "He also needs to know he's not completely alone."

Alder swallowed hard, guilt building a lump in his throat. "Shouldn't I be the one making sure he knows that?"

"No. He's kept you at a distance and used you as a punching bag for too long. Take that away from him and what does he have?" Skull chuckled. "An old man who sees right through him. He can't hurt me. And I know all his secrets. Which will force him to face them."

"If I knew—"

"You will. Your brother hides behind his ego, using the stage as his own personal pillow fort. Up there, in front of a crowd that adores him, he can pretend he's invincible." Skull shrugged. "Take away his toys and he'll join us in the real world. Where he's just a man. A man who needs to face his demons."

"Is that what I am to him?" Alder fisted his hands at his sides, wishing he got what the hell was wrong with Brave. What he'd done to earn his hatred. "One of his fucking demons?"

"No, my boy. You remind him that he'll always be vulnerable to them. If he keeps you at a distance, he believes he can avoid them as well." Sadness filled Skull's eyes. "I can't even blame him for wishing that was true. Which is another reason I'm staying. He doesn't deserve what started him on this path. His only fault was choosing to stay there."

Alder had always known Skull was a smart man, but this vague bullshit was frustrating. He didn't press for more though. He knew very well Skull had told him all he planned to.

"You'll let me know if there's anything I can do?" Alder raked his fingers through his hair. "I mean, there has to be more?"

"There isn't. You're doing what you have to. You're going home."

"Right. Taking my ball and going home is the perfect plan."

Skull laughed. "That's what you don't get. It's his ball, Alder. You've just decided not to play his game anymore. And it's about fucking time."

Slapping his back, Skull pretty much dismissed him.

On the whole drive to Detroit, Alder picked apart the old roadies words. And came to one conclusion.

He'd always known this was a game with Brave. He'd tried to follow the rules, even though they'd been set up so he'd never win.

But until now, he'd never considered he had another option.

He didn't have to play.

Which didn't mean he'd lose.

It meant the game would change.

Chapter Eighteen

Getting a couple of days away from the bus and the band was damn refreshing. Danica missed Alder, and she'd have put up with all the stress of the tour to see him again, but waking up to a message that he'd be home early had been a nice surprise.

Until she woke up enough to remember Winter's Wrath had a show scheduled this afternoon. In Indiana. They shouldn't be heading here until tonight, earliest. She hadn't really expected them until tomorrow.

Yesterday, she'd taken advantage of her free time to go visit her grandfather. They'd gone out to dinner with Ms. Mary Nitsch and then Danica had gone back to Grandpa's place. Alone. Her grandfather offered to cancel his plans with Mary, but Danica knew very well he'd been looking forward to spending the night at his new sweetheart's place. She refused to let him change everything because she'd shown up unexpectedly and promised to stop by to see him again as soon as she could.

Since she'd be staying at Alder's place, she decided to pack a few things, but nothing big. Showing up at his door with a bunch of boxes would be weird. She'd thrown in some warmer clothes for when they began the Canadian tour, but made sure not to bring anything impractical. Nothing she wouldn't need on the bus.

Halfway to Detroit, she started wondering if she should have brought more. Her one suitcase kinda made it seem like she wasn't actually committing on staying for any length of time.

Then again, *Alder* wouldn't be staying long. The tour wasn't over, they just had a little break.

That's suddenly a day longer?

Yeah, that was off. Was the band canceling their afternoon show? If so, why? She'd read over Alder's message over and over, looking for clues, but he'd sent it at almost 2:00AM and kept it brief. Knowing full well she'd have her phone on vibrate if she was sleeping—which she had been.

As much as she appreciated the head's up and the chance to see him this morning, she really wished she had an idea what to expect. Was someone hurt?

No, he'd have called.

But what other than one of the band members being injured would force them to disappoint their fans? Actually, even when one of them *was* hurt, they still found a way to go on. Tate had been pulled off stage and then split the drum parts with the drum tech to give him more time to heal.

Maybe Brave finally smartened up? If he'd gotten another 'gift', maybe he'd decided his safety was a priority?

Somehow, she doubted that. But stranger things had happened.

Pulling onto Seward Avenue, she double-checked the address Alder had texted her, then parked. This area of Midtown was pretty nice. Not that she'd expected him to live in a rundown neighborhood, but with how often the band traveled, the expense of an apartment like this didn't make much sense.

Unless he had a roommate? But would he have invited her to stay without asking them?

"Go upstairs and ask him. You're gonna drive yourself nuts overthinking everything." She stepped onto the sidewalk, sending Alder a quick message to let him know she was there. She'd left early this morning, so she hadn't texted him earlier, figuring he'd probably gotten to bed late.

His invitation had been pretty clear. And the one thing she didn't doubt was that he'd be as happy to see her as she was to see him.

That in mind, she quickly retrieved her suitcase and headed up the walkway.

She grinned when Alder met her in the entrance, wearing nothing but a black muscle shirt and black, plaid pajama pants. He looked deliciously rumpled, his hair loose around his shoulders and little creases on his face—probably from his pillow.

Her pulse sped up as he came toward her. She released the handle of her suitcase, laughing as he lifted her up in his arms and held her close.

"Fuck, I missed you." His lips covered hers in a deep, passionate kiss. She tangled her hands in his hair as his tongue touched hers, slanting her head so she could tease it with her own.

"Oh my." A gasp from behind him had Alder pulling his lips from hers to look over at the little old lady who'd stepped off the elevator. She arched a brow at him before stepping around them and making her way outside.

"Yeah…we should probably continue this in my apartment." Alder grabbed her suitcase with one hand, and her hand with the other. "I should warn you, Jesse is here. He spent the night. In Tate and Malakai's room."

"But they're not here?"

Alder let go of her suitcase long enough to press the call button for the elevator and shook his head. "They both spend most of their time in Detroit at Tate's grandmothers. We share the apartment just to have a place to call home. Both stayed with me more often when Tate was high all the time, but once he got cleaned up he missed being spoiled by her."

Danica smiled, loving the idea of Tate having someone to take care of him. "And Malakai?"

"Malakai spoils him too."

She snorted and smacked his arm as they stepped onto the elevator. "That's not what I meant. I'm curious why he'd go there too."

"Oh, he loves Tate's grandmother. She treats him like family and he's never had much of that." Alder gave her a grim smile. "Maybe some day he'll tell you more. Probably when he's drunk."

"Fair enough." She watched the numbers pass as they went up to the top floor. "I'd like to know more about what happened with you and Jesse, anyway."

"Nothing." Alder's brow furrowed. "I wouldn't cheat on you, Danica. I thought you knew me and Jesse are friends. And that's it."

"That doesn't *have* to be it." And *this* wasn't how she wanted to approach the subject, so she made a dismissive gesture, slipping past him when the elevator door opened. "Is Jesse all right?"

Stopping short, Alder put his hand on her arm. He shook his head and took a deep breath. "No. And I should probably catch you up before you see him. Something happened. Part of the reason we canceled the show."

"Is he hurt?" Maybe Alder *wouldn't* have called her. If it wasn't serious enough for Jesse to be at the hospital—well, then it wouldn't have been serious enough to cancel the show? She bit her bottom lip. "Please just tell me. I spent most of the drive trying not to imagine the worst."

Alder inclined his head. "Okay…well, there's no way to tell you that's not messed up. He—*we*—walked in on Brave with Connor. And Tate. They were smoking up and fucking in the back lounge."

She winced at the jolt of pain in her chest, imagining how Jesse must have felt. "I'm sorry, Alder, but your brother is an asshole."

Letting out a bitter laugh, Alder shook his head. "Things only got worse from there. He didn't stop and he decided to lash out at everyone. Malakai looked ready to kill him. He walked away though. Jesse got him calmed down."

"Focusing on someone else would have helped him. That was smart of you."

Alder shrugged. "Brave had done enough damage. I spoke to him alone and it's obvious he doesn't give a fuck anymore. The only thing that he even cared about was canceling the show, but we're getting to the point where he's going to do something he can't come back from."

Pressing her lips together, Danica touched the back of Alder's hand, which was fisted around the handle of her suitcase. "Has he?"

"Not yet. The guys will still hear him out when he's ready to fucking explain himself."

"Will you?"

He looked surprised. "Of course. He's my brother. Hell, I wasn't sure about leaving. I knew it was the right thing to do, but it took a talking to from Skull to get me gone."

The tightness in her throat loosened up and she inhaled, relieved. If anyone could get through to Brave, it would be Skull. "The next show is here, right? Maybe this will give Brave the time he needs to sort out whatever's pushed him over the edge."

"I hope so." Alder continued down the hallway, stopping in front of a door near the end and pulling out his key. "Jesse was still sleeping when I got up to meet you, but he's a light sleeper, so he's probably awake."

"Good. I'd like to speak to you both." Danica hesitated as Alder held the door open. "Do you trust me?"

Alder nodded. "Yes. But I have a very bad feeling about this."

She laughed, patting his cheek as she passed him. "Don't. You have absolutely nothing to worry about."

Taking off her mid-length, leather jacket, she folded it over her arm, blushing when Alder reached for it at that very moment. After handing it to him for him to hang it in the small, mirrored closet in the entryway, she slipped out of her boots and followed him into the living room.

The apartment had a nice open concept; the walls were all a nice, sharp blue tinted white, with modern, black furniture everywhere. The huge sectional splitting the living room from the dining room was matte black microfiber. The table and chairs in the dining room were black. The only thing not black were the massive appliances in the alcove kitchen, which were all stainless steel.

She spotted Jesse in the kitchen, leaning back against the counter, a mug tipped to his lips. Her eyes traveled down his bare chest, over all the hard muscles that tensed as though reacting to the touch of her gaze. She swallowed hard when she reached the V of his pelvis.

Then she forced herself to look away. He wore only a pair of snug, boxer briefs. And parts of him were wide-awake. *A* part anyway.

A part she needed to not be staring at before she and Alder had that talk.

"Good morning, Danica." Jesse set his mug on the counter. "Do you want some?"

She bit her bottom lip and looked over at Alder, who'd stepped up to her side. Why would Jesse ask something like that? He'd caught her staring, obviously. She couldn't hide that she thought he was fucking sexy. No wonder Alder had lusted after him for so long. Being on tour, seeing Jesse like this every day? Only a straight man, one who read the bible twice a day and had sex only for the purpose of reproduction, could ignore Jesse's allure.

But they had to discuss where their—relationship? Yes, relationship—they had to discuss how to handle it first. Jumping right to her 'wanting some' was wrong on so many levels.

He had to know that?

Yes, because he's suddenly become a mind reader?

He didn't have to be a mind reader to slow down a little.

Alder put his hand on her shoulder. "Are you all right?"

"Yes." She scowled at Jesse. "And no, I don't 'want some'. Not yet, anyway. Maybe not at all if you're going to be so blunt."

Jesse's eyes widened. "Umm…all right? Have I mentioned I don't understand chicks? Not sure how I offended you with coffee, but I'm sorry?"

Coffee?

Oh my god. Could you have any more of a one-track mind? She pressed her eyes shut as the little voice in her head laughed at her. *Dumbass.*

Well, since she'd stuck her foot in her mouth already, she should probably be honest before Jesse started wondering what the hell was wrong with her.

Too late for that.

She took a deep breath. "I didn't know you were talking about coffee."

"Oh." Jesse picked up his coffee. His brow furrowed as he brought the mug to his lips. Then his eyes went wide again as he spilled the coffee over his bare chest. "Oh—*Oww*!"

Shit! She hurried across the room, grabbing a dishrag from the handle of the stove and pressing it to Jesse's chest.

His mug slipped from his hand and crashed on the black tiled floor.

"Don't move." Alder joined them, crouching down to pick up the broken mug. "I think I've got it all, but be careful until I get the vacuum. While I clean this up, both of you go sit in the living room. And by the time I'm done hopefully one of you will be able to explain what the hell just happened."

Both Danica and Jesse took a wide step to avoid any little shards, going to the sofa as they'd been told. Only once she'd taken a seat did Danica dare meet Jesse's eyes.

The amusement she saw there made her want to throw something at him.

"Oh, don't get mad. I think it's cute that you've come up with some kind of crazy plan—" He paused at the sound of the vacuum. "A threesome? You clearly have no idea how to pull it off, but let me guess." Jesse leaned back into the sofa, thoughtfully scratching his scruffy jaw. "We all get 'some' and I'm out of Alder's system."

Danica shook her head. "No, that's not—"

"One problem though, sweetheart." Jesse continued, ignoring her protest. "Alder is with you. Which means he's not thinking about me at all."

"Do you really believe that? He just stopped loving you because he met me?" She leaned forward as Jesse dropped his gaze. "You're right. I don't know how to pull this off. That doesn't mean we can't."

"Why even risk it, Danica? You've got something great with Alder. Between the band, and the groupies, you both have enough of a challenge to make this relationship last." He rubbed a hand over his face. "Why add me?"

"You're not a challenge, Jesse. You're an amazing man. I can see why he loves you." She hated the way Jesse cringed when she said that. How could he not see it? Or was he just afraid to? "Right now, I'm on tour with the band, but I won't always be. You will."

"If you're afraid he'll cheat on you—"

"I'm not. I hate the idea of him seeing the man he loves with someone else. I can't stand him losing you again and again and never getting the chance to show you how he feels about you." She hugged herself, knowing she was going against what any other woman would do in her position. But Alder had put everyone else's wants and needs before his own for so long. He'd stood back and watched Jesse choose his brother.

And from what she'd seen, he'd done nothing but worry that Brave would treat Jesse like shit. Which he had. And Alder was being a good friend, supporting Jesse in every way possible.

She wouldn't bring up Brave, because that would be cruel after what Alder had told her. But she liked Jesse. A lot. She wanted him to be happy and he would be with Alder.

Jesse rested his elbows on his knees and lowered his head to his hands as the vacuum shut off. He let out a soft sigh. "He'll never go for it, sweetie. Even if I was willing to go along with this crazy idea of yours, he'll focus on the obvious. You don't think you're enough for him."

"That's where you'd both be wrong." Danica heard Alder putting the vacuum away. And spoke quickly, because this wasn't how Alder needed to be added to the conversation. "I can be all he believes he deserves. We *could* build an amazing life together. But when I love someone, I don't settle for what's easy. I want to give him everything. I want to help him be part of a band that will go down in history. I want him to look in the mirror every day and be fucking proud of the man he is, because he should be."

"And you can give that to him."

"I can. But you'll always be the one that got away."

"Only, I didn't get away. I'm right here."

"If you decide you want to be, then yes." She had to be very very clear with him. He was right about all the objections Alder would bring up. "The idea of you scares me a little. I'd be crazy not to wonder if he'll get to the point that he feels he has to choose between us."

A sharp throat clearing made them both jump. Alder sat on the back of the sofa behind her, arms crossed, lips drawn in a tight smile. "Well, that answers that question. I'm fascinated by how you're both planning this out for me. *Really*."

Jesse stood, holding his hands out in front of him like he wanted no part of whatever Alder thought was going on. "Not planning anything. Just crazy talk. And when did you get so quiet, man? You should really stomp a little when people are talking about you behind your back."

Alder chuckled. "Sit down, Jesse."

"Right." Jesse sat.

Danica scooted sideways to look up at Alder. "Please don't be mad. This isn't how I wanted to bring up the subject."

"Clearly." Alder shook his head. "I'm not sure how this even became a 'subject'. Aside from Jesse teasing you with details of us making out."

Scowling, Jesse moved to stand again. "I didn't—"

"*Sit.*" Alder's tone hardened as he pushed off the back off the sofa. Jesse staying put didn't seem to satisfy him. He paced like a wild animal that had shaken off the affects of a tranquilizer and found himself behind the bars of a cage. "I won't lie. I love you both, but right now, I'm fucking confused. Are you seriously considering the three of us being together?"

"Why not? You just said you love us both." Which meant he didn't hate the idea, right? Danica slid off the sofa, needing to be close to him. To make it clear, if he *did* hate the idea and decided he never wanted to discuss it again, she would accept that. She took his hand, relieved when he let her. "There are so many ways I could have done this better and I'm sorry I didn't. I've been thinking about it for a while, but I needed to see what we had was strong enough first. And then I wasn't sure if that mattered."

"Because if I wanted him, you'd let me go." Alder's eyes darkened with frustration. "That's what I can't wrap my head around. I love you, Danica. I told you I don't need anyone else."

"But you love him too."

"Yes. And I could live my whole life, loving him as a friend."

"What if you didn't have to?"

Alder pressed his eyes shut. He shook his head and let out a rough laugh. "Not something that would have ever occurred to me, but sure, let's go with that. I don't have to choose. I can have everything."

Now we're getting somewhere.

He cupped her cheeks in his hands, holding her gaze. "What about you? And him? You put up with one another to make me happy?"

She frowned. "Why not?"

"Because that will get old, very fast. I know what I have with you. I've considered what I could have with Jesse in the past." Alder's lips curved slightly. "But if we're in this together, what will you be to one another? Friends sharing a lover? Because I'm not okay with that."

"Jesse's gay. He's not interested in me." She had to be honest. Most of her fantasies had revolved around seeing Alder and Jesse together. She'd hoped Jesse wouldn't be uncomfortable with her time with Alder, but they could always take turns?

Jesse snorted. "Jesse would love to be included in the conversation."

"Jesse is more than welcome." Danica frowned at him, not liking that he was still sitting on the sofa, observing from a distance. His support would have been appreciated.

"Jesse prefers men. As far as I know, he's never been with a woman." Alder winked at her, sliding his arm around her waist as he turned to face his best friend. "Are you interested in my woman, Jesse?"

The amused smile on Jesse's lips faded. "She's with you, so I consider her off limits."

"What if she wasn't off limits?"

"I…" Jesse tugged his bottom lip between his teeth, which made it hard not to stare at his mouth. His eyes filled with lust as he met Danica's steady gaze. "I get what you see in her."

"Good. Then let's not make this all about me." Alder curved his hand around the back of Danica's neck, running his thumb up and down the side of her throat. "Maybe a hint that you're not completely repulsed by one another might be more convincing."

She wasn't repulsed by Jesse, but she wasn't sure what to do with Alder's suggestion. And the arousal Alder was stirring in her from touching one of her trigger points made it difficult to think.

Inhaling deeply to slow her racing pulse, she tried to focus. Making this all about Alder had been easy. He loved Jesse. She had been willing to step aside if Alder chose him, but she had no objection to an unconventional alternative.

But her and Jesse? Their friendship was new and tended to revolve around concern for Alder. She was attracted to him in the same way she'd be attracted to any man that could melt panties with a smile and looked like a wet dream with his shirt off. Several of those men strutted across the screen whenever she got the chance to watch her favorite TV shows, but if she met them in person?

From past experience, that kind of lust didn't translate to real life. Many fantasy men were best left as stroking material. Like the pages she bookmarked in her favorite books.

"If I had a fragile ego, her silence would wound me." Jesse put his hand over his heart as he stood, grinning when she shook her head. "Don't worry, I'm not offended. I've probably thought about fucking you more than you've ever considered touching me, but I'm a guy."

Not gay then? She wet her lips, forcing her eyes not to drift shut at the heat spilling down to her core. She wasn't sure she could take Jesse coming any closer with Alder touching her like this.

Was it still just his hand on her neck? Her nipples tightened as though they were being stroked as well.

"Look at me, Danica." Jesse tipped her chin up with a finger, not moving, not speaking again until she met his eyes. "Tell me what you're thinking."

She let out a nervous laugh. "I'm still stunned that you've thought about fucking me."

"Yeah, I was kinda stunned at first too. And I still don't understand chicks, but I've thought about you and Alder together. And you alone. And him alone. And…" Jesse ran his hand through his rumpled, overgrown blond curls. "Let me be perfectly honest. If not for him, me and you probably would never happen. But when he kisses you, when he touches you, I want to know how you taste. How fucking soft your skin is."

Drawing in a shaky breath, wondering when it had gotten so damn hot in here, she nodded. "I never thought two guys were hot together until I saw Alder and Malakai on stage."

Jesse's lips thinned. "Yeah, I like watching that a whole lot less."

Alder's hand still on her neck. "You're jealous of Malakai? That's fucking new."

"It's not a big deal. I get why you put on the whole homoerotic show on stage. For how 'straight' metal is, the fans have always gotten off on the man on man thing." Jesse folded his arms over his chest. "If I didn't care about you so much, I would have seduced you a long time ago. But I have a bad history with relationships. I don't go for the guy I might have a nice, stable future with. I go for the one that's so screwed up, there's no fucking hope of it ending well."

Danica reached out, putting her hand on his tightly crossed arms. "Do you know why?"

He made a face, shaking his head. Then released a shallow laugh. "Actually, maybe I do. I spent the first few years of my adult life angry and alone because my parents kicked me out. I was broken and no one could be bothered with me. I guess I look for broken and want to fix it. Works out *real* well for me."

That would explain what he'd seen in Brave. But she really didn't want him thinking about Brave right now.

Trailing his fingers up the side of her neck, Alder chuckled. "I guess it's good to know you don't consider me broken."

"You might be when I'm done with you."

There was no doubting the fear underlying Jesse's warning. Danica studied his face, hoping she'd find a clue as to what to do next. The longing in his eyes told her he wanted this. But if he didn't have to fight for what he wanted, he didn't seem to know how to take it.

She traced her fingers up the center of his chest, the edge of her lip quirking up. "You can't break him, Jesse. I won't let you."

"You think you can stop me?" Jesse's eyes closed as she brought her fingers to his neck, stroking him much like Alder was stroking her. "I don't mean it to sound like a threat."

"I know."

"My track record fucking sucks. I don't know how long this will last, but—"

"But you really need to relax. I'm pretty sure Alder's not expecting you to propose." She brought her other hand up to his arms to tug them apart. "Don't overthink this. Is the idea of kissing me so scary?"

The uncertainty in Jesse's eyes disappeared, replaced by pure masculine confidence. Relationships might not be his thing, but he had no doubt about his other abilities. His whole stance shifted, and goosebumps spread over every inch of her as he moved forward, trapping her between his body and Alder's.

"If it wasn't a little scary, it wouldn't be worth doing." He tucked a strand of hair behind her ear, so close she could feel his breath on her lips. "Are you afraid, Danica?"

She shivered. Were they really doing this? So much of her time had been spent running different scenarios over and over in her head. Some where her and Jesse shared Alder. Others where she was forced to walk away so she didn't come between them.

But she'd never let herself fantasize about how being between them could be one of the hottest experiences of her life. One that might change absolutely everything she'd thought she wanted.

Not only for Alder.

For herself.

"I'm terrified."

Jesse caught her chin between his thumb and his bent forefinger, flicking his tongue over her bottom lip. "Good."

There was something different about kissing in the morning. Not only the taste of coffee on hot lips, and fuck, Jesse had never realized a woman's lips could be so hot. Kisses at night tended to end the same. Great sex, usually after a few drinks, then finding a bed to crash in.

Alone.

Starting the day with a kiss often meant the night had gone well enough for another round. But this was where it would all begin. With a kiss that might lead to so much more.

He wrapped his arms around Danica's waist, lifting her up against his body, ignoring the pain of his hard dick being crushed to his stomach by her pelvis. He wanted to see if the rest of her was as soft as her lips. If those little sounds she was making in the back of her throat would get louder when he licked and sucked every fucking inch of her.

Bringing his mouth to her throat, he met Alder's eyes. And the surge of lust hit him so hard he had to fight to stay on his feet. He groaned as Danica took advantage of his momentary distraction and ran her teeth over the corded muscled of his neck. Afraid to drop her, he perched her on the edge of the sofa, holding his hand out to Alder.

Alder came to him, raking his fingers into Jesse's hair as his mouth covered Jesse's with the same fierce passion he'd shown the one time they'd kissed. He didn't hold back and Jesse felt the cold, protective shell he'd encased his heart in shatter.

Other men had fucked with his head. Had left him licking his wounds when they were done with him, but he'd always gone in expecting the worst since he'd chosen them *because* they were damaged assholes. Each and every goddamn one. He might have made stupid choices, but he'd never been foolish enough to let them in too deep.

This man, this amazing, selfless, loving man was already in as deep as he could be without crossing the line between friends and lovers.

That line was about to be fucking wiped out. There wouldn't be a trace of it when they were done.

If their relationship didn't work out, it wouldn't hurt Jesse. It would destroy him.

But, for the first time, he was willing to take the chance.

He caught Alder's bottom lip between his teeth, giving Alder a hooded look as he slid his hand under Danica's shirt. He palmed her breast over what felt like a lacy bra.

Fucking annoying thing. He groaned, leaning into Alder even as he pulled her shirt off. The black bra was molded to her skin, with delicate little straps he could probably break if he tried.

Or he could just move it out of the way. He dipped his fingers under the lace, bending over her as he shoved the material down. With his other hand, he shoved the strap off her shoulder.

"Just take it off, Jesse." Danica moaned as he sucked one hard little nipple into his mouth. "Oh god, the feels good."

Alder chuckled, somehow undoing the bra from behind her back. He let it fall to the floor behind the sofa. "I think we have a few things to teach him, my angel."

Danica murmured something that didn't sound like a complaint, so Jesse didn't stop. He moved from one breast to the other, squeezing the first since the stimulation had her writhing mindlessly as he lowered her to the sofa.

By his side, Alder worked on removing her jeans and panties. He knelt at the end of the sofa, pulling her thighs over his shoulder and spreading her glistening pussy with his fingers. Jesse's balls tightened as Alder licked her. He dipped his tongue right inside her, looking like a man feasting on the most delicious dessert on the fucking planet.

Laving right over those puffy little lips, Alder caught his eye, a playful glint in his eye. "She's so fucking wet, Jesse. You should taste her."

A tiny whimper escaped Danica as Alder pressed two fingers into her. He withdrew his fingers, holding them out to Jesse.

Evil fucker. Two can play this game. Jesse waited until Alder brought his mouth back to Danica's cunt then latched onto Alder's wrist. He swirled his tongue over the tips of Alder's fingers, savoring the sweet, heady flavor of Danica while he sucked.

He smirked when Alder groaned. He had to give it to the man though. His attention didn't shift from Danica until he'd used his fingers and mouth to bring her over the edge. She cried out, thrashing with her thighs clenched against Alder's face.

Ladies first I guess? Jesse had been with guys whose whole encounter—including prep and fucking—took less time than Alder had just spent getting Danica off. But he guessed it made sense. He might not know a lot about women, but he knew they could be hard to pleasure. And when they *did* come, they could go again immediately.

Suck a guy's dick until he came, and if he didn't bottom, he was useless.

Speaking of sucking dick.

"You're overdressed, Alder." Jesse stood and quickly stepped behind Alder. "Don't you think, Danica?"

Biting her bottom lip, Danica nodded. She released Alder, then sat up with her legs folded under her. While she tugged Alder's tank top over his head, Jesse knelt, drawing down Alder's black plaid, flannel sleep pants. He'd always hated these fucking things. Not that he should have cared what Alder wore to bed, but he'd only started wearing them when Danica joined the tour.

Jesse guessed he'd missed watching Alder walk around first thing in the morning in snug boxers. Fine, he'd decided not to have sex with the man, but he wasn't blind.

He wrapped his hand around the base of Alder's cock, tracing the ridge of the thick head with his tongue. Maybe it was fucked up to consider the last dick he'd had his mouth on right now, but he couldn't help notice that Alder was a bit longer. Not quite as wide, but the dark purple, swollen head of him more than made up for that.

Despite his aversion to bottoming, Jesse did like sucking dick. He took Alder in his mouth, loving the way the wide ridge of his head felt sliding over his tongue.

"Oh god, that's so fucking hot." Danica whispered. She made a soft sound of pleasure as Alder gave her a hungry kiss. As Jesse tipped his head back to take Alder further down his throat, she was nodding to something Alder said to her.

She stepped off the sofa and Alder pulled out of Jesse's mouth.

Jesse frowned. "What—?"

A sly smile on her lips, Danica nodded toward where Alder had moved to the other end of the sofa. "We should all get more comfortable."

Jesse shrugged. He'd been fine where he was, but he'd play along. He climbed onto the sofa, rising over Alder to give him a long, slow kiss before running his lips down the man's muscular chest. Alder might not believe it, but he had the body of an athlete. Maybe one during offseason, but it was still fucking sexy.

He grazed his teeth over the bit of extra flesh covering Alder's abs, palming his balls as he sank his lips over that long, hard cock he couldn't get enough of.

Cool air flowed over his own erection as Danica's small hand pulled him free of his boxers. He lost his rhythm as her lips slid over him.

"Fuck." He rested his forehead on Alder's thigh. He hadn't had anyone suck his dick in way too long and she was damn good at it.

No way was he going to embarrass himself by coming in her mouth this fast. And he was already close. He sat up, pulling her off the floor and bringing her up to straddle him. Her hot pussy slid over his over-sensitized dick. Which wasn't much better. He wanted to thrust inside her. To feel that hot cunt all around him.

But he needed a minute. Or ten. Hell, the way his heart was beating couldn't be healthy.

She squirmed, wrapping her arms around his neck and pressing her soft breasts against his chest. "Are you all right, Jesse?"

He gave her a crooked grin. "Yeah, just not as young as you two."

"Poor baby." She leaned forward, nipping his bottom lip. "Take your time. There's no rush."

Okay, there might not be a rush, but he wasn't *that* old. He just needed to not blow his load the second someone touched him.

Alder rose from the sofa, stepping behind Danica and kissing her shoulder. "Do you have any condoms in your purse, angel?"

Jesse cursed under his breath. The question was almost as bad as having Danica's lips, or her pussy, on him.

Danica shot him a curious smile. "No. But between the two of you, you must have some?"

"Yeah. I've got some in my room." Alder grinned at Jesse. "And lube."

Dropping his head back, Jesse banged his head on the sofa a few times. They were trying to kill him.

"Deep breaths, Jesse." Danica stroked her hand down his chest. Thankfully, not touching his dick. It hadn't gotten the message that he wanted to last a little longer. "I could go put my clothes back on if that would help."

"Don't you dare." Jesse barred one arm across her back before she could move. He lowered his gaze to her breasts, loving the gentle swell of them. They weren't as big as the ones usually bared for the band from the crowd, but they were a perfect mouthful. He bent her over his arm, running his tongue around one breast in smaller and smaller circles until he reached her nipple. He sucked on it, bringing his other hand between them to slid his fingers over her slick pussy. "Fuck, I need to feel you."

"Mmm, please, Jesse." Danica threw her head back as he slid one finger inside her. Her cunt was hot, tightening around his finger as he worked it in and out. "That feels so good."

"Yeah?" He was enjoying the control she gave him. Fine, he might not be entirely sure of what he was doing, but he was a fast learner. And tasting her on Alder's fingers hadn't been enough.

He twisted his body, lowering her to the sofa, his finger still inside her. And he brought his tongue to the cute little nub of flesh that peeked out past her pussy lips.

She jerked, her back bowing as she tugged at his hair.

He bent over her, twisting his finger, adding another as he focused on her clit. He sucked it harder and harder as her moans grew louder. Encouraged, he tugged it between his teeth.

She yelped and twisted away from him before sitting up.

Shit.

He licked his lips, trying to focus on what he'd done wrong rather than how good she tasted. "Sorry about that."

"I get that, but we have a new rule. You don't get to do that again until Alder teaches you how."

"Uh oh." Alder strolled into the room, a box of condoms and a bottle of lube in his hands. "What did you do, Jesse?"

Jesse's face heated. "Apparently women aren't much fonder of teeth than we are."

Alder winced. "Umm, no. Not unless you're very very careful."

So noted. Jesse ran his hand down Danica's thigh, hoping she'd forgive him. "I think she just put her pussy off limits for me."

"I did not. I said Alder will show you how it's done." She pulled her bottom lip between her teeth, eyeing the condoms. "Some other time."

"Agreed." Alder pulled out two condoms, then set the box and the lube on the coffee table. "But let him kiss you better."

She hesitated.

Alder took a knee by the sofa, gently pushing her onto her back. "He'll be careful. I'll supervise."

Danica giggled, hissing in a sharp breath as Jesse gave her pussy the same kind of deep, passionate kiss he'd give her lips.

He felt Alder's hand on his dick, covering him with a condom.

Then Alder's lips brushed his ear. "Fuck her."

Every drop of blood in Jesse's body flowed right into his dick. He curved his arm under Danica's waist, rising up even as he pulled her under him. He didn't need instructions to guide his dick into her hot body, but he wasn't a complete idiot. He pressed the head of his cock in gradually, watching her face as he sank in deeper.

Her lips parted as her hips rose, encouraging him to thrust in all the way.

The grip of a man's body was different, but he loved the way her cunt enveloped him, all those muscles within holding his cock as he slid in and out. She was so fucking wet. Nice and slick. He could easily pound into her, but he didn't want to hurt her again.

So he took it slow.

Alder curved a hand around the front of his neck, giving him a bruising kiss that made up for how careful he had to be. Danica might be delicate, but Alder wasn't. Which meant he could have a little of both.

He wasn't sure how he'd gotten to be so fucking lucky.

Or how long this would last.

But he wouldn't question it. He'd take every goddam thing he could while it did.

Alder hadn't expected seeing Danica and Jesse together to be such a turn on. If they'd suggested this any other day, he would have rejected the idea. He loved Danica. He would have been happy with her for the rest of his life.

Would he have regretted never getting a chance to explore his feelings for Jesse? Maybe. But he didn't have to worry about that anymore. He had them both and he would find a way to keep them.

He wasn't given much time to think things over though. Danica whispered his name, wrapping her hand around his cock when he approached her and pulling it to her mouth. While Jesse fucked her, she put all her focus on his pleasure. No matter what he said, she'd probably worry that he'd be jealous.

He should be. His best friend was fucking the woman he loved, but all he could think about was Danica was enjoying herself and Jesse seemed to have forgotten catching Brave with another man.

Danica made a soft, irritated sound, letting him slid from her lips. "He's distracted."

Jesse nodded, having slowed his steady thrusts at some point. "I can see that."

Alder frowned. He hadn't been distracted in a bad way. He wanted the two most important people in his life to be happy. They were, so he was more than satisfied.

Latching on to Danica's hand, Jesse pulled her up, kissing her even as he slipped out of her. He reached over, snatching a condom out of the box on the table. "Help me out, beautiful?"

"My pleasure." Danica tore the package with her teeth and rolled the condom over Alder's dick, grinning as he shuddered.

"You're evil." Jesse cupped her cheek, giving her a tender look that erased any doubts Alder had about the two of them feeling nothing for one another. This relationship would go nowhere if they didn't have a solid foundation.

He was confident they were building something strong. Not only for him. For them all.

"Alder, I need you. Here with us. Now." Danica grabbed his wrist and pulled him against her. "Completely."

"I am with you." Alder lifted her up against the back of the sofa, holding her there with one arm, kissing her as he guided himself into her tight, warm body. He held still as she clenched around him. She clung to his shoulders, bowing her head, gasping through parted lips as she kissed his throat. "I can't think of another place I'd rather be."

"Good. But, Alder?" She inhaled roughly, bringing one hand up to his cheek. "Stop thinking. Just feel."

He nodded, tensing as he felt Jesse move behind him. His dick throbbed as he considered the position they had just put him in. He'd be surrounded by the two people who meant more to him than anything else in the world.

But Jesse hesitated, pressing his lips to the nape of Alder's neck as he ran his hand up and down Alder's side. "We haven't discussed this, but I need to know. When's the last time you were with a man?"

Alder huffed out a laugh. "*So* the wrong time for this conversation."

"No, it's not. It's one I haven't…I haven't had as often as I should. I remember you having a thing with the drummer in that punk band, but that was almost two years ago. It ended when we stopped touring with them."

"Yeah. Still not seeing why we're talking about this now, Jesse."

"Damn it, Alder. Did you top or bottom?"

Running his tongue over his bottom lip, Alder sighed. "I topped."

He always topped. The men he'd been involved with expected him to take the lead. But he'd always wanted to give that control to someone else.

Jesse had been the first man he'd actually hoped would do so.

The hand Jesse was stroking him with went still. "Have you *ever* bottomed?"

"No." Alder's jaw tensed. "Is that a problem for you?"

"Only if you're not sure you want to do this." Jesse put his hand on Alder's hip, flattening the other in the center of his back when he moved to stand. "Don't get pissed. My first time, I didn't have a choice. And *that* we won't discuss now. I need to know you won't regret anything I do to you."

Alder's throat tightened. Damn it, how much had Jesse endured from the assholes he'd been with?

Danica's hand pressed against his cheek. She met his eyes with a penetrating gaze that seemed to reach his very core. Then she kissed him, whispering against his lips. "He'll be all right. We've got him. Just tell him how much you want him. That's what he needs to hear."

She was right. And he did want Jesse. He needed to give him everything. And to make sure Jesse knew he'd never regret a fucking moment of what they shared.

He drew away from Danica until only the head of his dick was in her sweet, tight pussy, then thrust back in. Letting out a soft moan, he lifted her up, so her back was on the sofa, but her hips were lifted. Putting himself at the perfect angle for Jesse.

"Others fucked this up for you, Jesse. But I trust you." He spread his thighs, opening Danica a little more as he thrust into her. And opening himself so Jesse would understand he was ready. "Fuck, I want you. I need this."

Jesse cursed softly. He moved away, returning to slide his fingers, slick with lube, over the tight ring of Alder's ass. Then he laughed. "Hold still. I have a bad feeling all the twinks you've fucked were experienced and didn't need prep. I don't want to hurt you."

"You won't." Alder wasn't worried. When he was younger, he'd used his fingers to get himself off. How difficult could this be? "Just do it."

"No, I won't, 'just do it'. Fuck. You're stubborn." He bit Alder's shoulder hard as he penetrated him with a single finger. "And so fucking tight. Try to relax."

"I am." Alder ground against Danica, sensing that she was close to the edge and needing to keep her there. She seemed to be turned on by what Jesse was doing to him. Which made it a bit easier to take the stretching as Jesse worked a second, thick finger into him.

But the burning pain had him tightening and jerking away.

"Distract him, Danica. Fuck, he's the worst virgin I've ever been with."

Alder scowled, trying not to tense even more because he was getting annoyed. He wasn't a fucking 'virgin'. What the hell?

"Jesse, sweetie, your pillow talk can use some work." Danica's tone held a hint of laughter. "Alder, I've never…a man has never fucked me *there*. But I want you to be my first. So you need to show me how it's done."

Since when did she use vague terms for sex? He grinned, smoothing her damp hair away from her cheeks. "I'll be gentle. And not make you feel like you're doing it all wrong."

"I don't mean to…" Jesse groaned, pressing his fingers in deeper as he lowered his voice, his lips against Alder's ear. "I want you so bad. But I need this to be good for you."

Panting as the burning became a deep heat that shot from his ass to his dick, Alder nodded. "I'll try to relax."

"Good." Jesse added more lube, his thrusting fingers building up a pressure so intense, Alder couldn't help moving with him. He drove into Danica, sweat beading on his temples, on his chest. The invading presence left him and he felt something firm and blunt spreading him open.

He ground his teeth as every muscle in his body stiffened.

"Press back against me, Alder." Jesse kissed his throat. "You're ready."

Pressing back, Alder's lips parted. The burning from before increased a thousandfold. He fought the urge to pull away. For a moment, the pain seemed even worse. Growing until Jesse withdrew. A cool spill and then more pressure.

He felt the head of Jesse's cock inside him. Pushing in slowly.

"God, Alder." Jesse latched on to his hips, gasping with his lips parted against Alder's shoulder. "Take me."

Those words sent a shot of emotion right into Alder's heart, and a jolt of lust right to his dick. He kept still, the pain nothing compared to having Jesse so close. He ground his teeth as Jesse pulled back again, but more lube and he slipped in with little resistance. Filling Alder so much that the warm heat of Danica around his dick, and the slow stretch of Jesse inside him was almost too much.

He needed to share this with them. To make it last as long as possible.

"Please don't move." He groaned as Danica clenched down. "Angel, that's not not moving."

"I'm sorry, but I can picture him inside you and it's so fucking hot." She delved her hands into his hair, her thighs tightening around him. "One day, I need to watch you two together. Can I?"

"If he doesn't kill me taking his time now? Sure."

"Impatient fucker. You said don't move." Jesse laughed, kissing Alder's shoulder. "I'm warning you, I won't last. You're so fucking tight, you feel so fucking amazing, I'm surprised I've lasted this long."

"What about you, baby?" Alder met Danica's eyes. "Aside from the fantasy, are you close?"

"I came when he told you you were ready." She blushed, clenching down on him again. "But yes, I'm close."

Jesse chuckled. "Good. Then let's see if I can get you both off. Move with me."

Alder wasn't sure what Jesse meant, but he figured it out before long. As Jesse slid back and thrust into him, he was forced deep into Danica. As the pace quickened, he found himself slamming into her. Harder than he'd ever done before, but the way she moved against him, she was enjoying every fucking second. Her pussy seized around his dick and she threw her head back, crying out.

Her pleasure threw him over the edge. He grabbed the back of the sofa, groaning as pleasure ripped through him, like a tremor powerful enough to break through the core of the earth and split continents. He came so hard his muscles tensed and the pleasure surged from the base of his spine, right into his balls, spreading until his whole body was shaking.

Jesse let out a low growl that seized him right by the balls. If he could come again, he would have. Instead, he gasped in air, struggling to keep his weight off Danica as his arms and legs and his whole fucking body went liquid.

He was so damn spent, he moved to lay down with Danica without thinking. But pulling away from Jesse made him wince. His ass was sore. Not in a completely bad way, but moving was a very bad idea.

"Shh. Don't move." Jesse pulled out, stroking Alder's side and speaking softly. "Give me a minute."

Alder frowned as he heard Jesse's quick steps. He kissed Danica, who looked like she was ready for a nap.

In less than a minute, Jesse was back, cleaning him with a soft, warm washcloth.

"Lie down with her while I clean up. I would snuggle with you, but there's not much space." Jesse took a knee by the sofa, his jaw tense. "Please don't think I'm leaving you."

"I don't." Alder was sleepy, but Jesse's words set off little alarms in his skull that he couldn't ignore. "What do you mean, cleaning up?"

Jesse bunched the washcloth in his hand. "Ah…just getting rid of this. Then I'll come sit with you or something."

Nope. Not good enough. Alder eased away from Danica. He pulled off the condom, using the trip to the trashcan in the kitchen to prove he could still walk. The pain in his ass made it a little awkward, but he managed.

Jesse seemed to be doing better with remaining vertical though.

"I feel pathetic asking, but…" Alder looked from Jesse to Danica. "Could you carry her to the bedroom?"

"I can walk." Danica protested without lifting her head from where she'd rested it on her arm.

"Nope. We're good for more than sex," Jesse said lightly. But he paused before lifting Danica into his arms and looked over at Alder. "You sure?"

"Sure about what? Letting you carry the woman I love after I just let you have sex with her?" Alder arched a brow at Jesse, not sure he understood the man at all. "Why wouldn't I be sure?"

"Because…" Jesse's forehead creased. He shrugged. "Hell, I don't know. I'm not good at the after sex stuff."

"You'll learn." Alder was happy he had something he could teach Jesse. Aside from how to go down on a woman. It was kinda sad that he had to show the man how people who cared for one another could lay in bed, enjoying the aftermath of hot sex, but it was a lesson Jesse needed to learn if he was going to be with Danica.

Alder might accept less for himself, but he wouldn't for her.

Thankfully, Jesse didn't seem to have a problem with learning new things. He laid Danica on the bed and reclined beside her, giving Alder a sleepy smile.

"You've told me you loved me before. Is it horrible to bring up now?" Jesse's eyes drifted shut. "I'm worried it might be, but

I wanted to tell you, I never thought it meant anything. I said it back like it didn't, but it did. I do love you, Alder."

Putting his hand over the one Jesse had rested on Danica's side, Alder smiled. "This is the perfect time to bring it up. And I'm glad you figured that out. Because Danica was right. I never stopped loving you."

He knew Jesse was asleep from his soft, steady breaths, but even if the man couldn't hear him, he had one last thing to say.

"And I never will."

Chapter Nineteen

The entire day was spent lazing around and making love. Danica was tired, but it was an amazing feeling. She still hadn't gotten to see Jesse and Alder together alone, but she couldn't complain. They included her in almost everything, but didn't hesitate to touch or kiss whenever they were close, erasing any concern she'd had about being an obstacle for them.

She was the only one who woke when their phones buzzed though. She thought it was funny they all had their phones on vibrate, but her amusement died when she saw the mass text message that had gone out.

From Brave.

> **BRAVE: I HOPE EVERYONE IS DOING WELL. AND I UNDERSTAND IF YOU CHOOSE NOT TO, BUT I WOULD LIKE EVERYONE TO MEET AT MY PLACE. IN AN HOUR. YOU KNOW WHERE I LIVE. WE NEED TO DEAL WITH THIS SHIT BEFORE ANOTHER SHOW IS CANCELED...PLEASE.**

Ignoring him would be easy. Both Alder and Jesse deserved one goddamn day without having to deal with his bullshit.

Except, making that choice for them felt wrong. What if Brave wanted to apologize? What if this was the defining moment for Winter's Wrath?

She knew the band meant so much to Alder. To Jesse. Who knew if Brave would be willing to reach out more than once?

Sitting on the sofa in the living room, she tossed her phone onto the cushion beside her and groaned.

What if this wasn't for an apology? What if he wanted to give them shit about canceling the show? Act like he was the only one who cared about the future of the band?

Does it matter?

She sighed, dropping her head to her hands.

No.

Besides, if he wanted to tell the guys off, why would he have added her to the text?

Going to the kitchen to fix some coffee, she poured two cups, not sure how Jesse liked his, but recalling Alder's preferences. She grabbed a tray, leaving one coffee black, settling on bringing a small mug of milk and another full of sugar and a spoon when she couldn't find any dishes dedicated to either.

Setting the tray on the night table, she bent down to kiss Alder's cheek. "You have to get up."

He groaned, pulling her closer. "No, you need to get back in bed."

"I brought coffee."

His brow creased. He opened his eyes. "What's wrong?"

"Coffee first. And wake Jesse up." She wrinkled her nose. "I would, but I don't know what he's like after a nap. He was always in the van, or sharing driving shifts on tour."

"He's fine." Alder nudged Jesse with his elbow. "Get up. Danica brought us coffee. And something's up."

Jesse shoved to a seating position, instantly alert. "What is it?"

Smiling, she pointed to the coffee. "How do you like yours?"

"Black with five heaping teaspoons when I need to be awake for something bad. Want to tell me what that is?"

Five? She shook her head as she shoveled the sugar into his mug. "I refuse to have conversations until everyone is properly caffeinated."

Both Alder and Jesse drank their coffee faster than she'd thought possible. She was still sipping hers when they stared at her expectantly.

Rolling her eyes, she leaned against the headboard, facing them both. "Brave texted everyone. He's called a meeting at his place."

"Great." Jesse sighed, throwing his legs over the side of the bed before he stood. "At what time?"

She checked the time on her phone. "About forty five minutes?"

Alder inclined his head. "He's only a few blocks away. We've got plenty of time." He gave her a knowing look. "How long did it take before you decided to tell us at all?"

Wrinkling her nose at him, she thought about pretending she'd never considered otherwise. Then she rolled her eyes. "Not long. I made up my mind before making the coffee and he said in an hour."

Biting back a laugh, Alder grinned at her. "Not bad. If it was me, we'd have about half an hour. Jesse would have us all getting there about twenty minutes late."

Jesse snorted. "Not true."

"Bullshit."

"Twenty minutes is generous. I'd keep the asshole waiting at least an hour."

All right, she didn't feel so bad about second-guessing telling them anymore. They did need to have a conversation about not making those kinds of decisions though. From what they'd just admitted, she wouldn't have been too pleased if she'd been the one being woken up.

They made their way to the kitchen, Jesse fixing himself a fresh cup off coffee before turning his attention to her. "I know Brave doesn't live far, but do you have enough time to do your girl thing?"

Danica glared at him. "Damn it, Jesse. Seriously?"

Alder sighed and shook his head. "And it begins."

Both Danica and Jesse stared at him. "What?"

"Jesse wasn't joking when he said he doesn't understand women. His sister is almost twenty years older than him. He grew up almost like an only child. His parents are…well, let's just say his father was ready to retire when he was born."

"According to him, I don't exist. And my mother is fine with that now that he's recovered from his stroke." Jesse put the bag of sugar away and slammed the cupboard door. "So can we not discuss my parents?

"I just wanted her to understand you're not trying to be a jerk." Alder gave Jesse a level look. "She's not going on stage. Or to a photo-shoot. So she doesn't put on more than lip gloss."

That Alder had paid enough attention to know that made her smile. She pulled out a fresh change of clothes from her suitcase, which was still in the living room; happy they'd taken a shower that afternoon.

Before having sex again. Twice. Condoms meant she didn't have anything much to wash off, but if she was going anywhere important, she'd want to wash again because…well, they'd all worked up a sweat. She was sure she smelled like both men.

Which wasn't a bad thing, going to Brave's place. He'd clearly moved on.

After they were all dressed, they headed down, taking her car to Brave's condo. It was only a few blocks, but it was damn cold out and why walk? She gave both men points for not asking to drive. She'd known a few men who seemed to feel less masculine with a woman behind the wheel. Alder and Jesse not joining those ranks made her very happy.

Both were way too quiet though. She parked, getting out to wait for them on the sidewalk. Alder looked determined, so she wasn't worried about him.

Jesse was pale and took his time getting out of the car.

Taking to his side, she grabbed his hand, lacing their fingers together. When he blinked at her, looking confused, she gave him a small smile. "I wish I could say this won't hurt, but…I'm here." Her smile widened as Alder came up behind Jesse to hug him. "We're here."

With a huffed laugh, Jesse leaned back against Alder and squeezed her hand. "Fucking lucky for him, because if you weren't, I wouldn't be."

A few minutes later, they stood in front of Brave's door. Malakai was the one who let them in and he led the way to the living room. The apartment was much older than Alder's and the rooms had a more closed setting. At the end of the long hall was a small kitchen, and the open doorway to the living room was halfway there.

Inside, Tate and Connor were sitting on opposite sides of a long leather sofa. Brave stood by the window, looking out.

Malakai cleared his throat as he plunked down in the spot between Tate and Connor. "Everyone's here, Brave."

Brave turned, crossing his arms tightly over his chest. There were dark shadows under his eyes, but for the first time in a long while, his golden brown eyes were clear.

He motioned to the empty, black leather loveseat. "Can you please have a seat?"

Danica settled in the middle of the loveseat. Sighed when Alder and Jesse remained standing at either side of her. She grabbed both of their belts from behind and tugged them down.

"Thank you." Brave shot her a grateful smile, then inhaled roughly. "Look, I know you're all pissed at me."

"Pissed?" Malakai let out a bitter laugh. "Try fucking furious."

"Fine. Furious." Brave bowed his head. "This isn't an excuse, but I owe you all an explanation for why I've been acting like a goddamn head case. If you can't forgive me, I get it, but I'll do anything to make this right. I can't lose this band."

"How about you explain first?" Tate suggested, looking more confused than angry. He rubbed his palms on his knees. "Is it the stalker? Because I'd be pretty freaked out if I had a stalker. Actually, maybe you were pushing all of us away to keep us safe, which would be cool of you."

Connor sighed and leaned forward to give Tate an exasperated look. "Will you shut up?"

Malakai glared at him. "You need to back the fuck off him, Phelan."

"Chill the fuck out, Noble."

"Guys, both of you get a grip." Alder slammed his fist on the arm of the loveseat and stood, eyes on his brother. "Tate's right. If you're losing it because of the stalker, then say so. But this shit you pulled? The fucking drinking and smoking? It stops now."

"Deal." Scratching his jaw and staring at the floor, Brave sighed. "But it's not really about the stalker. It's about Valor."

Alder sank back down to the loveseat, shaking his head. "Valor? Damn it, Brave, why didn't you say something?"

"I'm trying to." Brave's lips quirked slightly. "Shit, I didn't know it was fucking with me so much. The stalker seems like he was obsessed with our brother before he fixated on me. Maybe when I'm dead, he'll go after you."

Danica bit her lip as Alder tensed beside her. She put her hand over the one with a death-grip on his knee. "That's not funny, Brave."

"No, what's funny is the son of a bitch loved Valor, the fucking hero. His latest gift is a CD of LOST songs and pictures of Valor. And a poem that included Valor among the greats that we've lost too soon. I'm sure our brother would have loved being mentioned along with Kurt Cobain, Benjamin Curtis, and Buddy Holly." Brave combed his fingers into his hair with a broken laugh. "Of course, they actually did something worth remembering them for."

"So did Valor." Alder stood again, this time crossing the room and approaching his brother, putting his hand on Brave's shoulder and meeting his eyes. "As bad as things are between us, I'm fucking grateful to him for saving you."

Brave pressed his eyes shut and leaned his head back against the window frame. "He didn't save me. He almost got the whole band killed."

Everyone sat forward, staring at Brave in shock. Danica hugged herself, wishing she could go to Alder, because she didn't trust Brave not to lash out if sharing the truth about Valor ripped open an old wound. But Alder could handle his brother now, better than he'd ever managed before.

He wasn't the same man that Brave had used as a punching bag for years.

Alder gave his brother a little nudge when the silence lengthened. "What are you talking about, Brave? Is this about the van you guys had breaking down?"

"The van didn't fucking break down. Valor was high on PCP and walked out of the motel we were staying at in the middle of the night. The desk clerk came and got me because it was fucking freezing and she was worried." Brave turned, slightly, staring sideways out the window, but not like he was seeing anything other than what he remembered. "I tried to follow his tracks, but it was snowing so much…Skull dragged me back to the van and the whole band went looking. We kept stopping along the side of the road, then splitting up, calling for him. The cops were on their way, but it was a bad night, so they took forever. By the time they got to us we were all in rough shape. I don't even remember getting to the hospital."

"Jesus. Why the fucking story then?" Alder let his hand fall to his side, not sure if he was more angry about being lied to, or that he'd been standing in the shadows of a dead man who'd never deserved Brave's love. "I don't understand. I thought you hated me because I'm not him. You lost the brother you were closest to and got stuck with me."

"No, by the end I fucking hated *Valor*. I was so tired of dealing with his shit, with him getting more and more out of control, sometimes so violent we were all afraid to be around him. But I wanted the band to make it, so put up with whatever he threw at me. Sound familiar?" Brave's lips thinned. "That's why I went along with the story when Cole came up with it. The press ate up the idea of Valor being a hero. And Mom and Dad?

Fuck, they would have blamed me for what happened either way, but at least they could pretend their dead firstborn had been perfect."

"They couldn't be bothered with any of us for how fucking long? I don't think they would have cared either way."

Brave's brow lifted. "Our parents love you, Alder."

With a thin smile, Alder inclined his head. "They do now. As much as they can love anyone, and only because I go home and let Mom show me off to her friends, and let Dad brag about how Mathew expanded the shop."

"Yeah, I guess I haven't tried that."

"Why would you? You're right, they do blame you for what happened to Valor and it's fucked up." Alder shoved his hands into his pockets and gave Brave a hard look. "Is that why you hate me?"

"I don't fucking hate you. I need you to not be close to me. You fucking scared the hell out of me when we started Winter's Wrath, acting like I was amazing, like we could create another band just like LOST. That was the *last* thing I wanted." Brave hunched his shoulders. "It was easier to push you away. The worse things got, the more determined you were. You never touched hard drugs, you hardly ever got wasted. I was fucking proud of you. I still am"

Brave's words were like a punch in the gut. Alder's eyes burned and he blinked fast, taking an involuntary step back. "You're proud of me? Are you fucking joking?"

"No."

"You have a fucked up way of showing it."

"Yeah, well I'm fucked up. I figured we could work together, but it would be safer if you weren't like a brother. If you were just part of the band. That way, if anything happened to me, it wouldn't fucking destroy you."

Alder wasn't sure what to do with his hands. Wrapping them around Brave's neck was a good option. "So you let it destroy everything?"

"That wasn't the plan. It just kinda…hell, things just got worse and worse. This psycho stalker bringing up Valor, Cole wanting to write a fucking tribute to him."

"The stalker?" Tate asked suddenly, reminding Alder that there were other people in the room. "That's fucked up, Brave. This is all fucked up, but I like that you two are talking. Is everything better now? I really don't want to cancel the show tomorrow."

Brave rolled his eyes and shook his head. "Not the stalker, Tate. But that's a good point. And part of why we needed to meet as a band." He rubbed his jaw, his gaze going slowly over every man on the couch. Then shifting to Danica and Jesse. "And you're both important to the show as well, but first…I'm sorry. It's just a fucking word, but I need you to know I mean it."

"Sorry about everything? Even the sex?" Tate grunted when Malakai jabbed an elbow in his side. "What? Yeah, the timing was bad, but it was good."

Brave snorted. "Yes, Tate. Even the sex."

Alder noticed Danica holding Jesse's hand and speaking to him softly as Jesse ground his teeth. Shooting Tate a dirty look, Alder turned back to his brother. "Can we get back on topic?"

"That's a good idea." Brave shoved his hands into the pockets of his jeans. "It's simple. I was wrong. This band needs every one of you and from now on, we make decisions together. If you all want to cancel the show, consider it done."

Alder met the eyes of his band mates, one at a time. They all wanted to play. The show was in their hometown, and they hadn't performed here in over a year. But he understood why not a single one of them spoke up.

So he folded his arms over his chest, nodding slowly. "You've given us a lot to think about. How about we all head our separate ways, enjoy the rest of our day, and let you know our answer tonight?"

He wouldn't lie. The way Brave's jaw ticked as he surveyed the room and saw everyone nodding their agreement brought him a shallow satisfaction. Brave could say they'd make decisions together, but he was used to getting his own way.

If he was really sorry, he'd give them the time they needed.

"Fine." Brave sighed. "Don't make it too late though. Cole's already ripping about the show we canceled yesterday. Another one and he'll probably quit."

"Good. That will save us the trouble of firing him." Alder patted his brother's shoulder, a half smile on his lips. "A topic for some other time."

"Fuck you, Alder."

"Yeah, I love you too, Brave." He headed out, the calm front he'd pulled on out of habit slipping as he reached the sidewalk. His stomach twisted as he considered everything Brave had told him. He braced his hands on the hood of Danica's car, not sure what he wanted to do more. Puke or punch something.

A hand settled on his back, moving soothingly up and down. Danica slipped between him and the car, lacing her fingers behind his neck and bring his forehead down to touch hers.

"This was good, Alder. Maybe it doesn't feel like it now, but this was good for you," she said softly. "For the band."

"I hope you're right." He glanced over at Jesse. "You good?"

Jesse shrugged. "Better?"

His uncertainty reflected Alder's own. Years of things getting progressively worse couldn't be fixed in a day, but Brave had made a good first step. He said he wanted things to be different.

They had to give him a chance to prove it.

Chapter Twenty

In the back of the van, where they'd decided to hide out before the show, Danica slouched on the small mattress, her head on Alder's lap, smiling a little as Jesse rubbed her legs. He'd admitted the shoes she wore on stage freaked him out and asked if her legs got sore.

Might have been a line though, because he was obsessed with the little, red plaid skirt she was wearing.

As his hand moved up her leg, she pressed her thighs together. "If anyone touches my pussy today, they will die a painful death. I'm still sore."

Jesse gave her a crooked grin. "I'll be gentle."

"You and Alder were both gentle this afternoon."

Leaning over her, Alder sucked lightly on her throat, his hand sliding under her thin white dress shirt. "He could use his mouth. He still needs practice."

A surge of lust shot down to her core. Damn, that was tempting, but neither of them were satisfied with giving her one orgasm. And by the time they were done with her, her legs would be too shaky to make it across the stage, never mind dance.

It was hard to resist them, with Alder fondling her breast and Jesse taking advantage of her restlessly shifting her thighs. His fingers slid under her panties. He kissed along her inner thigh as he dipped his fingers into her.

He got three nice and wet. But only returned two to her

pussy. The other began to penetrate her back hole and she jerked away from him.

"We are *not* trying that in the back of a van, Jesse." She threw a pillow at him, making a face when she noticed the crusted sock that had been hiding beneath it. "Eww. Actually, we're not doing *anything* in here."

Alder watched her straighten her skirt and button her shirt, then arched a brow at Jesse. "What did you do?"

"Tried something from a song that I can't get out of my head."

"By who?"

Jesse gave Alder a guilty smile. "Steel Panther."

The sound Alder made was half laugh, half groan. He shook his head. "Try Gun 'N Roses. Hell, even Nickelback. They won't give you stupid ideas."

All right, Danica had no idea what they were going on about. She tried to think of a good suggestion from some of the older bands she'd started listening to. "How about Limp Bizkit?"

Eyes wide, lips parted, both Alder and Jesse stared at her.

"Did she just say what I think she did?" Jesse sounded absolutely horrified. "Because if she mentions *them* again, she's not allowed back on the bus."

He had to be joking. She frowned at him as Alder shook his head, happy at least he didn't look like she'd broken some serious rule. "What's wrong with Limp Bizkit?"

"Woodstock '99. Enough said." Jesse's brow furrowed. "Doesn't Alder teach you anything?"

She turned to Alder. "Tell me he's joking?"

"He's joking." Alder leaned over and punched Jesse in the shoulder. "He needs to learn to make that more obvious before I decide he's not allowed back in our bed."

Rubbing his arm, feigning a wince of pain, Jesse shifted closer to Danica. "No, I wouldn't actually kick you off the bus. But I do hate that band with a passion."

"So noted. I promise to never play them on the radio while we're driving." Danica rose up on her knees in front of him, kissing him softly. "We can stick to Adele."

His brow shot up. "Are *you* joking?"

She patted his cheek and grinned. "*Maaay-be.*"

"You two are going to drive me insane." Alder checked the time on his phone, then reached for the back door, throwing it open. "I can't referee your little fights all the time. Danica, you have to accept that Jesse is an idiot. Jesse, the one thing you need to know about women? They're always right."

Taking off her shoe, Danica tossed it at Alder, who ducked out of the way just in time to avoid getting hit.

"Dude, even *I* know you don't say shit like that in front of your girl." Jesse hopped down from the back of the van, retrieving Danica's shoe for her. He took a knee, right in the snow, and slipped the black and white Mary Jane stiletto onto her bare foot. "At least one of us is a gentleman."

"Yes, the one who just stuck his finger in her ass without warning." Alder walked backwards as Jesse helped her down from the van.

Almost backing right into Connor, who burst out laughing, slapping Alder's shoulder before they collided. "Damn, and I thought you were the boring one of the group. Danica *and* Jesse? Fucking sweet."

Danica's cheeks flamed. She hurried to stand by Alder. "Don't tell anyone, Connor. So far, I've got a colorful, but still somewhat professional image online. If this gets around—"

"I won't say a thing." Connor smiled at her, his eyes warming with understanding. "Just make sure Tate doesn't find out. That kid's fucking horrible at keeping secrets."

"Thank you!" She gave him a quick hug. "We better get in. My stylist is sick, so I'm doing my own hair and makeup and—"

"And I'm sorry, hon, but I don't care." Connor chuckled, setting her away from him. "You ever want to talk about sex, though, and I'm all ears."

She was happy he'd stopped her from rambling. She wasn't sure why she was so nervous and excited about tonight. Cuddling with Alder and Jesse had helped her unwind, but

Connor overhearing that comment from Alder reminded her that they'd never discussed how they would handle their relationship in public.

As Connor led the way into the back of the venue, Alder curved his arm around her, holding her close. "People can know as much, or as little as you want them to, angel. I'm not sure I'll ever love the idea of you kissing Brave on stage." He rubbed her arm when she wrinkled her nose. Damn, she'd forgotten about that. "But what we do out there, and what we do at home, are two different things."

He and Jesse walked her to the dressing room where she'd left her makeup kit.

Alder turned to Jesse. "Stay with her while she gets ready."

Jesse started to nod, then frowned. "And who's gonna keep an eye on you?"

"No one's after me, Jesse."

"Yet." Jesse pulled out his phone, sending out a quick text. "We've all got a job to do. You both get to look pretty and entertain the crowd. I do the grunt work and keep you safe."

"And we appreciate that very much." Alder backed Jesse into the dressing room, fisting his hand in Jesse's Winter's Wrath CREW T-shirt.

Danica licked her lips as she watched them kiss. She'd never get tired of seeing them together. They were gentle with her, most of the time, but with each other? They were so rough she sometimes worried one of them would get hurt.

And that was sexy too, which was messed up.

She jumped at the sound of throat clearing from behind her.

Alder and Jesse jerked apart.

And Skull looked them all over and laughed. "I've walked in on worse. Let's go, Alder."

"One minute." Alder grabbed her abruptly, covered her mouth with his, and kissed her until her head was spinning. He grinned as he lowered her back to her feet. "All right, now we can go."

It took her about twenty minutes to get her hair and makeup done. She and Jesse chatted about music—well, he mostly lectured her about *real* music, but he did have some interesting stories about different bands behind the scenes. Roadies gossiped with other roadies, but if they wanted to keep their jobs, that's where the secrets stayed.

So the bands he told her about were long disbanded, and she hadn't heard of most of them, but they all made the members of Winter's Wrath seem like choirboys in comparison.

Soon it was time to head on stage. Jesse walked her there, a pace behind her, which she hated. But she couldn't have it both ways. Alder was right. Up here, they worked together. Being lovers at home would have to be enough.

For now.

A familiar song started, which wasn't one of theirs, but one she—and clearly every member of the crowd—knew well. She grinned as Brave stepped up to the edge of the stage.

"I think you all know this one. Fuck it's good to be home!"

They played a cover of *Don't Stop Believing*, by Journey, and Brave let the crowd sing most of it. By the time they reached the end, the fans were pumped.

The heavy thump of Tate kicking the bass drum lead into the band's first official song.

Danica licked her lips, peering past the heavy black curtain. She wasn't sure what she'd expected to see. More tension with the band? Them messing up because they couldn't lose themselves to the music anymore?

Whatever she'd feared, as the guitars ripped out the melody and Brave began to sing, Winter's Wrath gave the crowd everything they always had. And more. They didn't need gimmicks, or lights, or her out there dancing. They gave their fans what they loved to hear. Music that spoke to them, that made them feel like they weren't alone in all their pain and rage and passion.

They might not need her, but she was part of this.

And she was going to enjoy every damn minute while it

lasted.

"Go get 'em, sexy." Jesse whispered in her ear.

Taking a deep breath, she skipped onto the stage, giving a little wave to the fans that called her name. A couple of songs went by, absolutely perfect. The guys were enjoying themselves and she'd never had this much fun. SLUT was still her favorite performance, now that she knew the choreography well enough to add her own different spin on it with every show, but Fallen Star was a close second.

Her heart beat a little faster as the familiar rhythm roared through the theatre. She threw her fist up in the air as she tossed her hair around and sang along. The mosh pit grew, filling with wild, thrashing bodies. Crowd surfers reached the stage, some coming over to give Brave high fives. Security got most of them off the stage quickly, but for every person that lingered, two more seemed encouraged to try.

She could hear the last one, speaking to Brave, his voice coming through Brave's mic.

"No one will ever forget you."

Then she saw the glint of metal in his hand.

A woman in the crowd screamed, her voice coming clearly over the dying sounds of the guitar. "He's got a knife!"

Security moved fast.

Alder got to his brother first.

Hands grabbed Danica and she struggled, losing sight of Alder in the mass of bodies. Yellow security shirts were all around him.

A bloody handprint was smeared on the sleeve of one of the guards that had gotten their first. Her heart lodged in her throat as the security guards backed away, their hands out in front of them, their voices calm.

The man who'd attacked Brave snarled. Between the guards, she spotted the knife still in his hand. Covered in blood.

With another tug, Jesse dragged her away from the stage. "Stay there! I need to know you're safe."

He waited for her nod then carefully approached the tense

scene in the center of the stage, circling as though looking for a way to get closer.

"I swear to god, I'll kill him! Back off!" The man shouted from somewhere in the middle of all the yellow shirts, his voice crazed. "He'll never be good enough. I encouraged you, I tried to make you better, but you're still making the same mistakes. He said we could make you a star."

"Then leave him. It's me you want." Brave's voice was even, without a hint of pain.

He's all right.

Which meant Alder had gotten to him in time.

So who was the man threatening? Where was the blood coming from?

"You have to know I love you. That's how he found me. I kept sending letters, but you never answered them." The crazy man laughed. "Now you get them all." He went quiet. "Tell them not to come any closer, I'll slit his fucking throat!"

"Back off!" Brave's voice broke. "Look at me…what's your name? You never signed any of the cards."

"My name doesn't matter. Will you come with me?"

"Yes. I'll come with you if you let someone take care of him. I'll do whatever you want." Brave's tone took on an edge of desperation. "Don't let him die."

Someone took her hand. She bit her bottom lip hard, glancing over to see Tate. That was good. Tate was safe.

Maybe Malakai was hurt. Tate loved him like a brother. Losing Malakai would destroy him.

"He'll be all right." Danica whispered, squeezing his hand. "He has to be all right."

"I know, but I should have done something." Tears spilled down Tate's cheeks. "Malakai dragged me backstage soon as things got crazy."

"So he's okay?"

Tate nodded, swallowing hard. "He's on the other side of the stage I think. Him and Connor are waiting to see if there's anything they can do."

Every member of the band was accounted for.

Bile rose in her throat. She dug her nails into her palm, shaking her head as tears blinded her.

Not Alder.

"I have to go to him. He's hurt. They're not letting anyone near him." She stepped forward, but Tate wrapped his arms around her, pulling her back into the shadows of the side stage.

"The cops are coming. If security can't deal with the guy, they will." Tate bowed his head to her shoulder. "There's nothing either of us can do but stay out of the way."

By the time the police got here, it might be too late. But Tate was right.

The crowd was being cleared out. Several uniformed officers spread out around the theater.

A firm voice came from behind them. "You're going to have to clear the area."

Danica stared at the officer that had slipped up silently to the side stage. She felt completely numb, but she knew she had to get out of the way. Let the police do their jobs.

Her and Tate made their way out into the dressing room hall. Another cop waved them on.

Bang!

Tate grabbed her arm.

"Move!" The cop in the hall shouted.

Bang! Bang! Bang!

Cold hit them as they rushed outside. Thick snow blinded her at first. Then all she could see were the red and blue lights flashing. More cops, two who came to lead her and Tate to one of the ambulances.

Someone asked if she was hurt. She shook her head.

"There was so much blood…" Tears hit the back of her arm as she hugged herself and a blanket was wrapped around her. "I just need to know he's alive. That's all that matters."

She couldn't hear any questions. Her pulse pounded in her skull as she whispered the same thing, over and over.

"Just tell me he's alive."

Chapter Twenty-One

"Find Danica."

Jesse pressed his fist against the brick wall. He'd followed the stretcher outside as they rushed Alder to an ambulance. He wanted to hate Brave for going with him.

But Alder had asked Jesse for one thing.

He could still speak, so he would be all right.

He had to be.

Lifting his hands to his face, Jesse's knees buckled as he saw the blood covering them. He shoved against the wall before he could hit the ground. He couldn't be weak. The blood would wash off.

He had to find Danica.

There were so many people; he didn't find anyone he recognized. He took out his phone, then shoved it back in his pocket. Danica wouldn't have had her phone on stage. The police had gotten everyone outside pretty fast. Especially when the crazy man that had stabbed Alder moved to stab him again and the cops started shooting.

He couldn't remember much after that. He'd been shoved out of the way. The guy was cuffed, even though Jesse was pretty sure he was dead.

And the paramedics had worked on Alder right there on stage, trying to stop the bleeding.

As soon as he was 'stabilized' they rushed him out on the stretcher. Jesse had needed to see Alder's eyes open. To hear him speak.

He'd gotten that moment right before they loaded Alder in the ambulance.

"Find Danica."

Even if Alder hadn't asked, Jesse would have focused on finding her. A few of the ambulances were transporting people in the crowd who'd been trampled. He prayed she wasn't among them. That she'd stayed where he'd left her until being evacuated.

Walking along the side of the theatre, he spotted Skull with Connor and Malakai. He ran over to them.

"Have you seen Danica?" Neither Malakai or Connor answered. They looked like they were in shock. They couldn't fucking go into shock until everyone was accounted for. "Fuck, pull it together! Where is she?"

Skull grabbed Jesse's arm. "She was seen with Tate. We don't know if they were brought to the hospital. We'll find out."

"Tate hates hospitals. He'd avoid going if he wasn't hurt and Danica wouldn't leave him alone." Malakai pressed a fist to his mouth. "It's fucking freezing out. Maybe they went to the van?"

Not waiting for the others, Jesse took off at a run. The van was still parked behind the theatre.

It was running. No one was in the driver's seat. He yanked the back doors open.

And there was Danica, sitting next to Tate, glaring at an open laptop. One of the most beautiful sights he'd ever seen.

She glanced up, her face losing all color as she looked him over. Then she gave her head a hard shake. "Neither of us have our phones, but a few people have tweeted about what's going on. Alder's on his way to the hospital."

"I know."

"Do you know which one? None of these idiots seem to have a clue."

"Yes. We'll head there now." He moved aside as Malakai joined him. "Get in. I'll drive."

After Connor got in the back with the others, and Skull jumped in the passenger side, Jesse pulled out of the parking lot. A cop stopped him to check his ID and ask where he was going. Doing his best to stay calm, Jesse answered all the questions.

Before long, they were at Henry Ford Hospital.

They found Brave pacing in the waiting room.

Danica sprinted right up to him and hugged him tight. "How is he?"

"He's in surgery. They brought him right in, but no one's told me anything yet. One of the paramedics stuck a needle in his chest and pulled out some blood. I don't know why, he's lost so much already." Brave brought a trembling hand up to his face. "I can't lose him, Danica. He needs to know I love him. I did a great job making him think I didn't. I need a chance to change that."

"You'll get one." Danica stroked Brave's hair as he lowered his head to her shoulder. "He's strong. He'll keep fighting and he'll make it through this. And then you're going to be the brother he's always needed you to be."

"Yes." Brave squeezed her, then lifted his head, looking around at the rest of the band. "Are you all okay?"

They all nodded. Except for Tate.

Tate shook his head. "There's so much blood. Am I the only one who's noticed everyone is covered in blood? I'm gonna be sick."

He bolted from the waiting room.

Malakai quickly followed him.

And Brave looked down at his clothes. He wore the same tight black jeans and black shirt he'd worn on stage, so the blood didn't show, but he had as much blood on his hands as Jesse, as well as splatters of it on his pale face.

"Jesse, you and Brave should go get cleaned up." Danica drew away from Brave and cupped Jesse's cheek. "I'll stay and wait to hear from the doctor. I'll come get you if there's anything."

Skull cleared his throat. "I'll go grab some clothes from the van for you both."

"Thank you, Skull." Danica smiled at him. She didn't seem to notice she was wearing nothing but the same little skirt and thin shirt she'd worn on stage. She had to be freezing, but she'd become the steadiest one among them.

She'd try to take care of them all. The distraction might keep her from falling apart, but someone had to take care of her. Jesse stepped up to the older roadie before he could take off. "Can you bring one of my hoodies for Danica? It's going to be huge on her, but it should keep her warm."

"I'd planned to, my boy." Skull clasped a hand behind Jesse's neck. "Connor and I will watch out for her. You keep an eye on him."

Inclining his head, Jesse put his hand on Brave's shoulder, leading him to the closest bathroom. They both scrubbed their hands in silence. When Skull brought their clothes, Jesse handed a stack to Brave, then quickly shed his bloody clothes, tossing them in the trash before putting on the fresh jeans and T-shirt. He pulled on the thick hoodie, feeling a little more stable.

Brave hadn't moved.

"Hey, look at me." Jesse faced Brave, hands on his shoulders, shaking him to get his attention. "You don't get to check out now, Brave. You might be a complete fucking dick sometimes, but you're one of the strongest people I know. Alder needs your strength."

Brave shook his head. "He needs you. And Danica. This isn't the time for him to worry about playing nice with me."

"Then show him he doesn't have to. You're going to be the first person allowed in that room to see him." Jesse held Brave's gaze, wondering if that was even a good idea. What if he went in there and made things worse?

He won't. He just needs a reminder that he's a tough son of a bitch.

"You go in there and you tell him he's going to make it. He needs that stubborn goddamn attitude that kept him from getting close to you for so long. But this time, you're going to use it to make sure he keeps fighting."

"He'll fight for you, Jesse."

"Awesome, but give him every reason you can think of. You, Danica, me. The band. Those dogs—hell, tell him the dogs will be at his place, waiting for him when he gets home."

Brave let out a shaky laugh. "My parents will be happy about that. They might not even mind seeing me if I'm there for the mutts."

Jesse went still. "Aren't they coming?"

"Maybe?" Brave's brow furrowed. "I figured they would be Alder's emergency contact—he has a file here from when he got his appendix out. But...he put my name down." His voice cracked and he lashed out suddenly, punching the wall. "That stupid fucker! Why would he throw himself in front of a guy with a knife? Especially for me?"

"You know why." Jesse latched onto Brave's wrist before he could land another punch. "Go call them. They might surprise you."

Pressing his eyes shut, Brave nodded slowly. "I doubt it, but he'd want them here."

Back in the waiting room, Jesse waited with the band, surprised when Danica slipped into his lap and let him hold her. He buried his face in her hair, loving that she'd stopped giving a fuck about public opinion. If she'd kept her distance, he'd probably have snapped. Either at Tate, who kept trying to sweet talk the nurses into giving them updates, or at Brave, who'd resumed his pacing.

Two hours after Brave called them, his parents showed up. Mrs. Trousseau hugged her son, but his father barely acknowledged him before going to hunt down someone who would 'give him some answers'.

"You boys are all over the news." Mrs. Trousseau took a seat beside Malakai, where she could face them all. "I couldn't believe it. Brave never told us someone was threatening him. How long has this been going on?"

"Almost a month," Connor said after a long silence. "We finally got security, but they...they couldn't stop the guy from

getting on the stage. There were so many people going nuts—
there always are, but they're just fans, having a good time."

"From what I've seen, this 'good time' is very dangerous.
Gallant is right. You're all old enough to find better jobs." She
glanced over at Tate. "Perhaps you aren't, but you should learn
from this. Before someone else ends up dead."

Tate's skin turned a sickly shade of green. He bolted from
his seat.

Malakai slammed his fist into the arm of his seat and went
after Tate.

Danica stiffened in Jesse's arms, tracing her thumb over the
silver cuff on her wrist. He rubbed her back as she trembled.
Forcing Brave to call his parents had been a mistake.

Mrs. Trousseau sighed. "I didn't mean to upset anyone, but
you have to understand, I've lost two sons to this crazy dream
and—"

"Alder is going to be fine." Brave stopped in the center of
the waiting room, staring at his mother. "Fuck, I don't
understand you. Don't you even care that he's fighting for his
life? I don't know why he bothers with you. Or why I didn't see
how hard he tries to keep this family together. When he visits, he
answers all your questions, knowing your just digging for your
next story."

"He's always respected my career." Her eyes went cold as
she stood. "I'm sorry you don't. And I wish I could say Alder
will pull through, but I'm a realist. All reports say he had been
bleeding for a very long time before they were able to get to him.
I clung to any hope that Valor would be found alive for days,
and look how that turned out."

Brave just shook his head and turned his back on her.
"You're here because Alder will want to see you when he wakes
up. But if you dare let him know you'd already given up on him,
I'll kick you out of his room myself."

Mr. Trousseau returned, his face drawn with the same weary
acceptance his wife was expressing. "There are complications.
They stopped the bleeding, and repaired the damage to his heart,

but he's in shock and showing signs of severe hypothermia from the blood loss. The chances of him ever waking up are low."

"But there's a chance?" The way Brave looked at his father, as though he was desperate for the man to tell him everything would be all right, broke Jesse's heart.

He already felt like a knife had slammed into the center of his chest. The way Mr. Trousseau shook his head twisted it even deeper.

"Not a strong enough chance to get your hopes up." He raked his hand through his hair, looking so much like both Brave and Alder that Jesse had to look away. Too bad he couldn't block out the man's next words. "I can't do this again."

"Can we see him?" Mrs. Trousseau asked. She almost sounded like a loving mother, but when her husband shook his head, she picked up her purse and took his hand. "Then we'll come back when we can."

They left. They actually fucking left.

Jesse considered his own parents and realized he wasn't all that shocked. At least Alder's parents had shown up. His wouldn't have bothered.

But that didn't matter, because this was their family. Right here. This band. Danica. The roadies who came in with coffee over the next few hours and asked about Alder. All of *them* had faith he'd pull through.

Hours later and a doctor approached them, asking to speak to Brave alone.

Brave shook his head. "They need to hear this too."

The doctor nodded. "All right, well I can say his condition has improved. He's a healthy young man, which works in his favor. The hypothermic shock increased the bleeding during surgery, but he's responding well to the transfusions. His heart stopped and along with oxygen loss it's difficult to say how extensive the damage is. He hasn't regained consciousness, but we're monitoring him closely. If he makes it through the night, I'm confident he'll make a full recovery."

"That's good news then, right?" Brave rubbed his cheek

irritably. "He's made it this far—"

"He's hanging on. I don't want to give you false hope, but if I was a betting man?" The doctor smiled and put his hand on Brave's shoulder. "Your brother isn't ready to let go. You can see him for a few minutes if you'd like, but I don't want too many visitors. Maybe one or two."

"His girlfriend and..." Brave looked over at Jesse and Danica. "I know it will help him to see her."

"And Jesse." Danica stood and took Jesse's hand, pulling him to his feet. "He'll need to know you're close too."

The doctor's gaze went to Danica's hand in Jesse's and he frowned. "I wouldn't advise anything that might cause him undo stress."

"He loves us both, Doctor." Danica hiked up her chin. "If I know him as well as I think I do, he'll be worrying about everyone else. He needs to know we're okay so he can focus on getting better."

Inclining his head, the doctor chuckled. "This is true. I almost forgot I was dealing with a rock star that likely leads an unorthodox lifestyle. Come on then. I've done all I can for the moment. What he needs now is something to fight for."

Brave went in first, and within seconds, Jesse was tempted to go drag him out of the room.

The last thing Alder needed was to be yelled at.

Danica held his hand in a firm grip, shaking her head when he let out a low growl and moved toward the door. "If Alder can hear him, he'll know how much Brave loves him. That's all he's ever wanted. He needs this."

Jesse arched a brow at Brave's next words.

"I'll seduce Danica. I'll take Jesse back. And I'll get Tate stoned every fucking night. Do you hear me?"

The man is insane.

"Alder, you fucking keep fighting. You're the only thing holding this band together. The guys won't put up with my shit anymore. You're the fucking star. And I am so proud of you. I've never told you that. You've done more than me or Valor ever could." Brave sobbed and Jesse swallowed hard. "I don't know how someone like you came out of a fucked up family like ours, but you make me want to be a better man. So you get through this. Get through it and let me show you I can be better."

Brave took a deep breath.

"I'll be here when you wake up, Alder. And I know you will. If not for me, than for that fucking beautiful woman and that amazing man who love you like you deserve to be loved."

After going quiet for a few moments, Brave stepped out of the room. He gave Jesse and Danica a small, sad smile. "Not sure if that helped. I was waiting for him to get up and punch me. Tell me to fuck off. *Anything.*"

Danica let out a shaky laugh. She brought a trembling hand to the silver cuff Alder had given her, rolling it around her wrist. "Give him a couple of days and you'll get your wish."

Nodding, Brave headed down the hallway, hands stuffed in his pockets, shoulders hunched.

Jesse let Danica go in next. He couldn't hear what she said, but she seemed much more relaxed when she came out.

"I could have been imagining things, but I think he smiled."

Squeezing her hand, Jesse nodded, then slipped into the room. He rubbed his lips with his hand as he looked over all the machines around the bed. All the tubes and wires attached to Alder's body.

The blue sheet covering Alder brought out the pallor of his flesh. There was a tube under his nose. His chest didn't seem to be moving, but after Jesse stared for a while, he caught the subtle rise and fall. The steady beat of the heart monitor reassured him a little, but Alder's hand was ice cold when Jesse took it between his.

He sat on the edge of the small, black padded metal chair by the bed and brought Alder's hand to his lips. "I'm sure Danica came up with something good to say. She's smart and she's good at showing people how much she cares. Brave sucks at it, but from the sound of it, he's getting better."

Jesse rubbed Alder's lifeless hand, hating that it was so damn cold.

"I wasted so much time not letting you get too close. I told you how much you scared me. You're a good thing I couldn't let myself have. But that was me being weak. I don't think I really understood what fear was until I saw you bleeding. Until I realized I might lose you."

He hadn't let himself cry before. He'd been strong for Danica. For Brave.

But he couldn't stop the tears now.

"You have so much to live for, Alder. So I'll say what everyone already has. You fight. And that shouldn't be hard, because even when you were in the background, getting no fucking credit for everything you've done, you were fighting. So you have to keep doing that, just a little longer." He looked at Alder's face, wondering if Danica had been right. Had Alder smiled? Heard any of them? "You're a fucking hero. Valor wasn't, and I know you always looked up to him, but you don't have to any more. Because you saved Brave—you saved him even before you stepped in front of that crazy fucker with the knife. He looks up to you. So does Tate, and Malakai, and Connor. And so do I."

The doctor had said no stress, so maybe this was a bad idea. He should find something to talk about that Alder could look forward to. Something simple.

His lips curved as he considered the one thing Brave had forgotten to mention. "I'm going to pick up your dogs and bring them home. When you get out of here, they'll be waiting for you. And you know they'll go fucking nuts when they see you. Think about it. You'll be coming home to your furbabies. To Danica." His throat locked as the door opened and a nurse quietly told him visiting hours were over.

Leaning close to Alder as he stood, he kissed his forehead.

"And me. Come home to me. You wake up and you fucking come home."

Chapter Twenty-Two

Slicing pain. Then cold. Shouting and pressure on his chest.

Alder struggled in the darkness, gasping for air. The man was trying to kill Brave. Where was Brave? He wasn't sure if he'd gotten there in time.

He jumped as he heard a loud *Bang!*

He opened his eyes and tried to sit up.

"Whoa, not so fast." A man in a white coat pressed a hand to his shoulder. "Try to relax. Breathe slowly."

"Where am I?" Alder winced at the sharp pain in his chest. "Shit, that hurts."

"I imagine it does. I've just given you something for the pain. Give it a moment and you should feel a bit better." The doctor checked the beeping machine by the bed and nodded with satisfaction. "Very good. Aside from the pain, how are you feeling?"

Fucking confused. And cold.

But that didn't matter. He frowned at the man he assumed was a doctor. "Where's my brother?"

"Asleep right there." The doctor pointed to a chair in the corner of the room that didn't look very comfortable, where Brave was passed out with his head on his bent knees. "He's been taking turns with a sweet girl and a very irritable man for the past few days and none of them have slept much. I'd hoped hearing that you were definitely going to live would get at least one of them to go home for a good night's sleep, but I don't think they were convinced, since you hadn't woken up and I had to inform them you likely weren't smiling when they spoke to you."

"Wait, did you say *days*?"

"Yes."

"The band is on tour! They can't perform without Brave." His head was spinning and he groaned as he brought his hand to his face. "Wake him up. Tell him he needs to go."

"Considering the amount of gifts and letters you've gotten from your fans, I believe they understand and are willing to wait for you to recover." The doctor grabbed a clipboard and jotted down a few notes. "If you'd like to wake your brother to tell him the band's tour schedule is more important than your health, you're welcome to it. But if you'd like my professional opinion? It's a very bad idea."

The doctor clearly didn't know his brother. Alder took a deep breath. "Does that mean I can get up?"

"Not yet. I'll come back in an hour or so and let you know if you're ready to get out of bed. For now, try sitting. Slowly."

Sounded simple, but the slightest movement turned Alder's stomach and his whole chest felt like it was going to rip open. He panted as the doctor adjusted his bed, then rested back against it.

"Very good. If you're ready for visitors, please let the nurse know. He'll be here in a bit with something for you to eat."

Alder's stomach growled. Fuck, he was starving.

"I'm guessing it will be soup or something? Like when I had my appendix out?" He sighed when the doctor nodded. He was pretty sure he could eat a fucking Big Mac with fries, but the best way to get out of the hospital as soon as possible was to do whatever the doctor said.

The doctor left and he looked around the room. Damn, there were a lot of flowers. Most of them black. Metal fans were weird. Rather than brightening up the room, all the black and red made him think of a Goth wedding. He even saw a few little voodoo dolls, one white, one black, and one red. They were cute, but...odd as 'get well' gifts.

By his side was a swiveling table with two empty coffee cups on it and a newspaper. He didn't want to bother Brave after the doctor saying he hadn't gotten much sleep, so he might as well entertain himself.

And maybe the paper would have something about what happened at the concert.

His mouth went dry as he read the headline.

'Winter's Wrath Manager Arrested For Endangering Lead Singer'.

What the fuck?

He continued to read, then started to wonder if he'd woken up in some kind of nightmare. This couldn't be true. Sure, Cole could be an asshole, but he wouldn't put Brave in danger. Not for fucking publicity.

The article didn't leave much doubt that that was *exactly* what Cole had done.

Alder ground his teeth. "I'm going to fucking kill him."

"Get in line." Brave crossed the room, pulled the newspaper out of Alder's hand, and leaned over him. Hugged him like he was made of glass. Then eased away slowly. "I forgot Danica left the paper there. That's not how I wanted you to find out, but the doctor had no idea when you'd wake up."

"Cole fucking *hired* a fan that was sending you crazy letters?" Alder shook his head. "Is it the same one that attacked you in Ohio?"

"No. Apparently there's a whole community online of people who were obsessed with LOST. I'm hoping not all of them are this nuts. The love letters they write to Valor are a little disturbing though." Brave took a seat on the edge of the bed. "The guy that grabbed me on stage in Ohio gave Cole the idea. He swears he didn't know it would turn violent. Part of his defense actually. He contacted the guy writing me the letters and said he could get him closer to me. He planned to use the whole thing as a way to get the band on the front page."

"Which explains why he didn't think we needed more security." Rage sped up Alder's pulse, which made his chest hurt.

ОК

Not as bad as before though. The meds must be working. "Did you find another manager? The band needs to go back on tour as soon as possible."

"Fuck that."

What? Alder blinked at Brave, sure he'd heard wrong. A nurse came in with a tray bearing a bowl of watery soup and a glass of water. He set it on the table without a word, then left.

Alder scowled at the soup, then turned his scowl on his brother. "What do you mean, 'fuck that'?"

"I thought it was pretty clear. We're not touring without you."

"Fine. Then start recording."

"Without our lead guitarist? How about no."

Shit. He sounds serious. Alder groaned, pressing his head back into his pillow. "How about we agreed future decisions would be made by the whole band. You don't get to make this one on your own."

Brave nodded, a sly smile spreading across his lips. "You're absolutely right. It's a democracy now, which means majority rules. And when I asked the rest of the guys about taking a break until you're all better. They agreed. Your vote wasn't needed."

"Fucker." Alder pressed his lips together. He'd talk to the other guys; make them see how bad the time off would be for the band. They'd 'voted' while they were worried about him. Once they saw he was okay, the success of the band would become priority again. "Have you been writing at least? We have three songs. We need at least ten for a new album."

"I'm aware of that." Brave grinned, then bent over and kissed Alder on the forehead. "I love you, you crazy bastard. How about you be awake for more than an hour before you get back to work?"

"Fine. Where's my phone, I need to call Danica. Is Jesse with her?"

"Yeah, they're at your place taking the dogs for a walk." Brave studied Alder's face, his brow creasing slightly. "Why are you so grumpy? Are you still in pain? Do you want me to get the doctor so he can up your doses?"

"No, I think they're already fucking with my head. You're being way too nice, you're not putting the band first, and I think I just heard you say you loved me."

"I did. And I do. Get used to it." Brave pulled his phone out of his pocket and handed it to Alder. "Now stop being all broody. That's my job."

Alder snorted and tapped Danica's number on speed dial.

She answered right away, sounding out of breath. And like she was walking through a wind tunnel. "Brave? Is Alder awake?"

"Yes, I'm awake." Alder held the phone away from his ear as she screamed. He grinned at Brave's chuckle. "Brave was just telling me you're taking care of my babies."

"Yes, I am. And I've fallen in love." The windy sound faded away. "Jesse, hurry up! You shouldn't let her drag you around then!" She laughed. "Alder just called. We're going to the hospital!"

"Who have you fallen in love with? Jesse or the dogs?"

"The dogs. Jesse is a pain in the ass. Did you know he can't work a dishwasher?" She giggled, which made Alder smile. He was happy she and Jesse had been taking care of one another. "And I'm going to ask my grandfather to take care of the puppies when we go on tour. Do you know your parents never took them for walks? They're horrible on the leash, but me and Jesse are training them. My grandfather will get some of the boys from the reservation to bring them out running every day."

Wind again, and then a car engine growling.

"We just dropped the dogs off at your place and we're on our way. But sleep if you're tired. How are you feeling? Fuck, I should have asked that first."

"I'm fine. The meds make me tired, but I've been asleep for days. I'll be up when you get here."

"Danica, give me the phone while you're driving," Jesse said.

Danica sighed. "I planned to. I just pulled out. Relax."

"Right. Remind me to never let you drive the bus."

"Alder, I love you. I'll see you in a few minutes," Danica said quickly. "Talk to Jesse. He's pouting."

"I'm not pouting." Jesse's voice came out clearly, as though he had the phone now. "Alder, your woman is driving me insane. Your house is fucking spotless though."

"So she's my woman? I thought we had a good thing starting between the three of us?"

"We do, but when she's being a nag, she's all yours. *Ow!* What the fuck was that for?" Jesse sighed. "I swear, I've got bruises everywhere. She's very abusive."

If this conversation was anything like the ones they'd had while Alder was in the hospital, he wouldn't be surprised. Jesse needed to learn some tact. Or at least when to keep his mouth shut.

"Other than managing not to kill one another, have you both been doing good?" Maybe he'd assumed they'd taken care of one another too fast. He hated the idea of them being miserable; sticking together because they thought that was what he wanted. "I'm guessing Malakai and Tate stayed with Tate's grandmother?"

"Yes, we've been fine alone. I know it sounds bad, but we haven't argued *that* much." Jesse's tone softened. "I would have gone crazy without her. Neither of us has slept a lot, but Brave suggested we try lying down together for a bit. Even just to get some rest because we'd be useless to you dead on our feet. It worked. No one could get him to leave the hospital for longer than it took to eat and take a shower though. We all tried."

Alder looked over at his brother, taking in the shadows under his eyes. He'd been shocked when Brave had said he loved him. His brother hadn't used those words since Alder was a teenager.

Saying them was cool, but he'd proved they weren't just words.

"Alder, you still there?" Jesse asked, sounding concerned.

"Yeah. You guys almost here?"

"We're just pulling into parking."

"Okay, I'll see you when you come up." He met Brave's eyes. "I need to talk to my brother."

Hanging up, he set the phone on the tray by his bed.

Brave stood. "Okay, I'm not sure what to make of that look. Whatever Jesse told you, he's lying. I haven't hit on him or Danica. I've only seen Tate in this room. And if he told you anything I said while you were unconscious, I was trying to piss you off so you'd wake up."

"I don't even want to know." Alder folded his arms over his chest. Which was a very bad idea. His stomach flipped as pain tore through him.

"What did you do? Do you need the doctor?" Brave started toward the door.

"No, just give me a sec." Alder took several uncomfortable deep breaths. The pain didn't disappear, but he didn't feel like puking anymore. "I want to thank you."

"Thank me?" Brave blinked at him, like he'd spoken in math terms that didn't add up. "For what?"

"For staying with me. For making sure Jesse and Danica were okay. Our parents aren't even here, but I don't care because you are." Alder shrugged, not sure Brave really got how much it all meant to him. "I swear, I won't mention it again, because I know how much you hate the sappy shit, but you were my fucking hero growing up. So…thank you."

Shaking his head, Brave came up to the side of the bed and hugged him. "Don't fucking thank me. I love you. You're the only family I have, and I'm lucky you didn't give up on me. Now, to top it off, I owe you my life."

"You would have done the same for me."

"Yeah, but unfortunately I wasn't fast enough this time." Brave ruffled his hair. "I get dibs on taking down the next psycho."

"How about we avoid the psychos?"

"That is a very good idea." Danica slipped into the room beside the doctor, holding her bottom lip between her lips and shooting the doctor a questioning look. When he smiled and motioned her toward the bed, she practically slid to Alder's side.

Her hug was even more careful than Brave's had been.

"You look amazing, Alder." She cupped his face in his hands and kissed his lips, slow and gentle, but the taste of her, her soft breasts pressing against his arm, made it very clear he'd regained enough blood in his body to fill his swelling cock. "Do you know how soon you can come home?"

"Soon I hope, because I don't need to see that." Brave exchanged a look with the doctor. "I think he's good to go."

"Not quite, but I'd say another day or so, if he remains stable, he can be released." The doctor stepped aside to let Jesse in. "I have to see to my other patients, but I wanted to speak to you both now that Alder is awake." He nodded his head toward Alder. "In my professional opinion, Brave should go home before he ends up needing to be admitted himself. If he could bring the fans that have been parked out in front of the hospital with him, that would be appreciated."

Brave snorted and grabbed his jacket off the back of the chair he'd been sleeping with. "I won't bring them all home, Doc. But I can manage a few."

Jesse laughed as Brave sauntered out of the room. He came around the bed to sit on Alder's other side. "I'd say he's gonna be fine. He won't be sleeping. For a few hours at least."

"And on that note, I'll leave you three to enjoy your visit." The doctor paused on the way out. "Not that it needs to be said, but Alder has not healed enough for any kind of physical activity."

Danica's face went red. "Of course, Doctor. We wouldn't... Umm, thank you."

The doctor inclined his head, then left.

Finally, he had Danica and Jesse alone. Which was weird, because it hadn't felt like they'd been apart until he found out how long he'd been unconscious. He wanted to know what they'd been doing.

But his body was not cooperating. His eyelids felt like they had bricks weighing them down.

Lying on her side on the edge of the bed, Danica brought her lips close to his ear. "You need your sleep, Alder. Don't fight it. We need you all better so we can bring you home."

He felt Jesse's hand on the back of his neck, rubbing gently.

Which made him even more tired. But he fought to stay awake. "I missed you. And I slept for a long fucking time."

"We're going to be right here." Jesse kissed his temple. "Don't argue with us. One of the benefits of a threesome is you're always outnumbered."

"Always?" Alder's whole body got heavier. Danica's soft breaths and Jesse's massage lulled him closer and closer to sleep. "That doesn't sound fair."

"What happened to you wasn't fair. Us making sure you're left with nothing but a battle scar? Couldn't be more fair." Jesse's voice deepened, becoming low and soothing. "The next few days are nothing. Danica and I had a crash course on how to live together. When you get home, it will be the beginning of a whole bunch of awesome. And sex. Lots and lots of sex."

Alder didn't hear much more after that, but damn, he couldn't wait to have it all.

Actually, he didn't have to wait.

I have it all now.

Epilogue

Ordered perfection,
Ugly as sin.
Paint the world in dull hues.
Leave the monster under my bed.

Three months later

Black paint covered every inch of Danica's body. The long black nails on her fingers classified as lethal weapons. The process of putting her costume on took almost four hours and three theatrical makeup artists.

Every day. For the past week.

But getting all done up, in a warehouse designed to look like a dollhouse built in the pits of hell, was the most fun she'd ever had. She couldn't freaking wait to see how the music video turned out.

With her makeup done, she was allowed to go watch the guys for a bit. So long as no one touched her. Or kissed her. Or so much as breathed too close.

The last time Jesse had snuck a quick kiss backstage, the head of hair and makeup had called Sophie *and* the band's new manager.

No way in hell would she risk getting that lecture again. Reese Griffith, who'd been the manager of Winter's Wrath for almost two months, was considered by the band as Sophie's evil twin. She ran the band like a drill sergeant, had hired bodyguards, and promoted Jesse to tour manager. In other words, she was a godsend.

And as much as the guys grumbled about the routine drugs tests they were now forced to take, and the strict schedule that she'd set up for recording the new album and their upcoming European tour, they all worshiped the ground she walked on.

This music video alone was proof that the band had made a breakthrough in the music business. She promoted them so well, their dwindling sales had spiked within a week of hiring her. They were headlining every single one of their future shows.

Their music had hit the top of the metal charts. Including *Subsist*, which had been released as a single last month. And was getting the band's first big budget music video.

Hearing the long, creepy notes sent a shiver up her spine. She'd heard the song a hundred times, but she still loved it. The message was deep and twisted, stolen innocence, wanting to keep the dreams and the nightmares rather than face a conformed reality. She played the demon and the innocent girl in the video. The girl scenes had been filmed already, and she'd gotten a peek at the footage.

She'd done an awesome job, if she did say so herself. Sophie had talked up her acting abilities to Reese when the manager decided to re-evaluate all the contracts Cole had drawn up.

Reese had watched some of her old performances and looked over her profile. Then said the sweetest thing.

"I was afraid the band was settling on you because they didn't want the expense of hiring a more experienced actress." Reese passed the contract she'd already gone over with Sophie across the desk in her office and smiled at Danica. *"Now I believe they were lucky to find you before you got a better offer."*

The contract left time for 'better offers', but ensured she'd be available for all the band's bigger shows. Which was absolutely perfect.

Actually, everything was pretty much perfect.

"Fuck, I can't get over how hot you look." The words sounded like Jesse, but it was Alder. He came up from behind her, looking like he desperately wanted to touch her. But Reese had trained them all well.

"You're looking pretty damn sexy yourself." Danica's gaze took in his wiry body, his wide, bare chest covered with fake blood, the bruises painted on his face making him look rugged and wild. Even his torn jeans turned her on. She wanted to rip them the rest of the way off.

"Too bad that makeup is so uncomfortable." He circled her, the hungry way his eyes trailed over her, and the way his breath brushed over his skin as he got as close as he could without touching her, sent lust pooling in her core. "I'd ask you to leave it on tonight."

She licked her bottom lip. "I could leave my nails on. If you don't mind a few more scars."

"And if you want to look like you've been mauled." Jesse stepped out of the set that looked like a little boy's room. "Sorry to interrupt, but you're scheduled to be jumping on the bed now. If you don't do it within five takes this time, the director said he's hiring a body double."

"Why can't they just use Tate's clips? He looks like he's having fun." Alder rolled his eyes at Jesse's blank look. "The rest of us feel stupid. We put it to a vote and—"

"Reese heard. She vetoes your vote." Jesse smirked. "Tate breaking the walls with a guitar wouldn't make any sense. Just fucking get it over with so we're not pulling another twelve hour day."

"Yes, you know Jesse needs his beauty sleep." Danica batted her eyelashes when Jesse frowned at her. "And you know I'm never on your side when you're being a jerk."

"I'm not being a jerk, I—" He cut himself off and glanced over at Alder. "Is this one of the times where I have to tell her she's right?"

"If you haven't figured that out yet, Jesse, you never will." Alder chuckled at Jesse's heavy sigh. "Do you need me to step in again?"

"Please do."

"You both better be joking or I'm out of here." Danica moved to cross her arms, stopping just in time to save her earning the hatred of her makeup crew. "And I was going to put up with this—" She trailed her hand down her side, carefully touching nothing but air. "—for a few more hours so we could enjoy my last night as a demon."

Jesse tugged his bottom lip between his teeth in a way that she found fucking erotic. It reminded her of how fucking talented he was with his mouth. He let out a low groan.

Then abruptly flashed her his most charming smile. "You're so right, gorgeous. I'm being a jerk. Doing my job, but still being a jerk."

"No you're right. Alder, go jump on the bed." She winked at Jesse when his lips parted. "I love you."

She also loved how easy he was to fuck with.

Making her way to her own set, which was a girl's room with a *huge* bed that she'd spent a lot of time crawling out from under, Danica thought over how much her life had changed. She'd gone from being a model struggling to find work, to having a contract with one of the biggest up and coming metal bands in the music industry. From not having any desire to let a relationship get in the way of her career to finding two men who supported her in every way.

Loving them both wasn't something she'd ever planned on, but she couldn't picture her life without them anymore. And didn't want to. Even when Alder got quiet and overthought everything, or when Jesse was messy and said the kind of things that belonged in a men's locker room, she loved them.

That the sex was incredible and they still couldn't get enough of each other was a definite plus.

Yep, she'd definitely be wearing the paint tonight.

The End

About the Author

Tell you about me? Hmm, well, there's not much to say. I love hockey and cars and my kids...not in that order, of course! Lol! When I'm not writing—which isn't often—I'm usually watching a game or a car show while networking. Going out with my kids is my only downtime. I get to clear my head and forget everything.

As for when and why I first started writing, I guess I thought I'd get extra cookies if I was quiet for a while—that's how young I was. I used to bring my grandmother barely legible pages filled with tales of evil unicorns. She told me then that I would be a famous author.

I hope one day to prove her right.

For more of my work, please visit:
www.Im-No-Angel.com

You can also find me on Facebook, and Twitter

Also by *Bianca Sommerland*

Made in the USA
San Bernardino, CA
22 November 2017